Ink
&
Sigil

Ink & Sigil

KEVIN HEARNE

DEL REY

NEW YORK

Published in the United States by Del Rey, an imprint of Random House, a division of Penguin Random House LLC, New York.

DEL REY and the HOUSE colophon are registered trademarks of Penguin Random House LLC.

LIBRARY OF CONGRESS CATALOGING-IN-PUBLICATION DATA
Names: Hearne, Kevin, author.
Title: Ink & sigil / Kevin Hearne.
Other titles: Ink and sigil
Description: First edition. | New York : Del Rey, [2020]
Identifiers: LCCN 2019056896 (print) | LCCN 2019056897 (ebook) | ISBN 9781984821256 (hardback ; acid-free paper) | ISBN 9781984821263 (ebook)
Subjects: GSAFD: Mystery fiction. | Fantasy fiction.
Classification: LCC PS3608.E264 I55 2020 (print) | LCC PS3608.E264 (ebook) | DDC 813/.6—dc23
LC record available at https://lccn.loc.gov/2019056896
LC ebook record available at https://lccn.loc.gov/2019056897

Printed in the United States of America on acid-free paper

randomhousebooks.com

2 4 6 8 9 7 5 3 1

First Edition

Book design by Caroline Cunningham
Title page: antique pen: iStock/InaSchönrock; flourish: iStock/Terriana
Frontispiece illustration: Galen Dara

For Weegies

AUTHOR'S NOTE

Some of the language used in this book reflects the charming and unique way Scots employ English, and some of it is specifically Glaswegian (or Weegie). Accents and pronunciation can vary greatly in regions of Scotland, and even though Glasgow and Edinburgh are less than fifty miles apart, their accents are quite distinct. The East End London accent is sometimes incomprehensible to Americans, so to give you an idea, folks from the East End of London sometimes find Glaswegians incomprehensible. I remember when Kimberly and I visited Glasgow and got a cab from the airport to our hotel. We felt absolutely terrible that we had to ask the driver to repeat himself several times, even though we were supposedly speaking the same language. We got the hang of it after a few days—you do get used to the vowel shifts and so on—but it can be disorienting at first.

The written version of it can be disorienting too, so I want to provide a quick guide here. I didn't try to be exhaustively accurate in representing the spoken language but rather wanted to give a general idea of its flavor. The narration and texted conversations will largely conform to standard spelling rules, but the dialogue will contain the words listed below, and I'm providing some pronunciations so that you can more easily hear it in your head.

Ye is pronounced like *yuh,* or with a schwa sound, almost never *yee.* It's used in place of *you,* with two exceptions: *You* is employed and pronounced as *yoo* for emphasis, but *ya* is used whenever calling someone a name, as in *ya steaming gobshite* or *ya tiresome tit.*

    Daein' is usually pronounced with two syllables that rhymes with *payin',* but when folks are excited or in a hurry a syllable gets lost and it sounds like *dane,* and this is in lieu of *doing.*

    Tae is pronounced like *tee* and is used instead of *to* in spoken language.

    Gonnay is just like *gonna* in informal English, but it is pronounced with a long *a* sound at the end, and yes, Weegies really do pronounce it that way. I'm spelling it thusly to make the difference in pronunciation clear.

    There seems to be a general aversion to saying the word *not* out loud, so there are several ways that Scots avoid that. All verb constructions like *would not* or *did not* become contractions and *not* is replaced at the end with *nae,* pronounced like *knee.* So she *didnae* say anything, or she *wouldnae* do that, or she *cannae* afford a yacht. Sometimes on social media you will see these spelled as *didny, wouldny,* or *canny,* which saves a character, but I'm using the older spelling that's in wider use. In other constructions where the contraction cannae be made, the *t* will be dropped off the end of *not,* and thus you will see phrases like *she'll no ever come back* or *I'm no paying for ma drink* or *I'm no gonnay get in the van with ye, ya spooky serial killin' bastard.* Which means that ye will no see the word *won't* very often, but curiously you'll see *don't.* (There are always exceptions to rules, eh?) Perhaps to make up for the extra *no*s inserted into their language in place of *not*s, the Scots often say *naw* instead of *no* when answering a question. And sometimes *nae* is used in place of *no,* as in the phrase *nae bother.*

    The *th* in the middle of *something* is eliminated entirely in the speech of many Weegies, and as a result the word is spelled and pronounced like *sumhin*.

The English contractions *ain't, isn't,* and sometimes *aren't* are written and pronounced like *in't.*

Sometimes in spoken language the word *my* is replaced with *ma,* more accurately reflecting its pronunciation.

The word *what* in Weegie pronunciation often sounds like *whit,* so in dialogue you will occasionally see it spelled as *whit. Wot* is obviously a different vowel sound and a more familiar variation of *what* to many readers, and that is also used in places by certain characters.

Head is pronounced like *heed* in spoken language and some-times even in thoughts, but this is spelled as *heid* throughout to avoid confusion with the actual word *heed.* Likewise, *dead* is pro-nounced like *deed* but spelled as *deid,* so watch out: It's the first word of the book.

Police is spelled the regular way in written language and on the back of official vests and so on, but Weegies pronounce it like *polis,* sort of rhyming with *bolus,* and often spell it that way in spoken language and in their more colorful graffiti messages that encourage all passersby to FUCK THE POLIS!

And in Scotland, a dog is often called a *dug.* Regardless of how it's spelled, they are all good dugs.

The surname of our hero contains a Gaelic spelling, so the *Bh* is pronounced like a *v,* and the *i* before the final *s* means it's pro-nounced with a *sh* sound at the end. So *MacBharrais* is pronounced as *mac VARE ish,* emphasis on the middle syllable.

Likewise, the Gaelic *bean sídhe* is going to be pronounced as *ban shee* (shortened and anglicized to *banshee* in some cases).

A couple of Scottish slang terms for you:

Rammy is a noun that means fracas or brouhaha.

Gallus is an adjective that means stylish and impressive.

You'll also see the phrase *and that* in place of *and such* or *and so on,* as in "Angus had eggs, sausage *and that* for breakfast."

And in case you missed it or were unaware, the protagonist of this series, Al MacBharrais, did appear in the Iron Druid Chronicles in *Besieged*, in a short story called "Cuddle Dungeon." I don't recommend sharing that particular story with the kids, though.

Enjoy!

—From a flat and frozen landscape in Canada that looks not unlike the rest of this page

February 29, 2020

Ink
&
Sigil

CHAPTER 1

———— • ————

Scones Should Come with a Warning

Deid apprentices tend to tarnish a man's reputation after a while. I'm beginning to wonder when mine will be beyond repair.

Fergus was crushed by a poorly tossed caber at the Highland Games.

Abigail's parachute didn't open when she went skydiving.

Beatrice was an amateur mycologist and swallowed poison mushrooms.

Ramsey was run over by American tourists driving on the wrong bloody side of the road.

Nigel went to Toronto on holiday and got his skull cracked by a hockey puck.

Alice was stabbed in a spot of bother with some football hooligans.

And now Gordie, who was supposed to be my lucky number seven, choked to death on a scone this morning. It had raisins in it, so that was bloody daft, as raisins are ill-omened abominations and he should have known better. Regardless of their ingredients, one should never eat a scone alone. Poor wee man.

None of their deaths was my fault, and they were completely unrelated to their training in my discipline, so that's in my favor, at least. But still. People are starting to wonder if I'm capable of training a successor.

I'm starting to wonder too. And I'd like to have a successor soon, as I'm past sixty and rather wishing I could spend my time on sunny beaches, or in sunny gardens, or indeed anyplace where I might see the sun more often.

Scotland is not known for its sunshine. The Highlands get two hundred sixty days of rain per year. But it's no fun for people in other countries to think of us as perpetually drenched, so I believe the popular imagination has painted us with kilts and bagpipes and unfortunate cuisine.

The muscle-bound constable standing outside Gordie's flat in Maryhill and doing a fair job of blocking the entrance held up a hand as I moved to step around him and reach for the door. He was in no mood to give me a polite redirection. "The fuck ye daein', bampot? Away an' shite," he said.

"Ram it up yer farter, Constable. Inspector knows I'm comin', so get out ma way."

Oh, yes, and colorful language. Scotland's reputation for that is well deserved.

My cane is in fact a weapon that a person of my age is allowed to carry around openly, but I pretended to lean on it as I pulled out my "official ID" and flashed it at him. It was not a badge or anything truly official but rather a piece of goatskin parchment on which I had written three sigils with carefully prepared inks. Any one of them alone would probably work, but in combination they were practically guaranteed to hack the brain through the ocular nerve and get me my way. Most people are susceptible to manipulation through visual media—ask anyone in advertising. Sigils take advantage of this collective vulnerability far more potently.

The first one, Sigil of Porous Mind, was the most important, as it leached away the target's certainties and priorities and made them open to suggestion. It also made it difficult for the target to remember anything that happened in the next few minutes. The next one, Sigil of Certain Authority, applied to me, granting my personage whatever importance the constable's mind would plausibly accept. The third, Sigil of Quick Compliance, should goad him to agree to almost any reasonable order I gave next and make him feel good about it, giving him a hit of dopamine.

"Let me pass," I said.

"Right ye are, sir," he said, and smartly stepped to the side. There was plenty of room for me to enter now without contact and no need to say anything more. But he'd been a tad rude and I believed it deserved a proportional response, so I shouldered past him and muttered, "I pumpt yer gran." He flashed a glare at me but said nothing, and then I was in the flat.

The inspector inside did not, in fact, know I was coming. She was middle-aged and looked a bit tired when she swung around at my entrance, but she was a good deal more polite than the constable. She had decided to let her hair go grey instead of dying it, and I liked her immediately for the decision.

"Hello. Who are you, then?"

There was a forensics tech of indeterminate gender taking digital pictures and ignoring both of us, an actual camera pressed to their face instead of a phone or a tablet extended toward the victim. I deployed the official ID once more and gestured at the body of poor Gordie, blue in the face and sprawled on his kitchen floor. Years of training, his hopes and mine, all spread out and lifeless. "Tell me what ye know about the man's death."

The inspector blinked rapidly as the sigils did their work and then replied, "Neighbor in the flat downstairs called it in because the victim fell pretty heavily and pounded on the floor—or the neighbor's ceiling—a few times before dying. A choking accident, as far as we can tell, unless the tox screen comes back and tells us there was something wrong with the scone."

"Of course there was something wrong," I said, looking at the half-eaten remainder sitting on a small saucer. "It had raisins in it. Anything else of note?"

She pointed toward the hallway. "Two bedrooms, but he lived alone. One bedroom is full of fountain pens and inks. Never seen the like. Bit of a nutter."

"Right. That's why I'm here. I need to send that stuff in for testing n' that."

The inspector's features clouded with confusion. "He didnae drink any of it."

"No, no. This is part of a different investigation. We've been watching him for a while."

"We? I'm sorry, I didnae catch your name."

"Aloysius MacBharrais. Ye can call me Al."

"Thanks. And you're investigating his inks?"

"Aye. Toxic chemicals. Illegal compounds. That sort of rubbish."

"On ye go, then. I didnae like that room. Felt strange in there."

That idle comment was a huge warning. Gordie must have had some active and unsecured sigils inside. And all his inks—painstakingly, laboriously crafted with rare ingredients and latent magical power—had to be removed. The last thing the world needed was some constable accidentally doodling his way to a Sigil of Unchained Destruction. I'd secure them and preserve them for later analysis, keeping the successful decoctions and viable ingredients, and destroying the rest.

I turned without another word and went to the hallway. There were three doors, one presumably being the loo. Layout suggested that was the first door on my left, so I went to the second and cautiously cracked it open. It was his bedroom, and there was a desk as well with a small collection of pens, inks, and papers—all for normal correspondence. I snatched a sheet of stationery and selected an Aurora 88 pen from my coat pocket. It was presently filled with a rust-colored ink using cinnabar for the pigment and a varnish infused with ground pearls, fish glue, and the vitreous jelly of owl eyes. I drew a small circle first to direct the effect at myself, then carefully but quickly outlined the shapes of the Sigil of Warded Sight, which looked like a red eye, barred and banded over with simple knotwork. Once completed, the sigil activated and my sight changed to black and white, all color receptors dormant. It was the most basic defense against unsecured sigils: I could not be affected by them until this one wore off—or until I destroyed it myself. It had saved me too many injuries to count.

Putting the pen away and hefting my cane defensively, I kept the sigil in my left hand and crossed the hall to open the door to Gordie's study. A waft of foul, funky air immediately punched me in the nose, and I wondered why the inspector hadn't said anything about it before. It smelled like a sweaty scrotum. Or maybe ten of them.

"Gah," I said, and coughed a couple of times to clear my lungs. I heard titters coming from the kitchen and realized the inspector had left out that fact on purpose. No wonder she'd told me to have at it. Her politeness had been a ruse to draw me to an olfactory ambush.

But I'd been wise to guard my vision. Gordie had far more than a few sigils lying around. The room was full of them, warding against this and that. The walls were lined with raw wooden workbenches and chairs, and cubbyholes full of labeled inks and ingredients glinted on the left. The main bench for ink preparation was opposite the door, and it was stained with pigments and oils and binders and held stoppered bottles of yet more inks. There was also a labeled rack of fountain pens and trays of paper and cards for sigils, along with sealing wax, a melting spoon, and a box of matches. Several cards pasted on the wall above the workbench had recognizable sigils on them for selective sight and attention that should make me—or anyone else who entered—completely ignore what was on the right side of the room. That's why the detective inspector had felt so uncomfortable. She felt something was going on in there and most likely saw it, but the sigils wouldn't let her mind process it. My warded sight made the sigils ineffective, so I had no difficulty seeing that there was a hobgoblin grunting and straining to work his way out of a cage placed on top of the workbench. That was a sight I never thought I'd see.

Different from pure goblins and more mischievous than outright malevolent, hobgoblins were extraordinarily difficult to capture as a rule, since they could teleport short distances and were agile creatures as well, with impressive vertical leaps aided by their thick thighs. This one was trying to reach one of several sigils placed around his cage on little metal stands, like draught-beer lists placed on pub tables. His long, hairy-knuckled fingers waggled as he stretched for the sigil nearest him. If he could reach one of them and tear it up, he might have a way out, since the sigils were more of a prison for him than the actual cage was. He froze when he saw me staring at him, openmouthed.

"Wot?" he said.

I closed the door behind me. "What are ye *daein'* here?"

"I'm in a cage, in't I? Ye must be the cream of Scottish intelligence. Cannae be anywhere else if I'm no free, ya fuckin' genius. But at least ye can see an' hear me. The bird who was here before couldnae."

"I mean why does he have ye caged?" The fellow didn't appear to be an unusual hobgoblin worthy of capture or study; he was short and hairy, square-jawed, his face adorned with a fleshy nose and eyebrows like untrimmed hedgerows.

"He's a right evil bastard, that's why. Or was. He's deid, in't he? How'd he die?"

"Raisin scone."

"So it was suicide, then."

"Naw, it was an accident."

"He didn't *accidentally* eat a raisin scone, now, did he? So it was suicide."

I shrugged, conceding the point. "Who are you?"

"I'm the happy hob ye're gonnay set free now. Unless ye're like him."

"I'm no like him. I'm alive, to begin with. Answer ma questions truthfully and no more dodges. Who are ye and why did Gordie imprison ye here?"

"Said he was gonnay sell me. He's a trafficker in Fae folk, so he is. Or was."

"Nonsense." I stamped my cane on the floor. "Tell me the truth!"

The hobgoblin stood as straight as he could in his cage—he was only about two feet tall—and placed his right hand over his heart, deploying the phrase that the Fae always used when they were swearing the truth or asserting reality. "I tell ye three times, man. He's got a buyer. I'm s'posed tae be delivered tonight. And I'm no the first he's sold. There was a pixie in here a couple of days ago, didnae stay long." He pointed to a slightly smaller, empty cage sitting next to his.

This information was more of a shock to me than Gordie's death. I'd had apprentices die on me before, but none of them had used their knowledge of sigils to traffic in the Fae. Carrying away the inks and pens of my old apprentices had always been a sad affair, because they'd been pure souls who wanted to do good in the world. This situation suggested that Gordie hadn't been such a soul. Trafficking Fae? I didn't know such traffic existed.

"But . . . we're s'posed tae boot the likes o' ye back to the Fae planes whenever ye show up here."

"*We*, did ye say? Oh, so ye *are* like him. Just with a twee dandy mustache, all waxy and twisted."

I squinted at him, considering how to respond. Hobgoblins tend not to take well to naked aggression, but they have that pubescent sense of humor young boys have, which I can deploy rapidly when occasion demands. "It's no twee," I said. "It's luxuriant and full-bodied, like yer maw."

The hobgoblin cackled at that, and I noted that his teeth were abnormally bright and straight. It wasn't a glamour, because my sight was still warded. He'd had some work done. Since when did hobgoblins pay for cosmetic dental work? And his clothing was notable too. I couldn't identify colors in black-and-white vision, but he wore a paisley waistcoat with a watch chain leading to the pocket, but no shirt underneath it. There was a triskele tattooed on his right shoulder, the sort I've seen associated with Druids. Black jeans and chunky black boots. Maybe he was an unusual hobgoblin after all. His eyes glittered with amusement.

"Come on, then, ol' man. Let us out."

"I will. But ye still have no told me yer name."

"For wot? Are ye gonnay send me flowers for the Yule?"

"I need to bind ye to leave this place safely."

"But then ye can bind me for anythin' else ye want in the future. I'm no letting ye have that power. Ma current situation has made me a wee bit distrustful."

"Well, I don't want tae set a hobgoblin loose in a room fulla binding inks. Do ye know who's s'posed to be buyin' ye? Or for why?"

The hobgoblin shook his head. "I don't. But yer lad Gordie had some papers over there he liked to shuffle around an' murmur over. The bird had a look an' said they were nonsense, but maybe they're no to an ol' man. Ye look like ye went tae school back when yer hair wasn't white as lilies."

I moved to the workbench and scanned the papers I saw there. Gordie had been preparing sigils for later use, but there was no helpful explanation of his business dealings. The hobgoblin might be making this all up, and I hoped he was, because otherwise Gordie *had* been an evil bastard and I'd been a consummate fool. But the fact was, Gordie had done some impressive sigil work in this room. Work that should have been impossible for him. There were sigils I hadn't taught him yet—like the Sigil of Iron Gall—which meant he'd also crafted inks for which I hadn't taught him the recipes. He'd obviously been keeping some secrets, which didn't bother me, because apprentices are supposed to do that. What bothered me was that someone was teaching him behind my back.

"I think I know who ye are," the hobgoblin said. "There's s'posed tae be a Scottish sigil agent with a waxed mustache. Are ye called MacVarnish or sumhin like that?"

"MacBharrais."

"Ah, that's it. Heard ye were sharp. But if ye had that wanker Gordie tossin' around behind ye, maybe ye're no, eh, pal?"

Maybe not. On a scrap pad where Gordie had scrawled lines in different inks to make sure the flow was good before drawing sigils, he had written: *Renfrew Ferry, 8 pm.*

"Ye said ye were s'posed tae be delivered tonight? Was it at eight?"

I got no response except a grunt and the sound of torn paper. I turned to see a triumphant hobgoblin freeing himself from the cage, one of the sigils that dampened his magic having been destroyed. He couldn't have reached it physically—I saw him fail as I entered—so he must have managed to exert some magical pull on it to bring it to his fingers. That was precisely the sort of thing that should have been impossible with multiple copies of it around him. The only explanation was that their potency must have waned significantly, the magic all leached from the ink, and with Gordie dead and obviously not paying attention, it was little wonder.

Cackling and flashing those white teeth at me, the hobgoblin leapt off the table and made for the door. I was out of position and woefully slow; there was no time to even break the seal on a prepared Sigil of Agile Grace.

"Laters, MacVarnish!" he said, and bolted out the door. A thud and screams followed shortly thereafter, and there was a shouted "I'm glad yer deid!" before a shocked silence settled in the kitchen. I emerged from the room, far too late, to see the inspector and the tech on the ground, holding their noses. The hobgoblin had leapt up and punched them for the fun of it, and Gordie's body now lay twisted in a much different position, having recently been kicked. I could still see his face, though, a look of frozen surprise that this was his end, that his brown hair was mussed and he had a few days' stubble on his neck and jaw, blue eyes widened in horror that he would be literally be caught dead wearing his Ewok pajamas.

"What in the name of fuck?" the inspector cried. "What was that just now, a pink leprechaun?" She'd had no difficulty seeing the blighter once he'd exited Gordie's room. I'd not seen the hobgoblin's skin color with my vision limited, so I filed that information away for future reference. Her eyes lit upon me and anger flared in them as she rose from the floor. The constable from outside burst into the room, also holding his nose. I needed them out of there right away, because Gordie's entire flat had to be scoured for clues. The official ID came out before they could lay into me and I gave them what for.

"Clear this flat now! Leave immediately and return tomorrow. That's an order. Go! Work on sumhin else!"

They scarpered off under the sway of the sigils and would probably return sooner rather than later when they remembered someone had punched them and they wanted answers. I needed to get answers of my own before then; Gordie had caught me napping, but I was fully awake now.

CHAPTER 2

Item Number One

I couldn't stop blinking once the police left, and it became distracting after three seconds or five. I supposed it was some kind of instinctive reaction, an attempt to clear my vision after I'd been so clearly hoodwinked. But it also told me that my mind was awhirl and I'd do no one any good this way when I needed to be calm and analytical. So I removed my topcoat—a long, tan cashmere job that made me look fancy and scrubbed, even when I wasn't—planted my cane, and began the laborious process of lowering my ancient bones to the hardwood floor. Once seated, I used my arms to pull my blasted shanks into a lotus position, cartilage complaining, and then I breathed in slowly and exhaled, over and over, focusing only on my breath, until my mind quieted. Meditation does wonders for me that sigils cannot; it's a different way to hack the brain.

Calm and prepared for the work ahead, I rose with a series of grunts and chose to interpret the symphony of pops and crackles in my joints as a mark of extraordinary character. I checked the time on my cell phone: 14:45 in the afternoon. So Nadia was still on the clock. I Signaled her terse instructions:

Situation in Gordie's flat on St. George's Road. Need you to motor here soonest.

I stepped over Gordie's body to the kitchen sink and opened the cupboards underneath; there was a bin full of sardine tins—Gordie's unfortunate relish that made him stink eternally of fish—and a box of rubbish bags next to it. The smell reminded me of my first apprentice, Fergus, who'd liked sardines also, and I felt a twinge in my chest, a prickle at the corners of my eyes. Live long enough and people from your past will echo, calling back to you years after they have left you behind.

Wiping impatiently at my eyes, I took out a few bags and headed for the study. The phone vibrated in my pocket and I checked it.

I'm supposed to have the day off. If you make me late for my brother's wedding, Nadia warned, *I'll have your bollocks slow-roasted and served with mayo.*

I winced. I'd forgotten she wasn't on the clock. Her place wasn't all that far away—she was very close to Kelvinbridge subway station—but traffic never cooperated. *Drive fast, then,* I typed with my thumbs. *Not that you even like the woman he's marrying.*

Aye, she and her manky fanny can perish in an industrial accident, but I love him, ye know?

Don't text while driving. Because you're already driving, right?

I'm gonnay shave you smooth as a dolphin, she replied, and I frowned. Nadia only threatened to do that when she was seriously upset. She had yet to flash her straight razor at me, but I didn't want to ever make her feel like she had to either.

Wear the hat I gave you to fool the cameras.

That's it. Tell your upper lip it's gonnay be nude.

I supposed she'd liked Gordie and might take this news hard. I'd liked him too, until these last few minutes, when I learned he'd been using my training to exploit others and enrich himself.

First thing I did in Gordie's study was to destroy all his sigils. I gave them a tear down the middle, and into the bag the scraps went. That allowed me to rip up the Sigil of Warded Sight and restore my vision to normal. But I noted which sigils he'd successfully created without my aid: I took notes in an app on my phone. There were only four people in the world who could have taught him besides me, and I'd be giving them a sharp questioning.

Next I went to his rack of cubbyholes and ruthlessly plundered them, one by one, every single stoppered pot of ink, carefully labeled. The inks I'd never taught him matched up with the sigils he shouldn't have known. I wasn't particularly worried the inkpots would break as I tumbled them into the bag: They were made of very thick glass, and a genuine effort would be required to break them.

He also had a stash of ink ingredients that went far beyond what he should have possessed. He certainly hadn't been given leave to collect chambered-nautilus ganglions for Manannan Mac Lir's ink or the time to seek out banana-slug slime for the rare ink known as Vermilion Beard. And how in nine hells had he got chambered-nautilus ganglions anyway? I didn't have any of those myself! If he had a supplier, I wanted to know who it was. Regardless, he was shelling out quite a few pounds for all this, and it had probably come from trafficking. There had to be ridiculous money in it, or I can't imagine why he'd ever take the risk. Into another bag the sturdy ingredient containers disappeared.

I swept up his pens and assorted inkpots on the workbench too and wondered where he'd been stashing his trafficking money. Some forensic accounting would need to be done—some hacking as well, no doubt. Moving into his bedroom, I dumped Gordie's laptop, phone, chargers, and a couple of flash drives I found into another bag, along with notebooks and correspondence, anything he'd actually written on.

Fortunately, I knew someone willing to perform the required hacking for a few prepared sigils: an absolutely batty but otherwise reliable bloke who went by the outlandish alias of Saxon Codpiece. I wasn't sure whether he sold the sigils later for enormous sums or kept them for his own use, but the ones I gave him were not inherently dangerous.

I knew Nadia had arrived when I heard her swearing at the front door.

"Oh, no, Al, ye lost another one? Poor Gordie! What happened this time—oh, ya daft shite. Raisins! What a senseless way tae go tits up."

Usually Nadia sheathed herself in a symphony of black, including some black lipstick cheerfully branded as Father's Ashes and a shade of nail polish she swore was called Satan's Blackest Hole. But she was dressed for a wedding today, the brightly colored clothing and jewelry of a traditional Indian ceremony, with sari and sandals and the works. Her hair—normally spiked up in the middle and bald on the sides—was artfully plastered to her skull so as to make it seem like she hadn't shaved most of it off and then further disguised with a sort of bejeweled headdress shaped like a swimmer's cap. She'd taken the trouble to apply cosmetics beyond eyeliner, and she'd even painted her lips and fingernails a bright red. That last was clearly what bothered her the most, as her eyes followed mine to where she gripped the hat I'd told her to wear into the building.

"No a word 'bout my nails, Al. Or anything. This situation here is only because I love ma wee brother and need tae convince his bride's family that I'm totally normal and no involved with the occult, plus I'm pretending that ma uterus desperately wants a ten-month lease from some man's seed but I'm just too busy at the moment, awright?"

I nodded and opened my text-to-speech app because Signal seemed impersonal when we were in the same room. Nadia hadn't heard me speak aloud for most of the ten years she'd been my manager, because a curse laid on my heid meant that I couldn't speak very long with anyone with whom I wished to continue having a relationship. After a few days they would begin to hate me, and more so with every sentence I uttered.

I can report that it is a terrible way to lose a family.

I lost my son to it and most of my friends before I realized what had been done to me. At first, I thought maybe I was just insufferable. That was plausible and even probable. But then I reasoned that the Scots have suffered a lot worse than me, so there might be something else at work. A friendly witch in the Highlands was able to recognize that I'd been cursed but couldn't dispel it or even tell me who did it. Now I'm careful to be functionally mute with most everyone until I can be sure the curse is gone.

The text-to-speech app didn't have a Glaswegian accent available, but it had a London accent, so I at least sounded like I was from the UK.

[Thanks for coming,] the app said for me in a slightly stilted delivery. [I need you to take Gordie's inks and that somewhere secure, then go to your brother's wedding. See you in the morning. We'll talk then.]

"Fuck." She pinched the bridge of her nose as if to ward off an incoming headache. "Awright, where's this shite ye want stowed? Is that it there?"

I handed her the bags in question and nodded my thanks at her.

"I want a raise, Al."

My thumbs flew across the phone screen, and the app's voice said, [Okay. Item number one in the morning.]

Her eyes widened in a promise and she pointed at me with two fingers, thumb cocked. "Item number one."

She didn't know it, but she could have anything she asked for. She kept my secrets and the shop's books and kicked what arses occasionally needed kicking. She was, in other words, the perfect manager and, more often than not, the boss of me.

With Nadia gone, I had only the computer, phone, and papers to take with me, which were easy enough to sling over my shoulder. But there were two cages as well, which I might be able to use to track either the pixie or the hobgoblin. I couldn't take both and I highly doubted I'd have the chance for another plunder before the police returned, so I chose the hobgoblin's cage, since I knew he was still alive as of a few minutes ago. The pixie's fate was more doubtful.

I paused before leaving, considering Gordie's still form, and spoke aloud to him, since it didn't matter anymore.

"Well, I'm off tae find out just how giant a turd ye were behind ma back. I'll no doubt have plenty of cause tae curse yer name soon enough. But I'll say this now, Gordie, if yer ghost is lurking around: I wouldnae have wished yer death for anything. Chokin' on a raisin scone, all alone and knowing there's no helping it, ye're gonnay die in the next minute—well, it's horrific. I'm more sorry than I can say. I might wish for ye tae be roastin' in hell once I figure out what ye were up to, but for now I hope ye're at peace."

The door to his flat shut with a final click that echoed in the hallway, and I paused to wipe at my bloody eyes again. Moments like that—the smothering, quiet aftermath of deaths, when I'm intensely aware of being a little bit more alone in the world than I was before—always hit me harder than the moment when I first hear the news.

Seven apprentices, damn it.

CHAPTER 3

Don't Be John MacKnob

Hamlet was right when he told Horatio that there are more things in heaven and earth than he dreamt of in his philosophy. There are far more planes than heaven and earth, for one thing. There are the Fae planes, the Norse planes, the planes of any pantheon ye care to name, all teeming with creatures and spirits and deities who need to work out their rights regarding visitation to earth. The general rule is that the humans in charge don't want them coming to earth at all, because that would sort of ruin the idea that the humans are in charge. We don't have to consult every new administration that comes along; that's been the position for centuries. Any visits extraplanar entities *do* make are supposed to be shepherded, or at least monitored.

But the reverse holds doubly true. Humans who just wander into other planes by accident or by really screwing up their arcane rituals rarely come back. They need a guide and permission. I look at the Internet as a sort of plane in the sense that it has plenty of rules and one shouldn't be mucking about there without some expertise. Even if you only shop there or post selfies, you're being traced, and your personal data is being mined and sold. If you want to walk into the hell of protected data, you're absolutely going to need a hacker, the way Dante needed Virgil.

When I informed Nadia about my need for a hacker several years ago, she took a few days to get back to me but eventually gave me a name, a time, and a rendezvous point.

"Saxon Codpiece, noon, at Tchai Ovna."

[His name is . . .]

"Saxon Codpiece. He likes it if ye kind of half-shout each name as an exclamation, like he's a superhero or sumhin in the cartoons. Like, *Saxonnn! Codpiece!* Do it like that and he'll take a shine tae ye."

[Is he undergoing treatment for anything?]

"I dunno. I've never met him. But I think he's doing one of those absurdist bits where ye make people think ye can't exist because it's too ridiculous."

[Right. I thought that hackers had numbers in their names or some rubbish like that.]

"That sort of thing is like buying a fast red car and daring the polis tae catch ye. This guy is in it for the long haul. Just go. He's no supposed tae be dangerous."

The man who loomed across from me at Tchai Ovna—a Czech teahouse near the university that was always in danger of being demolished and redeveloped—was fully two meters tall. Wiry and dark-haired with hazel eyes, he wore what the kids called vintage and I called clothes. By that I mean it was seventies punk, the sort of thing I was into when I was young: ripped jeans and safety pins and lots of zippers and buttons on his leather jacket. Judging by his pallor, he lived with a perpetual vitamin D deficiency, which he attempted to disguise with some lurid sleeve tattoos on his arms that began at his wrists. The bottom of his nose was red and he sniffled, wiping at it with a handkerchief.

"Sorry about the cold," he said, folding himself into a chair without invitation but thankfully neglecting to offer a handshake. "All systems are susceptible tae viruses, eh?" He peered at me and a corner of his mouth turned upward. *"Fantastic* mustache, mate. Al, is it?"

"That's right."

"Gaun yersel'! Right, well, here's ma card."

He placed a maroon-colored card on the table in front of me and tapped it a couple of times for emphasis. There were just two lines of text, centered in an all-caps, sans serif font, the first line significantly larger than the other:

SAXON! CODPIECE!

PROFESSIONAL WANKER

I scoffed. "What, then, the rest of us are just amateurs?"

"Unless ye're getting paid for it like me, yes, ye're an amateur."

"Ye must hang out in the darkest places of the Internet."

"I do, on occasion. But I spend a good deal of time in the lighter places too. Cat videos, ye know. Full-grown screaming goats, dancing baby goats, or any goats, really, are endlessly entertaining. Rejuvenates the soul."

"Fine. But are ye discreet?"

"About ma wanking? No, in fact I'm anything but discreet. I film it and make a sizable income from it, because I have a sizable—"

"No, no, no. Shut yer gob. I'm no here for that. I mean about your other clients and the information ye come across."

"Oh, yes. Absolutely. Congratulations, ye passed the test."

I hadn't known there was a test at all, but if someone says ye passed it already, no need to bother. We turned to the business I needed done at that time. He did it quickly and well and I paid him the same way, but I offered him alternative payment the second time we met over tea at Tchai Ovna, because he asked me what I did for a living and I told him.

"Officially I own a printshop on High Street. But truly I'm a sigil agent."

"Whit?"

"It's like yer own business. Officially ye're a professional wanker on the Internet. But truly ye're a hacker."

"Right, but I meant whit's a sigil agent?"

"I write and enforce magical contracts using sigils, which are symbols infused with power that can do some remarkable stuff. The enforcement part's where all the fun is. Would ye like a demonstration?"

"Ye mean like card tricks?"

"No, I mean like this." I pulled a prepared Sigil of Certain Authority out of my coat and popped the seal in front of him, lifting the flap to reveal the sigil underneath. He flinched, gulped, and then I demanded that he give me all the money in his wallet. He had about five hundred quid. Impressive. I left it on the table.

"Thank ye."

"Of course, sir," he said. I waited, and then after about ten seconds, Saxon blinked rapidly. "Hey. Why did I call ye *sir*? I haven't called anyone that since childhood."

"I used a sigil on ye tae make ye obey a single command. There are many sigils with different kinds of effects. That particular one is not open for discussion, because as ye have just learned, it can too easily be abused. It does, however, prove that I have something tae offer ye besides money. Please, take yours back. It's all there."

He snatched it up and returned it to his wallet, shaking his head with a smile. "Christ, that's stonkin'. I'd say I didnae believe it, but it just happened. I never call people *sir*, much less give them money for nothing. This is wild. I always wanted tae meet a wizard."

"I'm not a wizard. Common misperception, though. I get called that a lot."

"How come I've never heard of this sigil business before?"

"There are only five of us in the world, and we don't advertise. If ye would like tae be paid in sigils—ones that ye can use yourself or on others—I'm open tae that, if ye can keep secrets."

After that meeting, I stopped talking and used my app, since I'd established that magic and therefore curses were real. We have worked well together ever since and do our best to avoid mentioning our official jobs to each other. It was true that Saxon usually requested to be paid in Sigils of Sexual Vigor, but I steadfastly refused to inquire what use he made of them.

Saxon's place was hidden underneath Tartan Greenhouses, a twenty-four-hour industrial operation based in a warehouse in the shadow of the necropolis, growing all sorts of organic vegetables in hydroponic beds. He owned it through various shell corporations and used it, along with similar operations scattered around the country, to launder his various streams of illicit income. I was one of the few people he trusted enough to enter his work space, an underground lair of crisps and beer, Faraday cages and an old Dig Dug video game from the eighties that he admired because Dig Dug "blew up bullies and got paid."

To access it, I entered the office that functioned as a lobby, strode through the door marked EMPLOYEES ONLY, skipped the locker room, and headed to the toolshed, wherein a pegboard waited on the back wall with assorted tools mounted on it. By lifting a saw blade, I revealed a small intercom speaker with a call button. I pressed it and a voice demanded a password, which changed weekly and Saxon sent to me via Signal's encrypted text.

It was always some combination of an adjective followed by a food noun. Last week it was Languid Eggplant, and the week before it was Complacent Taco.

[Urgent Cake,] I had my phone say, and the pegboard slid aside to reveal a narrow staircase descending into the earth. With my cane and bag clutched awkwardly in one hand and the hobgoblin's cage in the other, I took it slow.

"Awright, Al?" Saxon rose from a chair behind a semicircle of monitors and keyboards, crumpling up a bag of haggis-and-pepper crisps and tossing it into a nearby bin. He had black jeans on and a T-shirt with a portrait of Margaret Thatcher crossed out by a red *no* symbol—those circles with a backslash through them. He'd grown a small field of black whiskers on his chin since last I'd seen him, like angry iron shavings. I simply nodded my greeting, which he was used to by now.

"Can I get ye sumhin to drink? I have most of the basics, ye know." He gestured grandly toward the bar, which was fully stocked and far beyond basic. He even had a couple of local craft kegs on tap, the Black Star Teleporter from Shilling Brewing and Bearface Lager from Drygate Brewing.

[Maybe just an Irn-Bru,] I typed, already shuddering at the thought of the sugary, caffeinated stuff, but pretty sure Saxon would have some on hand. [We have work to do.]

"Excellent!" He clapped his hands together once and rubbed them with glee. "Irn-Bru and work. I like it. Ye just made my day, Al."

He scurried to the bar—as much as a two-meter giant can scurry—and poured us drinks while I began unloading the bags. I left the cage at the bottom of the stairs, then put the laptop, phone, and flash drives on his crowded desk. I took the papers over to the bar and dumped them out on the cherrywood while Saxon bizarrely garnished my Irn-Bru with a grapefruit wedge.

"There we are. So! What are we daein'?"

[Breaking into a laptop and phone. The owner was trafficking Fae, and we need to know who was buying, or who was selling, or both.]

"Yes!" He executed a lanky fist pump before pointing at me. "That is *wild*. I knew it was gonnay be. I love yer weird shite, man." He grinned and slurped his soda noisily while I composed a reply.

[My weird shite keeps people worrying about economics and politics instead of the possibility that trolls might steal their children for breakfast, so I think we should accord it a smidgen of gravitas.]

"Awright, I can pull a smidge of gravitas from somewhere. Ye have any passwords at all?"

[Not yet. Maybe something in this rubbish here. I'll go through it.]

"Right. I'll proceed without them until ye say different."

He went digging around for gadgets to help crack the devices, while I sifted through the papers on the bar. Lots of it was bills, but there were a couple of old-fashioned letters, a mess of receipts, some small yellow squares with to-do lists on them like *get milk and scones,* and a half-sheet concert flyer for a punk band called Dildo Shaggins. There were several blank-papered journals, sadly left uninked except for one, which was about half filled.

That contained all sorts of scribblings, notably *Al is a clueless git* and *MacB has the brain capacity of a nuthatch.*

Some other notes, like *must find nautilus ganglions,* had obviously been reminders that he had followed through on, and the observation that *pixies are nothing like the cartoon ones* must have come after he'd caught one. Much of the rest were practice sketches of sigils made with normal inks. He'd been having trouble remembering the Sigil of Dampening Magic, which was not surprising since I hadn't taught him that one. But on page ten, near the bottom, I found something potentially useful: the heading VAULT and then what must clearly be a randomly generated password, thirty-two characters long and composed of numbers, letters, and punctuation marks.

"Oh, aye, that'll be helpful once I get in," Saxon said, busy clipping something with wires and lights to the laptop. "But if it says VAULT, that's no the password tae unlock his computer."

[How long until you can get in?]

"Depends on how long his password is. Could be a few minutes, could be hours or days."

[I might be needing a beer, then.]

"Sure. Help yourself."

I circled around behind the bar and plucked a pint glass from a drying rack. The Black Star Teleporter, I discovered, was a delightful coconut porter without too much foam. The quantity and quality of foam becomes important when one cares for an impeccable mustache.

The gadget attached to Gordie's laptop bleeped after a few swallows, and Saxon yelped in surprise.

"Ha! He only had a six-digit password! Not too bright." He tapped a key and said, "Awright, I'm in. Here's his vault."

[His vault?]

"Password vault, mate. An app that contains all his passwords. We'll type that thirty-two-character monstrosity into it and then we'll own him, whoever this is."

I left the beer on the bar, because it was time to work again. Saxon's eyes widened as he scanned the contents of the vault.

"This guy has multiple offshore accounts. Account numbers and usernames and everything here in the notes. Ye don't bother with accounts like that unless ye have a lot of scratch tae move around."

I typed instructions. [I want to check balances in each account, but don't move anything. And then let's get into his email.]

"Right ye are. Here we go."

Gordie had a hundred thousand quid in each of six different accounts in various tax havens.

"Know what's strange? These are all recent accounts. Deposits made, but he hasn't touched them or even had time tae earn much interest, except in one."

I took note of the account names and numbers and the dates they were opened, then told Saxon to move into email. He scanned the vault.

"He's got three accounts. Which one dae ye want tae start with?" He pointed at the screen and I recognized only one of the addresses. One was a gmail account, and I doubted he'd keep anything sensitive there, but the other was composed almost entirely of numbers.

[Start with the dodgy numeric one.]

"That's where I would have started too. Okay, let's see . . . yep. It's fairly new, only ten conversations, no spam. And have a keek, man—it's all from the same guy. This account exists solely tae communicate with whoever this is."

[Open the oldest one, please.]

I looked over his shoulder as Saxon clicked on the oldest conversation, with the subject heading ARRANGEMENTS.

Please bring first subject to the north shore of Renfrew Ferry, 9 p.m. Friday. My representative will meet you. Upon transfer of subject, funds will be deposited into an account you name.

—Bastille

Gordie replied:

Will do. Please transfer to First Cayman Bank, account number 9842987241. But I must ask: What are subjects being used for? I inquire for ethical reasons.

I snorted and typed, [If there was anything ethical about this, he wouldn't have had to use numbered accounts.]

"Right? But it implies he's got some line, at least, that he won't cross."

The reply from Bastille was short:

Science. Glorious, lifesaving science.

"That is strange," Codpiece murmured. "I mean the *why*, not the what."

[What are you on about?]

"Ye said this was about the Fae, right?"

[Aye.]

"Well, the reason behind human trafficking is usually either the sex trade or the labor industry, like janitorial services or sumhin like that. But this looks like Bastille wants test subjects. Which means yer boy Gordie was serving up high-priced lab rats tae evil scientists."

[Evil scientists? Really?]

"Sure. They happen sometimes. I mean, there's a spectrum, in't there? Most scientists try tae work on things tae help us understand the world, or else they shout and bawl quite rightly about how we're all doomed and have been choking the planet tae death since the Industrial Revolution. The scientists in the moral grey area tell ye tobacco is just fine, not harmful at all, or they take money from oil companies tae tell ye climate heating is nothin' to worry yer heid about. But occasionally ye get pure bastards who work for governments, and what kind of science do governments want, eh? Evil shite like truth serums and hallucinogens and bombs and chemical weapons tae protect their nation against whoever they think the bad guys are. They've got the money and the facilities and the leverage tae make it happen. So it makes me wonder, Al: Who's this Bastille bloke that's doin' this? Isnae a government, 'cos they can snatch any ol' snatch they want for experiments, right? They don't have tae do *this*."

I grunted at him because I didn't want to explain that maybe they did. There's not a government I know of that has access to the Fae, and that's because sigil agents made damn sure they didn't in the treaties drawn up between our peoples long ago. And, of course, because Brighid wanted it that way. Gordie might have been giving them access, though I didn't know how. I didn't know much about this business at all, but I'd have to learn quickly.

[What you were saying earlier. About focusing human trafficking on the sex or labor industries. How do they go about it?]

"Shenanigans, mostly. This really isn't my line of business, but from what I understand, there's an assortment of cons they use tae trick people intae traveling somewhere, usually for love or money—oh, lookit all this green grass over here on the other side, they say, ye can leave yer shite life behind—but it's a bait and switch every time. Once their marks get to where they're going, the promises made are disregarded. If the victims are in a situation where they're being paid—a job in a restaurant, maybe—they're loaded up with debt they can never pay off and they're trapped. Sometimes these shiteweasels take their victims' passports and make threats, shut them in rooms without food for a couple of days, and then they're afraid and trapped in a different way. But the bait part is why the authorities cannae catch them when it's happening. People are traveling willingly, for the most part. Because of the telly, the public thinks trafficking means they're kidnapping people off the streets and sending them in shipping containers across borders, but if that is happening—I'm no saying it isnae—it's the exception rather than the rule. Most of the travel is done legally, and then the hammer falls on the victims when they arrive."

[Bollocks. So Gordie—or somebody—was convincing the Fae to come here under false pretenses. I'm sure they weren't lured by the promise of becoming a science experiment.]

"Right."

[Okay, regarding common trafficking: If somebody's supplying it, then someone's demanding, it, right? So who's demanding modern slavery?]

"There's the thing. They usually don't know that's what they're daein'."

[How can they not?]

Saxon gave a shrug. "If it's someone in a restaurant cooking up yer appetizer, or some invisible person who cleans yer hotel room after ye leave, how would ye know? But as an example, let's take it from the sex side of things: Let's say ye're a sad sack of shite named John MacKnob and ye're going tae a convention for sad sacks in Liverpool and ye want tae get yer end away while ye're there. Ye go online—people know where tae find these sites—and ye schedule it. Since ye're John MacKnob, ye assume that yer escort is in it for all the money ye're paying them. Ye think they're just so incredibly hot for sad sacks that they've voluntarily entered the industry tae shag some. Sometimes John MacKnob will even ask, and when he does, the escorts will of course always say they're in it because they like it and no because if they try tae escape or say anything like the truth they'll be punished or killed, or their families back home will. And therefore John MacKnob's vague wisp of a conscience is easily reassured that he's no daein' anything wrong. He gets tae tell himself that he's entered intae a consensual arrangement. If he had half a brain, he'd stop to consider how the way he set up the encounter would give him a broad hint at the independence of the worker. If he contracted with the individual on their own, then they're probably running their own show. If he contracted with a third party, however—if he set it up with a hotel clerk or a call service or sumhin—then the likelihood of trafficking is much higher. But it's John MacKnob we're talkin' about here and he's just thinking about his knob, in't he? That and covering his own arse. And tae do that, he orders four or five escorts at a time and brings his friends along."

[Seriously?]

"It's a party, see? John MacKnob and his sad-sack industry buddies are gonnay have a good time. Entertainment is a business expense. They can actually pay for trafficked people on company credit cards and it gets written off their corporate taxes."

[Are you having a laugh at me now?]

"I'm not. It might not be as widespread as it used tae be, but these traffickers are savvy. They know how tae make it look legal. It's going on in plain sight. Conventions of any kind are where most of the sex trafficking happens. Them or big sporting events. Get a bunch of men together with disposable income and ye're going tae have trafficking. Arseholes scheduling parties and plenty of singles also. And on the labor side, it's hotels or other businesses with large buildings contracting for janitorial services. The hotels aren't intae the trafficking, but they subcontract their labor, and those subcontractors are in it up tae their necks."

[So how do we stop it?]

Codpiece spluttered and sighed. "I wish I knew. The problem is with the John MacKnobs of the world and late-stage capitalism. They're creating the demand, see? Traffickers will find a way tae supply that demand as long as it's there. Focusing on the traffickers might make ye feel good, and it gives the polis and the politicians something to point at and say they're making progress, but they're no really addressing the root cause. Someone else will step in tae make that money, because rumor has it they're hauling in thirty thousand pounds a week on average tae ruin people's lives. Best thing we can do is not be a John MacKnob. Employers can stop doing all this contract work and—" He paused, blinking as a thought hit him. "Actually, I suppose that's where we could do some good. Hit them in the contracts. That will slow things down on both the sex and labor sides of the market."

I liked the sound of that. Contracts were exactly my line. [How so?]

"These conventions require contracts between the hotels and the companies holding the event. Vendor contracts, ye know what I mean? If there's a clause in those contracts that's anti-trafficking, that will change behaviors. They tell their employees they'll be fired for anything like that. They'll be auditing entertainment expenses. They'll have a meeting in the break room and tell their employees all kinds of fire will rain down upon their heids if they're perving out on company time."

Well, Gordie didn't get fire raining down on his heid, but he got a raisin scone lodged in his throat for his trouble. It made me wonder: Were *all* my deid apprentices trafficking in the Fae and slain by a stroke of bad luck, or was it on purpose, like a curse? I knew from experience how subtle a curse could be. Maybe my apprentices crossed the Fae and got themselves cursed with an accidental death—just a bad-luck hex cast on them when they weren't looking. But on the other hand, if all my apprentices were mucking about like Gordie and inviting such curses, I needed to either retool my oversight or just retire.

The way I saw it, there were two things to pursue—no, three: First, who was luring the Fae to earth? Because it probably wasn't Gordie; he'd have no way to contact them. Second, who were the John MacKnobs in this scenario, paying for the Fae to be trafficked—who was Bastille, in other words? And third, where the hell did that nose-punching hobgoblin scarper off to?

The rest of the emails from Bastille just dealt with new transactions, establishing rendezvous times for new subjects. Each of these corresponded in terms of dates with deposits to offshore accounts. The hobgoblin had told me the truth: Gordie was a trafficker in the Fae.

[Can you trace the origin of Bastille's emails?]

"I can try, but I'll bet you six biscuits it's just a bunch of prox-ies."

[Can you get into Gordie's phone and get his contacts and calls?]

"Aye. Androids are easy. I mean, it'll take a while, don't get me wrong, but I'll get it done."

[Okay. Please see what you can to do track down Bastille, find out who he might be. Anything to narrow it down. Keep me posted.]

"Awright. And regarding payment . . . ?"

I knew what he wanted. I got out my pens and cards drew him five Sigils of Sexual Vigor and sealed them for later use with a Sigil of Postponed Puissance. Usually I paid him only four.

[This is important. I'll draw you another bonus one for quick work.]

"I am *on* it, Al. Always good to work with ye."

[Thanks, Saxon.]

I took the hobgoblin's cage with me and climbed back up to the humid hydroponics operation. It was a bit past 17:00 and time for dinner and a chat with someone from Tír na nÓg. I imagined they'd only have questions for me, but I hoped they'd have some answers too.

CHAPTER 4

---◆ ∙ ◆---

Illicit Spirits

Scotland is justifiably renowned for its rich and varied whiskies, but there is another spirit at which it excels, due to the botanicals available here: gin.

The Scottish gin industry in recent years is almost as varied as the whisky—so much so that it allows for the existence of Gin71 in Merchant City, an establishment featuring seventy-one craft gins from Scotland, all using local botanicals. They have savory profiles, sweet sloes and berries, or even floral notes, depending on the botanicals used. I was always impressed that they grouped gins by flavor profile and garnish on the menu and even went so far as to offer a range of flavored tonics. But for all that, there was another reason I frequented Gin71. Owing to the history of bustling human activity near its location, it was almost on top of an Old Way leading to Tír na nÓg and therefore a point of contact with the Fae.

It was a bit of a walk from Saxon's place to Virginia Court, site of the Tobacco Exchange back in the days when Glasgow basically received all the tobacco from Virginia and then shipped it to the rest of Europe. It staggered me at times to think of how much money and cancer had flowed through that relatively small area, a metaphor for all of capitalism's glories and evils. The tobacco merchants were all long dead now, their moldering bones entombed in the Glasgow Necropolis, their engraved markers testifying that once, more than a century ago, they had worn fancy clothes and eaten whole hogs and shat in only the shiniest of chamber pots. A portion of their product had been stolen by the Fae and given to grey-bearded wizards, along with lengthy hand-carved pipes as gifts, a tradition that eventually worked its way into popular imagination, much to the amusement of the Fae.

To enter Gin71, one walked through a set of double doors that was basically a hallway leading to a number of delights. To the right was a tapas bar called Brutti Compadres, an orange-and-yellow-lit space that sold many Aperol spritzes. Straight ahead was a spa, and to the left was my rendezvous point.

Once I was through the door, the bar stretched immediately to my right, and the table and booth seating was to the left. I was going to take a booth, but I wanted to catch the bartender's attention first. To humans she was known as Heather MacEwan, but her real name—the name I'd written on her work visa allowing her to be employed on earth—was Harrowbean. She was a faery loyal to Brighid, First among the Fae, and she served as my direct line to the Fae Court whenever I needed it. She was ethereally beautiful, of course, a flame-haired vision of strength and delicacy, and an outstanding mixologist whose drinks had been reviewed as "magical" in the Glasgow papers and food blogs, though they decried the fact that she was essentially working with only one spirit instead of all of them. She kept her wings folded and out of sight underneath a spotless white shirt and a purple-black brocade Victorian waistcoat stitched with silver thread and accented with a silver ascot tied at her throat. She tended to get tipped fantastically well.

"Awright, Al?" she asked.

[Awright, Heather. I need an Illicit Gin right away, please. I'll take a seat over there.]

"You need it fast?"

[As fast as possible.]

"Coming right up."

Normally I ordered a Pilgrim's, a fine gin with the traditional suite of juniper botanicals, which paired very well with Fever Tree Mediterranean tonic and a blackberry garnish, though in fairness it paired well with almost any tonic you'd care to name. Heather MacEwan, the human-seeming bartender, always managed a perfect pour. If there were any messages from Faerie to deliver that didn't come via the usual post to my office, she would deliver them to my table with my standard drink. Illicit Gin, on the other hand, was made under a railway arch in Glasgow, with notes of cinnamon, clove, and orange peel. Ordering one of those was our agreed-upon signal for Harrowbean to summon Coriander, Herald Extraordinary of the Nine Fae Planes, and ordering it fast meant it was an emergency.

She ducked out from behind the bar, exited the restaurant, and then began walking about Virginia Court in a pattern that may have seemed random but was not at all. The specific steps, the turns and length of them, transported her on an Old Way to the Fae Court in Tír na nÓg, until she disappeared from this plane and appeared there. Heather would be Harrowbean for a brief while, summon Coriander, and return the way she came to resume her bartending duties.

I took a seat and waited, reflecting morbidly that my profession as a sigil agent basically made me akin to those hygienic shields in public toilets, what the Americans called an "ass gasket": a thin tissue-like layer of protection between an arsehole on one side and a bowl of shite on the other. When it came to humanity and the Fae, I honestly didn't know which was which, and I supposed it didn't matter. My job was to keep them apart.

Harrowbean returned in a few minutes, transitioning flawlessly to her role as Heather MacEwan the bartender, and fixed my Illicit

Gin along with the favored drink of my coming guest: a Garden Shed gin and tonic, proceeds to benefit the preservation of bees.

By the time she had them made and brought them over, Coriander had appeared in Virginia Court and was entering the bar.

Like Harrowbean, he was beautiful. He appeared to be either a handsome woman or a pretty man, very easy on the eyes regardless of one's orientation. He was a universally appealing biped and asserted the use of the male pronoun when I asked. He wore a Victorian-style waistcoat as well, grey with hints of pale blue in the pattern, which matched his ascot. In the Fae Court he wore a powdered wig, because Brighid favored it, but he ditched it whenever he came to visit me, allowing his blond hair to splay about his skull, artfully mussed.

Coriander slid into the seat across from me, nodded to the bartender, and took a sip of his drink as I took a sip from mine. Once that was done, glasses placed carefully back on cocktail napkins, he met my eyes and spoke in his calm, measured, musical voice with an Irish accent.

"Hello, Al. What's the emergency?"

I told him of Gordie's death and the alarming news that he was trafficking Fae somehow.

[Can you ask around the Fae Court,] I typed in my app, [and see if any of your people have disappeared mysteriously? This would be only the last six months.]

"Of course. Anything else?"

[Has Brighid started teaching sigils to anyone else besides sigil agents recently?]

"If she has, I haven't been made aware. I will ask, though I would be highly surprised if the answer was yes. She has been satisfied with your performance and would have no need."

Hearing that she was satisfied was good, but it meant that Gordie must have learned his extra sigils from one of my colleagues. I dutifully informed the herald that someone had shared unauthorized sigils with Gordie.

[I'll try to get to the bottom of that, but perhaps you could investigate on your side too.]

Coriander nodded. "Of course."

[Also: There's a hobgoblin loose in Glasgow.]

"His name?"

[I don't know. Gordie had him in this cage.]

"What did he look like?"

[I overheard someone say he has pink skin—I had my sight warded when I saw him, so I only saw a shade of grey. Thick, dark eyebrows and hair. Shiny, perfect teeth that weren't glamoured— he's had actual work done. Paisley waistcoat, no shirt underneath. Triskele tattoo on his shoulder.]

Coriander shook his head. "He doesn't sound familiar."

[No matter. Can you set a barghest on him? I'll write out the contract now.]

"Of course."

[Please impress on the barghest that this isn't a hunt. This is a fetch. The hobgoblin is not to be harmed.]

"Fetching a hobgoblin is easier said than done."

[He'll tire out eventually and be unable to teleport. The barghest will win.] From the many inner pockets of my bespoke topcoat, I pulled out the proper pens for contract work, a folded piece of blank paper, my sigil-agent seal, and an embossment inker. It was a bit of a production, but it beat going back to the office to do everything.

"Understood. And where is the barghest to bring the quarry once found?"

[To the office in my printshop on High Street. I'll head straight there to wait.]

"May I assume that this cage you've brought is going to provide the source scent?"

[Yes.]

"Very well. Will you excuse me for a moment while you write the contract? I need to have a word with the bartender."

I nodded and Coriander slid smoothly away, taking his drink with him while I got to work.

Barghests didn't usually perform harmless fetches; they were ghostly warhounds typically employed on seek-and-destroy missions. As long as the hobgoblin didn't put up too much of a fight, he'd probably escape serious injury. The problem was he'd have no idea that the barghest was instructed to deliver him unharmed and would assume he was in a fight—or a flight—for his life. Still, the best way to find a faery in a human city was to use Fae methods. I probably wrote a barghest contract at least once a month to find a rogue faery or some other being from the world's pantheons, and the other sigil agents probably did it at least as often or even more. Besides being outstanding trackers, barghests had the extraordinary ability to shut down the magic of anything in their jaws, so they were quite nearly perfect solutions to many problems.

I used an emerald Visconti fountain pen for contract language and the Sigil of Contracted Labor that needed to appear at the top. The ink was a carbon black derived from pine soot with finely ground bits of stag-beetle carapace mixed in—honestly the most pedestrian ink recipe I had, the exoskeleton additive being the only thing that made it different from normal inks. After I drew the sigil, I wrote out the barghest contract and signed it. Then I had to switch to a flashy pen by Caran d'Ache that amused me to no end: The barrel was wrapped in leather and the cap was a sculpted rhodium skull, a limited-edition piece of gothica in honor of American architect Peter Marino. It was a fitting delivery system for an ink that contained pit-viper venom and cochineal to power the Sigil of Dire Consequence, which did not actually slay those in breach of contract but rather ignited all their nerves with pain so that they wished they were dead. My seal was last, applied with a handheld embosser that included my name worked into a Sigil of Binding Law. The finishing touch was a stamp of dry ink, a circle of solid pigment containing many rare ingredients that would cover the embossed ridges of my seal and power it up—which in turn would power up the other sigils, which didn't activate except in the presence of Binding Law. There wasn't any actual sound effect when the sigils activated, but I always imagined one, like a *voom* vibrating under a shiver of bell chimes and a harp flourish. There was, however, a visual effect: The ink took on a glossy, iridescent sheen it hadn't possessed before.

Satisfied, I returned my pens and seal to my coat and informed Coriander that the contract was ready. He finished his conversation with Harrowbean, leaving his drink at the bar, and came back to fetch the contract and the cage.

"Remain well, Al. I wish I could linger to socialize, but I'd better see to this immediately."

I waved farewell to him and took a few deep breaths once he'd disappeared in Virginia Court, trying to banish a gathering sense of dread. This business would get worse before it got better. I grabbed my Illicit Gin and murmured to it in a parody of Hamlet before draining it dry: "But what is your affair in Glasgow? We'll teach you to drink deep ere you depart."

It was a very good emergency gin.

CHAPTER 5

The Buck Stopped There

High Street is one of the older streets of Glasgow, and it has suffered many refurbishments and its share of gentrification while retaining much of its original character. My printshop, MacBharrais Printing & Binding, was sandwiched in the middle of a row of businesses including a yoga studio, a travel agency, and a chip shop. On the side of the building at the north end of the row was a mural of a dark-bearded man in a woolly hat gazing down at a finch resting peacefully on his index finger, his hand curled into a gentle fist, and I found it an inspiring reminder that we should always consider the welfare of others and think of the smallest and weakest first. It was a modern look at Glasgow's patron saint, St. Mungo, painted by an Australian artist. Even though I usually approached my shop from the south, because that's where the train station was, I often took the extra hundred steps or so required to gaze upon this gentle giant and be conscious of my purpose: to love and cherish and protect the beings of this plane, and to be kind to its visitors until they prove they won't respond to kindness.

It was already too dark to indulge in my pastime, however, and

I had a visitor besides. A small figure about the size of a toddler sat hunched over in a wee grey hoodie on a set of steps next to the entrance of MP&B. The steps led up to the entrance of a residence located above the shop next door. I halted and looked around for anyone nearby who might look vaguely parental. Stopping and uttering a mild oath, however, drew the attention of the figure, who looked up and pulled back the hood to reveal a pink, snarling visage in the yellow light of streetlamps.

"About time, MacVarnish!" the hobgoblin said. "I've been waiting here an hour, at least."

I dug out my phone and noted that he was instantly on guard. I didn't know if I was going to talk for long to this hobgoblin, but it was best to be prudent. [Oh. Hello,] I typed. [Guess I didn't need to set that barghest on you, then.]

"Wot? Why aren't ye using yer gob like a normal human?"

[I'll explain later. And don't worry, the barghest is not supposed to kill you. He's supposed to bring you to me for a wee chat. So when he gets here, we can declare mission accomplished and let him go home. Just relax and talk to me. Why are you here?]

"Because the game's a bogie. I've got nowhere else tae go."

[Bollocks. You have nine Fae planes.]

"No, I don't, ya sad, shriveled ballsack of a man! If I did, dae ye think I'd be sittin' here waitin' for ye?"

I sighed. [You'd better come in.] When the hobgoblin cocked his head and narrowed his eyes, I added, [If you want to, that is. If you'd rather talk about Fae shite out on the street and get us in more trouble than you already are, that's fine.]

"Swear ye won't try tae bind me like yer apprentice did?"

[I swear.]

"Awright. But you go first, and keep yer hands away from that coat. If ye try tae reach for a sigil, I'll punch ye in the nuts and scarper."

[Fair enough. But I need to get my keys out of the coat.] We had presses running around the clock but the main entrance was locked after business hours.

"No, *I'll* get them. Where are they?"

I pointed to my right outer pocket and raised my arms away from my sides. He darted forward, fished out the keys, and tossed them up into the air for me to catch before scooting away again. Damn Gordie for making him so suspicious.

He stepped aside as I unlocked the door. A wood-paneled reception area greeted us, where customers could come in and ask for quotes and debate the merits of various paper stocks. I strode past that and pushed through the swinging door that led to the actual shop floor. The printers were humming and clacking, the night shift just a few hours into it, and I waved at the foreman before taking the metal stairs to the right that led up to the offices on the first floor, which looked from outside like sandstone-faced flats as the rest of the street did but served us as a warded set of rooms— three of them, in total, accessed by a balcony, and the rest of the floor was open to the ground.

"What is this? A trap? Those steps have iron in them!"

[Good thing you're wearing shoes. Come on. We can talk up here and it won't be so noisy.]

My office was a refuge from the presses, an insulated study of ink and glue and wards. Bookshelves lined the walls to the left and right; the one on the left slid open to a safer, secret office in which I kept my magical inks and a sizable store of prepared sigils. Beyond that was Nadia's office, where most of the printshop's actual work got done.

This space was largely devoted to receiving rare guests, like the hobgoblin, or more usually customers and vendors from the mundane world. Paper salesmen, I had noticed, loved to visit me. Near a window that looked down on High Street I had a mahogany desk, at which I did practically nothing; it displayed some props to make it look like I did things there, but mostly it was a place for me to store business cards and hide the button that would open the bookcase to my real office.

In front of the desk, closer to the door, were four brown leather upholstered chairs arranged around a piece of furniture we called a "coffee table" from three A.M. to noon and a "whisky table" at all other times. (The paper salesmen, I had noticed, tended to visit after noon.) Right now it was a whisky table. A crystal decanter and glasses waited on a silver tray.

[Drink?] I asked, taking a seat that faced the door. The hobgoblin leapt nimbly onto one opposite me after first rotating it slightly so he could keep one eye on the door.

"Sure. But you go first."

I poured us a finger each and gestured toward a mini-fridge lurking on the side of my desk. [Rocks?]

"Neat," he said. I shrugged and took a sip. The hobgoblin watched this, checked the level in my glass to make sure I'd actually swallowed, then sniffed at his suspiciously. "What is this? Something from the Highlands?"

[It's an Islay that drinks a bit like a Highlands, goes easy on the smoke. Eighteen-year Bunnahabhain.] The speech app had no bloody idea how to say Bunnahabhain correctly, but the hobgoblin appeared to recognize the name anyway.

"Not bad." He took a sip, held it in his mouth awhile, and swallowed. "Ahh."

[Let's start over, shall we? I'm the sigil agent Aloysius MacBharrais. What's your name?]

"Ye can call me Buck Foi."

[That's not your name.]

"I know that, ya tit. I said it's what ye can call me."

[Fine, Buck. Tell me how you came to be in a cage in Maryhill.]

"I was promised real work, the kind hobs used tae get before the Industrial Revolution. Domestic service, all legal, permits signed by you."

[Signed by me, you say?]

"Aye."

It took me a while to type a response. [I'm not saying that never happens anymore, Buck, but it's rare. I haven't signed a contract for domestic service in seven years. It didn't occur to you that it might be a fraud?]

"Seemed legit tae me. They gave me these clothes ahead o' time, said they'd last me for years."

[Did they fix up your teeth as well?]

"Naw, that was ma own idea. Ye get further with humans if ye have a nice smile. Thought it worked too. Thought that was the reason they offered me the contract."

[The big question, Buck, is who are *they*?]

"Oh. Well, it was a bunch of bean sídhe, but I don't know their names. And Clíodhna, o' course."

I'd been about to take another sip of whisky and nearly dropped it. For the bean sídhe, or banshees, to do anything but wail in advance of someone's death was strange enough. But Clíodhna was a deadly Irish goddess who should have nothing to do with arranging domestic service for hobgoblins. I set the remainder of my Bunnahabhain down carefully before composing a reply, because it was old as a full-grown adult, and I also didn't want the trembling of my fingers to spill any. I didn't want any of this to be true. [Clíodhna of the Tuatha Dé Danann—we're talking about Clíodhna, the Queen of the Bean Sídhe—gave you forged permits to come work on earth?] The app mispronounced the Irish Gaelic words horribly, but Buck was able to follow along. The Tuatha Dé Danann might not have been so tolerant—the members of the Irish pantheon did have their pride—but a hobgoblin cared nothing for bungled names.

"That's right. And, no, before ye ask, I couldnae be mistaken. It was Clíodhna. I tell ye three times."

[Methinks I need a double, wee man. You want?]

"Aye. I'll say this for ye, MacVarnish: Ye don't pour a shite dram."

I poured us two more fingers, took a fine, burning mouthful, letting it linger on the tongue to detect all the flavors, and leaned back in my chair with my phone. [Okay, you think the contract's legit because it's Clíodhna who's offering. That's understandable. I don't suppose you have those permits with you?]

"Naw. Yer boy Gordie took 'em off me."

[That grimy bawbag.] I hadn't seen anything of the sort in the papers I pilfered from his flat, but, then again, I hadn't been thorough, occupied as I was with getting into his laptop. Maybe the faked documents were still hidden there somewhere. More likely, he'd destroyed them. I could use some proof—I would need it before I made any accusations. [Very well, then, how did you get here from Tír na nÓg?]

"I was given ma permits, and one of the bean sídhe led me through the Old Way that ends in Kelvingrove Park. Ye know it?" I nodded and gestured that he should continue. It wasn't used as often as the one in the necropolis or the one in Virginia Court, but I'd known about that path to Tír na nÓg since I was an apprentice myself. "Gordie was waiting there for me, and he introduced himself as yer apprentice. Like I said, I'd heard o' ye before and yer name was on ma permits, but I didnae know anything about ye otherwise except that ye were based somewhere in Glasgow and looked like an older man. Never had any reason tae look ye up before now. I've been tae Glasgow a few times, ye understand— I used tae run errands for Manannan Mac Lir and Fand if they needed anything from here or Edinburgh."

I held up a finger to interject and typed out a query. [What kind of errands?]

He raised his glass. "Stealing whisky like this, mostly." I nodded. Such little breaches of the law were common. The Tuatha Dé Danann observed the treaty well in most cases and rarely came to earth—the Morrigan had been a notable, pants-ruining exception, because Choosers of the Slain tended to do what they wanted and she had never agreed to the contract—but as a group, the old Irish gods often sent various Fae to steal whatever luxuries they desired, and if the Fae got caught by one of us, it didn't matter to them. They remained out of our reach in Tír na nÓg.

"Anyway, I thought Gordie was bringin' me tae see ye and I didnae know where ye lived or anything, and I had no reason tae be suspicious then. He took me tae that tenement of his and I thought it was all proper. I was gonnay see the sigil agent I've heard about and he was gonnay tell me all the rules for living among the humans. But once we got through the door, Gordie popped a sigil in front of ma eyes and I woke up in the cage next tae the pixie. At least it was an aluminum cage."

Gordie couldn't have come up with this scheme on his own. The shape of it, though still masked from me, was already larger than his intellect. It was quite possible he had learned his extra sigils and ink recipes from Clíodhna and that the other sigil agents weren't the cause of the leak. That didn't relieve me of the necessity to ask the others about it, but it made more sense to me than my colleagues being shadier than a mine shaft behind my back.

[Did you cast any kind of curse on Gordie?]

"Naw. Never had the chance. Had me locked down tight with his sigils until he choked tae death and the juice in them wore off. He was pretty good for an apprentice, ye know."

[I do know, aye.]

"That's not tae say I wouldnae have cursed him if I had an opportunity. I woulda loved tae give him a nice set of colorful boils on his arse. Maybe drop a piano on his heid. But he was already deid, ye see."

Well, that exploded my budding theory about how all my apprentices died. Maybe they really were tragic accidents. After all, there is nothing so deadly, so ultimately terminal, as being alive.

The door to my office rippled, darkened, and clouded with an oily black mist, and I raised my hand, palm out, to warn Buck.

"Stay very still," I said out loud, not having time to type.

"Wot? Why? Ye suddenly remembered how tae talk?"

If Buck just slid his eyes right he'd see it, but his gaze was focused on me. I just widened my eyes and waggled my hand at him, emphasizing the command. The black mist poured in, solidified, and took shape as it floated up behind Buck's chair and advanced to the right arm. Red eyes and sharp yellow teeth appeared, then a snout and floppy ears and the square head of a mastiff. The rest of the body then filled in, silently, and Buck didn't see it because he still thought I was the dangerous one in the room and he shouldn't even blink. But once corporeal, the barghest licked his chops, and Buck heard that. His head whipped around and he startled, jerking his hand and spilling a few precious drops of Bunnahabhain.

"Gah! Fuck ma ears, it's a barghest!"

The ghost hound—now a very real and solid hound—growled and drooled impressively, slobbering on my fine carpet. Slobber was all well and good; it's the blood you can never wash out properly, so I really didn't want him to be taking a bite of Buck.

"Just don't move or piss yerself!" I told Buck, then spoke to the hound. "Barghest! I'm the contract holder!" I pulled my copy of the contract out of my coat with the sigils still glowing and pulsing with puissance—a phrase that drove Nadia mad, so I used it all the time. "Ye were supposed tae fetch the hobgoblin tae me. Ye can see he's already here. I hold yer contract fulfilled. Understand? Ye've done yer job. That's a good dug. I would scratch yer ears if ye wouldnae bite off ma fingers."

The barghest looked at the contract, and then at Buck, and back at the contract, and whined. He'd not had even a *little* bit of fun.

"Here. I'll get ye sorted," I said as I hauled my carcass out of the chair. "A little sumhin for the road—but take it tae go, eh? I do no want tae listen to yer slobbery gob macking the shite out of some poor coo's remains." I went to the mini-fridge, which did in fact contain the ice I'd promised Buck if he wanted any but also contained a sirloin roast wrapped in paper. I unwrapped it and tossed it in the air to the barghest, which caught it neatly in his jaws.

"Off ye go, then, back tae Tír na nÓg. Thank ye kindly for the service."

The barghest whuffed around the roast and dissolved into oily black smoke, departing through my door the way he came. Buck stared at me and waited until I sat down again before speaking.

"What kind of diabolical shite was that?"

Emergency over, I went back to my phone. [I told you earlier that I'd sent a barghest after you.]

"I don't mean that. I mean the mini-fridge with a bloody roast in it!"

[I am a practical man. My fridge contains ice and roast and that's it. Always good to have something for the dugs when they visit.]

"The dugs, eh? Ye work with barghests on the regular, then?"

[I do. All sorts of troublemakers come visit us from the planes, and barghests track them down better than most anything. I like to keep on their good side, so meat is my friend.]

The hobgoblin glared for a moment, then his eyes dropped and he scooted back in the chair and sighed, sadness almost visibly exhaling from him like motor exhaust in winter. "What am I gonnay do, MacVarnish?"

[That's not how my name is pronounced. But you'll go home, I expect.]

"I can't. They'll kill me."

[Who are *they*, again?]

"The bean sídhe! They're up tae their screechy necks in bats and cats, and they don't want me tellin' anyone about it, see? I'm livin' proof that Clíodhna is selling out the Fae tae some kind o' horrible trafficking shite, so they'd rather I wasnae living anymore. Why is that so hard for ye tae understand? I am fucked on the altar of any religion ye care tae name, that's how unforgivable I am just by continuing tae exist! And I don't have anywhere tae go on earth. All I know is where tae steal whisky an' sausage in Glasgow an' Edinburgh."

[One could argue that's enough.]

"It's not, awright? I can get smashed on stolen hooch an' shudder with the meat sweats, but I cannae sleep sound anywhere ever again. Neeps and tatties, man, if I don't find a safe place tae hide, I'll wind up like that roast, in the mouth of another barghest!" His eyes rolled about and then focused with laser intensity on the decanter. "I need some more."

[Easy now,] I said, as he downed his last swallow and slid off the chair to pour another shot, already unsteady in his movements. [Let's calm down and think.]

"Oh, calm down, eh? Easy fer ye tae say when it's not *your* bollocks in the barghest's jaws." He grappled with the neck of the decanter and it wobbled in his grip. Realizing he might have already drunk more than his wee body weight could process, he let it go and set down his glass, his pink shoulders slumping as his hairy caterpillar eyebrows knit together in consternation. "I am a fool and a failure."

[Naw, you're a hobgoblin on a Wednesday.]

Buck looked up at me, unable to tell if that was absolution or condemnation. I gestured that he should wait and typed, because I knew the sort of immature shite that would cheer him up: [You're no better or worse than an old man with a mustache. A mustache that's soft and plush and parted in the middle, like yer maw.]

Buck's expression changed to delight. "Haw! That was a good one, ol' man."

[Sit back down and let's think about it. My office is warded against the entrance of barghests I didn't contract myself. Spectral Abeyance all around. You have nothing to worry about here.]

"Awright." Buck climbed back into the chair and lay down on his side, curled up. "Think away."

[Who were you supposed to be serving?]

"I dunno. It was a master tae be named later, and I didnae care, because it was my legal ticket out of Tír na nÓg. And it's no matter now, is it? Obviously, it was a load of shite."

[But did you even read the contract?]

"I read the parts that said how I'd be paid and lodged, what freedom of movement I would have, an' how I could be released from the contract."

[Aye, and what did those parts say?]

"Let's say they were barely satisfactory but that I'd be free tae move about as long as ma work was done."

[The trick there would be to make sure you never finished your work.]

"I know, but I made sure ma service was limited tae a single master in a single house and all tasks he assigned had tae be capable of being accomplished in a single day. There was a bit where they couldnae loan me out tae anyone else. I reckoned one house would be manageable and I'd be free for a good portion of the day."

[Maybe so. And if you managed to secure this freedom to move about, what would you do with it?]

"I'd see a fucking sight or ten, wouldn't I? Revel in the fact that I'm not going tae be constantly watched by some Fae or other. Relax among the stupid humans, maybe tell an Arsenal fan that I've seen gumdrops longer than his cock an' then run tae have a laugh. Steal something besides whisky and sausage! Maybe a fruit or a vegetable, just tae go wild and stave off the ravages of scurvy. Get tae know the city better."

[And how could you be released from the contract?]

"The primary exit was death, I believe."

[That's not a good contract, Buck. I would never sign such a thing.]

"I didnae know a single thing about what might be normal or no. All I knew was that sigil agents oversaw such matters, and if yer name was on it, then it must be proper and fine."

[Clearly, I need to impress on the Fae Court the necessity of educating the Fae about these things. Not knowing leaves you vulnerable to exploitation.]

"I certainly feel vulnerable now," the hobgoblin said in a tiny voice, all curled up on my office chair.

[Would you still be open to the idea of domestic service on earth if it was a proper contract?]

"Aye, that would be great, for the two hours or so before the barghests came."

[I'm offering it to you now, Buck. The real thing.]

The hobgoblin slowly rose to a sitting position on the chair. "What are ye sayin' now? Real domestic employment?"

[Aye. Be my hob, Buck. I can draw up the legitimate permits, seal them with the proper sigils. But it does mean real service, you understand? And working for me is going to be more dangerous than working for some stuffy swell.]

"Dangerous how?"

[I will send you on errands for me. These errands may require you to track or even confront Fae, or other beings, who come to earth illegally. And, of course, there is the danger of iron anywhere you go in this world. We should get you a coat and gloves. Maybe a scarf.]

"Aye, that's fine. I mean, let's not be sendin' me tae subdue a troll all by ma self or back tae Tír na nÓg for any reason, but if it's a mission I can expect tae survive, that's a good idea. At least I won't be bored. But can I make Buck Foi ma real name now? Because then they cannae use ma old one against me. I need protection, MacVarnish."

"MacBharrais!" I said aloud, then typed furiously. [I know that you know how to spell it and say it, or you wouldn't have found my office. Since you're so concerned with names, you will say my name correctly if you're to work for me.]

"Aw. Can I no take the piss out o' ye a bit? That's part of the deal when ye employ a hob."

[I understand that, and I heartily approve of the practice in general terms. But you must find some other way to take the piss than purposely mangling my name. I expect high-quality, creative, and nondestructive pisstaking. I am a quality employer and require the best hobgoblin in all of Tír na nÓg. If that's not you, then let's move on.]

Buck's eyes narrowed. "I see this is not yer first negotiation with the Fae."

I shook my head. [It's what I do for a living.]

"Are ye gonnay tell me why ye're using that rectangle thing tae talk, then?"

I told him about the curse and that he'd be required to carry a phone to receive messages from me. And then the negotiations began in earnest. And it *was* a good-faith negotiation: Thanks to my late wife, who'd been a labor representative before her accident, I tried not to be the sort of exploitative employer she spent her working hours fighting against. Happy employees, I've found, are loyal and productive and do quality work. Even Nadia, who rarely smiled except when she got to hit someone in a mosh pit or right before she used her straight razor on someone harassing her, insisted to me that she was very happy, in my weekly meetings with her wherein I asked over a dram what I could do to help. Most of those meetings consisted of her claiming to be happy and me not believing her. Maybe it was because she snarled at me as she said it.

"I'm fucking happy as fuck, Al," she'd say. "Really. This is ma happy face."

Her happy face looked like she wished my immediate death.

[So everything is fine?] I'd ask.

"Absolutely fine. If it wasnae fine, I'd say so. I promise. And I'd say it when I thought it. I wouldnae save it up for the weekly dram. Ye know this already."

But I asked her and every employee each week anyway if I could do anything better. Because if I stopped asking, they'd think I'd stopped caring. And sometimes there genuinely was something I could do, in spite of Nadia taking care of most everything before it got to me.

I warned Buck in the strongest terms possible not to mess with Nadia or the running of the shop in any way or she might summarily slay him. In return, I'd ask Nadia not to treat him like an employee but as a guest of mine.

[Can we agree in principle, then, the text to be reviewed before signing a contract?]

"Aye, MacBharrais, it's agreed in principle, pending review," Buck said, finally saying my name correctly. We spat in our hands and shook on it.

[Good.] I checked the time on my phone: 19:29. Thirty-one minutes to the rendezvous. [Now, let's go to Renfrew Ferry and meet the lovely people who wanted to buy you, shall we?]

"Wot?"

CHAPTER 6

Renfrew Ferry

Before I could answer Buck, my phone vibrated in my hand. It was a texted Signal from Saxon Codpiece.

Gordie's phone just chimed. Message badge said, "Confirm Renfrew at 8." Mean anything?

Yes, I Signaled back. *Whoever it is thinks he's still alive. Thanks. You didn't get into the phone, did you?*

Not yet. But come by tomorrow.

Will do.

I rose and gestured that Buck should follow. I wasn't sure whether they meant the actual ferry or the restaurant of the same name a few miles away, but I was gambling that they wouldn't want to do this in a restaurant. The ferry site was fairly isolated and saw very little traffic anymore, since most people used bridges now to cross the River Clyde. But it was still a fair chunk of land set aside since the days when there were no bridges and the only way across was by ferry—big wide ones that didn't operate anymore. Nowadays there were just wee aluminum boats that could carry ten or so people for a pound or two.

We hailed a taxi and sat in silence for a couple of minutes as the driver guided us west down Dumbarton Road. But soon enough, Buck had questions.

"So this is a taxi, eh?"

[Aye.]

"Why is there glass between us and the driver?"

[Because arseholes are a thing that exist in the world, and drivers don't want to be swallowed up by one.]

"Are ye sayin' there are man-eating arseholes on earth? Like, just arseholes, unconnected tae anything, roaming around and eating people?"

[It does seem that way sometimes, but I was speaking metaphorically.]

"Oh. Wot's that weird building there? With the segments?"

[That's the Hydro. People call it different things. It's a place for concerts and other special events.]

On it went until we took a left off Dumbarton onto York Street, which shortly curved around to the right toward the ferry as we passed a cluster of tenements. The entrance to the ferry was ringed by a steel-barred gate painted blue, with the gate thrown open to reveal a sloping ramp toward the River Clyde, paved with old stone bricks. The taxi driver parked outside the gate and didn't want to wait. He took my cash and put the car in gear, rolling down his window to give us a warning.

"Careful goin' in there, now. All kinds o' stuff ye could step on. Get yerself a case of tetanus."

I scanned the ground in the dim yellow light of streetlamps as the cab rumbled away, and his warning appeared to be a case of friendly hyperbole. It was not a site littered with proverbial rusty nails. It was littered with just about everything else, however. Fast-food wrappers and napkins blown by the wind up against the fence. Plastic bottles. A disturbing number of used prophylactics. Bizarre clumps of hair. And here and there across the docking ramp, broken glass from bottles. No doubt many diseases could be contracted here—variations on a theme of hepatitis, for example—

but tetanus was unlikely so long as one's parents had been sane enough to get their spawn vaccinated and one kept up with the periodic boosters required.

I checked the time on my phone. A few spare minutes before eight o'clock. I pulled out a sticky note and a Montblanc pen filled with the Ink of Trollskin. I quickly drew a Ward of Kinetic Denial on the note and stuck it to my coat, then resumed typing on my phone.

[Have a good look around. This could be dangerous. Have you ever seen a gun?]

"Aye."

[If they point one at you, get out of the way.]

"I know that! I've seen how it works on the telly. This is basic *Starsky and Hutch* stuff ye're talkin' about."

[That is a really old show, Buck.]

"Yer a really ol' man. And I'm older than I look."

I cast a skeptical eye at the gate leading to the ramp. [Can you do something to make sure this gate stays open and no one can close it behind us?] Hobgoblin magic could be powerful, but they rarely did the practical thing with their power unless someone gave them a hint. They tended to err on the side of flashy.

Buck squinted at the gate. "Naw. Too much iron." He peered through the dark at the area surrounding the ramp. "Is this iron fence all around the ferry dock?"

[Looks like it.] There were several tenements bordering the perimeter of the ferry area—newer ones too—but the builders had wisely ensured that few windows looked out upon the dock, since it was an eyesore. The windows faced the river or else the street they were on. They were also a good thirty or forty yards away from the perimeter. If anybody screamed, no one would hear it. Or if they did, they would assume it was a drunk. No one would come to investigate, because that would be asking for trouble and maybe even a bespoke bacterial infection.

The thrum of a motor warned us first, and then a light speared the gloom, signaling the approach of the ferry. The distant mumble of voices could be heard reflecting off the water.

[Stay close to me,] I typed, [because we're supposed to be giving you away. But the moment it looks dodgy, pound the shite out of them.]

"Looks dodgy now," Buck replied.

[Not yet. Let's have a talk first.]

"How much talk, exactly? Because whatever shite they're carrying, the moral thing tae do here is tae pound it out of them right away. The sooner the better."

[I will say the phrase *Now would be good*.]

"Awright, then. I hope ye say it soon. They're buyin' Fae for some reason, and it's a crime that deserves punishment. What's in it for them, I wonder? It's no sex, I hope? You humans have a thing for pink parts and so maybe they thought, well, Buck's nothing but pink parts, let's have a go at him?"

[I'm trying to figure it out. It's why we need to talk. Stow your pink parts and focus. Follow my lead.]

"Right. Right ye are."

When the ferry pulled up at the bottom of the docking ramp and extended its wee courtesy bridge to let passengers off, three hooded figures of varying sizes stepped off. None looked like casual Glaswegian commuters. They looked like escaped characters from an assassin video game, their features shadowed and their muscles, in at least one case, bulging ridiculously.

One of them, walking on my left, wasn't much taller than Buck, and I wondered if that might not be another hobgoblin. The middle figure looked closest to a normal human, perhaps an inch shorter than me if anything, and I'm only five ten. On the right was a towering slab of muscle with skin on his fists that either looked grey in the wan light of the docks or might actually be grey. The wee man on the left looked white, judging by his fists, but the middle figure was wearing gloves and I couldn't see anything else, except that he was somewhat unsteady on his feet, weaving on wobbly knees. They stopped a few yards away from Buck and me, the ferry behind them still idling and waiting, and the middle one spoke.

"You're not—urrrp!—shorry. You're not . . . uh. Gordie."

"Naw, I'm his master. Who are you?"

"His *mashter*?" The voice was clearly drunken and unwilling to answer my question. "You're the agent guy? The MacVarnish guy?"

Buck sniggered and I sighed. "MacBharrais. Yes. Who are you?"

"You know." The figure raised a hand and waggled his fingers at us in a strange manner. Had he just cast a spell? Was he waving at us? Or was he making sure his fingers still worked? "Bashtille sent us. Now, hand over the hobgob—urrp!—goblin."

"Does Bastille know you're drunk?"

"Of coursh! Coursh he doesh. Hee hee! 'M alwaysh . . . drunk. 'Swhat a clurichaun does, after all."

"A clurichaun?" They were besotted faeries with rather impressive martial capabilities because they moved unpredictably and were often too drunk to feel pain. "What are ye daein' here?"

"Here for the hobgob. Lin."

"I want to talk to Bastille."

"An' I wanna 'nother drink. Gobhob now, ol' man. I gotta pish."

"We're not doing this until I talk to Bastille."

"Ha! It don' work like that. Lash chancesht. Gimme the gob or we take him." The wee man and the giant shifted a little. It didn't look like the drunkard was going to be helpful.

"Awright." I reached into my topcoat for prepared Sigils of Agile Grace and Muscular Brawn and said, "Buck?"

"Aye?"

"Now would be a good time." I popped open the sigils and felt my accumulated stiffness of sixty years slough away, my body temporarily invigorated with Olympic athleticism. As I did so, Buck launched himself vertically at the speaker and laid him out with a cross to the jaw in that shadowed face.

As soon as Buck landed, the small figure shouted "Oi!" and

tackled him, tiny fists flailing as Buck wrestled to throw him off but succeeded only in removing the hood from a freckled face.

"A fucking leprechaun?" Buck cried out in disbelief. And then the blighter was pummeling him and cackling madly, blue eyes blazing underneath an unruly mop of red hair.

The large brute charged me as the drunkard clambered unsteadily to his feet. I saw the anvil of a fist coming my way and did my best to roll with it since I couldn't avoid it, for all the good it did me. It cracked my ribs despite the Ward of Kinetic Denial applied to my coat—I felt them break—and sent me flying to crash some distance away.

When you see that sort of thing happening in movies—stuntmen and actors flying on wires and brittle sugar plaster breaking behind them on impact—it makes you think flesh and bone will somehow win out over masonry. But it doesn't. I fell on the brick of the ramp, and it hurt like hell.

Kinetic wards can stop most anything if you have enough of them layered on top of you to do so. Coriander is famous for being untouchable in combat. But while the simple ward I'd crafted took some of the sting away, it couldn't match the force behind that fist.

"Haw!" the big bastard barked at me, pulling back his hood so I could see his gruesome nightmare of a smile. There were gaps in the teeth and maybe some bits of flesh trapped between them. "Trollskin wards won't protect you from me!"

"No, I guess they wouldnae," I admitted. For the speaker was in fact an actual troll, the kind that used to guard bridges and terrorize travelers with their threats of violence and inevitably foul breath. They were thick enough in the head that most sigils wouldn't work on them. Might as well try to hack the brain of a rock. But a ward made in part from a troll wouldn't affect a troll at all. I was lucky he hadn't put his whole fist through my torso.

Bastille had been smart to send a troll to confront a sigil agent. I didn't have a lot of options, and that fist was coming back for an encore.

Something tore inside as I rolled away from another hammer

blow. The troll grunted as his knuckles smashed into the stones, but more out of frustration than pain.

I gasped and wheezed as I scrambled to my feet, trying to think of some way to defeat the monster and coming up blank. I backed away in an effort to put some space between me and those fists and saw that the clurichaun had lost what little patience he had. He was standing knock-kneed and attempting to figure out how to make the gun in his hand work, shaking it and peering at it.

"Gonna kill ye," he promised. "Shoon ash I can figger out thish fucking ting."

Thank the gods for safeties, I suppose. My ward wouldn't stop bullets any better than a troll fist.

Buck and the leprechaun were biting and snarling and rolling around, each trying to get advantage on the other and failing, while they shouted grave insults about the sexual predilections of their close relations.

I thought my only chance was to help him out. If I could get the leprechaun or the clurichaun to retreat, perhaps the troll would go with them. There was nothing I could do to him at this point except get out of his way.

So when he charged me again, I charged back, which he had not expected. He tried, belatedly, to adjust, but I pitched forward into a somersault, ribs grinding as I rolled between his legs and came up with nothing between me and the clurichaun but the shards of bottles thrown down on the dock by sozzled twats like him.

He saw me coming, and his eyes flicked over my shoulder, where the troll was no doubt turning around and reacquiring his target. All the clurichaun had to do was stand his ground long enough for the troll to catch up. I raised my cane in an obviously telegraphed swing that he could easily duck, but it was all a feint. As I began to bring it around, he planted his feet and ducked, and that is when I teed off and punted him in the privates.

He curled inward with a noise somewhere between a gasp and a moan and toppled over, dropping the gun to cradle his bruised bollocks with both hands. I gave the side of his head a good whack with the cane to concuss him as I passed, then scooted sideways toward Buck and the leprechaun to make sure the troll couldn't zero in on me.

Twirling the cane once, I whipped it around at the leprechaun. It caught him on the back, and he cried out and disengaged from Buck before I could do it again. He scarpered away to regroup, cursing all the while, leaving a bloody hobgoblin behind. I caught his gaze and lifted an eyebrow.

"Can ye pluck out an eye for me?" I asked, and he grinned with bloody teeth before disappearing with a small pop of displaced air.

Another pop announced his appearance above and in front of the troll's head, where he simply thrust three stiff fingers into the ugly brute's eye before dropping to the ground. Not so much plucking but effectively blinding.

The troll roared as he clutched at it, black blood fountaining from the wound, but it wasn't long before his remaining good eye searched for us.

That shouldn't have happened. We should have gotten a good thirty seconds of cursing and bellowing before he thought seriously about striking back. Trolls were not normally so focused, and neither were clurichauns or leprechauns. Nor were any of them in the habit of working together. Everything about the encounter was wrong. With my internal injuries, I wasn't prepared to extend this, and I wouldn't be getting any answers anyway, so I suggested to Buck that we leave while we could. He had a bloody nose and split lip and assorted other cuts. No one was going to go home pretty; simply making it home was the best possible outcome.

While the leprechaun and clurichaun were content to watch us scramble for the gate, the troll voiced a loud objection and lurched after us. He realized after a few steps he'd be too slow to catch us, so he threw something he'd picked up at my legs—I don't know what, but it tripped me up like a baton suddenly stuck in the spokes of a bicycle wheel.

My ancient carcass smacked into the pavement again.

As a rule, pensioners don't like falling down. Ask any of them. It hurts.

Senior citizens traveling at high speed with broken ribs really, really don't like it.

I made noises like the clurichaun did when I dropped him, the pain too much for me to muster anything more. Buck paused and looked back at me, the troll roaring in triumph and his heavy footfalls growing closer. I pleaded with my eyes for the hobgoblin to do something to save us, because I'd clearly not come prepared to take out a troll.

"Come on, MacBharrais," he said, his pink hand clutching my shoulder, and then that strange popping noise happened again, my stomach flipped like it does when a lift descends too quickly, and we weren't at the ferry docks anymore but sprawled in an alley that I bet wasn't far away. The troll's roar of frustration could still be heard, albeit at a volume that reassured me he wasn't in easy striking distance.

"That's it," Buck said, collapsing near my head. "I'm out of juice, boss. That was the meanest leprechaun I've ever met. Strongest too."

I groaned and rolled gingerly onto my back. I fished out a couple of prepared sigils from an interior pocket and checked to make sure they were the right ones. I handed one of them to Buck and began to reach for my phone, but it felt too far away, and it would be too much effort in my condition. I spoke aloud instead.

"Pop the seal on that and look at it."

"Wot is it?"

"Healing sigil." I said no more but popped the seal on mine and felt the first soothing bliss of my brain pumping happy dope into my system. There would be magic following close behind, but I doubted I'd remain conscious for any of it.

We'd gotten our arses kicked and learned absolutely nothing about Bastille except that he had powerful friends and a drunk faery on his payroll who didn't know how to fire a weapon.

———— • ————

Water Bears

Water bears are micro-animals that have survived pretty much all the mass extinctions and will probably survive us too. Lots of folks call them tardigrades, because that is in fact what they're supposed to be called. But I have always preferred the colloquial name for them, since I conflate the word *tardigrades* with the time my secondary school English teacher took three months to grade my essay on Hemingway's festering misogyny and simply wrote *Indeed!* in the margins.

They look like telescoping donuts, or maybe ravenous swimming penises, with eight chubby legs and claws. They're only half a millimeter long when they're full grown, and they can be found snacking on most mosses and lichens. That makes them extraordinarily easy to find in Scotland, since you can grow moss and lichen on most surfaces without even trying, but I require a large number of them for any ink used in healing sigils. A full teaspoon. And they are pure hell to separate out from the moss and lichen. Half a millimeter or less, remember, and squishy. Your typical tweezers aren't going to do the job, except to mash their wee guts into the moss.

To be truthful, you can't really get hold of enough of them in a reasonable amount of time without the help of a Druid or the Tuatha Dé Danann. They can bind a load of them together and collect a teaspoon without harming them. But neither Druids nor members of the Tuatha Dé Danann are readily available for such work. It makes crafting those inks near impossible unless you know someone who can help. Which is, of course, the point. Brighid doesn't want just anyone making healing sigils and curing themselves of diseases and wounds that are only doing their jobs at culling the population. She wants such magic available to only those few mortals who have labored on her behalf.

Which was why, when I was an apprentice, I spent nine days cursing as I scraped off moss and tried to collect a teaspoon of the little bastards, before I got some help. The key was that they had to be alive all at once, and it took so long to get any that by the time I'd gotten enough at the end of the week, the ones at the beginning of the week had died. I was trapped in a hell of water-bear collection.

And then Coriander came to me and introduced his glorious self. He gave me a small bottle with more than enough.

"You needed to learn how difficult it is to collect this ingredient," he said, "before we simply gave it to you. Proceed to make your ink and draw your healing sigils in advance. If you ever wind up needing them, you probably won't be able to draw them on the spot."

That was excellent advice.

CHAPTER 7

⸺ ◦ ⸺

The Sigil Agents

Someone shook me awake and my eyes opened on daylight. A familiar voice said, "It's the polis," and an unfamiliar one said, "Are ye all right, sir?"

Blinking, I sat up and squinted up at a florid constable staring down at me. I nodded at him, but he wasn't satisfied.

"What are ye daein' in this alley with this, uh . . . this person?"

"That's right, I'm a person," Buck affirmed. "Well spotted."

I pointed first to my mouth and then made a slashing motion at my throat to indicate I couldn't speak.

"Oh, ye cannae tell me? Well, let's see. Ye're covered in blood, and it might no be yours. In the interest of public safety, I should probably find out whose it is and how it got there. So I'm givin' ye both a free ride to the station so we can sort it out. Come on, let's go."

I nodded and rose to my feet, noting that my ribs still ached but there wasn't the sharp bright pain I'd experienced last night.

We didn't have a good explanation for our appearance, of course, and I didn't want to create any kind of incident report. I pulled out my sigils of authority on the goatskin and flashed them at the constable. When his eyes focused on them, I said, "Walk away and forget about us."

He blinked and did precisely that.

"When do I get some o' those sigils, then?" Buck asked. "Tae aid me in the performance of ma duties, y'know, workin' the will of MacBharrais on the world?"

I quirked an eyebrow and pulled out my phone. [You're never getting these. You'd tell humans to jump in the Clyde.]

"Well, maybe, but only for a laugh. I'd never do it maliciously."

[The distinction hardly matters.]

"What now?"

[Haggis, neeps, and tatties. I'm hungry. How about you?]

"Sure, I could eat. Probably wash up. That healing sigil closed up the cuts, but I feel like a mess. Home, then?"

[No, the office. There's a kitchen and washroom in the basement.] I also needed to draw some more sigils, and most of my rare inks were there. And it was past time to contact the other sigil agents; they needed to know what was going on.

We hopped onto the train at Garscadden station and pretended not to notice people staring at us. They were interested in either my mustache or Buck's strangeness. I imagined they weren't sure he was quite human, but while they had no problem staring at him, they were too polite to question his origins out loud. Or maybe they were just worried about the dried blood and dirt all over him. Much of it was his, but some of it was no doubt the leprechaun's.

When we got off at High Street not far from my shop, I made sure to compliment him.

[That was good fighting last night. Thanks for getting us out of there.]

Buck snorted. "I suppose it was good in the sense that we're still walking around afterward. But I have no had ma arse kicked that badly in a long time."

[Have you fought leprechauns before?]

"Aye. That one wasnae normal. Sumhin different about him.

Maybe he just inhaled a barrel of amphetamines on the ferry over, but I think he was different in a permanent way, if ye know what I mean. He's been . . . altered."

Thinking of my conversation with Saxon Codpiece regarding the idea that someone was performing experiments on the Fae, I nodded and typed in a question. [Did the clurichaun and troll seem altered as well?]

My hob shrugged. "Dunno, MacBharrais. I didnae have a square go with them like with the leprechaun. The clurichaun was as drunk and daft as the rest of his kind. If the troll was juiced up, it didnae help out his eye, y'know?" I simply nodded, and Buck continued in a quieter voice. "I know he was yer apprentice, but I'm doubly glad Gordie's deid. I wouldnae want tae be handed over to that lot last night. Bloody horrors, so they were. Like clowns and cauliflower."

[Like what, now?]

"Nothing. Recurring nightmare."

My receptionist, known to everyone except customers as Gladys Who Has Seen Some Shite, was cool and professional when we entered the office and greeted us like nothing was unusual at all about me walking in with a bloody hobgoblin. It was that utter unflappability that distinguished Gladys Who Has Seen Some Shite from all other Gladyses in the world. She has greeted everything from deities to demons with the same cool professionalism, and I suspect that she may also be immortal and invincible but simply left those facts off her CV when I hired her. She always dressed in conservative tweeds, her grey hair pinned up on the sides, and peered over her desk through a pair of bright-red horn-rimmed glasses. That grey hair, though—plenty of it actually white—was not an indicator of her age. Her face somehow retained the wrinkle-free skin of youth. I judged her age to be anywhere between thirty and three thousand and knew better than to ask, because she had been referred to me by Coriander and if she wasn't Fae she was something else more than human. According to her official papers, however, she was Canadian.

[Morning, Gladys. Coffee on downstairs?]

"Yes, Mr. MacBharrais. I believe there's some Danish out too if you're hungry." Her pleasant alto came with a Nova Scotia accent and she knew I liked it whenever she pronounced *out* like *oat,* so she usually left something out in the downstairs kitchen just so she'd have a reason to say it in the morning. Gladys Who Has Seen Some Shite is simply the best. "Do you require anything for your guest?"

[No, but thanks. This is Buck. You'll be seeing him around from now on.]

"Welcome, Buck."

My hobgoblin surprised me and bowed. "Thank ye, Gladys. It's an honor tae meet ye."

I thought we'd slipped downstairs to the employee area unnoticed, but my manager found me after a few minutes, obviously looking for me, because she called my name as she clomped down the stairs.

"Al? Ye down here? Fucking hell, what is that?"

The wedding finery was gone. Nadia was in high goth metal that day, her strip of hair spiked and the rest of her attire following the pointy theme. She had a choker on her neck with chrome spikes radiating out from it, a black vinyl corset that descended into a wide studded belt, and a filmy coal-black tutu over jet leggings that disappeared into chunky leather boots with silver buckles and three more dangerous spikes on the toes. She also wore black studded bracers and finger gloves with pointed studs on the knuckles. Yesterday's red fingernails were black again, but they had a glossy sheen to them that meant it was a color called Negative Sun rather than Satan's Blackest Hole. I am an expert on black nail polish, thanks to Nadia.

I had ignored the Danish left out in favor of making a fry-up on the stove and put down the spatula to type a reply. [It's breakfast.]

Nadia pointed at Buck standing on the break room table and chugging a beer he'd purloined from the fridge.

"No, Al, I mean who is this wee pink man covered in blood and shite who's drinking ma beer? And am I gonnay have tae be seen with him? Because ma family is no gonnay believe anything I say about his existence or why I'm anywhere near him."

[We haven't worked out protocols yet. But this is Buck. Buck, this is Nadia.]

"Buck who?"

[Buck Foi.]

"Are ye joking?"

[No. Why?]

"Because it's Fuck Boi with the initials switched, Al! How did ye no notice this?"

[I suppose I'm old enough not to give a toss. If he wants to be called Buck Foi, that's his name.] I noticed Buck trying to suppress a fit of giggling and largely failing as I typed. [That doesn't mean he's not a bawbag, though.]

"I am also his hobgoblin n' that," Buck added. "As of last night."

Nadia's jaw dropped and she looked to me for confirmation. I nodded and said, [He's supposed to stay out of your way.]

My manager did not think that point could be emphasized enough. "Aye, wee man, you do that. Ye come at me and ye'll leave with missing body parts."

"Well, hello there," he said.

"I don't say hello tae bastards who boost ma beer. Ye want tae get along with me, ye'll replace that and then some."

Buck wisely checked with me to see if she was serious.

[I'd do it. I may have neglected to mention last night that Nadia is a battle seer.]

Those perfect teeth flashed at me. "Naw! For reals, ol' man? A battle seer? I'm gonnay have tae confirm that."

Before I could warn him again—I *had* warned him against messing with her—he dropped the empty beer can, belched, and popped off the table with his little disappearing trick. Nadia, who was standing just inside the doorway leading to the stairs, took one step forward and spun, throwing her fist into empty space. Except when it got to the space where her head had been, Buck's face materialized and promptly got crunched with her studded knuckles. He grunted and crashed to the foot of the stairs, his nose broken and perhaps a tooth knocked loose as well.

"Is that confirmation enough, ya wanker?" she said, and was satisfied with a weak moan in reply. She nodded once and turned to me, hooking a thumb in Buck's direction. "Honestly, Al, I'm no impressed. He's no very bright, trying to pop behind me like that."

[He's a hobgoblin,] I replied. [They have to learn the hard way sometimes. Come sit for a second, please.]

Nadia moved forward while I fetched a plate and scooped my fry-up onto it, turning off the stove before joining her at the table.

"Aw, thanks, Al," she said, neatly stealing my tomato, which I let happen without comment. "Do I get an explanation, then?"

Instead of answering, I asked, [How was the wedding?]

"Auch, it was a nightmare. Surrounded by straight people. Pretending tae be their idea of normal so the bride's family could feel smug. The worst. Except ma brother was happy and he thanked me at the end for being so kind tae him. And I got the phone number of the hot bridesmaid, just to remind myself that I still got it. How was your night?"

I shoveled in a mouthful of haggis and typed while I chewed. [Got my arse kicked by a troll and woke up in an alley. Might not have made it without the hob.]

"So that's why you're all askew! Shite. Is the troll still around? Ye want me tae take care of him?"

I shook my head. [Rematch later. I need you to give me an alibi for the time of Gordie's death up to when you arrived. The police may come calling.]

"Ye want to run that program that Codpiece gave us for the security tapes?"

I gave her a thumbs-up with one hand and ate some more with the other.

"Awright. But we've discussed several items already besides item number one. That will no do."

She got a fond smile for that and a gesture to continue. In response, she pulled a rolled piece of paper out of the top of her corset and slid it over to me. It had some numbers on it, respectable ones but less than she was worth, and I wondered when it had become taboo to speak of money out loud. There always seemed to be this business of writing figures down. We could and probably should blame the English.

Considering what Nadia had already done for me and would continue to do, I pulled out a pen and wrote my counteroffer. Her eyes widened when she saw I'd written a larger instead of smaller figure.

"What's this for?"

[Putting up with my hobgoblin. He's deathly allergic to iron. I need the iron surfaces covered up as much as possible—especially the stairs and balcony. And thank you very much for wearing gloves with chrome studs on them today. Your steel ones might have killed him with that punch.]

Nadia turned to gaze with narrowed eyes upon Buck's prone form. "I might still kill him later if he's no careful around me."

Buck moaned again, and I snorted in amusement. [I think he'll be careful.]

"MacBharrais!" he wailed. "Ye got any more o' those healing sigils?"

I retrieved one from my coat and handed it to Nadia. A small smile appeared on her face, which was the equivalent of incandescent glee for her, and once she took it she briefly laid her gloved hand on top of mine and squeezed, an admission of genuine affection.

"Yer a good boss. That number will be fine. And I'll get on those things for ye."

I typed quickly as she rose from her seat, and she waited for me to finish. [I also need a conference call set up with the other sigil agents when I'm done here. Tell them it's an emergency.]

"Right." I kept fueling myself and watched Nadia move over to

Buck. She squatted down next to him and held the sigil in his vision.

"Listen, wee man. Ye made a mistake with me, but it's easy tae forgive as long as ye learn from it. So can we agree tae this? Ye get me a growler of a very specific craft beer tae replace the can ye stole from me and we'll start over. We both have work tae do here, and we don't need bad blood simmering between us."

Buck was suspicious. "What's the craft beer? Something impossible tae find?"

"Naw, it's easy. It's called Drink Beer Hail Satan, and though it's brewed in Nottingham, they have it right now at Shilling Brewing in town as a guest tap—6.66 percent ABV, of course. It's a black IPA with blackberries, black currants, and sour cherries."

"Sounds good."

"Yeah? Awright." Nadia's hand disappeared into her tutu or something—everything was so black I couldn't really see if she had a pocket or a hidden belt pack or what, but she produced twenty quid and held it up next to the healing sigil. "In that case, when ye get me a growler, ye can buy yourself one on me."

"I was just going tae steal them."

"Of course ye were. Still, take it. Buy sumhin else tae make ye smile. Are we good, wee man?"

"Aye."

Nadia handed over the sigil and the money and said she'd be happy to talk more about beer later, but she had to get to work. She took the steps quickly as Buck broke the seal on the sigil and sighed in relief.

"Where in the nine planes did ye find her?" he asked.

[An underground fight club. She was destroying men twice her size and using her winnings to pay for college.]

"So a prizewinning pit fighter was what ye were looking for in a printshop manager?"

[Precisely. Not the typical inclusion on the CVs of most applicants. But this is not a typical printshop.]

I finished my breakfast and fried up some more for Buck. [Clean up when you're finished, then you'd best go get that beer for Nadia. But return as quickly as you can.]

He grunted around a mouthful of food and I went upstairs to the offices. I told Nadia I was ready for the conference, and she said they'd show up on the monitor in my office.

The sigil agents came on one at a time, and since we were scattered around the globe it always meant that somebody was going to be sleep-deprived and irritable as a result. In this case, nine A.M. in Glasgow meant the U.S. Eastern time zone was about four A.M. So my colleagues in Philadelphia and Chattanooga would show up last, no doubt, and be in a foul mood.

Wu Mei-ling in Taipei appeared first, and we politely inquired after each other's health. She had looked to be in her fifties for about forty years now, a petite woman in a traditional Chinese dress whom I fully expected to outlive the rest of humanity. She had a cup of green tea at hand and radiated calm. A younger, earnest face blinked at me behind her right shoulder.

"May my apprentice listen in, Al?" she asked, her English only slightly accented. That apprentice would most likely take over Mei-ling's territory upon her retirement.

[Forgive me, Mei-ling, but this particular emergency should be kept between full agents only.]

She gave the barest nod and then dismissed her apprentice in Mandarin. Said apprentice, a woman who was in her second year of training, bowed and departed.

Lin Shu-hua was next, dialing in from Melbourne. She had been Mei-ling's first apprentice and now had an apprentice of her own and an active agency throughout that part of the world. She asked the same question about her apprentice, and Mei-ling answered abruptly in Mandarin, obviating my need to reply.

Shu-hua was dressed in western men's clothing, a suit and tie tailored to her size, with her long hair pinned up on top of her head. Like her former master, she had a cup of green tea at hand. Once her apprentice left, she poured more tea from a pot into her cup.

"Now you've got me curious, Al," she said, her voice lower than Mei-ling's and speaking English with an Australian accent. "Turning up the dial on the theatrics already."

[I wish it was nothing but theatrics,] I typed. [But if it was, I wouldn't have needed to bother you.]

Diego Salazar came online next from Chattanooga, knuckling sleep from his eyes and still looking unfairly handsome with a few days' stubble on his square jaw. When he wasn't being a sigil agent, he sparked rich fantasy lives by simply walking around town. He dressed sharply as a rule, but at the moment he wore SpongeBob SquarePants pajamas and still looked sultry enough to grace the cover of a steamy novel.

He had a faint Spanish accent I envied, as he hailed originally from El Salvador. "What's the emergency, Al? I like these conferences better when you're the one losing sleep."

[We're still waiting on Eli,] I said. [How goes your search for an apprentice?]

He blew a raspberry and shrugged. "I have a couple of leads. Trying to figure out how to tell them the Fae are real without them pretending to remember something they need to do anywhere else but where I'm at."

That had already happened to him a few times. Diego had no problem finding people willing to listen to him, since he had tremendous personal charisma, but when he started speaking of the Fae, they inevitably said they knew he was too good to be true and exited with alacrity. Looking as he did, people were willing to believe a limited number of things about him and fled when he didn't conform to any of them.

Chattanooga seemed at first to be an odd location for a sigil agent, but the Fae preferred the Appalachians and Smoky Mountains above all else in the western hemisphere, and he was quite busy as a result. Plus, there were plenty of American Civil War ghosts to contend with. He traveled as needed to handle contracts and disputes with other pantheons in Central and South America.

Eli Robicheaux finally appeared from Philadelphia, pouring a cup of coffee for himself, which he'd obviously taken time to brew before showing up. He wasn't in pajamas but wore an old Wu-Tang Clan concert shirt with the sleeves cut off. It was the most casual I'd ever seen him; usually he dressed formally, like me, except better. He was from a large African-American family in Louisiana and most of his relatives were still there, but he had come to Philadelphia for college and got recruited into the world after he stumbled across a ghoul in the Laurel Hill Cemetery and defeated it with his bare hands. He would have died shortly thereafter from the pestilent wounds the ghoul gave him, but the sigil agent he eventually replaced arrived on the scene and healed him. He still had scars on his torso and had nightmares about the undead, but he was the most capable fighter among us.

"S'up everybody," he said, his voice a deep bass thrum. "I don't need my apprentice here, do I? 'Cause it would take him like a half hour to get here."

[No, we just need you,] I said. [I have bad news and worse news. The bad news is that Gordie is dead.]

They each expressed dismay at that, and I nodded at their sympathy and well wishes while I typed the rest, holding up my phone when I was ready to hit RETURN so they would know to stop and listen.

[The worse news is that Gordie was trafficking Fae for some kind of scientific experimentation. I have proof. The person he's selling them to goes by the name of Bastille. Does that ring any bells for you?]

I had to catch them up and answer plenty of questions after that, but the takeaway for me was that they didn't know who Bastille might be and they were as flabbergasted as I was by the concept of trafficking Fae. The truly awkward bit was when I had to broach the subject of Gordie's illicit knowledge.

[Gordie somehow knew how to make Sigils of Iron Gall and Dampening Magic and also had the ingredients to make the inks for them. I had not taught him either the sigils or the ink recipes. So my first question is: Did any of you share those with him? And my second is: Have you taught those sigils to your apprentice yet? Answer one at a time, please, beginning with Mei-ling.]

Wu Mei-ling's face shifted subtly to hardness. "I did not share them with him, of course. And I just taught the Iron Gall recipe to my apprentice last week, so she could not have passed on the information to him before that."

Lin Shu-hua replied that she did not share anything with Gordie and had yet to teach Iron Gall and Dampening Magic to her apprentice. Diego had also not shared them and remarked that he was faintly offended I even needed to ask. Eli's reply was identical to Shu-hua's, but he had some extra thoughts to add.

"Hey, Al, I can see everybody's being polite here, and I don't wanna speak for anybody else, but I'm gonna say it for myself: You pissing me off with this. Insinuating we'd break the rules or step over the line like that is messed up. It's your apprentice who did some shady shit and got killed, and then you wanna come at us like it's our fault? Step back, man."

[My apologies, Eli, and everyone. I didn't think any of you did anything improper. I'm only eliminating possibilities. I know this is my problem and I will work on solving it. However, since someone is obviously trying to traffic Fae and there's a buyer out there, either you or one of your apprentices may be approached next. I wanted you to be aware.]

Diego said, "Gracias, amigo. Also—just so I'm aware—how many of your apprentices have died now? Because this isn't the first, am I right?"

I held up seven fingers.

Diego whistled. "Seven? Mary mother of God, Al. I appreciate your help on contracts and disputes and kicking the occasional cabrón off the planet, but whenever I do get an apprentice, I won't be coming to you for advice."

[Understood. Last thing is that Gordie had some ink ingredients I'd never given him and he'd never had time to collect, like nautilus ganglions. So you might want to inventory your ingredients to make sure everything is still there.]

Mei-ling hissed at that and logged off without saying goodbye, and Shu-hua's eyes widened in response.

"Wow, Al. I've never seen her do that before. Looks like you've been missing a lot right under your nose lately, so I don't want you to miss this too: She's incredibly angry with you. I am also, but I hope you'll make it right somehow later." She switched off as well, leaving me to face Diego and Eli. Diego rested his chin on his fist and stared at me with a silly grin, and Eli shook his head before bursting into laughter.

"You know this shit is going to follow you forever, right?" he said. "It's gonna be the thing we use to cover our asses for years. Like if Coriander ever gets snippy with me, I'll say, *Yeah, I done fucked up, but at least I didn't pull an Al MacBharrais, right?* And then he'll say I'm right and I'll get away with whatever it is because that's how bad *this* shit is. I almost wanna go out right now and do something stupid, because you've practically given me a free pass. It's just too damn early."

I nodded, understanding that I'd earned the abuse and taking it was a small part of the penance I'd have to pay. Eli took a swig of coffee and continued.

"Look, I'd love to stay and chat some more, but I've been in-formed I need to inventory all my ingredients, so I better get on it. Later." He switched off and I was left staring back at Diego, who had blinked a couple of times but otherwise had not moved.

[What?] I typed. No response. Just that sappy grin. Slowly, I realized he was enjoying the awkwardness and seeing me shamed, and he was staring at me to savor and remember it. [Fine. I hope you get a pox on your cock,] I said, and he laughed as I reached to turn off the monitor.

I paused to take a few deep, calming breaths, then I Signaled to Nadia. *Where'd you put all of Gordie's inks and stuff?*

The reply came back quickly: *I hid them because you nicked it all from a crime scene.*

You are brilliant, I said.

I know. Did you want to go through it now?

The thought had little appeal, and I needed a shower and a change of clothes. Besides, it was Thursday, and I had a long-standing date.

No, keep it secret. Keep it safe.

Am I supposed to be Frodo or something? You telling me the One Ring is in that stuff?

What? No.

Just asking, boss. The shite you get into tends to be either deep or weird or both.

I sighed, suddenly tired. It wasn't yet ten in the morning, but I felt weary. Chastised. Dressed down. Chewed out. An impending tornado of self-loathing and recrimination was spiraling in my frontal lobe, and I needed to vacate the premises before it touched down and obliterated my mental landscape.

Going home to clean up. Mind the shop?

I always do.

CHAPTER 8

The Grand Librarian

I fetched Buck from the basement. He was still cleaning up after breakfast, staring at the bottom of a skillet in befuddlement.

"How do they get the nonstick coating to stick to the aluminum?" he asked me. "Can we conclude that they're lying because obviously it *does* stick, or is it magic?"

[It's chemistry. Come on, I'm taking you home. After you know where it is, can you pop in and out of there?]

"Near there, I imagine," Buck corrected. "Because I'm assuming you have it warded tighter than a Puritan's dry and puckered hole."

[I do indeed. Safest place for you until this business is over. I'll get you a key. But don't forget to grab that beer for Nadia today. Sooner is better.]

"Naw, I won't be dallying on that chore."

My flat on Howard Street hovered above some businesses in a three-story building that was built in Glasgow's more prosperous times. The sandstone exterior still bore witness to decades of car exhaust and coal soot and angry pigeon shite, but as with my shop offices, the interior had been gutted and remodeled to my liking, a nice modern place furnished mostly in repurposed wood and granite rather than laminates and such. The natural materials took the wards better, held them and even amplified them in a way that plastics and composites never would.

I opened the door and let Buck step through first. I closed the door behind me, shrugged off my coat and hat, and hung them on the hooks next to the door, then typed, [Welcome home.]

"Aw, thanks, MacBharrais. Nice digs ye've got here."

[Behold the door,] I said, and he stopped his perusal of the living area and kitchen to turn back with his eyebrows raised.

"Awright, but I already saw it."

[Except you didn't look at it. Do you see the wards?]

"Holy shite."

[Exactly. Every door in the flat has them and the walls too. Keeps all kinds of things out, but especially barghests. They can't ghost their way in here. So it's important that you don't ruin those wards, accidentally or otherwise, and keep all the doors closed.]

"Got it."

[Parts of my flat contain iron, especially in the kitchen but the bathroom plumbing as well. So you'll find gloves underneath the sink.]

The hobgoblin whooped and sprinted for the sink, finding the gloves fairly quickly and snapping a pair on.

"I've heard of this plumbing business! Very kinky. Let's do this!"

[Kinky? What kind of plumbing do you think I mean? I'm talking about pipes and water and that.]

"Oh. Well, that's boring."

[It's the first and best luxury of modern living. Now come on. You need to see everything iron so you can avoid it. And you need to know how to use the plumbing, trust me.]

I showed him how the shower worked, because he needed one, how the toilets and sinks worked, and where the cleaning supplies were stowed in case he felt like impressing me.

"So correct me if I'm wrong: Plumbing is a human invention tae wash away all yer shite, and then ye have tae wash the plumbing?"

[That's a decent summary, yes.]

The hobgoblin's face fell. "Bollocks. That's not what I thought it was at all."

To cheer him up I introduced him to Netflix. [You won't be so bored if you have some entertainment to watch.]

I left him scrolling through shows while I cleaned myself up and gingerly prodded my ribs, wincing at the remembered impact of that troll's fist. It was still genuinely a bit tender, but at least I wouldn't be immobile for a month.

I half-expected something to happen while I was in the shower—the first of many pranks to come from a hobgoblin eager to push boundaries. But he let me clean up in peace, no towels mysteriously missing, no ink on the combs, nothing.

Shaving with a brush and soap was a self-care ritual I rather enjoyed, regardless of how old-fashioned it might make me seem. But since there was a hobgoblin in the flat, I eschewed the straight razor this time and used a safety razor instead. Once finished, I splashed on some stinging aftershave and some skin conditioner and shaped my mustache. I reemerged from the back of the flat, dressed sharply, to find a hobgoblin sprawled on my couch with a chicken drumstick hanging from his mouth as he stared wide-eyed at the television screen. He was watching *The Fellowship of the Ring*.

"Hey . . . MacBharrais." He flopped a hand toward Frodo and the gang hiding out from the dark riders. "Where did this happen? Which one of the Fae planes? Was it Mag Mell? Because I've never seen a wraith like that."

[None of the Fae planes. Middle Earth does not actually exist.] Unless, of course, it did. I couldn't be certain.

"But . . ." He pointed at the screen as evidence I was clearly wrong.

[That's fiction.]

"Ye mean ye cannae get there from here?"

[That's right. Let me give you a key before I go.]

Buck paused the show, which I thought a remarkable feat. I

could never make the remote work when I wanted it to. "Go? Go where?"

[I have to do some research.]

"Fine, but can ye no just use the Internet?" Buck asked.

[What do you know about that?]

"I've . . . heard of it."

[I can use it for lots of things, sure. But there are people who can find what you need faster than an old man pecking around a search engine.]

"Yeah? Who?"

[Librarians.]

"Ohhh, aye. I've heard o' them too. They always know where the secret room is with the treasure in it. They like tae go plumbing in there, if ye know what I mean."

[I don't know what stories you've been hearing in Tír na nÓg, but that's not what a librarian does. And neither do plumbers.]

He waved a hand dismissively. "Whatevers, MacBharrais."

I didn't have the time to give him a thorough demonstration and a safety warning about cleaning products, so I didn't remind him about them or ask him to tidy up the place. Instead, I said, [Don't drink the bleach—or anything under the sink, for that matter. Beers are in the fridge, which I see you have already found. Speaking of which, don't forget to pop out and get Nadia's beer.]

"I won't forget. Quit nagging."

After fetching him a duplicate key and making sure there was a rubber grip on the handle end to protect him from any small iron content it contained, I departed for my Thursday ritual.

I can't tell you how empty you feel after your love has walked the world with you and then gone home to sleep forever. It's not the emptiness of youth, of never having loved; that's different. That's the sort of thing where you know you're missing something but you're not sure what it is, when you listen to love songs and think it must be fine but you don't fully know what they're on about.

Naw, it's more like suddenly losing a tooth and you feel the absence keenly, a hole in your body that used to be filled, except it's much bigger than that. It's an empty room, an empty chair, a pillow next to yours that doesn't bear the soft round impression of the dear head who dreamt so many dreams by your side. It is an emptiness like no other, because even if it is filled with some other thing later on, it's a final subtraction that no addition will mend.

To distract from the yawning nothingness, you keep busy. Gardening. Walking the dog, or just walking and petting other people's dogs. Reading, smoking, and drinking. Doing your job. Finding a friend or three to have tea with or a morning gab over breakfast, where you can all agree that the world is shite—present company excluded—and if someone could only find a way to apply enough suction, maybe Parliament would finally get its heid pulled out of its arse and do something sensible for once.

These aren't solutions to the emptiness. They are merely harnesses, safety lines tethering you to the cliff face as your bollocks dangle over the abyss. Absolutely vital to survival, but never a replacement for the great lost love of your life.

I lost my wife to an auto accident when we were fifty. I've been dangling ever since.

Part of my routine was to visit the Mitchell Library on Thursdays. I walked up from my flat to the Queen Street train station and took it to Charing Cross, breathed out a small sigh of contentment when I emerged from underground and saw the green dome, and made my way across to the entrance. And on the fourth floor, which contained their collection on the occult and which I was steadily working through, I greeted a fine soul who's been dangling like me.

[Good morning, Mrs. MacRae,] I typed, though it was just barely so, the clock edging toward noon. I've never spoken a word aloud in her presence. To her, I am mute due to a medical condition.

"Good morning, Mr. MacBharrais."

She smiled at me and I removed my hat, bowing my head. She'd lost her husband to cancer seven years ago in Oban. She couldn't bear to continue living there, because the memories were too thick, the weight of them compounding her grief, so she relocated to Glasgow. Together we walked the world alone, and on Thursdays we each checked on the other.

Her first name, displayed on a badge on her black wool wrap coat, was Millie. But I'd never presume to call her that. Maybe some bonny day when the curse is lifted, I'll say it out loud. That would be very fine, but until then we would be formal. She tended to carry herself soberly, with faultless posture that communicated that she was on duty and there to help, by gods. She had a pair of reading glasses perched precariously low on her nose but not the clacky beaded tethers some folks wore to make sure their spectacles wouldn't fall to the floor. I imagined this hinted at the soul of a daredevil. Her dark hair, pulled back gently and pinned to sweep behind her ears and fall to her shoulders, was going grey at the temples, and her brown eyes were large and warm.

Placing my derby hat on the counter, I typed, [I wonder if you might help me with something unusual today.]

"Oh?" She smiled to let me know she was teasing. "Coming from a man who likes tae read about witches and cults and the like, that could be a bit frightening."

[It is a frightful subject, unfortunately. I've been made aware of the problem of human trafficking recently—the modern sort—and wonder if the library might have something about it in the stacks somewhere.]

"I'm sure we must have something." Her fingers danced across the keyboard in front of her terminal, and I noticed her colorful scarf. She had a different one every time I saw her but always the same black attire otherwise.

[Are those forget-me-nots on your scarf? Very nice.]

"They are, thanks." She hit RETURN on her keyboard and scanned the results that came up, then grabbed a pen and started to write some information down on a sticky note for me. When she finished, she peeled it off and handed it to me. "There ye are. Different floor, but once ye get tae that section, you'll find plenty on the subject."

I replaced my hat on top of my head and tipped it at her, mouthing a silent thank-you.

"Ye're welcome, Mr. MacBharrais. Always good tae see ye."

[And you as well. I appreciate your help.]

I wished I could think of some way to extend the conversation, but it would seem oddly cavalier of me to begin with human trafficking and then switch to a fluffier topic, like clouds or poodles or anything else, really.

Turning on my heel, I withdrew to the elevators and followed the directions on Mrs. MacRae's note to a different floor and a stack that had seen very little custom. There I found a whole shelf dedicated to books on human trafficking, many of them quite recent, as the issue became stark only in recent years and academics realized there were careers to be had here as well as a scourge to be identified, classified, and explained.

There were some rather weighty tomes that would probably take a long time to wade through, but some of them were ineligible to be checked out and must remain on-site for research purposes. I'd have to peruse them later. But one title, a slimmer volume called *In Our Backyard: Human Trafficking in America and What We Can Do to Stop It,* by Nita Belles, looked like it would give me a good overview, and it was available for checkout, perhaps owing to the fact that it was not about Scotland. I was certain that the principles of trafficking explained therein would apply to Scotland as well, so I pulled it out, a whisper of paper hinting at secrets to be revealed later. I resolved to get through it and thank Mrs. MacRae next week for the help.

CHAPTER 9

The Right Hat Makes All the Difference

It was surprising to step out of the Mitchell Library to find two detectives about to step in. They pulled up when they saw me and exchanged a glance.

"Oh, that's a happy coincidence," the man on the left said. Which meant they were looking for me and it wasn't a coincidence at all.

I gingerly wedged my book underneath one arm, kept my hat cradled in the crook of the other, and stole a glance at the position of the sun in the sky before I typed on my phone. [Detective Inspector Macleod. Good afternoon.]

I'd dealt with him before. D.I. Macleod was a thin and prematurely wrinkled man of middling years, his face deeply lined by years of cynicism and tobacco smoke and not averse to a pint on the job, I'd learned. He approached life with a wry grumble, vaguely disappointed by everyone but willing and perhaps even hoping to be surprised in a pleasant way. I thought he was a good man who appreciated my help when I was able to give it, on the few occasions when my job revealed some activity that the human police could get involved in. He favored tweed suits and cashmere scarves to keep off the chill, and he also had a derby hat similar to mine.

He was with the detective inspector I'd met at Gordie's flat, the one who'd let her hair go grey. Macleod introduced her as D.I. Munro, and I merely responded with a tight nod and a blank expression, waiting for them to initiate anything further.

"Yer office manager said ye'd be here," Macleod said. "We need a word."

[Certainly,] I typed, and shifted off to one side so that we wouldn't be blocking access to the library door.

"Why are ye using that?" D.I. Munro asked. "Yesterday ye spoke."

[I beg your pardon? Have we met before?]

"Yesterday, yes."

[I don't recall that, sorry.]

She blinked. "Do ye recall that Gordon Graham died yesterday?"

[Yes, I heard. Very sad.]

"He was an employee of yours, right?"

[Yes.]

"When did ye last see him yesterday?"

[I didn't see him at all.]

"But I saw ye there in his flat."

[I'm certain I wasn't.]

I hated lying, specifically this kind—the gaslighting sort. But I couldn't tell the truth and avoid being placed in jail, could I? I had to break the law sometimes to do my job properly—it kept interplanar wars from happening and casualties from accidents down to a minimum—but it condemned me to being a lying bastard with the mortal authorities. In this case, I was hoping the sigils I'd used on my "official ID" would get me out of trouble here. My respect for D.I. Munro, already considerable, increased markedly. She must have an extraordinary brain to remember me after I'd inflicted Porous Mind on her twice in the same hour.

"But someone who looks just like ye and introduced himself as

MacBharrais came in to the flat. Said they were gonnay take all the inks. Then I'm no sure exactly what happened—a strange little person came out of nowhere and attacked us and we wound up leaving the scene. But when we returned, Gordon's flat had been robbed."

I looked at Detective Inspector Macleod with widened eyes, wondering if this sounded as bizarre to him as it did to me. He said nothing, so I blinked at him a couple of times and typed, [I can't be sure what happened either, since I wasn't there.]

D.I. Munro scowled. "I'm sure I saw an actual man, a short man, in a blue paisley waistcoat. He came out of that room ye went into, kicked the body, punched me in the nose, and took off."

I just chuckled and let them grow embarrassed at how ridiculous it sounded. D.I. Macleod began to apologize for wasting my time, but Munro held up a hand to stop him.

"Hold on, I want an answer first. If it wasn't you in his flat, Mr. MacBharrais, where were ye yesterday afternoon?"

[In my shop, working on the offset press. It broke down and needed repair. You can confirm with my manager, Nadia, if you like. She'll show you the security footage. Let me give you my card.]

Macleod waved me off. "No need, we already know where yer office is. We were just there."

I nodded and typed, [Apologies for the confusion. I have one of those unfortunate faces that get recognized everywhere. I am a dreadfully typical Scottish man.]

"Were ye close with Gordon?" Munro persisted, deciding to ask about relationships since she couldn't place me at the scene until confirming my alibi.

[Not especially.]

"But he'd worked for ye for a couple of years?"

I nodded.

"A good worker, then?"

I took the trouble to type out [Yes,] wondering where this was going.

"Any enemies?"

That question seemed like the sort one asked in a murder investigation, so I pasted on a look of concern. [I don't understand,] I replied. [Was his death not accidental?]

"So far as we know right now, yes," D.I. Munro said. "Just being thorough."

[If he had enemies, I was not aware of them.]

D.I. Munro nodded. "Ye don't have any plans to leave town anytime soon, do ye, Mr. MacBharrais?"

I shook my head.

"Good. We may have more questions for ye later. We'll be in touch." She plucked a card from her breast pocket and handed it to me. "If ye think of anything in the meantime, please don't hesitate tae call or text."

Her card bore the name Tessa Munro, and I nodded and flashed a tight-lipped grin.

"Take it easy, Al. Good tae see ye," D.I. Macleod said, and they were off. I waited and watched them go before moving, then purposefully turned in a different direction from them. I walked for a couple of blocks before returning my black derby hat to my head, the one with the black sigils on it that disabled any cameras pointed in my direction, for they were Sigils of Swallowed Light.

The Sigil of Swallowed Light became necessary as the world edged ever closer to constant public surveillance. Cameras everywhere were fantastic for deterring and solving crimes but not so great for keeping the secrets of extraplanar visitors. So Brighid invented the sigil in the seventies, and agents have worn black hats emblazoned with them ever since.

The sigil specifically makes camera lenses black out while the sigil is in the picture. To the observer looking through the lens or at a developed photo or at security footage, it appears to be a glitch, or as if someone had switched off the power—or, in the case of a still photo, poor exposure. It is an aegis of privacy in the era of Big Brother.

I am a normal human with only twenty or thirty years left if I beat the odds, but if I have anything close to a modern-day super-power, it is this: I cannot be surveilled in the surveillance state unless I allow it. The police therefore have no footage of me from yesterday walking into Gordie's building or out of it, nor of Nadia arriving and then departing with a bag of stolen inks and pens.

Without such evidence—and in the face of the timestamped video footage Nadia would show them of me supposedly fixing a broken press during that time—they'd have no way to prove I was there. They would have to get me to admit I had been in the building, and I wasn't about to do that.

Not that I expected them to pursue this much longer; Gordie's death had been an accident, after all, and the Sigil of Porous Mind had affected everyone in the place, making their recollections of what exactly had been in the building a bit fuzzy. They might nibble on the bone of the mystery a bit more, or let it gnaw at them before they went to sleep for a couple of nights, but another case would come their way and they'd forget about me soon enough.

That, or D.I. Munro would outthink me. She clearly had a mind to be feared.

CHAPTER 10

Sometimes, Ghost Dogs Are Not Enough

I was making my way to Tartan Greenhouses to check in with Saxon Codpiece when Coriander glided up next to me. He appeared to walk, that is, but his feet didn't quite touch the ground. He came across as the smoothest walker of all time. His knees must feel amazing, never having to take the impact shock of millions of steps over the years, and I admit that envied him for that.

"Good afternoon, Agent MacBharrais."

I gave him a nod and then a raised eyebrow as if to say, *What news?*

"After investigating at your request, it turns out that there have, in fact, been some suspicious disappearances of rather dangerous creatures from the nine planes. A more than usually bloodthirsty leprechaun among them."

That prompted me to get out my phone. [Aye, we met him last night. He gave my hobgoblin a beating.]

"Indeed? Well, our course of action seems clear. Provide me the contracts and I will send barghests after them."

[I don't think that would be wise in this case,] I said. [If your missing Fae have all become like the leprechaun, you won't be getting your dogs back.]

"What do you mean when you say *become like the leprechaun?*"

[The leprechaun wasn't normal. Neither was the clurichaun or the troll that attacked us last night. They were all stronger, meaner somehow. It touches on something I didn't get to tell you when last we met.] I pressed SEND on that and then held up a finger to indicate that there was more coming. [The hobgoblin is now legally in my service, and he told me that he was lured here under false pretenses. I have a theory that it's for scientific reasons.]

"Science?" Coriander curled his lip and shuddered.

[I can't be certain, but I believe that whoever's behind this is augmenting the Fae somehow. So giving them more Fae in the form of barghests would be a terrible idea. I'm sure they're going to be waiting for something to come at them—after our encounter, they know that at least one sigil agent is aware of their presence here. If they have half a brain, they'll have an ambush or a booby trap ready for anything we send their way.]

"So we require reconnaissance only."

[Aye. And, look, I can't prove it yet—all I have is the word of a hobgoblin—but he's saying that Clíodhna is offering fake contracts for domestic service to lure the Fae here.]

"That is . . . uh . . ."

[Something I need to prove without a doubt, aye. I'm working on that. Have you got something insubstantial to send after the missing Fae that the bastards can't turn into a hopped-up monster? A nice phantom, maybe?]

"More insubstantial than a barghest? They'll forget what they're after before they're halfway there."

[Aye, you're right.]

Coriander snorted. "We could ask Clíodhna to help and send some of the bean sídhe to look. Her reaction might be instructive."

[It might at that. Of course, if she agrees, we'd have banshees floating around Glasgow doing who knows what on her behalf and scaring the living shite out of people. And she can simply report to us afterward that the banshees found nothing.]

"I wasn't being serious."

I nodded at him by way of saying I knew that and then sighed as I typed my reply. [Brighid should at least be informed.] The Irish goddess of poetry, fire, and the forge carried the title of the First among the Fae and ruled from an iron throne. Or used to. Rumor had it she ruled from a throne of wood now, since the Fae had been offended by the iron and mounted an ill-fated rebellion a while ago.

"Of course. Did you find out if any of your colleagues taught your apprentice the sigils out of turn?"

[I don't think they did. Clíodhna may or may not be involved in that. But somebody is leaking secrets.]

"The First among the Fae might wish to speak with you in person regarding these matters," the herald said. "Prepare yourself."

Suddenly I felt anxious and uncertain. [What do you mean? How do I prepare? Do I need a shave or what?]

Coriander chuckled musically. "I forgot you've never actually met Brighid. Preparation is at once simple and impossible: You must be ready to tell the truth and be told it."

[Do I bring a gift? An Irish whiskey?]

"Not necessary. Bring a healthy sense of wonder and dread. That should be the right frame of mind."

[So there's nothing I can do or say to smooth the way?]

"She might appreciate a poem. She is a goddess of poetry, after all, but few honor her that way anymore."

[I am guessing she would not want to hear a dirty limerick, though.]

"You guess correctly. Something of your own creation would do nicely. An emotional piece."

[Bollocks. I'm no poet.]

"She will be aware of that, I assure you. But as a gesture she will appreciate it."

[Shite. How much time do I have?] I felt as if I'd just been given some horrible homework.

"I have no way of knowing. When she wants to set up a meeting, she will of course send me to arrange it. Hopefully you will be available."

[My schedule is infinitely adjustable to hers.]

"Excellent. We shall speak again soon."

And then Coriander glided gorgeously away, ignoring all the humans who told him in passing that he was handsome and pretty.

CHAPTER 11

The Oral Tradition

I lifted the circular-saw blade on the wall of the Tartan Greenhouse shed and had my phone say "Urgent Cake" at the hidden intercom.

"Incorrect password," a smooth female mechanical voice replied. "Tosser," she added, because of course Saxon Codpiece would have a security system that insulted people.

I checked my Signal app and saw that I'd missed one from Codpiece. There was a new password waiting for me there, and I typed it in.

[Melancholy Charcuterie.]

The secret door opened and I began my descent. The hacker had changed his lighting concept to the violet and magenta end of the spectrum, and a glass disco ball, unseen earlier, had somehow been installed. It spun slowly and threw glimmers of reflected spotlights on the floor below. A groove funk anthem from the seventies was playing loudly, the bass vibrating up through the soles of my shoes, and I paused on the stairs, unsure if I wanted to see what Codpiece was up to at the moment. I might be interrupting something.

I doubted that my ability to shout would be loud enough, and my text-to-speech app definitely wouldn't be, so I Signaled him and hoped the phone would light up or vibrate or otherwise catch his attention.

Is it safe to come down? I'm on the stairs, I sent to him. He answered in less than thirty seconds.

Sure, he replied. And then the music turned off and I continued down, the lighting returning to a fluorescent white for business. I didn't see Codpiece immediately, so I drifted toward the bar, assuming that when I did see him I might be in the mood for a drink.

Sure enough, he emerged from the back of the basement, running long fingers through his hair and his face flushed. I went ahead and pulled myself a pint without asking.

"Awright, Al?" Saxon called. "Glad ye came by. I have news. What did ye learn?"

He entered his half circle of monitors and keyboards and gadgets the way a rock drummer nestles into his trap kit. I drank half the pint before answering.

[Found out that Bastille is definitely doing something to the Fae. Juicing them up somehow, like steroids but more permanent. Augmenting them.]

"Oh, aye? It's a government ye want for it, then," Codpiece said. "Bastille's working for a government."

[Why a government?]

"Because this in't mad science being conducted in a misguided attempt tae help the planet, is it? This Bastille guy isnae a tragic Dr. Frankenstein type where a man of lofty ideals thinks he's daein' the right thing. Whoever's daein' this is up tae evil shite, and they know it. Only way ye get scientists tae do that is with a government behind them. They'll use carrots or sticks or both tae make 'em work, but regardless it's gonnay be, *Let's go, lab coats, we have work tae do, your country needs ye,* et cetera."

[Why can't it be an evil-industrialist type?]

"All kinds of reasons. Ye've seen too many Bond films. Look, if ye're a billionaire oligarch, ye already rule the world, in the sense that ye can go anywhere and do anything ye want. It's complete freedom. Ye don't dream of ruling the world if ye already own it—if ye can buy politicians or even entire elections, why do ye need tae do the actual ruling? And why do ye need science tae accomplish yer goals? Ye don't. Ye just go 'round being fancy and above the law on yer yacht in international waters. There's even a subgenre of romances dedicated tae how hot and desirable billionaires are—very hot and desirable, in case ye were wondering. I'm a fan. But government employees, mate? They dream of ruling the world. Because their day is full of hierarchies up and down and all around, and they all want tae be on top because they all know how tae fix things, by God."

[It's a fair point,] I admitted.

"I'm not saying it's this president or that prime minister or that royal highness behind it all. But it's somebody on the spooky side of things with a secret budget, who's been looking at the world and thinks they can fix it with a few good monsters."

[But what for?]

"I dunno, MacBharrais. Ye need to ask 'em when ye find 'em."

[Could it be they want perfect assassins?]

"Naw. Too much attention around assassinations, in't there? That's not how ye win. That'll get people pissed off and shootin' back, maybe start a war. But I know I've never heard of an actual secret organization daein' shite."

[Well, if you had, they wouldn't be secret.]

He snorted derisively. "Awright, let me put it this way: All the truly evil scientific discoveries that we live in fear of—I'm talking nuclear weapons and that—were invented by groups of scientists working at the behest of a government. And a lot of that science is still mostly secret. The things that are actually killing us—plastics and fossil fuels and opioids and so on—were developed for the purpose of profit and sold tae us tae make our lives easier. Either way, it's not the Masons or the Templar Knights or the Illuminati or whatever criminal organization ye care tae name that's killin' us. They don't do mad science, because they've got their rituals and candlesticks and mystical symbols. It's governments and corporations that do science. And when billionaires want tae rule the world, they don't bother rounding up a bunch of people with advanced degrees. They just go buy the governments and make their politicians change the laws to suit them. I'm tellin' ye, it's a bureaucrat who wants to change things that's behind this, not one of these oligarchs."

I nodded because it was the polite thing to do. He might well be right. But there *were* secret societies out there who did shite. I was in one of them. And there were eccentric billionaires who did something because they could, not because they should, and told themselves they were being philanthropic.

[What's your news?]

"Got into Gordie's phone. No calls or texts that scream conspiracy tae me, but he's got some photos in a hidden album that are unbe-fucking-lievable."

[How so?]

"Things that are no human. Pretty sure they're Fae, though I'm no actually sure what I'm looking at."

[Show me.] I beckoned to him and he came over with the phone while I finished off the pint. The folder had only seven pictures in it, and the last one was of a snarling pink hobgoblin of my recent acquaintance. But I recognized some of the others as well. The leprechaun, clurichaun, and troll, for example. There was also a pixie, presumably the one that had departed shortly before Buck, along with a fir darrig and what I supposed must be an undine. Six portraits of Fae corresponding to six payments in Gordie's numbered accounts, plus one more that wound up being a failed delivery.

Had they all been offered bogus contracts to serve on earth, as Buck had? And how in the world had Gordie smuggled a troll here without me noticing?

[This is an insufferable pile of mince.]

"No argument here."

[Where'd you put all those documents I had from his flat?]

"I stashed them out of sight, because I had some other clients coming 'round. Ye want them now?"

I nodded. [I want to take time to go through them more thoroughly, if that's okay.]

"Nae bother."

While he disappeared into the bowels of the basement and made rummaging noises, I pulled another pint.

I settled myself at the bar and wondered what kind of poem Brighid might like from an old man she'd never met. Something singing her praises? It couldn't possibly be genuine. What could I offer that she hadn't heard before? My observation that iced tea—

[Saxon!] I typed as he approached with a bag of Gordie's documents.

"Yeah?"

[Have you ever noticed that iced tea creates a stronger, more urgent need to pee than any other drink?]

"Oh, shite yes! That's why I won't drink it often. Iced-tea pee is no joke. People tend tae drink lots of it fast, and high quantity combined with the diuretic qualities of caffeine double-team your bladder and create extraordinary urgency."

[Thanks.] I raised my beer in a salute, a beverage one could hold on to for quite some time before evacuating it. [I'm glad I'm not the only one.]

"Nae damage."

So iced-tea pee was real. Maybe Brighid hadn't heard about that in Tír na nÓg. It was an aspect of modern existence that may have eluded her up till now. Maybe I could write a poem about that? Coriander said it should be emotional, though. I didn't have any emotions associated with peeing except relief. And somehow I didn't think it was appropriate material to offer to anyone, much less a goddess.

I shook my head as I emptied out the contents of the bag Saxon brought. I was going to be rubbish at poetry if this was all I could think of. Then I remembered something and typed it before I dove in.

[I need Gordie's phone and sim card utterly destroyed. Computer too. Can't have the police looking at that.]

"Right ye are. Anything else ye need off it first? Contacts? Recent calls?"

[All of that. And all the passwords and account numbers from the vault, anything about banking information.] Holding up a hand to stay him, I pulled out the proper pens and a card and drew him another Sigil of Sexual Vigor before sealing it for later use.

"Thanks, Al! I'll put those contacts and calls on a spreadsheet for ye, give ye a flash drive with all the data ye want. Then the evidence will be destroyed and disappeared, no worries, and take all the time ye need there."

It was slow going, checking all of Gordie's bills and notebooks for small notes, anything I might have missed before, but it turned out to be worth it. My jaw dropped when I found a small rectangle of paper pressed between the sheets of a cell-phone bill, with the recipe for Manannan's ink written down—a gigantic no-no in a discipline handled by oral tradition—and it wasn't in Gordie's handwriting. This was a transgression beyond unauthorized teaching; it was the sort of thing that could get a sigil agent disappeared.

Manannan's was the ink that required chambered-nautilus ganglions, and it allowed one to draw the Sigil of Aquatic Breathing—the western variation of it, anyway. Mei-ling and Shu-hua had their own sets of inks and sigils, since they had a different, older system invented by Chinese deities, and their inks were solid ink sticks rather than liquid. To draw their sigils, they had to grind the ink sticks on a stone and mix with water, then use brushes to paint their sigils, always sealing them for later use if they weren't intended as wards. The disadvantage to their system was that they couldn't really draw sigils on the fly like I could with my fountain pens. The advantages were that they had a lot of wards and blessings we didn't have and their ink ingredients weren't quite as difficult to obtain. Our few overlapping sigils that performed the same functions using nearly identical inks, albeit in solid and liquid forms—like the Sigil of Iron Gall—were treasured bridges across the gap between us. While the Sigil of Aquatic Breathing

existed in the Chinese system, its form and its ink were both different from the western one.

Why had Gordie needed that sigil? Ah: The undine, right. So
someone had not only helped Gordie with the Fae-trafficking scenario, but they had helped him with the sigils he'd need to pull it
off.

Gordie was just a festering pustule on the surface of a deep infection. If he hadn't been daft enough to eat a raisin scone, who
knew how long they would have gotten away with it?

There was nothing else. Saxon had a fireplace down there, back
where he had built a cozy set that weirdly resembled a hunting
lodge, and there were some cameras pointed at it. He let me feed
all of Gordie's papers into the fire. I kept only the proof that someone was writing down secrets. I figured I'd show that to Coriander,
at least, and maybe he'd be able to identify the handwriting before
destroying it.

It was dark when I emerged from Saxon's seedy basement with
a flash drive of Gordie's contacts, recent calls, and the contents of
his password vault. Saxon had turned up the funk and turned
down the lights as I ascended the stairs, so he obviously had his
evening planned.

"Tits," I muttered into the darkness, realizing I'd have no rest
when I got home. I'd left Buck Foi alone there all day.

CHAPTER 12

Homework

I expected one of two things when I got to my flat: It would either be a bloody shambles, or it would be incredibly clean and tidy except for one glaring thing out of place, like a screaming goat shitting on my couch. Hobgoblins had to do something wrong to balance out all the right they did by you; their constitutions wouldn't let them do otherwise. If you wanted an angel, you shouldn't employ a hobgoblin.

I opened the door to the flat cautiously, making sure there wasn't a booby trap to land a bucket of goo on my heid. It looked clear. And the place itself looked spotless. So nothing obvious in the living area or kitchen. Maybe there would be a surprise in the bedroom or bathroom, then.

"Oi! Is that you, MacBharrais?"

I got out my phone and typed [Aye,] and Buck appeared from the hallway that led to his bedroom.

"Welcome home. What's new, then?"

I closed the door and locked it before removing my coat and hat and hanging them on the pin. [I've got homework to do.] I explained that I might be meeting Brighid soon and maybe it wouldn't go so well for me, considering that I'd apprenticed a bag of shite that had taken money to traffic Fae. Coriander had suggested a poem to honor the goddess of poetry. [I haven't written a poem since I was in school.]

"Oh, aye? What did ye write back when ye didnae have wrinkles?"

[A terrible sonnet. Does Brighid like sonnets?]

"Not especially."

[How long do I need to make it, then?]

"Well, was there no an American poet who said, *Brevity is the soul of shit,* or sumhin like that?"

[The line ends in *wit,* not *shit.* And that was Shakespeare. Polonius said that in *Hamlet.*]

"I don't care who said it, MacBharrais. I'm trying to tell ye no to make it short. She likes epic poetry."

[I don't have time to write an epic! Not to mention the skill. What's the bare minimum I can get away with?]

"Nine lines. The Tuatha Dé Danann are obsessed with nine of this and nine of that. Nine Fae planes. Nine Druids dancing in the dark. Nine ways to Nancy."

[What? Who's Nancy?]

"I dunno, but there's nine ways to her, so she's probably centrally located. I bet she's in a train station."

[I'm serious, now. I have to figure this out.]

"Well, I can't write it for ye. If you're looking for the minimum, I told ye true: nine lines."

[What have you been doing all day?]

"Toiling at domestic chores for about five minutes. Got that beer for Nadia and some more for us; it's in the fridge. Finished that movie—that cave troll looked familiar, eh? And since then I've been watching a show called *Avatar: The Last Airbender.* Have ye heard of it?" I shook my heid, and Buck's eyes lit with excitement to tell me about something new. "Fantastic Fae creatures in it, man! Sky bison. Platypus bears. There's one mental bastard who's got an obsession with cabbages. And the main character has a blue arrow tattooed on his bald heid. Thinking of getting ma self one of those on a trial basis. People will point at me and then say, *Look! It's the Avatar!* And after that it's even money whether they give me gifts or try to kill me deid. It's an exciting life, I imagine, either gifts or death everywhere ye go."

[Let's have something to nibble, and maybe I'll watch an episode with you before getting to work on my poem?]

"Aye, that sounds grand. What are we having, then?"

[Halibut with a lemon butter herb sauce. Let us begin your culinary training in matters beyond whisky and sausage.]

He required a stepladder to access the stove, but he took to the task with gusto, and after dinner he sat next to me and wrote dirty limericks as I struggled to write a poem with some true feeling behind it. I think he was far more successful than I was at getting work done.

When I yawned hugely and checked the clock, I realized I'd stayed up past my usual retirement. It was quite fine, I realized, to have someone around at night with whom to spend the sepulchral hours. It had been a long and lonesome time.

CHAPTER 13

First Among the Fae

In the morning—refreshed and astoundingly prank-free—
I taught Buck how to make tea and waffles. I told him where he
could steal maple syrup when we ran out, because he felt better
about things when there was theft at least tangentially involved.
Stealing had been his only reason to visit the plane until now, and
it was my hope that giving him some small acts of larceny to perform on my behalf would prevent him from performing larger
ones for a laugh.

I impressed upon him the importance of staying in-house for a
while, though, since it was warded against the barghests that he
was worried about, and I thought it prudent for the short term to
lay low. [Clíodhna or whoever's behind this will be after you soon,
so don't open the door for anyone. You just pretend you're not
here.]

"What am I s'posed tae do all day, then? House is already clean.
And it's Friday—all the humans are gonnay be out and ready for
mischief."

That was when I introduced him to microwave popcorn and

suggested he watch some more shows. Netflix was made for people who were shut-ins by choice or necessity.

"Isn't sitting around all day gonnay be bad for ma health?"

[Yes. But not as bad as a barghest tearing you to pieces.]

"Ye have a keen mind, ol' man. Off ye go, then."

On the way from the train station to my office on High Street, Coriander found me again.

"Brighid does wish to speak with you. At the violet hour in the usual place."

He waited only so long for me to nod, and then he glided away somewhere else. That meant I had until twilight to get my poem ready. Or not. Would it matter, I wondered? I was probably in trouble regardless, and if I delivered a shite piece of verse on top of my other trespasses, the goddess of poetry, fire, and the forge might decide there was nothing left to do but light me up.

The mystery of Bastille hung over me like the sword of Damocles at work, where I retreated to my desk to work on the poem, having accomplished little the night before. Lyrics about cashmere and ascots were discarded, as were paeans to mustache wax and haggis. The brief spark of an idea about sigils winked out almost immediately, for while I knew plenty about them, they didn't carry any emotional weight for me at the moment. They were merely tools of my trade and inspired no passion, except to find out who was sharing their secrets inappropriately.

When I finally settled on an adequate subject, it was midafternoon, and Nadia had long given up on trying to engage me with the business of my actual business. She kept everyone out of my office, explaining that I was "in a state" and couldn't be seen.

Finally finished, I nipped back home to check on Buck and freshen up before my meeting with the First among the Fae.

"How'd the poetry go, then?" Buck asked when I entered. I hung my coat and hat and typed a reply.

[It took me all day, but I finished nine lines. How people manage to make a career out of it is beyond me. It's excruciating work.]

"Are ye familiar with the Irish poet William Butler Yeats?"

I nodded at him.

"I had to memorize a bit of his stuff—well, most of it, really. Brighid requires some poetry of her Fae, ye know, if ye can believe it. Ye made me remember a passage: *A line will take us hours maybe; Yet if it does not seem a moment's thought, our stitching and unstitching has been naught.*"

[I wonder how long that took him.]

"Pretty sure he wrote it in the loo."

I showed him how to bake a tray of nachos with bacon and green onions, a recipe I learned—along with waffle batter—during a trip to America. It yielded a far superior product than microwave nachos if one had the time, and I took the opportunity to wash my face and re-wax my mustache while he shredded the cheddar.

When the nachos emerged from the oven, Buck said, "They look splendid, MacBharrais, but these will probably kill me faster than the binge-watching, eh?"

I nodded. [But not as fast as raisins. Avoid them, you hear? Only pain and suffering follow after.]

We devoured some melted fat and grease on chips with a sprinkling of greenery on top, and then I had time enough to brush my teeth before heading to Gin71. It would not do to meet Brighid with onion breath.

It rained on me the whole walk there, but the coat and hat did their thing and I arrived a few minutes early, since "the violet hour" was somewhat imprecise and I didn't want to keep Brighid waiting.

She and Coriander arrived together via the Old Way hidden in Virginia Court. Coriander was wearing his full green-and-silver livery and wig, since he was operating in his official capacity and had just come from the Fae Court, but Brighid had dressed down to blend in. She wore blue jeans and a white top that featured enough diaphanous layers so as to appear simultaneously transparent and opaque. It was a localized fog bank, a garment of mystery.

The goddess of poetry, fire, and the forge did not blend in, however. She was too beautiful to go unnoticed. Flame-haired, green-eyed, and toned, she would stand out in anything that didn't hide her features.

Coriander remained by the door so that we could have privacy, and once Brighid stepped in, Heather bowed so low behind the bar that she disappeared from view. I stood to greet Brighid and put a hand over my heart, not daring to offer any contact.

"Brighid, it's an honor."

"Aloysius," she said, beaming at me and giving me a nod. "At last. Thank you for being here." As if I would be anywhere else.

"Please." I gestured to my booth and we sat across from each other. I took out my phone and jabbed a finger at it before typing anything. "Did Coriander tell you about my curse?"

"He did. But put aside that silicon horror for this meeting. Let us risk it and have a look at your aura. Coriander said he can tell there's a curse but not much else. Perhaps I can perceive something beyond that."

I returned my phone to my coat and Brighid cocked her heid to one side and then the other, examining each of my temples.

"Yes, you've certainly been cursed. It's not Druidic, however, so you can put that out of your mind. None of the Tuatha Dé Danann were involved. It's strange magic, and I think there's more to it than this gradual process of your speech turning people against you."

"More?"

"Yes. Let me try to figure this out. Hold still."

She leaned a bit closer, and deep in the pools of her irises I saw a blue-white flame kindling there. The corners of her mouth pulled down in concern.

"Have any people close to you met with misfortune?" she asked.

I almost said no automatically, but then considered. "Yes. Every single one of my apprentices has had a fatal accident."

"They weren't accidents. Well, they were, but they only happened because that's another curse on your head. You've been doubly cursed. Very subtly too, and by the same person, or at least people wielding the same sort of magic."

I temporarily forgot to breathe, and then when I did, it sounded unnaturally loud in my ears, as did my words. "You mean . . . all seven of my apprentices died because of a curse on my heid I didn't know was there?"

"Yes."

"So . . . it's my fault. They died because of me."

"No. Scour that nonsense from your mind right now. Whoever laid this curse on you is at fault. They have committed murder as surely as if someone had left a hook binding to summon a demon here."

"Intellectually I understand that." I clenched my fists, as if that would help me control the volume of my voice. "But I should have discovered this long before now, instead of letting seven apprentices enter into a relationship that would end their lives prematurely. I should have asked for your help years ago. But why didn't—" I stopped, recalling the circumstances of how I learned about the first curse. "Yes, why didn't the Highlands witch see this second one?"

"I'm honestly surprised she saw the first one. These are extraordinarily subtle curses. If you hadn't told me something was there—if I hadn't specifically been looking for them—I wouldn't have seen them myself. They're blended into your aura. Allow me an analogy to help you understand. Most curses are clumsily tacked onto a person and make no attempts at disguise. They are like reading a text into which someone has pasted a passage in a different language that's also in a different font, a larger size, and a different color. It's ugly and glaring, it draws attention, and you know immediately that it's wrong. But your curse is crafted well, like everything is set in the same text except that there are a few words in a smaller size than the rest of it, as in eleven-point type rather than twelve. It's practically seamless. The curse isn't tacked or pasted on; it's part of who you are now, folded into your aura instead of warping it."

That didn't sound good at all. I took a moment to consider a response before asking, "Can you remove either of the curses?"

"I'm afraid not. This is some other system of magic and not one I can readily identify. Druidic bindings are obvious to me; other magics are also bindings in the sense that they bend and shape reality to their will, and while I can glean their purposes, I cannot unmake them without first knowing how they were made. You will have to review your acquaintances and speculate as to who might have done this to you."

I snorted. "They might be deid. My apprentices have been busily dying for many years."

"Whoever did this is not dead. If they were, you wouldn't be cursed."

"I beg your pardon?"

"Some curses endure long after the deaths of the caster. The Egyptians were particularly good at that sort of craft. But most of them, like this one, last only so long as the caster remains alive. That ill will—that animosity or bad blood—is necessary to keep it going. Find them and kill them and you'll be free of it."

"I . . ."

"I wouldn't take on any new apprentices until you clear that curse."

"No, no, of course not. I just wish I'd known earlier."

"And don't take on any servants either."

"Hmm? What?"

"You don't have any servants, do you?"

A cold fist of dread clutched my heart. "I just took one on. A hobgoblin named Buck Foi."

"His life is in danger, then. You have some time—years perhaps. Whoever's done this to you wants to give you time to become attached. But eventually the curse on your head will fall on his neck."

"Gods below," I said, though the goddess across from me was the first among them all. "And what about employees? Does the curse apply to them too?" I worried about Nadia. She'd been with me for a decade now. If the curse applied to her, she had to be near a fatal accident of her own. But the goddess shook her head.

"It shouldn't. That's a different relationship than between master and apprentice or this situation with your hobgoblin, where you're responsible for his well-being. You are merely contracting for their services and paying them. They should be safe so long as you maintain that professional distance."

I sighed in relief, that extra weight removed from my conscience. But then another replaced it.

"Would these accidents that were not accidents . . . did they . . . did it kill my wife?"

Brighid narrowed her eyes. "I doubt it. When did she pass? Before or after your first apprentice?"

"Before."

"Hmm. And when did you notice people starting to hate you? Before or after her death?"

"After. I thought at first maybe Dougal—my son—blamed me somehow for her death. I couldn't explain his anger otherwise, until I knew about the curse."

"Well, the curses are intertwined. They were placed on you at the same time. If they had been in place in time to affect your wife, then it would have made her despise you first, yes? And you can deduce that the curse causing fatal accidents doesn't target your loved ones, because they are all, save your wife, still alive after all this time. So it was truly an accident."

"But why target my apprentices?"

"Perhaps someone does not wish you to have a replacement."

"But both Eli and Shu-hua have apprentices who can replace me. Mei-ling too, technically, though she will probably take Mei-ling's territory when she's achieved her mastery. And I'm sure Diego will find an apprentice eventually."

"I'm going to visit the other sigil agents and make sure they're not cursed as well, but my suspicion is that only you were cursed."

"So I need to find and kill whoever did this to me and I'll be free." I said it as an affirmation as much as a confirmation.

"Yes. Or else they must voluntarily remove the curse. But if they cursed you once, they can do so again. If I were you, I would not accept an apology for this. I would burn the responsible party to ash."

Casual discussion of murder is not normal for me, but my head was already nodding in agreement. Because someone had murdered my apprentices so deviously, I had not even recognized them as murders until now. Their deaths had appeared to be such freak accidents that I'd never considered not getting another apprentice, thereby feeding the appetite of what must be the most passive serial killer ever.

"Is there anything you can tell me about who might have done this? Even by way of eliminating possibilities, as you did with the Tuatha Dé Danann?"

"It's someone highly skilled, who demonstrates such mastery over magic that I doubt that it's anyone human. It's conceivable that it's the work of a god. Which would make killing them a difficult proposition."

". . . Yes."

"But if all else fails, you have work-arounds, right?"

"How so?"

"This enemy may be too powerful to confront. But you have already figured out how to use technology to get around the first curse, which turns your friends to enemies. The second is easily defeated by not taking on any new apprentices."

"True, but then they win. I want the curses gone. I can't get my apprentices back, but maybe I could have friends again. Talk to my son again. And teach an apprentice who'd actually make it to mastery."

The goddess nodded. "I would wish that. It's a quest worth pursuing. I cannot promise to help you along the way, except to be receptive when you ask. I may have to tell you no because I have obligations and responsibilities to other pantheons, many of which you are already aware of. Without knowing who your enemy is, I can only be vaguely supportive."

"I understand and think that is very kind."

Brighid raised her finger and caught the eye of Harrowbean—or Heather MacEwan—and then twirled her finger, nodding as she did so, to indicate that we were ready for drinks. That was a signal for a change of subject, I realized, and I would have to stow away these revelations and emotions for now and unpack them later. We did have other business to discuss.

The bartender brought me my usual Pilgrim's and tonic and brought Brighid a Boë violet gin garnished with a bit of grapefruit. A violet drink for the violet hour.

The First among the Fae beamed her gratitude at Harrowbean, and once the bartender had retreated, we poured our tonics over the ice lounging in a gin bath and enjoyed the pleasant bubble and fizz.

Brighid held up her glass, and when she next spoke, there was a bass and a soprano note riding along with her typical alto. I'd heard legends about that triple voice: She could tell no lie when she spoke that way, for it was speaking three times all at once. "I appreciate you seeing to so many contracts and enforcing our treaties over the years, Mr. MacBharrais," she said. And then her voice returned to normal. "I wanted you to hear that from my own lips and know that it was sincere. Sláinte."

Stunned into silence and perhaps a bit of panic, I realized that this would be the ideal time—if any time was ideal at all—for me to present my poem to her.

"I've, uh—" I cleared my throat of a sudden obstruction and begged her pardon. "It's been my honor. And I don't know, uh . . . if it's right. I certainly mean no offense, but I wrote a few lines in your honor, just some doggerel—"

"A poem?" She brightened. "For me?"

"Well, yes, for you in the sense that I wished to honor one of your aspects, but not about you, and it's just nine lines, hardly a poem at all, but—"

"That's perfect. Sometimes they can drag on a bit."

"Oh. Well." Apparently, Buck was misinformed as to Brighid's preference for epic poems. Either that or he'd outright lied to me.

"Do please share."

"Right. Uh. Let me see." From my coat, I pulled the folded sheet of paper that represented hours of ludicrous effort, tried to smooth it out, and began to read my own handwriting.

The soft scrape of a heel on pavement
Can trigger again my bereavement;
I often remember her laugh or her face
At any inconvenient time or place
And weep salt tears for the years we've lost
And the boundary that only she has crossed;
But what I shall forever cherish—

At line seven I realized that something had gone horribly, horribly wrong, and I stopped. It was not my writing anymore. Or, rather, it looked like my handwriting, but I had certainly not written that down.

"What? That's not all, is it?" Brighid asked. "It sounded like there was supposed to be more. At least two more lines about what you'll cherish?"

"Well, yes, but they're not my lines."

"Don't be modest, Mr. MacBharrais."

"They are seriously not mine. My hobgoblin has clearly changed them, and they are now tremendously profane."

The goddess grinned. "Your hobgoblin changed the last two lines of your poem?"

"Yes," I admitted. "I'm sorry." I was also furious. While I had gone to the bathroom to freshen up, or while he was supposed to be shredding cheddar for nachos, he'd obviously made the switch.

She clapped her hands together three times in excitement. "This is great! I can see you are acutely embarrassed, so your hob has done an excellent job. Let's hear it."

"I don't think they're appropriate to be read aloud."

"In poetry, Mr. MacBharrais, every word is sacred. None is profane. You have my assurance. Read them to me without delay."

How could I refuse? I couldn't. I took a deep breath and said the last three lines, since they were one single phrasing.

But what I shall forever cherish
Are the ripe, overgrown, and garish
Pubes around the knob of Al MacBharrais.

Brighid made the tiniest effort to stifle a giggle but wound up snorting and then laughing uproariously. She pounded the table. She startled everyone in the restaurant. She pointed at me and kept laughing.

"Your mustache! Is glowing! Because your face! Is so red! Ahahahahaha!"

I felt it heating up even more after that. I'm not sure I've ever been so embarrassed, and this was a significantly less dignified meeting than I'd hoped for.

Brighid eventually wound down and wiped at a tear on her cheek.

"Oh, I haven't laughed like that in centuries." People said that all the time as hyperbole, but in Brighid's case it might have been true. "That gift of laughter was at your expense. You have my sincere gratitude and should feel only goodwill from me, Mr. MacBharrais. What were the last two lines of your poem before your hobgoblin changed them?"

"Something about how my love for the late Mrs. MacBharrais would never perish. I can't remember the exact phrasing."

"Oh, my. He hobbed your mourning poem? That's a pair of brass bollocks he's got." She sniggered and then tried to master herself. "I mean, I am of course very sorry for your loss. Your sentiments for her were expressed very well for someone who's not a deft hand at verse. But still. As far as taking the piss out of your new employer is concerned, you have to admit: Buck Foi has made a spectacular debut."

I sighed and managed a weak chuckle. "I did tell him to be creative and nondestructive."

She laughed again. "So he followed your instructions! And he wasn't here to enjoy your discovery of the switch. Iron and forge, that's a rare hob indeed! You've managed to snag an excellent one. I know you might not appreciate it at this moment, but you are to be congratulated, Mr. MacBharrais. I don't think I've ever seen a more sophisticated pisstaking from a hobgoblin."

"Thanks," I said tightly before finishing my drink and ordering another. Brighid likewise drained hers and twirled a finger for a second round.

"Right. We have actual business to discuss, do we not?"

"We do." I caught her up with all I had learned and suspected of Gordie and the mysterious Bastille, who had paid for the trafficking of a clurichaun, troll, leprechaun, undine, pixie, and a fir darrig. I informed her that my hobgoblin was supposed to be next and he claimed that Clíodhna of the Tuatha Dé Dannan had offered him an employment contract with my alleged approval.

"Clíodhna is behind it? That is a serious charge."

"Yes."

"One that we'll not be able to solve without some proof. A hobgoblin's word cannot be taken over Clíodhna's, and she will certainly deny it."

"Understood. I just wanted to make you aware that this happened to Buck and may or may not have happened to the others. But they were tempted to this plane somehow, then Gordie trafficked them to Bastille. What is particularly alarming from a sigil-agent perspective is that someone wrote down an ink recipe for Gordie. I found it in his papers."

Brighid's eyes flashed with blue flame. "They wrote it down, you say? Which ink?"

"Manannan's."

I withdrew the scrap of paper and pushed it across the table to her. "Do you recognize the handwriting?"

"No, but I doubt Clíodhna would do this herself. She would have made one of the bean sídhe do it for her. It still bears investigation. I will give this to Flidais—have you met her, the goddess of the hunt?"

I nodded and said, "Aye, we've met before, in Edinburgh."

"I will ask her to track down whoever it was. She's much better than a barghest. If it's possible to track the author, she will do it. Why are you making that face?"

I hadn't realized I'd been making one but quickly attempted to correct it. "It's nae bother, really. Flidais calls me the Scots wizard, that's all. But I'm no a wizard."

Brighid smiled. "Take no offense. She calls anything that's not Druidry either wizardry or witchcraft. We'll see what she can find."

She tucked the paper away and then placed her hands flat on the table on either side of her glass. "So. I have not been to this plane since that business with Loki required my presence."

She was referring to the Norse god's failed attempt to trigger Ragnarok the year before. Plenty of deities came to earth without permission that day but informed me of the visit and cited an emergency clause in their contracts to avoid Dire Consequence. I'd had to fly up to Sweden and throw around a lot of sigils to shut down the investigation of the aftermath and keep it from blowing up in the mainstream press.

"Perhaps it's because I've had a couple of drinks," Brighid continued, "but I'm not quite ready to go back without first punching someone. This news that someone is trafficking Fae has annoyed me, and I shouldn't go back to my throne that way—the Fae will sense it immediately. So tell me, Mr. MacBharrais: Where can I go in Glasgow to find someone who deserves a good thrashing?"

That is how I wound up going to a pub full of football fans with a pagan goddess and telling her that she could easily start a fight in Glasgow by blaring a certain song on the speakers. Neither of

Glasgow's two top teams, Rangers or Celtic, was playing that night, so the crowd was mixed and watching other teams on the telly. All Brighid had to do was somehow get Tina Turner's hit song "The Best" to blast in the pub, and since it was the entrance music for Rangers, all the Rangers fans would immediately start to sing along. That would enrage the Celtic fans, and violence would shortly ensue, guaranteed.

"Ye might have a fight just getting it going, because no pub in Glasgow will play it on purpose unless they know the whole house is full of Rangers fans."

"I appreciate the challenge. Where would I find this song?" I pointed to a DJ booth in the far corner that was used for late-night dancing, and she immediately strode to it. I nearly asked if she knew how to run modern entertainment systems but on second thought kept my mouth closed, on the principle that it is never wise to ask a deity if they know something, lest they take offense at the implication that a mortal knows something they do not. She did, however, know how to operate the system. She started the song—and therefore the brawl—without delay, and I stepped outside to wait while she ended it too.

"Most invigorating," she said when she emerged smiling a few minutes later. She did not appear to have actually been in a fight, except for a spot of blood on her top. "Very salutary. Just what I needed. I can find my own way back to Tír na nÓg, Mr. MacBharrais. You will hear more soon via Coriander." She kissed three fingers and touched them to my forehead. "Go. You have my blessing."

I did not know what that meant, exactly, but I felt better than I had in a long while as I bowed and took my leave.

—•—

Fish Glue

The boiling of fish bladders, tendons, and skin to make a gooey and rather smelly adhesive must periodically be undertaken. It's used in small amounts in many inks as a low-level binder. It's a pain to make—especially descaling the skin. There's no quick way around it, and the scales get everywhere, much like glitter. You wind up finding them in your cracks and folds days later, and it can be mortifying when someone points out that you've got a bit of fish in your dimples. But taking pains to make fish glue and using rare ingredients ensures that no one is accidentally creating inks potent enough for sigil work.

Whipping up a batch of fish glue is a perfect task to assign to an apprentice. It's a chore I'd set for all seven of them, who were doomed to die before becoming masters because I didn't realize I was lugging a deadly curse around on my heid.

I'd have to do it by myself from now on, and I figured that for all its inconvenience, it was a wee penance to pay for a truly massive cock-up. I know Brighid said I bore no responsibility for the deaths of my apprentices, but I felt guilty anyway and knew I always would.

CHAPTER 14

A Dram to Build a Dream On

It only took half a block for the euphoria of Brighid's blessing to wear off. My dizzy heid was busy reevaluating all my years as a master sigil agent, thinking I was shepherding my apprentices to greatness while I was in fact ushering them to their doom. Reviewing the progress of their education before they'd passed, I didn't see a correlation between them learning something specific and then dying soon afterward; the curse must use some other benchmark than sigil training to know when to trigger. I should have asked Brighid more questions about the mechanics of it, and I winced the way one always does when a moment's passed and you suddenly wish you could go back and say or do the perfect thing you thought of twenty minutes too late.

I didn't know the precise trigger conditions for my other curse either, but I always remembered the moment when it did trigger, because it was never a gentle ghosting when someone decided they didn't like me anymore. They let me know about it. Loudly, often with bared teeth and occasionally a thrown fist.

Eleven years ago, when I was in my fifties and my dear wife had already passed, and I was stuck in a morbid Shakespearean fugue where every third thought was of the grave, and I was wondering if perhaps I should find an enforcer like Nadia, the curse went off for the first time. Dougal, my own son, landed a right cross on my jaw, said he hated me and never wanted to lay eyes on my worthless carcass again and I shouldn't call or text. This was at his house: He'd just given me a cup of tea, I had said, "Thank you," and that did it. I left bewildered and gave him some space, and after it happened again and again with friends that I spoke to in my distress, I tried to speak to him once more to see if time had reduced his anger at all.

It had not. If anything, it was worse. His face turned red, spittle flew from his mouth, and he promised to kill me if he saw me again.

I made sure he didn't see me after that, but I checked in on him from time to time. After the revelations Brighid had bestowed on me, I thought he was due for another checkup.

Dougal was a bartender at a nice pub called The Citizen on St. Vincent Place, an easy walk from Queen Street station, and only ten minutes' walk away from my own flat. The pub was often busy, and it was now, so he never saw me come in. The press of bodies around the bar was too thick and he was too slammed with work to look up and scan the faces.

I ducked in and asked for a table, was led by a pleasant hostess past the mixed gabbling horde of business folk and tourists to a small place in the dining room beyond the bar and out of sight, and there I ordered a finger of seventeen-year-old Balvenie Double-Wood, which Dougal would eventually pour for me.

He was busy shaking a cocktail as I passed him by that night, perhaps a Last Word or a Bee's Knees. He looked well, and that was all I really needed to know. I ordered my drink as soon as I was seated and it arrived in six minutes, whereupon I asked for my bill.

I examined the dram, curling the glass and tilting it in my fingers, the amber liquid swirling inside representing the only commerce I'd been allowed with my son for eleven years now. It was a sad pour for a stranger, and that was what the curse had made us: strangers. I did not know if he followed football anymore or how my grandchildren were doing in school. I didn't know who they wanted to be when they grew up or what hopes Dougal and my daughter-in-law held for their futures.

That and so much more had been stolen from me. And despite Brighid's assurances that a member of the Tuatha Dé Danann hadn't performed the actual curse, the truth was, one of them was as likely to be responsible as anyone else. The Tuatha Dé Danann could have hired the work out, and most certainly would have done if they intended to curse me, knowing that their work could be inspected and possibly identified by anyone with magical sight.

You had to pay attention to what the Tuatha Dé Danann didn't say as much as to what they did say.

Whisky, at least, had its own language, and I could pretend that Dougal would have intended the dram's notes for me back when there was warmth between us. Honey and apples in the nose, a bright and luxurious crispness. Flavors of vanilla and honeysuckle on the tongue, and a sweet, lingering finish of caramel and old wood. It evoked feelings of camaraderie and compassion.

Perhaps we would enjoy those things together again someday, if I could figure out who'd done this to me and end this curse by ending them.

I wanted my family and friends back.

CHAPTER 15

Sometimes, Ghost Dogs Are Too Much

ards are like insurance policies in that you have them in hopes you'll never need them. For one thing, if you need them, you're being attacked. For another, you sometimes think you're covered against something only to find out when it's too late that you're really not.

Standard procedure in my flat was to close all the doors, all the time, because they're all warded. The windows leading outside were warded too. When the doors in the flat were closed, it functionally made my kitchen and living area the keep of the castle. Something might get past the outer walls, then—a distinct possibility, since I liked keeping windows open for fresh air as much as possible—but they'd still have to get past the warded doors to threaten me.

Saturday morning, I was in the kitchen with Buck, teaching him how to make French toast, when we heard snuffles and growls coming from the hallway bathroom. Buck caught my eye and said, "Is there sumhin ye'd like tae share with me about who ye brought home last night?"

Buck had been snoring on the couch when I came in late, and I found him still there when I came out to make coffee. I poked him awake and congratulated him on a spectacular pisstaking the night before and relayed both my acute embarrassment at the time and Brighid's compliments. That brightened his morning immediately, but he looked less sanguine now.

I shrugged and shook my head, snatching up my phone.

[Do not open any doors, period.]

"Okay. What in nine hells is happening, then?"

I turned off the stove and removed the skillet from the heat before answering. [The bathroom window must have been open. Something got in.]

Buck followed me as I walked over to the door to listen a bit closer.

"Like what?" he asked. "That bathroom window is a wee thing, good for nothing but ventilating the noxious fumes of yer hole. Nothing can get through there but a pixie."

[Or barghests.] With the ward rendered impotent by the open window, they could flow through the small space in their ghostly form and take on solid flesh when they had room to do so. The ones in my flat now snuffled at the crack beneath the bathroom door and growled again. One of them even scratched at it. The only thing stopping them from entering the open living area was the Ward of Spectral Abeyance I had on the door. They'd already be in the kitchen and tearing out Buck's neck otherwise.

My hobgoblin turned a much paler shade of pink.

"Oh, shite," he breathed. "Shite shite shite fuckity shite! They're here for me, in't they?"

[I imagine so.]

"What do we do?"

[Wrap some towels around your neck in case they get in. As many as possible. Deny them that target.]

Buck ran to the drawer where I kept them. "What else?"

[We need to determine how many there are and if they're in the bathroom only or the other rooms as well.]

"How?"

[We listen. And don't touch the doors.]

We crept forward together. Judging by the snuffles and Buck's counting of noses near the floor, there were three barghests in the bathroom. I doubted there were more—even two was overkill in most cases—but it would be best to be thorough. No noses at the bottom of my master bedroom or the study. No noses at the bottom of the guest bedroom either, which was now Buck's bedroom.

[Good job keeping the door closed,] I said. [This is exactly why we do it.]

"Well, aye, I'm gonnay follow the rules of the house, in't I, when it's gonnay keep me alive. The question is why ye left the bloody bathroom window open!"

[Noxious fumes of my hole, as you said.]

"But there's people who want tae murder me!"

[This is actually good, Buck.]

"How? How is it good?"

[They're not in the hallway of the building, terrorizing my neighbors. And since we know where they are and they have only one way forward, we can do something about them. We can craft a plan.]

"The plan is to wait until they get bored, right?"

[They won't get bored. They're on a contracted hunt. This is about meat and teeth and tearing into the first with the second. I can't make them stop, because I'm not the contract holder.]

"Fine, we'll just never use that bathroom until they starve tae death."

[They'll go out and eat in shifts. They're single-minded but not stupid.]

"So you go out and fix it somehow."

[You want me to leave you in here alone?]

"Fuck no! Don't you dare leave me here alone!"

[Okay. I couldn't go outside to fix this anyway. Think it through. We have a little time because they can't get through that door until they shred it.] The scratches we heard were multiplying.

Buck took a deep breath and considered. "Well . . . could they get recalled by the contract holder?"

[Yes. But the contract holder is most likely Clíodhna. She would not show up at the home of a sigil agent to call off an illegal contract, because then she would be liable for a violation of the treaty between the Fae and humanity. So that's out.]

"If I leave the flat, they'll know it, right?"

[Definitely. They can smell you now and they're locked on. Exit the flat and they will exit the bathroom and keep coming after you until you're in their jaws.]

"Can ye put 'em in a magic jar or sumhin? A box made of wards?"

[Naw. Can't be done. Spectral Abeyance keeps things out, not in. Line a container with the ward and then the ghost can't get in the container. They're not going to get in a container and politely wait for me to paint the wards inside to trap them.]

"So, what do we do? Kill them somehow?"

[Yes. Or we let them tear you apart. Those are the only options.]

"But I thought ye liked dugs."

[I do. All the dugs who aren't trying to kill my friends and me. I feel the same way about people. I think they're great until they try to kill me.]

"Won't Clíodhna just send more?"

[Maybe, but I doubt it.]

"Why?"

[Barghest contracts vary in value, but sending three of them at once is very expensive. It indicates that there's some doubt that one or two will be enough and there might be loss involved. That ups the price considerably. And if all three never come back, well, there's going to be a cost for that. The barghest handlers won't want to deal with a person who's going to send their animals out to be killed.]

"Ah, so she'll have to try something else."

[That's my guess, yes. But first we need to solve this problem. Three barghests is a significant one.]

"Too right it is. How do ye kill one of them, much less three?"

[Same as any Fae: with iron.]

"I cannae use iron."

[Yes, you can. You've been using my steel knives in the kitchen because you grip the wrapped handles. Pick two. I'm going to draw Sigils of Iron Gall on them and put that on my cane as well.]

A Sigil of Iron Gall would take the normal damage from a steel blade and, to paraphrase the immortal guitarist Nigel Tufnel, turn it up to 11—at least when applied to the flesh of the Fae. It accelerated the poison of iron in the blood and hastened their disintegration into ash.

"So yer plan is to open the door, let the dugs come at me, and I just stab them?"

[It's a little more complicated than that.]

"Wot's the plan, then?"

[Barghest fishing with Buck bait.]

The hobgoblin didn't just shake his head; his entire body quivered with a shuddering negative. "Naw naw naw, see, the general idea in fishing is that the bait gets swallowed. I'm no gonnay stand for that."

[Didn't say you'd stand for it. Was rather hoping you wouldn't.]

I filled him in on the plan and then left him in the kitchen to up his armor class with towels while I ducked into my study to paint sigils on the blades and my cane.

My fingers trembled with the brush as it hovered above the first knife, and I withdrew my hand and took a few deep breaths to calm down. I'd presented this to Buck as a quick fight, easy to win, but it wasn't going to be easy at all. It would, for sure, be quick, one way or the other. Barghests do not circle around their prey or play with their food. They simply attack.

Sigils completed, my intestines made hungry noises. If we were going to be meals in a wee while, we might as well have our last meal. Insisting that it was necessary and I required the calories and blood sugar, I finished making French toast while the barghests bayed and scratched at the door, occasionally pounding at it with their huge paws. It rattled in its frame.

"I'm no hungry," Buck said when I put a slice in front of him and poured on some maple syrup.

[One bite,] I said.

He groused but did it and gave me no compliments on its taste.

I tried mine, attempting to relax and enjoy it as murderous hounds howled for blood less than twenty feet away, but the toast tasted of tension, and I knew after a single bite that I wouldn't be finishing it either.

Buck noticed and gestured to the door. "That shite affects the appetite, eh?"

I nodded and studiously did the dishes and set them to dry in the rack as Buck paced back and forth on top of my kitchen island, now swaddled in layers of towel around his neck and face, which might do very little to save him. But he gripped the two knives in his fists and looked willing to use them.

[Ready?]

"Almost," he replied. "Look, ol' man. If they get me, well . . . I just want to thank ye for a few extra days of life. Thank ye for try- ing tae make things right. It's only been a wee while, but I can see I would have had a good thing going here. Ye've been kind tae me when ye didnae have tae be."

Nodding an acknowledgment, I moved to the bathroom door, which faced the end of the kitchen island on which Buck stood. When I opened the door, the barghests would have a straight shot at him. And I would have a shot at them as they came out.

The living room would be stretched out along to their left from the kitchen area, giving Buck some room to operate.

Since it might be the last thing I ever said to him, I asked aloud, "Are ye ready?" The hounds sensed that they were going to get their chance soon. Their barking and tearing at the door intensi- fied. Buck took a single deep breath, exhaled, then nodded.

I gave myself strength and agility sigils, twisted the handle, and pushed just enough to break the seal of the ward, and that's all the barghests needed. They didn't require the door to be flung wide open. They turned to ghostly mist and streamed over, under, and through both sides of the door. And I madly swung my carbon-steel cane with the Sigil of Iron Gall on it through the lot, hoping it would do some damage to them in their incorporeal form.

The barghests would have to become flesh in order to do Buck any damage, but they typically waited until the last possible moment to do that, since the relative invulnerability of ghostliness was something anyone would take advantage of if it was available.

As the first began to coalesce, Buck popped away from the island to the far side of the living room, thereby drawing the barghests away.

The clatter of the knives on the counter revealed a fatal flaw in our plan.

"Shite!" I heard him say. "I couldn't teleport the iron, ol' man!"

"Pick them up when ye come back!" I said. "Proceed as we planned!"

"This is gonnay be dodgy!"

"No way around it!"

Scrambling to the island as the ghost dogs banked left to pursue Buck, I planted myself in front of it, facing the living room and waiting. Buck popped himself back to the island as the hounds solidified and crashed into the far wall, their target gone. The hobgoblin muttered, "Shite, shite, shite!" as he scrambled to pick up his knives and the hounds whirled around to locate him.

My defensive strategy was to put myself between the hounds and Buck, and he'd put his back to mine on one edge of the island. The barghests could flow around me and over the top, perhaps, but the plain fact of the matter was that only one of them could fit on the island at a time. Buck would have a shot at using those knives and surviving the exchange if only one barghest could come at him.

That left the prospect of two coming at me, however, in their attempt to reach Buck from the floor.

Handling one was within the realm of possibility for me.

Not two.

The trio of ghost hounds growled, seeing me standing there with Buck peering over my shoulder at them and perhaps assessing their best options. They seemed to confer, exchanging glances and some assorted growls and barks. If they were feeling any of the Iron Gall I'd swiped at them in their ghost form, they weren't showing it.

"Fuck," Buck whispered. "Fuckity fuck fuck."

"Steady," I said.

Two of the barghests turned incorporeal and whooshed our way, while one remained flesh and charged straight at me. Out of necessity my focus had to remain on him, and I brought my cane down hard on his head and snout, causing him to cry out, and I realized a split second later that he was just taking one for the team. One of the other two barghests materialized just to my left and batted a massive paw at my face, claws raking down my cheek and nearly taking out my vision on that side. Buck and I and a barghest behind me all screamed at nearly the same time, albeit for different reasons.

As I staggered to my right, clutching my face with one hand and my cane in the other, the barghest who'd raked me eyed a spring at Buck, who cried out in pain as the bargest who'd taken shape on the island tried to bite him in half. The hound took two knives to the shoulders for his trouble and released the hobgoblin to wail about it, and once out of its magic-dampening jaws, Buck was able to pop away to the other side of the room, thwarting a pounce from the barghest who'd scratched me, leaving the one I'd conked on the head growling and clearly considering switching targets to me.

The barghest that Buck had stabbed kept yowling as the Iron Gall corrupted the very magic that allowed him to exist and systematically shut down his being. The other two swung their heads around to locate Buck, and as they did, the knife handles clattered back to the countertop. The barghest had turned to ash. One down.

Buck had not escaped unscathed. The barghest's teeth had penetrated, and multiple puncture wounds bled through his clothing but thankfully not through his swaddled neck.

The poor wee man looked ready to collapse, though. I probably didn't look much better.

"Again," I said, and lunged forward, swinging with everything I had at the barghest who'd first charged me. He yipped, and this time, between taking another strong dose of Iron Gall and the sheer force of my magically boosted strength, he collapsed and crumbled to dust. Buck popped back to the island countertop and picked up the knives again, breathing heavily. The multiple teleports combined with his wounds were draining him quickly. The last barghest became mist as I tried to bat him down and missed so badly that it threw me off-balance. I crashed into my coffee table, but it wasn't the easily broken sort you see in films. It was solid wood and sharp on the edges. Pain spiked in my back where I hit, and my right side went numb, a nerve cluster having been struck. The table won that battle, and Buck was on his own. I could push myself up to wish him luck and watch what happened but could do nothing to help in time.

The barghest swirled in a circle around him, trying to decide where to take shape—preferably behind him—and Buck waved his knives around and spun, refusing to give the hound a stationary target or a free shot at his back. He was wheezing and running on pure adrenaline, or whatever the hobgoblin equivalent to that was.

Buck eventually lost a step and the barghest thought he saw his chance. The hound became solid, his head cocked to one side and jaws opened wide, and he closed them on Buck's body, trapping his right arm against his torso. The top row of teeth sank into Buck's back and the bottom into his front, with the arm trapped in the middle, only possible because the hound was large and Buck was small. The barghest's magic nullification prevented Buck from teleporting away.

The hobgoblin screamed as the barghest lifted him up in his jaws, but Buck's left hand stabbed repeatedly into the side of the barghest's neck and the top of its shoulder, because that's all he could reach. The hound shook him left, then right, testing his weight, and what came next would be a rapid-fire thrashing about in an attempt to break Buck's neck. But the hobgoblin flew out of the maw on the next shake to the left as the barghest came apart under the iron poisoning and added its ash to that of its companion.

The wee man flew, trailing blood, until he landed with a pained grunt on the sofa not far from me.

"Buck!"

"Auggh," he groaned. "Ghost dugs are ma least favorite kind of dugs."

"I understand. But at least we're still here."

"Maybe . . . not much longer. Auggh! It hurts."

"Here." I pulled out a Sigil of Healing and a Sigil of Knit Flesh, opening both before his eyes. "Have a look at these and stop bleeding on my couch."

There was a soporific and an anesthetic quality to the healing sigil that sent Buck into unconsciousness after a few seconds, and his breathing steadied soon afterward; I was confident that he'd close up and get better from there.

The sigil cards in my hand were covered in blood because my hands were. The barghest's claws had scratched deeper than I'd thought, perhaps reaching down to my neck, and I was starting to feel a bit dizzy from blood loss. I found another Sigil of Knit Flesh for myself to close everything up, but I was out of healing sigils and couldn't make any more. Those inks were all at my office.

The strength and agility sigils wore off about the time that my wounds began to close up, and I felt drained and unsure if I could actually get to my feet. I struggled at it, however, using my cane to help, and once I was mobile I limped and moaned my way to the bathroom, where I closed the damn window. We did not want another pack of dugs or anything else coming in.

The interior of the bathroom door was shredded to splinters. It would have to be replaced, but it would hold for now. I took some multivitamins to aid my healing the old pharmaceutical way and drank plenty of water to replace my fluids, carefully not looking in the mirror, because I was scared of what I'd see. Then I exited and closed the door firmly, renewing the ward's seal.

There was so much else to do—sweeping and sponging and mopping and calling Nadia to come and help—but I sat down on the couch next to Buck, or rather half-crashed there, for a short rest, since I could afford one now.

My hands began trembling after about twenty seconds and tears sprang up in my eyes, immediately stinging the wounds on my cheek. We had come so close to losing that one. And though what I'd told Buck earlier was true—we'd likely see no more barghests after this—I worried about what Clíodhna would send next.

To calm myself, I began inhaling deep lungfuls of air and exhaling slowly. I focused on my breathing, internalized the truth that I had utter control over my reaction to this crisis, and knew that I would heal and set things right.

I fell asleep soon afterward, blood-soaked skin and clothing and all, and dreamt of the most delightful French toast with sliced bananas, my mind trying to find a happy place while my body tried to deal with its trauma.

Usually my Saturdays went better than this.

CHAPTER 16

The Train to Edinburgh

"Hey, MacBharrais," Buck said.

[What?]

We were sprawled on the couch, trying not to move while our bodies tried to heal, and watching Kenneth Branagh's *Hamlet* from 1996, since we were feeling so tragic. It was not my favorite way to spend a Sunday morning, my face on fire and wanting waffles yet not wishing to move, but I supposed I was fortunate merely to be there and not enjoying it, instead of being in chunks and coursing through the mystic bowels of a barghest.

"How come ye're the guy? I mean the sigil agent. Why does the goddess at the top of the Irish pantheon have an ol' Scottish man working for her?"

[I wasn't always old.]

"But you've always been Scottish."

[True, but being Irish isn't a prerequisite. A sharp memory and the ability to keep secrets are more important. And besides, the Scots have their own grand portion of the Fae too. Witness this fine hobgoblin here named Buck Foi.]

"Still, why is it you slingin' sigils for Brighid and not some earnest freckled dude in Dublin?"

[My master was Irish, and he picked me to be his apprentice. That's pretty much it. The sigil agents in the United States aren't Irish either. One's from El Salvador and the other is African-American. The agents in Taiwan and Melbourne are also not Irish.]

"So why'd he pick you?"

[He ran across me hunting for gall nuts to make ink. That was his first clue that I might have the aptitude and disposition to be a sigil agent. I learned later that he was in Scotland pursuing a hobgoblin like you who'd pulled off some rather large heists.]

"Heists, ye say? I like him already."

[Her.]

"Her? Ye wouldnae be talkin' of Holga Thunderpoot, now, would ye?"

[That's the one.]

"Ah, Holga! A heroine of the hobgoblins. He didnae ever catch her, though, did he?"

[Naw. He found me instead. Not sure what happened to her in the end.]

Buck's expression turned dark. "I do. When Fand had her little rebellion against Brighid a while back—I assume ye heard about that—Holga was one of many who died on that field outside of Manannan Mac Lir's castle."

[I'm sorry. Was she a relation?]

"Naw, just a heroine, like I said. I always wanted tae pull off a heist like hers someday. A few bottles here and a few sausages there are all very fine, but she'd steal entire barrels of master distillers' reserve, barrels that were old enough tae vote, ye ken? Then she bottled it under her own label, Hobgoblin Heist, and she gave it away in the Fae Court. Had a bottle myself once, and the label made me laugh. Under the name it said, *The Very Finest of Purloined Highlands Whiskies,* and then under that it said, *Aged a Long Bloody Time,* ha ha. For tasting notes, it said, *Discuss*

Amongst Yourselves, but It's Delicious Because I Fucking Stole It. And she was right."

I chuckled at that, which led to a mild coughing fit, and the coughing hurt. But I typed, [She sounds like a legendary hob. Why don't you honor her and yourself at the same time?]

"How d'ye mean?"

[You could create Buck Foi's Best Boosted Spirits and include a little homage to Holga Thunderpoot on the label. We can easily print them in my shop.]

"Are ye serious now?"

I shrugged. [Hobgoblins are going to steal. If you decide to steal and then give away the stolen goods in a sort of Robin Hood scenario, and you make sure to never take so much that the distiller can't recover or bear the loss, well, it's almost virtuous, isn't it?]

"I like the way ye rationalize theft, boss."

While I was typing a reply, we heard three soft knocks on the front door, followed by a rustle of paper. Buck looked at me with wide, panicked eyes.

"Ye're gonnay make me go look, aren't ye?"

[Somebody has to move their arse off this couch.]

"Can we play Cock, Vapor, Knickers for it?"

I frowned. [You mean Rock, Paper, Scissors?]

Buck scoffed. "Naw, that's boring, that is."

[Yours sounds a bit too exciting. I can't play whatever that is in my condition.]

"Gahh. Whatevers, MacBharrais. I see where this is headed. I'll go. Wauugggh!"

He went, but not without a dramatic series of groans and grunts that highlighted what great personal pains he was enduring for my sake.

"There's a sealed note slipped under the door here," he called eventually. "I'll bring it over. Don't move now, ol' man. Wouldnae want tae get yer mustache bent out of shape. Just wait."

The moaning and groaning resumed, and I typed, [Thanks,

Buck. My mustache is perfectly bent at the moment, just like yer maw.]

"Heh! Ow. Don't make me laugh."

After a marathon session of pained grunting, he crawled back up on the couch with me and handed over the note. It bore Brighid's seal, so I opened it immediately.

Mr. MacBharrais:

Flidais traced the scrap you provided to the airport. Whoever gave Gordie that ink recipe flew into or out of Glasgow, or both. The scrap has now been destroyed.

Brighid

That was strange. I had fully expected that trail to lead to one of the Old Ways in Glasgow. I would have put money, in fact, on the Kelvingrove Park one, near Gordie's flat. My thinking had been that Clíodhna had sent one of her bean sídhe over with the information. But an airport meant someone human—most likely human, anyway—was getting directly involved in the business with Gordie and Clíodhna. The only other person involved that we knew of was the mysterious Bastille. If it was him, where was he located that he needed to fly into Glasgow?

I had an idea to pursue, but it would mean moving. I felt like shite and there were plenty of reasons to stay half-sunk into the cushions of my couch. A long, soft time watching Shakespeare was precisely what I needed and probably all I had the energy for. But I also had a mystery to solve and some justice to serve. I couldn't do any of that without moving.

The grunting and moaning that ensued as I tried to rise from the couch outraged Buck no end.

"Oh, now ye move, after ye make me go tae the door and back? If ye were gonnay get up anyway, ye could have gone tae the door yerself!"

I waved him off and waddled stiffly to my coat, knees protesting the entire way. I retrieved the flash drive Saxon Codpiece had given me Thursday with Gordie's phone information and passwords on it and then plugged it into my laptop, once I'd fetched that and returned to the couch. I should have looked into this earlier, but what with Brighid's visit taking up my entire day on Friday and then getting attacked yesterday, I'd had no opportunity.

"What are ye daein' now? We were watching Claudius sugar o'er the devil himself, and what could be more important than that? We were gonnay have a rare moment of introspection, I could feel it."

I pulled up the files and opened a log of recent calls, and one had a +1 prefix, which meant a call from the United States or Canada. It was from the 571 area code.

Looking up the area code on the Internet took two seconds: 571 was a small, concentrated area of northern Virginia next to Washington, D.C. Plenty of federal workers lived in that area code. It was a stretch, but it fit with Saxon's idea that someone in a government job was behind all this. And as far as I knew, Gordie didn't know anybody in the States. No relatives there, no friends at all. Perhaps this was a legitimate clue.

Calling that number would require an excess of caution. If it was attached to anyone involved in this trafficking business, it was probably a burner phone. They probably wouldn't pick up and definitely wouldn't return a voicemail—not that I would leave one. If they were connected to the government, as Codpiece hypothesized, they might have the ability to track any call made to them. A certain amount of skulduggery would be required, then. Some protective tradecraft. And all probably for nothing. But it needed to be done.

[I'm going to go out for three or four hours,] I told Buck.

"Just going downstairs, eh? At the rate you're moving, you'd better allow five."

[Going to Edinburgh on an errand. I doubt you'll see another attack so soon, but just in case, don't let anybody in.]

"Aye, nae worries on that score."

Groaning theatrically again for Buck's benefit and because it made me feel better, I levered myself off the couch and shuffled to the bathroom to look at the damage to my face. The three slashes were red and puckered and angry with me but fully closed up, thanks to the Sigil of Knit Flesh. I gingerly applied some water and soap to it, wincing all the while, and patted dry with excessive care.

Pulling out my phone, I Signaled Nadia. *Can you let bartender Heather MacEwan at Gin71 know that three barghests attacked me at home last night? She doesn't have a phone.*

Her reply came quickly, with some pepper and vinegar in it. *What the hell, Al? That's twice you've been jumped this week and didnae call me!*

Wasn't time. I'm scratched but okay.

Well, the polis came on Friday, like you said they would. I showed them the doctored footage, so you should be in the clear.

Thanks, Nadia. You're the best.

I didn't have the inks at home to draw healing sigils, but my study did contain the ink for a Sigil of Hale Revival, so I drew myself one of those. It didn't heal anything, but it gave me some energy and the feeling that I was in great shape when I wasn't. It would get me through the day, I hoped, and I could crash later.

Since it was possible that we were dealing with a member of U.S. intelligence services, I left my phone behind so that there would be no digital record of me leaving my flat. I wore the derby hat with the Sigil of Swallowed Light on it to cover my trip to Edinburgh, leaving from Queen Street station. It was only a fifty-minute ride from Glasgow, and trains left regularly.

Once in Waverley station in Edinburgh and confronted with its vast panoply of shops, it was a simple matter to find a store willing to sell me a burner phone and a debit card that I could load with cash to activate it. No one would ever be able to trace me, with my hat shutting down cameras; all they'd be able to establish was that the call originated from a cell-phone tower in Edinburgh.

I charged the phone in a café and called the number in Virginia, fully expecting to get no answer. In all likelihood the phone had long been tossed into a river or lake or incinerator.

A man surprised me by answering gruffly. "Hello."

"Ah, yes, I hope I have the correct number. I'm looking for a Mr. Bastille?" It was a calculated gamble. He could claim it was the wrong number or simply hang up. "I have some rather sad news. I'm calling regarding the death of Gordie Graham. Have ye heard already?"

"Who is this?" That question, I realized, was why he'd answered the call. He wanted to know who had this number and probably how I'd gotten it.

"I'm Peter, a friend of the family," I lied. "Services will be in Edinburgh in two days. I don't suppose you'll be able tae make it?"

"Edinburgh? Your accent's from Glasgow."

Wow. Most Americans couldn't tell English and Irish accents apart, let alone Scottish accents by city. This man had obviously spent some time in country. "Well spotted, Mr. Bastille, but my accent has nothing tae do with the memorial site. How did ye know Gordie?"

"I didn't. You've got the wrong number."

He hung up on me. Well, that was a load of shite. He most certainly did know Gordie. What I didn't know about him was quite a bit, however. I felt certain I had been talking to Bastille, but I still didn't know his real name. I didn't know if he was actually in Virginia either, only that his phone had been activated there and given that area code. But that bit where he recognized the difference between a Weegie and an Edinburgh accent was a solid clue. He had the generic western American accent that one heard on their television, so for him to spot the difference in Scottish accents meant he was either a student of linguistics or he'd spent significant time here. I was betting on the latter, since I had difficulty believing that linguistics specialists would be involved in a Fae-trafficking scheme. And someone had flown to Glasgow to give Gordie that recipe for Manannan's ink, and most likely other inks as well.

Though I supposed that if Saxon Codpiece was right—that Bastille was someone in the government and likely in the intelligence field—linguistics training might be part of their background.

Still: I had enough information to attempt a search through my friendly neighborhood hacker. Even if Saxon couldn't pinpoint who Bastille was, he'd most likely be able to narrow the field and give me a list of names to pursue.

I tossed the phone into a bin and bought a ticket back to Glasgow. Let Bastille search for "Peter" if he wished. He'd find a single call made from a local cell-phone tower and glitchy cameras in Waverley station, if he was the sort of person who could access such information. Nothing that would lead back to me.

Except my Glaswegian accent. Damn.

It occurred to me that an extra dose of cautious paranoia might do me good. A smart man with access might start looking for security-camera glitches today between Edinburgh and Glasgow. If so, they could follow me back to my neighborhood by following the glitches. There was already a record of where I started if they traced backward from here, so it was key not to return there with my hat on, because that would give them a tight little area to search, and who knew what they would find if they did that?

I sighed. Paranoia and tradecraft were exhausting. But I didn't want to lead anyone back to my neighborhood, where they might eventually figure out who I was. I'd have to disappear—or, rather, reappear—anonymously somewhere else. Getting off the surveillance grid so that I could safely get back on it would take some time, however. The reliable way to do it was to get the hell out of the city.

I bought a ticket to Stirling and kept the hat on; there were not only cameras in the station but on the train too. If I took it off, they would have me. In Stirling I went to the bus depot outside the train station and took the first one going out to any village. I wound up going to Kippen, about nine miles west of Stirling. Once there, I walked out of the wee quaint place and kept walking until there was nothing but me, sheep, and the occasional grouse in a meadow. Finally confident that I was no longer under surveillance, I took off my hat and coat and draped the latter over the former. Then I stuck out my thumb and tried to look like I wouldn't murder anyone. Normally that wouldn't be an issue, but my scratched face was probably a red flag for many people. It took a dozen autos or so, but eventually a farmer in a fertilizer-scented lorry picked me up.

"Where ye headed, then?" he asked, politely not asking what had happened to me.

"The next town with a bus or train station, thank you." I brushed some potato crisp crumbs from the seat before sitting down and closing the cab door. My savior was an older gentleman about my age, with burst capillaries on his cheeks and the bulb of his nose. He liked his gin and whisky more than the average man, I guessed. I'd wager a fiver that there was a bottle in the glove compartment.

"Fancy coat like that, I'd have thought ye'd have yer own auto," the man said, with an upward twist to his mouth to let me know he was teasing. "Maybe yer own driver."

"It is fancy, in't it? Fancy enough that people feel safe picking me up for a lift. Don't need an auto that way."

He chuckled. "Fair enough. I'm Hamish."

"Aloysius. Ye can call me Al."

"I'm a farmer that does some micro-distilling on the side."

"G'wan, now. Whisky or gin?"

"Bit of both. Just a few barrels. But the whisky is aging, and I hope tae try some before I go tits up."

"That sounds grand. D'ye ever find yerself in a hurry tae do the things ye always wanted before the final hour?"

"Aye. But I assume I'll no do most of them. Nothing tae do now but the sheep." He blinked, realizing he may have given the wrong impression. "I mean, nothing tae do now but *take care of* the sheep. And the ducks and the farm and that. Shite, that didnae come out right at all."

"It's awright, I take yer meaning," I said. "I'm in the printing business."

"Flyers and whatnot?"

"Aye, but also books, magazines, bottle labels, ye name it."

We chatted amiably the rest of the way into Arnprior, a village even tinier than Kippen, and I enjoyed the freedom of it. I would never see Hamish again after the ride, so there was no need for me to get out my phone to talk. He dropped me off a block away from the bus stop and caught my eye before I closed the door.

"Hey, Al. I can see ye're on the run."

"I beg your pardon?"

"Fancy men with scratched faces dinnae hitchhike for the fun of it. I dinnae know which is the truth, so I'll say it both ways: I hope ye get away if ye're a good man who lost a fight with a bastard, and if ye're the bastard, I hope they catch ye."

"A wish for justice," I said, nodding in approval. "Thanks, Hamish. I hope the micro-distilling goes well. But do stop shagging yer sheep, awright? They cannae give consent."

I closed the door and grinned at him through the window. He was shouting something profane and raising two fingers at me. I laughed as he sped away and kept my hat carefully concealed beneath my coat. From here to home I'd be under surveillance. But I'd be a random person going to Glasgow from a point outside of where the mysterious glitches stopped happening. It was a good wait for the bus back to Stirling and then another train ride back to Queen Street station, and my three or four hours away had turned into six; it was late afternoon by the time I got back to the flat. Buck paused the show he'd been watching and stood up on the couch to peer over the back of it at me.

"Where ye been all this time, MacBharrais? Did ye stop for a pint or seven in Edinburgh?"

I fetched my phone from the counter where I'd left it and typed a reply. [No. I've been to Stirling and hitchhiked with a farmer who may or may not have been sober. Anything happen here?]

I meant anything dangerous, but Buck interpreted it as a request to be caught up on what had happened in the remainder of *Hamlet,* as if I was unaware. "Well, I've learned that if ye're eavesdropping on people in a confined space, ye shouldn't ever shout and reveal yer presence. And ye should run away screaming from any prince dressed all in black, unless yer name is Horatio. I mean, Hamlet flat out murders his so-called friends from school, Rosencrantz and Guildenstern, and he didnae have tae do so. He could have simply ditched them, but he made sure they got kilt, and at the end this old English guy comes in, everyone is tits up except for Fortinbras and Horatio, and he says that Rosencrantz and Guildenstern are deid."

[That's the title of a brilliant play by Tom Stoppard.]

"Wot is?"

[*Rosencrantz and Guildenstern Are Dead* retells *Hamlet* from the point of view of literature's most hapless duo.]

"Why?"

[Many reasons. Meditations on theater and free will and absurdity and plenty of wordplay. Worries about identity and how much of it is self-generated and how much is assigned by others.]

"Hey. I chose ma own name. Buck Foi is who I am now. Not the old name assigned by ma parents."

[That is true. You have surpassed Rosencrantz and Guildenstern in that regard. They're confused most of the time, conscious that something larger than themselves is happening, but unable to achieve the proper perspective to grapple with it, much less alter their destiny.]

"That sounds grim as all fuck."

[Life tends to be. But it's also a comedy.]

"Maybe I'll watch that tomorrow, then. I cannae handle any more tragedy today. I need some light entertainment, one of those game shows where people get knocked down a lot."

I found him a channel full of such shows, and he was guffawing soon enough at people sent tumbling into pools of icy water.

[I have to text my hacker and might have to go out again. Carry on.]

I opened Signal and asked Saxon if he was available to discuss a big job. He responded that he was, and I requested that he meet me at a pub rather than his place. The anonymity and noise of a crowd would suit us well.

We met in a dark footballers' pub, where the game was on and nobody paid attention to us. I still wrote everything down on actual paper, typing nothing into a device.

"Awright, so what's the job?" Saxon asked when we were seated and had our pints in front of us.

Need to find males who flew into Glasgow Airport and put a 571 area code into their reservation in the last three months. Most likely they would be flying out of D.C.

Saxon gave a low whistle and requested my pen to reply.

Hacking airlines is not going to be easy. It's much closer to impossible, not to mention extremely risky.

I nodded solemnly and wrote, *Can you do it, though?*

"Maybe," he said aloud. "If I get a list, then what do ye want?"

I wrote, *Look them up and see which ones fit the profile you came up with. Government workers with connections to intelligence and an ax to grind.*

"Jesus suffering fuck," he said. He picked up his pint and chugged the whole thing. "Can't answer now," he continued when he set the glass down. "Need to figure it out first. If it can be done, I'll Signal you with a price."

I nodded, and he left. I used the candle at the table to burn the paper we'd written on, and a few football fans saw that and realized I must have burned something damning, because why else burn something when you could toss it in the bin? They regarded me uncertainly and I stared back at them, daring them to say something. They decided to ignore me and returned to their pints of Tennent's lager and shouting at the television. Well done, sports fans.

I took my time with my pint, abruptly worn out and feeling miserable, my face throbbing. I worried that the scratches might be infected. I needed to draw some new healing sigils tomorrow, but mostly I needed sleep. I Signaled Nadia.

Going to be late tomorrow morning.
Get in when you feel like it. Or take a day off.
Thanks.

It was a slow walk back home, and when I got to the flat I told Buck I was knackered and just needed sleep. He turned off the telly and said that was fine by him.

"I don't s'pose ye swung by the office and picked up any of those fine healing sigils?"

I shook my head. [Need to make more tomorrow. Haven't had a string of injuries like this in a long time.]

The hobgoblin winced, gently probing the tender bits where the barghest had bitten him. "Do ye have anything to help me sleep, then?"

I nodded. [Get into bed and I'll give you a sigil.]

He popped out of sight and immediately called from the bedroom, where he'd teleported. "Hurry up, ol' man, I'm ready."

I fetched two sigils from my study and took them into his room. I broke the seal on a Sigil of Restful Sleep in front of Buck's eyes, and they immediately began to droop.

"Oh, that's dreamy, that is . . ." And he was out. The other copy of that sigil was for me. Sometimes sleep is all ye need. Sometimes it's not, but it will just help a whole damn lot.

When I woke in the middle of the next morning, there was a message on Signal for me from Saxon Codpiece, but it had been sent only a few minutes ago.

It's done. But I need £20K and twenty sigils. You get one name. The right name.

It's a deal, I replied. *I'll make the arrangements. Who is it?*

Naw, payment first. I'll draw up an invoice for the printshop. Make the draft to Tartan Industrial Supply.

That must be one of Saxon's many shell corporations that he used to launder his hacking income. *Right. Caffè Nero behind St. Enoch subway station, one hour.*

I splashed water on my face and got dressed, taking time to check the many pockets of my topcoat to make sure that the sigils that were supposed to be there still were and noting which pockets needed refilling. I also made sure my official ID was safe.

Buck was knuckling sleep out of his eyes in the kitchen when I emerged from my room. "What's up, MacBharrais? Feeling better?"

[Rested, if not well. Still aching and sore. You?]

"Same. What's for brekkie?"

[Whatever you like. I have to go out quickly and meet someone and then go to work long enough to make healing sigils at the very least. I'll try to get back early. Remember not to go out. Whoever sent those barghests might try to get us again, now that they can assume the hounds failed.]

The hobgoblin's shoulders drooped, and he looked a bit forlorn. "Okay. Bye."

I felt bad at leaving him so cooped up on his own, but I didn't have a choice. He'd not have a reasonable assurance of safety until we broke up Gordie's trafficking ring on all sides. And beyond that, he wouldn't have a reasonable chance of surviving his acquaintance with me for more than a year if I didn't find out who'd cursed me.

There was a Barclays bank not far from my flat. I had just enough time to walk there and then to Caffè Nero. My printshop account had enough padding to handle Saxon's significant fee, but only just. I realized I might be able to replenish it with Buck's help. Surely there was a massive corporation somewhere that wasn't paying enough taxes on their profits. Draining some of those and laundering the proceeds as large press runs would do the public some good, as I was protecting everyone from invasions of Fae and other undesirables, and Buck's mental health would be improved immeasurably if I gave him a to-do list that included stealing. Nadia was well used to adding ghost jobs to our presses and our books by now; I had a lot of strange expenses and stranger streams of income, and she juggled it all.

Once I got the draft, I stuffed it into an envelope and then spent a few minutes quickly drawing twenty Sigils of Sexual Vigor at the little station where people filled out withdrawal and deposit slips. It was probably the most sexual vigor ever displayed in a bank lobby. I couldn't seal them with wax as I normally would—I had the kit in my coat, but banks tended to frown on candles and flames and the like—so a thumb's length of Sellotape served instead. I crammed them into the envelope with the draft and slipped it into my left coat pocket.

The Caffè Nero behind St. Enoch station was housed in the old brick ticket depot for the tube, at once a crass repurposing of a lovely old building and a wonderful way to make sure the building got visited and loved. When I entered, I spied Saxon Codpiece sitting in a bench booth along the back wall and gave him the tiniest nod of hello as I got in line for coffee. I hadn't had anything to eat or drink yet, and I needed to fortify.

Before I could make it to the counter to place my order, however, someone tapped my right shoulder.

"Mr. MacBharrais? Fancy meeting ye here. What a strange coincidence."

I turned around and saw the smirking face of D.I. Tessa Munro.

CHAPTER 17

Lattes and Bugs

There was nothing fancy or coincidental about it. D.I. Munro did not frequent this café, or I would have remembered seeing the grey hair before. The fact that she came in directly behind me meant that she'd had the place staked out—which suggested that she had done some significant investigative work on my habits already.

There was no doubt plenty of archived surveillance footage demonstrating that I liked this particular café. The staff knew me as a regular and asked me if I wanted the usual and all I had to do was nod and pay. It saved me the trouble of having to get out my phone to talk. Living with this curse meant that I tended to frequent places that accommodated me and provided the closest thing to a frictionless experience I could have. Habits like that made me easy to find, though. I gave her a tight grin and nod with a small tug on the brim of my sigil-free hat to greet her and turned back around, knowing that she wouldn't be dissuaded from talking to me but making it very clear I didn't wish to talk to her. If she wanted a conversation, she'd have to work for it.

"My goodness, Mr. MacBharrais, what happened tae yer face? Did someone rough ye up?"

I got my phone out of my right pocket and launched the text-to-speech app, still turned away. [I'm fine. Thanks for asking.] That reply didn't answer her question, and I planned to give her that sort of answer as often as I could.

"Running a bit late to the office today?"

It was nearly ten A.M. I shrugged. Owner's prerogative.

"I'm glad I ran into ye, actually. I have some more questions about your employees. It appears that Gordon Graham was not the first of yours tae die. Turns out that seven of them have died in the past eleven years, all very young people in their primes."

I shrugged again. There had not been an actual question there.

"All of them were accidents, supposedly, but it's an extraordinary series of misfortunes. A string of deadly accidents like that would make most workplaces shut down, don't ye think?"

[If they had occurred in the workplace, sure.]

None of my apprentices had died on the job. I knew now that they had been indirectly murdered, and I wanted to know who was responsible even more than D.I. Munro did. We were on the same side in that regard. Except I had no ideas about who might be responsible for their deaths and she was obviously thinking I had something to do with them. I supposed she wasn't wrong, since my curse had done them in, and I certainly felt my own share of guilt for it. But the true murderer was whoever laid the curse on me.

"Right, right. But ye look at the tragic ends of these young bright lives and the common denominator is you."

[Their deaths weren't part of a neat math equation, D.I. If anything, they demonstrate chaos theory,] I said. It was my turn to order, and the server smiled and asked if I wanted my usual. I nodded and stepped forward to tap my bank card on the pay terminal, then slid down past the pastry case to wait for my standard order, a medium hazelnut latte. I had about thirty to forty seconds before the D.I. would join me and ask another question, so I typed out something and waited for her to arrive. After she paid for her order and came down, opening her mouth, I pressed the little playback button.

[I contribute some scraps of information to D.I. Macleod occasionally and might be able to do the same for you. Would you be interested in some information about human traffickers if I could find some?]

"Macleod mentioned ye'd helped him out here and there. That makes me only more curious about ye. How does a printshop owner nearing retirement know so much about the criminal underworld?"

[I've cultivated a rich and varied garden of friends.]

"I'll give ye points for horticultural metaphors. I like a fine bed of tulips ma self. Whatever information ye have, I could pass on tae someone who handles it. You're intae human trafficking, then?"

[No, I'm not.]

"Neither am I. I'm intae murders. Solving them, that is. Have any of those lying about?"

[Celtic murdered Rangers last week at the football stadium, but that was to get back at Rangers for murdering them the year before. That's all I know in the way of murders, D.I. Munro.]

My drink came up and I plucked it off the shelf, slipping my phone into my pocket, effectively ending the conversation. D.I. Munro noted this and smiled wryly.

"Right. Well, have a good day, Mr. MacBharrais. Do call if ye think of anything."

I turned away and very purposely sat at a different table from Saxon Codpiece, giving him a tiny shake of the head. I removed my coat, draped it over the back of a chair, and then sat on the opposite side, where I could see the detective inspector pick up her coffee, raise it briefly in a mock cheers, and exit.

That encounter was entirely too strange. She hadn't staked me out and confronted me just to get a coffee and bring up my dead apprentices. I mean, that was part of it, sure—she wanted me to know she'd been sniffing around me and would continue to do so. Buck had crunched his fist into her nose, and she remembered me being in Gordie's flat and wasn't going to let it go. A visit like this was likely intended to goad me into some action that would reveal secrets she was sure I was hiding. But that couldn't be all. She was fishing hard. What had been her game there?

She sort of snuck up on me—oh. I blinked a couple of times, replaying the encounter and letting my paranoia work. I made eye contact with Saxon and held up a hand, telling him to wait. I fetched my coat from the table and began to examine it minutely, especially the shoulders and back. Nothing. But deep in my right-hand pocket, where I typically kept my phone, there was a little nugget of something. I had difficulty getting hold of it, for it was narrow and trapped in the crease, like a flexible toothpick. My fingers were able to detect its presence but not lay hold of it easily. I was patient and kept at it, eventually extracting a thin filament of something that wasn't natural at all. It was a bug, one of the sleek modern ones. She must have slipped it in after I'd pulled out my phone and began typing replies to her. I placed it in the crease of the seat cushion behind me. Let them listen to a day's worth of café noise and conversation.

I wasn't satisfied, of course, that I'd found everything. I'd do a much more thorough search later. For now I'd conclude my business with Saxon. We needed to do it out of sight of any cameras, though. I tossed my head minutely, indicating that he should follow me, and he nodded. I put my coat back on and went upstairs to the bathrooms and waited. He came in less than a minute later. I removed the envelope from my left pocket and proffered it to him, raising my right finger to my lips. Once he took it, I texted him via Signal.

No words. I'm worried about bugs. He checked his phone and nodded, then opened the envelope to confirm its contents. Satisfied, he sent me a Signal back.

Simon Hatcher is your man. He flew in and out of Glasgow about six weeks ago—and may have made other trips too, but you asked for just the last three months. Saxon included a home address in Reston, Virginia. *He's CIA. Maximum caution, Al. I might disappear for a while and see if anyone comes after my usual hiding places. Recommend you do the same. He can bring heat.*

I nodded and Signaled, *Thanks. Be safe. If you need something to do while you're gone, I'd like to take out some human traffickers.*

Why? It won't solve anything.

It'll save some victims, maybe give them their lives back.

Saxon nodded. *What do you want? Names?*

Local raid targets. I'm going to set the polis on them.

He gave me a salute and I tugged at my hat brim and left him in there. I had a name to work with, at least. Was Simon Hatcher the mysterious Bastille? I had two different ways to find out.

The first was that I could request the aid of Flidais once more. She could travel to his place in Reston and confirm by scent or whatever magical means she used that Simon Hatcher was the same person she'd trailed to the Glasgow Airport using that scrap of ink recipe. If he was the same person, then the advantage would be that we'd have found clear evidence that he'd violated a strict taboo of the Tuatha Dé Danann and could proceed accordingly.

The major drawback to that was that the Tuatha Dé Danann did not do such favors for free. They required payment, and it was never a cash transaction. It was always something else, something you never wanted to pay. Brighid had requested Flidais's aid earlier at her own expense; she either called in a favor Flidais owed her or promised to do a favor in return. I wasn't ready to put myself in any kind of debt to the Fae or the Tuatha Dé Danann. It rarely worked out well for any human who traded with them.

My other option was to contact Elijah Robicheaux—my colleague in Philadelphia, who was currently annoyed with me—and ask him to confirm on his side of the Atlantic that a CIA agent was up to something dastardly with the Fae. He owed me a favor or two. Calling one in now would only annoy him further, but he knew his own backyard better than I did.

I Signaled him. *Calling in a marker. A CIA agent named Simon Hatcher may be Bastille. Can you look into him, please?* I gave him the address in Reston. The reply came back as I was contemplating the mural of St. Mungo on High Street, thinking that I should do more than just report traffickers to the police. There was no question that I would do something if the opportunity presented itself; the moral thing to do would be to seek out an opportunity. I needed to crack open that book I'd borrowed.

I do have my own shit going down, Eli's text read. *But fine, Al, if you want to use a marker on this, I'm on it.*

CHAPTER 18

Ogres Wear Layers

"Ouch. Ye weren't kidding about getting yer arse kicked," Nadia said as she stepped into my office only a few moments after I'd entered. I figured that Gladys Who Has Seen Some Shite must have let her know I'd arrived. "I'm assuming that's after you've already used a healing sigil on yourself?"

I shook my head and retrieved my phone, opening Signal rather than text-to-speech. *A detective tried to plant a bug on me this morning. I need the office swept for bugs before we say anything.*

Nadia frowned, pulling her phone out of her back pocket as it buzzed. She was in black jeans and her studded jacket today, and the boots were low-heeled jobs with no spikes on them, but she still had her favorite gloves on with the studs on the knuckles. "Shit," she said. "Awright, I had things to tell you, but hold on."

I did not have a sigil for destroying electronic devices or jamming radio signals. Brighid had created the sigil system before electricity was in wide use, and once it was, she realized that anything shorting out electrical systems could do more harm than good. So she added sigils very sparingly, like the Sigil of Swallowed Light, to counter very specific modern inventions that constrained our ability to do our jobs. The Ward of Muffled Conversation was from the Chinese system and essentially soundproofed my office, so I didn't need to worry about directional microphones pointed at my windows (though it did require me to install a doorbell, since I wouldn't hear any knocks). For bugs inside the room, however, we needed the sort of countermeasures anyone else would use. We had a bug-sweeping kit in the basement, and Nadia went to fetch it while I took off my topcoat and draped it over one of the chairs around the coffee table, then inspected the brim of my hat. I didn't find anything, but that didn't mean I was bug-free.

I stopped. Something about my desk was different. Maybe it was the huge pile of sealed envelopes there. The Monday morning post was unusually large. I went over to start sorting it by seals: deities, officers of deities, denizens of other planes, boring old humans who used stamps and self-adhesive envelopes, and bloody junk mail. If people were punched in the junk every time they sent junk mail, I bet we'd see a lot less of it. I refused to print any of it, on principle.

Nadia returned with the bug-sweeper and started prowling around the room as it beeped and shrieked and whirred. She gave me the once-over, my topcoat as well, and then I did the same for her. All clean.

"Can we talk now?" she said. I nodded, and the tension drained out of her shoulders. "Thank fuck. While ye were gone, the little delivery pixies kept coming and dumping letters on yer desk, plus there was a woman who claimed tae be a selkie, who was just unforgivably beautiful. I am seriously never gonnay forgive her, Al. I think she did some Fae shite tae me, because I'm pretty sure I'm pining here, ye know what I'm saying? Pining like the wankers in poems are always on about. Is that a thing selkies do, make ye pine?"

[Their beauty is a defense. The idea is that humans won't want to hurt them if they're extraordinarily beautiful.]

"Really? That seems like an epic misjudgment of humanity."

[Well, do you want to hurt her?]

"No, I want tae take her tae a bed-and-breakfast for a week and slather her in fondue."

[Well, there you go. What did the selkie want?]

"She said tae tell ye the banshees are distraught."

[Of course they are. They're banshees.]

"No, it's because they cannae perform their function. They're wailing and screaming but there are no any names, just a bunch o' random syllables. And someone named Cleo, or Cleaner—bollocks, does that sound familiar?"

[Clíodhna?]

"That's the one. She cannae explain it, and I guess she's the expert."

[Okay. Thank you.]

"Is that all? Anything ye want tae tell me about the twenty thousand ye withdrew this morning? I got an alert from the bank."

[Oh, yes. Please add twenty thousand in jobs to the books to replace it.]

"Where is the actual money coming from?"

[I don't know yet. I might set Buck on it.]

"Are ye serious?"

[He got your beer, didn't he?]

"It's a bit different, Al. Steal a growler and the bartender might not even notice. Steal that kind of money and ye get the polis involved."

[Don't worry about the cops catching him. Just keep the books pristine and ready for audit. They will be looking at our finances too.]

"Awright. Did ye have a go at fixin' yer face while I was getting the bug-sweeping kit? Because it still looks like a slapped arse."

The pain flared at the mention of it. I really did need to draw a proper healing sigil as soon as I got into my ink room. [I only used Knit Flesh, but I'll deal with it soon. And it's not over. They really want Buck, so there might be more of that trouble on the way.]

"Hope they come looking for him here. I'll get on the books and let ye get tae the mail. But if that selkie comes back, tell her I'm serious about the fondue."

There was no way in any of the hells of the infinite planes that I would tell anyone my manager wanted to coat them in fondue, but I reckoned Nadia understood that and I didn't need to type it out.

She left and shut the noise of the printing presses behind the door, since half the first floor was open to the ground. I returned to my desk and opened the deity letters in case they were urgent. They weren't. They were either formal requests to visit the plane for recreation—there was some good skiing in Switzerland at the moment, apparently—or informing me of official visits that were allowed under their respective treaties with humanity. The letters from representatives of deities were more of the same. Just a lot of skiing. Enough to suspect that there was more to it than recreation. A business meeting among various parties, perhaps, disguised as a vacation from the workaday drudgery of paradise? I decided to let that percolate in my subconscious, along with the problem of the banshees, while I got to my real reason for coming into work at all today: sigils. I ignored the rest of the letters on my desk and pressed the button hidden underneath my desk inside the top drawer. The bookcase to my right pushed forward and slid toward the front of the office, revealing the entrance to my ink room. It felt like ages since I'd been in there.

The welcome smells of dusty paper, briny solutions, and lemon from my sealing waxes wafted into my nose. My ink room was a well-ordered space, with racks of wooden cubbyholes and shelves all around with jars of ink ingredients waiting on them; completed inks were arranged in and above my writing desk, an old Victorian-era job with plenty of cubbyholes already built into it. A stack of cut cardstock waited to be inscribed with sigils, and I had a little burner set underneath a mounted brass spoon to melt sealing wax. I got that going; I vastly preferred it to the messy portable setup I had in my coat.

I selected the fountain pen labeled *Loch Lomond,* which was the name of the ink required to craft a Sigil of Restorative Care, and tested the ink flow on a scratch pad. Satisfied, I drew the circular triskele design on a card in the wet cool-blue ink and held it in front of me as I waited for the ink to dry and the sigil to become potent. When it did, I felt the burning of my scratches begin to fade. I drew three more of those, folded down the tops, and drew a Sigil of Postponed Puissance, sealing them for later use.

Then I switched pens and inks as required and drew up additional sigils of Restful Sleep, Hale Revival, and Knit Flesh, in case we had to deal with slashing or puncture wounds.

There was no doubt I'd require additional battle sigils as well, and both Nadia and Buck could probably use them too, so I set to it. There wasn't enough Dexterous Ink left for the Sigil of Agile Grace, however, so I had to whip up a fresh batch of that. The ink-prep station was really just a sink and countertop along the wall to the right as one entered, and it had cost me nothing to plumb since this room would have been the kitchen if the first floor had remained a flat. I had a mortar and pestle, beakers, and measuring spoons and the like, and it allowed me to craft the majority of the inks without leaving my office, so long as I had the ingredients on hand. I'd have to find time to go through Gordie's stores soon; perhaps I could do that after seeing to the remainder of the mail. During that half hour of careful mixing and decanting, I pondered why the banshees might be babbling incoherently.

Banshees mourned the dead in advance. They were the worst sorts of harbingers, crying out the names of the soon-to-be deceased. Sometimes they kept wailing after someone passed, but it was different then, a sort of "told you so" kind of moan. The incoherent syllables sounded consistent with heralding an impending death, but why wouldn't they be able to cry out any intelligible names? The answer came to me as I was drawing my fresh batch of ink into the reservoir of a Montblanc pen. I blinked and stood up straight, startled as an answer presented itself like a gymnast at the start of a floor exercise.

"They can't name the doomed because the name changed and

they don't know what the new one is," I said out loud. And I knew a member of the Fae who had recently changed his name. "Oh, no. Buck."

I scrambled for my phone, which was still in my coat, and sent a Signal to Buck.

Are you still safe? You're in the flat?

I had a tense thirty seconds to wait for a reply.

Aye.

Don't leave for any reason. Stay there.

That was the plan, old man.

That was a relief, until I realized that Buck might get himself killed accidentally messing with human things in my flat.

Keep fully clothed, I Signaled him. *Watch for iron in the house. And eat some fruit. An apple or an orange.*

Why are ye so worried? And what is with the fruit?

I'm just being careful. And you need fruit because scurvy is a terrible way to die.

You're a fucking nutter, MacBharrais, he replied, which told me he was just fine at the moment.

It would be wise to renew my wards, both at home and here in the office. The last thing I needed was for one of them to fail when we might be under assault at any time. The Wards of Spectral Abeyance had taken a beating with the barghest attack.

That prompted a search for the Chinese inks made by Mei-ling for such purposes, the solid cakes that I'd need to grind down and mix with water before painting them on my doors, windows, and walls. I pulled out eight different ink cakes, each molded into the shape of a Chinese dragon or other mythological creature and nestled in its own little box, and set them aside. I'd need to fetch a bag from the production floor to pack them for travel.

The office phone on my desk rang and I hurried out to punch the speakerphone. I tapped the desk twice to let Gladys Who Has Seen Some Shite know that I was on the line.

"Mr. MacBharrais, there's a gentleman here to see you on what he says is urgent agency business."

I tapped the desk twice more for message received and hung up. *Agency business* was the phrase visitors were supposed to use to indicate that they were not from earth and they needed to see me as a sigil agent rather than a printshop owner. I Signaled to Nadia that we had a visitor in reception and asked if she could escort whoever it was up to the office.

On it, she replied. I dashed back to the ink room, grabbed a card and the Montblanc pen, and drew a Sigil of Agile Grace in case I needed it. Once completed, I scooted back to my desk and pressed the stud underneath the top drawer to close the bookcase and conceal the ink room.

Moments after the bookcase slid into place, Nadia rang the office bell and I opened the door, inviting her and the guest in.

The man had to duck to get through, and he loomed over the two of us in a trench coat, wide-brimmed hat, and a scarf covering much of his features on top of what looked to be a vest over a turtleneck. Nothing matched, and the entire ensemble might have been stolen from a lost-and-found bin. What little I could see of the skin around his eyes was of a distinctly greenish tinge.

"Here we are," Nadia said. "Please come in, take off your coat. Can I get you something to drink?"

"Naw," the giant said, his gravelly voice muffled though the scarf. "Just need tae talk tae MacBharrais."

"Very well. Al, this is Durf from the Fae planes."

Durf was one of the top-ten most popular ogre baby names about forty years ago, so that fit with the greenish skin. I nodded at him and pulled out my phone, raising my brows significantly to Nadia. She took her cue to explain.

"Durf, Al is going tae use that device tae talk tae ye, since he has a bit of trouble with his voice right now."

"Huh? Okay. Whatever. Listen, there's a hobgoblin loose somewhere here in Glasgow. Name of Gag Badhump. I'm here tae get him."

I shook my head. [Don't know that name.]

"Well, I was told ye would. And ye'd know where he is."

[Who told you that?]

"Nunna yer business. Ye've no seen him? Wee pink guy."

[I may have seen him.] Apparently, Buck's former name was Gag Badhump. Even for hobgoblins, who tended to have horrific names, that was spectacularly unfortunate. No wonder he hadn't wished to tell me.

His voice dropped and lost its clarity. "Well, hee zere immee gull."

[Pardon? It's difficult to understand you.]

"I said—bah." Durf unwound the scarf from around his face and revealed that he was, in fact, an ogre, with a bulbous nose and a mouth full of yellow and brown teeth with something mossy growing on them. His voice, however, was much clearer now. "Said the hobgoblin is here illegally."

[Perhaps. That's my call to make, however, not yours. Until you tell me who sent you, the argument could be made that you're here illegally.]

"Huh? Look, I'm here on official business."

Nadia knew enough about the treaties to answer quickly. "It's not official business if ye dinnae say who sent ye. We need to know the official, awright?"

The ogre scowled down at her, and she took a few steps to her right, placing herself between the ogre and me. Durf followed her with his gaze and growled a reply.

"It's quite simple. Gimme the hobgoblin and I'll leave. We'll both be out of here. Nae bother."

"The proper way tae deal with such matters is tae hire a barghest with a contract. Now that we know his name, ye can just leave the matter tae us."

"Naw, I cannae do that. Barghests were already sent and Badhump kilt them. He's a nasty one."

Nadia looked over her shoulder at me, pretending to be surprised. "Have ye heard of any barghests getting kilt, Al?"

I nodded and she turned back around to Durf. "So ye're who

they send if the barghests fail? Ye're meaner and deadlier than they are?"

"That's right."

"How's that?" Nadia challenged. "What ye packing, eh, that will give ye the edge on a murdering hobgoblin?"

"Well, I have all these wards sewn intae ma clothes. He cannae slap me with his goblin magic."

"Whaaaat?" Nadia gave a teasing laugh and waved at him. "Get out o' here! Ye're full of shite."

"It's truth! I tell ye three times. Lookit." The ogre began to undo the belt of his trench coat, and Nadia stretched out a hand to stop him.

"Wait. Ye have trousers on under there, right?"

"Aye."

"Okay, go ahead. Show me these wards."

He was telling the truth. He had magic-dampening wards sewn into the lining, using thread dyed with the proper inks. He had them in his trench coat, his waistcoat, his shirt, and Nadia stopped him there because we didn't want to see or possibly smell his undershirt. Regardless, I'd never seen an ogre wear so many layers. I wouldn't know how effective the wards were without a practical demonstration, but I didn't think they needed to last long. They only needed to keep the ogre upright long enough to get hold of Buck, and then it would be pretty much over. Buck wasn't going to overpower an ogre, and neither was I. The brute was a lorry full of muscle tissue.

But while Durf was very scrupulous about not revealing his employer's name, he was not so bright about keeping his defenses a secret. We knew now that whoever was behind this would be prepared for Buck's magic and we could employ tactics to counter this. Tactics like standing behind Nadia.

I typed on my phone as Nadia congratulated Durf on his battle preparedness against hobgoblins.

[The individual you seek is now under my protection, and he remains on this plane legally under a contract I drew up myself.

You may tell your employer that and be satisfied. Without official reason to be here, I must ask that you return to the Fae planes immediately, in accordance with the treaty.]

The ogre flinched, as if making a request of him was a physical blow. "Wot? Naw, I cannae leave without Gag Badhump. If ye won't help, I'll just go find him myself."

[I can't allow that.]

Durf flashed his rotten teeth at me. "How're ye gonnay stop me?"

Nadia glanced back at me with one eyebrow raised, and I nodded to give her permission.

"He won't stop ye. I will," she said, and she pulled her straight razor out of her jacket pocket and unfolded the blade. The ogre's expression turned incredulous, then amused.

"Haw! I've got toothpicks bigger than that."

"Just tae be fair, Durf," Nadia said, "have ye ever heard why Al is the most feared of all the sigil agents?"

The ogre's amusement faded. "He's supposed tae have a battle seer or sumhin like that."

Nadia winked. "Atta boy. And have ye heard about the battle seer's weapon?" She twisted the blade so that the light flashed along the flat side, where painted sigils could be seen.

"It's supposed tae have a Sigil of Iron Gall on it." It had more than that, but Iron Gall was the one that mattered to the Fae. His shoulders slumped.

"Aye, ye're a bright one, in't ye? I can see ye're puttin' it all together now."

"No one told me the battle seer was a woman who worked in his office."

"Aye, I can tell ye weren't briefed properly. I'm givin' ye a fair chance tae change yer mind now. Go back home and eat some nice pixies, forget all this."

He shook his head. "I cannae go back without the hobgoblin. They have ma family. So there's no hope for poor Durf now."

I frantically typed [Who are they?], but its sound was lost in

Durf's roar as he lunged at Nadia, arms wide to prevent her escape. They collapsed together and she wasn't there, having ducked and rolled to her right, toward the office door. I backed away but not far enough, as Durf's momentum propelled him forward and he delivered a beefy shoulder to my upraised arms. It slammed me back against the bookcase hard enough to dislodge some volumes, and I groaned, my bruised ribs crying out at the renewed punishment. But Durf was getting his, off-balance from his lunge. Nadia had rolled to her feet and slashed him three times on his upper left arm, swish-swish-swish, right through his layers. They weren't deep cuts, but they didn't need to be. The steel of the blade had iron in it, already deadly on its own, but the Sigil of Iron Gall made it ten times worse. It burnt him badly like acid, his flesh instantly blistering and even bubbling, and he flinched, twisting his left side away so that Nadia couldn't keep slashing at him there.

But she had, of course, foreseen his withdrawal, knew where she could press her attack, and she did. Durf had removed his scarf earlier, and now his face and neck were unprotected. Nadia darted in and opened up a red line on his throat with her razor. Durf gurgled, his eyes going wide and his right hand clutching the wound, bloody bubbles leaking out from his fingers. The fight was already over, and he knew it. There was no coming back from those cuts; they would never heal. While he could in theory amputate his left arm and stanch the bleeding at the stump, he'd never get the chance. He'd bleed out long before that.

Durf surrendered, falling to his knees and bleeding onto my carpet, and Nadia stood ready should he try anything else.

"I'm sorry it hurts," she said quietly to the ogre, compassion in her voice now that the battle was won. "I tried tae make it quick so ye wouldn't suffer long."

He nodded weakly, understanding in his eyes, along with tears. I had time for one last attempt at learning something.

[Who has your family, Durf? I can try to help them.]

His eyes rolled to me and he shook his head, twice, then keeled over, the lights in his eyes extinguished. The iron from the sigil continued to work at dissolving the magic in his being, burning and consuming his flesh in the process, and soon his body began to crisp and then crumble into ashes, a fine rotten mess gone grey in a heap of clothing.

Nadia sighed. "He was a pretty nice bloke as far as ogres go. Damn shame."

[Whoever sent him is a pure bastard.]

"Ye got that right." She folded her razor closed and returned it to her pocket. "Shite. I'll go and get a vacuum and call the carpet cleaners."

———◆•◆———

Having the Gall

The Irishman who found me near Aviemore in Cairngorms National Park and made me his apprentice was hunting the same thing I was hunting: gall nuts.

He was also hunting the hobgoblin Holga Thunderpoot, though I didn't learn that until much later. At the time, we were both startled to find someone else into the same hobby.

Gall nuts are growths on oak trees caused by gall wasps laying eggs in the buds at an important early stage in their growth. These nuts—which are not really nuts at all and have the look and feel of a gourd more than anything else—contain tannic acids essential to the production of black inks since the Middle Ages. Many inks used to be made with gall, and gall-nut production has become industrialized the same way silk production has: Groves of oak trees are exposed to gall wasps and the insects do their thing, just as silkworms turn mulberry leaves into silk. The tannic acid is used for all sorts of things, not merely ink.

But I was in a wild area—or as wild an area as anyplace could be on an island continuously occupied for millennia—and the gall nuts were scattered and needed to be sought out rather than easily spotted in a grove.

"Beggin' your pardon," his voice called to me from some distance away in the forest. "Ye wouldn't be huntin' gall nuts, now, would ye?"

"I am," I said, surprised but also guarded. He was dressed fancy in a white suit and hat, not the sort of outfit one typically wears into the forest. It was the sort of getup one wore to polo and cricket matches, sipping mint juleps and laughing at the silly struggles of the working classes.

"Oh, well, in that case, I'll stop. I'm not local and can find some elsewhere. Were ye planning on making ink with them?"

"I was," I admitted, my surprise increasing.

"Ah, excellent! Would ye mind sharing your recipe? I'm a bit of an ink enthusiast."

It was already the strangest conversation I'd ever had at the time, and I thought I might be hallucinating the whole thing. Was I really about to shout an ink recipe to a stranger in a white suit?

"Are ye taking the piss?" I said instead.

The Irishman laughed. "I'm very serious, I assure ye. But, look, I don't mean to make ye uncomfortable, and I can simply leave. I know talking to strangers is probably a low priority for ye, so I won't take it too hard."

"What's your recipe, then?" I asked. "I mean, if you're really here for gall nuts, you'd know an ink recipe and could share it right now. Otherwise I guess ye're here hoping to run across a nice boy to murder."

"Right, right. Well, I use a cold bath rather than a boil for the gall, and then I use iron sulfate and gum arabic like anyone else, plus a couple other things." He listed the ingredients and proportions to me, and I felt a smile splitting my face at the thought that we might have created a new hobby: ink shouting.

"That sounds like a better recipe than mine," I said, and shouted my ingredients back at him.

"Ah, yes, I've heard that one before. Look, what's your first name?"

"Al."

"Okay, Al, I'm Sean FitzGibbon. I'm going to leave a business card here in the crook of this tree, and I hope you'll give me a call, because finding people who are into making inks by hand is rather rare these days. I might have a job for ye—a really good one—so let's have tea together soon in a nice public place, and you bring along some friends or whatever ye need to feel safe, and we won't need to shout anymore. All right?"

"Aye, that sounds good. But the shouting's been fun too."

"Ha ha. Excellent. Good hunting, then. I'm off."

He waved, and I watched him go and then retrieved the card. We had tea together two weeks later in Glasgow, and that's how I became apprenticed to an Irish sigil agent and learned that the Tuatha Dé Danann were bloody dangerous.

CHAPTER 19

·—·—·

The Spy Who Mauled Me

My phone buzzed with a message from Saxon Codpiece. *Up for a brew? I have news.*

Sure, I sent back.

Bier Halle on Gordon St. at half past noon, he replied.

Right you are, I said, and smiled at his choice of venue. The Bier Halle was an underground pub, which fit with Saxon's preference for subterranean living. I'd thought I wouldn't hear from him for weeks, since he'd given me the impression a couple of hours ago that he'd be dropping out of sight entirely, but apparently something had come up.

The Bier Halle had over one hundred bottles from around the world on their menu and an impressive tap list too. It was a sort of cement bunker filled with wooden tables and squat, square stools with brown leather upholstery. They served pizzas, pretzels, and a list of other foods that skewed toward German tastes. Saxon had secured a table in the corner and waved at me when I reached the bottom of the stairs and stepped into the dining space. We shook hands and I got my phone out.

[What happened to disappearing?]

"Still at the top of my list of things tae do. After lunch, though. Ye feel like slamming down a bevvy?"

I nodded, and when the server arrived I pointed at my menu, to a German beer called Fürstenberg and then to the giant pretzel with mustard. Saxon asked for a sausage dog to eat and ordered a Krombacker Pils on tap. Then he pulled out his laptop and grinned.

"Got yer tinfoil handy? Tear off a few sheets and sculpt it lovingly around yer crown. Have a keek at this." He pulled up a news article with the headline MONSTERS ATTACK VILLAGE IN UKRAINE and pointed at it. "Someone is taking down shacks and flats in the Ukraine that we're pretty sure are occupied by Russian intelligence. And by *we* I mean British intelligence."

[British intel? You have access to what they think?]

He smirked at me. "Let's just say I have multiple reasons to go intae hiding right now."

I shook my head in wonder and gestured that he should continue. "The thing is, they have no idea who did it. Eyewitness reports are claiming they were monsters, and one person is even quoted as saying there was a flying faery. A small humanoid with wings. That could be yer pixie, eh?"

I shrugged. It was possible.

"I was just thinking of those pictures on Gordie's phone. If that crew was wrecking shite, then I could see people thinking they were monsters. That troll's face was like an arse with hemorrhoids and teeth, and I wouldn't be surprised if someone thought he was a monster. He bloody well *is* a monster."

[True,] I admitted.

"And it fits with that bloke I told you about this morning. If he's CIA and he wants to flex with his pet Fae super squad, then why not take out some targets of the old enemy?"

[I suppose it's possible.]

"Anything's possible, sure. Absolutely. But what I'm saying is that it's *likely*. This is what it's all about, Al: winning the spy game. It's an addendum to what I said before."

[What's that?]

"I said they wouldnae go around assassinating folk because that draws too much attention. But killing spies is different, in't it? If ye're a nation with spies and some of yer spooky bastards get kilt, ye don't go squawking about it in the press and expelling diplomats and threatening war. Ye try tae find out who got ye and then get 'em back all soft and shady. But Russia cannae find out who got 'em in this case because they're bloody Fae. They slipped in and out of there, no travel records, no facial recognition, no fingerprints or anything. So Russia's stuck with floating a monster story. It's a better distraction than admitting they got rolled. It gets people thinking about where the monsters came from rather than what was going on in those flats."

I nodded because that much was true, at least. Putting MONSTERS in the headline would distract from everything else. But while this theory might make sense on the human side of things, it made zero sense on the Fae side. Not to take anything away from Saxon's analysis: He simply didn't have all the facts. Whoever was running things in Tír na nÓg—whether Clíodhna or someone else—they wouldn't give a single nugget of dry crumbled shite about the squabbles of human nations. Since I couldn't investigate there, however, I'd have to work on the human end and pass along the information in hopes it would illuminate something on the Fae side. The pints arrived, and we clinked glasses and enjoyed a cold swallow before Saxon continued.

"I have tae admit this is some wild and woolly bollocks, Al. We're only ontae this because of yer boy Gordie. If it weren't for him, we'd be as clueless as the Russians right now. We'd be looking at this article and saying *what the fuck* like everyone else, eh? Ye can bet there's a Russian intelligence officer screaming, *Who's got monstrous assets in this area? Who?* with spittle flying and a vein bulging in his temple and borscht erupting out his backside. It's cheerful, in't it? I mean, besides all the death, o' course."

[All the death does tend to dampen the joy,] I said, then I pointed at the article with a question in my brows, and Saxon nodded.

"Be my guest, mate," he said, nudging the laptop in my direction. I pulled it a bit closer and squinted against the glare of the monitor's screen.

MONSTERS ATTACK VILLAGE IN UKRAINE

Six people are dead and three buildings are cinders after a string of early-morning attacks by what eyewitnesses describe as "monsters." Residents of Kercz in Crimea awakened to fire alarms in the early hours of Sunday morning, as strangely shaped humanoids of varying sizes were reported at each site, and in one case a flying creature was said to be involved.

Police have not identified the victims yet but have stated that they were first murdered before the attackers set fire to the buildings. Two victims were missing limbs.

A string of eyewitness accounts followed, including one that claimed to have seen a small flying creature working in concert with the hooded assailants. I took that to mean that the pixie was now involved in these operations.

The most interesting part of the article was buried at the end, where the target locations were listed. [These flats—can you map them for me in relation to any parks or green spaces in Kercz?]

Saxon looked bemused but shrugged and said, "Sure. Why?"

[If the monsters in the article were the Fae, they'd use bound trees to get in and out of the city.]

"Bound trees?"

[The Druids bind trees on earth to Tír na nÓg. One can shift planes that way. If we were Druids or Fae, we could go down to Kelvingrove Park and shift to Tír na nÓg, then take a different bound tree wherever we wanted to go. Melbourne, Tokyo, Denver, wherever there was another bound tree. It's a sort of transit system.]

"That's . . . pure stonkin'. It's like teleporting."

[Close, yes. That's why people thought Druids could teleport.]

"Okay, give me a minute." He tapped away at his keyboard for a while and I tried to figure out why Clíodhna—or anyone in

Tír na nÓg—would have an interest in allowing the Fae to be used this way. Had they chosen sides in human concerns? It seemed unlikely; it would be akin to us choosing sides between warring hives of termites.

"There. Is that what ye mean?" He pointed to a city map of Kercz with a green blob in the middle of it and three red pinpoints around its perimeter. "That park in the center of the fires—I can't pronounce the name of it, but it has trees."

[That would do. I don't know if there's a bound tree, but if there is and the monsters were Fae, they entered and exited the city that way.]

"That's an amazing data set. They could do multiple strikes a night around the world."

I nodded, and Saxon grabbed his beer and leaned back in his seat. "Holy shite," he breathed, and took a much longer pull on his pint.

[Is that the news you had for me?]

"Aye, that was part one. Ye made a request of me and it didn't take long tae get results. Thought I would take care of it before I disappeared. Felt like I needed tae do it."

Our food arrived, and Saxon said we should eat first so our appetites wouldn't be ruined. We fell to and Saxon started talking again after a couple of bites.

"So ye already know that I'm technically what ye call a sex worker on a part-time basis. I mean, it's just me, or a part of me, online," he said, as he gestured significantly to his sausage in a bun, "and I get a modest revenue stream from that. But I'm the exception tae the rule in terms of being in the business voluntarily and completely in charge of my own situation. Or maybe it's changed and I am part of the rule now—I think that might be true. There are lots of folks like me who just do things on one side of the camera because that's safe, and there are lots of niche services that fall short of the full shebang, so tae speak, that allows people tae do it as a side gig tae help pay the bills while they keep their day jobs. The thing is, plenty of people are *not* in it by their own choice, but because some *are,* people who pay for sex like tae think that everyone's consenting and that if they're committing a crime it's a victimless one. But, no, victims of sex trafficking have been tricked, manipulated, and abused every step of the way, and that's a situation that's ongoing. They have little tae no control of their lives, and that's the way their pimps want it." He paused, shook his head, and tore into his sausage sandwich. Around a mouthful, he said, "I fucking hate pimps, Al."

[Understood.]

"So I'm going tae give ye two names and two addresses, and you do whatever ye're going tae do with it. The names are pimps, and I want them tae be punished. The addresses are where their victims are living, and I want them tae be treated like people who need help instead of people who need tae be arrested."

[Agreed.]

He handed over an envelope and I put it into my coat. "I'll contact ye when I return. If the pimps are in jail and their victims are no, I can give ye more later."

[Thanks, Saxon.]

"Right. Well, I best be off. Need tae stay out of jail ma self. Can ye get the check?"

I nodded, and he beamed at me before cramming the rest of his food in his mouth.

[What if your place is raided?]

He chuckled and swallowed before answering. "I have a Plan B. And also C through Z. Backups for my backups. Good luck, Al," he said, and unfolded himself from the seat, securing his laptop.

[You too.]

"I'll Signal you from a new number when I'm back."

[Okay.]

He gave me a salute, I tugged my hat brim, and he left first this time. I wondered if it was too soon to contact D.I. Munro with these names. It almost certainly was, but I didn't want to wait long. Now that I knew where there were people in need of saving, I didn't want to let them suffer any longer for the sake of appearances with a detective. I scanned the restaurant and discovered that everyone was ignoring the old man in the corner. Public places can be spectacularly private at times.

I withdrew the envelope, opened it, and read the contents. One of the addresses I recognized: It was Nadia's tenement. She'd be livid if she knew that there were sex-trafficking victims being housed underneath her nose like that—as livid as I was that Gordie had trafficked Fae under mine.

It was all around us.

I took out one of my Retro 51 pens filled with a basic blue ink recipe that had no magical potential; it was for correspondence only. I wrote a note to D.I. Munro:

Dear Detective Inspector,

Our brief meeting this morning filled me with boundless civic pride, awe of your commitment to public safety, and admiration for your professionalism. You mentioned that you may be able to pass certain information on to relevant parties in pursuit of human traffickers. The National Human Trafficking Unit, perhaps, as I believe it's called? Regardless, it is my dearest wish that your colleagues focus on the traffickers and not their victims, who have been trapped and manipulated into most unfortunate circumstances. Below you will find the names of two such traffickers, and I hope your colleagues will move quickly to prove their criminal activity and arrest them so that their victims may be free of their bondage.

I am trying to discover where these men are housing their victims; should I find out, I will relay the information to you.

I purposely left out the addresses because I wasn't sure yet if she'd move on this at all, and I didn't want the D.I.'s colleagues to begin with the victims. This would be a test for both of us: They had to confirm that my information was true, and I had to confirm that they'd act responsibly.

Checking the card she gave me, I saw that D.I. Munro was operating out of the Maryhill station. It was a bit out of my way but not difficult to reach via train and a pleasant stretch of the legs. I'd be back home before the close of business, so that worked well.

I left the letter for the detective inspector at the front desk of the station, wondering if anyone was still listening to the bug I'd left in the coffee shop and if they'd try to retrieve it at some point. I didn't imagine they had an unlimited budget to burn through those. They had probably already figured out what I'd done, and my name had no doubt been roundly cursed already. Perhaps the note would go some distance toward mending fences.

CHAPTER 20

—— • ——

The Weegie Goth

When I got home, Buck was in a state, and he immediately yelled at me without saying hello.

"Why did ye make me watch *Rosencrantz and Guildenstern Get Deid*?"

[I didn't make you do anything.]

He pointed a pink finger at me. "J'accuse! Ye said it was a comedy!"

[That's because I thought there were funny bits.]

"It's too close tae the bone, MacBharrais. They were summoned and they came and once they got there they were trapped. There was no exit for them except the final one, and they never figured out why. What if I'm like them?"

[You're not, Buck.]

"But I am! I'm stuck here in this flat and cannae leave. I don't know why Clíodhna targeted me. I don't know what she has planned."

[I'm working on it.]

"They were working on it too, ol' man. It did them no good. Did ye see how Rosencrantz kept discovering scientific principles way before his time? Things that Galileo and Newton got the credit for later?"

[Yes, I thought those episodes were amusing.]

"They were no! They were awful! He's a potential genius in the making if he only has the time, but instead his fate crushes him and all his potential is snuffed! Think of it, ol' man!"

[I've thought about lost potential more than a little.] Beginning with all my apprentices. [War, disease, famine. They've ended so many lives.]

"I'm no talkin' about falling tae mischance. This is different. This is Rosencrantz and Guildenstern being targeted and having no help for it. They can sense there's a big wheel about to roll over them, but they cannae get out of the way. And I feel like that is ma situation here."

Brighid had been right: Buck was a rare hobgoblin. They weren't usually so self-aware.

[The difference, as I've been trying to tell you, is that you have friends. Like me and Nadia. I'd make friends with Nadia if I were you.]

Buck blanched. "Friends? Why?"

[She took out an ogre this morning that was sent here to fetch you back to Tír na nÓg.]

The hobgoblin went a paler shade of pink for a moment but then scoffed. "Ogres aren't so tough. Big, but easy to handle."

[This one had layers of clothes with wards against your magic. I think you might have found him tougher than usual.]

"Oh. And she took him out, ye say?"

[Aye.]

"Do I write her a thank-you card or sumhin?"

[Some beer and a verbal thank-you would do very well. Speaking of beer, do we have any?]

"Aye, we do. You sit and relax and let me work. I've had nothing tae do all day but worry ma fool heid."

I sat at the kitchen island with a sigh but immediately got up again as I remembered I had a better solution at home for my curse than my phone. I had a laptop with some expensive text-to-speech software on it that actually had a Scottish male voice built in. It was expressive and clear and five billion times less annoying to listen to than the English voice on my phone. It wasn't a Weegie accent—it sounded more like an Edinburgh man with a roll of paper towels crammed up his anus—but it was a balm to the ears by comparison.

I typed a sentence in the new Scottish voice, named "Stuart," as Buck placed a pint of black beer next to my right hand.

[Thanks, Buck. How does this voice sound? Better?]

His face split into a perfectly capped grin. "That's pure dead brilliant, so it is! Why haven't ye used that before?"

[This voice is only on my laptop. Can't get it on my phone. But I can type faster this way and say more too.]

"I like it. Tell me a story, then, while I fix us some dinner?"

[Sure. What are you making?]

"It's a surprise. I watched a cooking show and realized ye had everything here already."

He was getting out the rice cooker, so that gave me a tiny hint. Maybe he was planning a curry. [What kind of story do you want to hear?]

"I want tae hear how ye met Nadia and she became yer manager, since ye say I need tae befriend the woman who broke ma nose. Make a proper story out of it."

[All right. I can do that. Here we go.]

I discovered Nadia by accident on an underground platform of the old abandoned Botanic Gardens railway station. It's located along a line they closed off decades ago, back when I was wee in the sixties, and the station building itself labored on as a nightclub until it burned down in 1970. They ripped up the tracks to use them elsewhere, so what you see down there now is a cement platform and a wide trough of hardpacked dirt. Plants and trees are growing underneath the ventilation shafts, where the sunlight and the rain drops down. On the walls of the platform, you have these layers of algae and spray paint from rather pedestrian graffiti. It smells of rust and piss and creeping mold.

It's not all that difficult to get down there and explore. Bit of a squeeze through some fencing, sure, and you need a flashlight to find your way in the dark, and be ready to fend off anyone who thinks it's a great place to attack someone else. But you won't find a lot of law enforcement. That's why it's a grand location for the underground pit-fighting circuit, since it's literally underground and the trough where the tracks used to be makes a great pit while the spectators cheer from the platform.

But you don't descend into an abandoned train station if you're afraid of the dark or what might be hiding in it, or if you're the sort who will let a fence and a sign stop you from doing what you want to do. Since I needed someone who wasn't afraid of those things to help me with physical work as I aged, that's where I went looking for help. Anyone who was there automatically passed my first filter, and anyone who made it past a few rounds in the pit would probably do just fine as my muscle.

I didn't have high hopes, however, because I needed a brutally effective fighter who wasn't also a shite human. I didn't want or need a paladin, mind; I just needed someone who wasn't actively evil.

On my way in, a couple of youngsters tried to mess with me and discovered that my cane was extraordinarily painful when whipped at speed into their bollocks. Further application to their temples prevented them from taking out their frustrations on someone else, and perhaps, when they woke, they would reconsider their lives of assault and petty thievery.

The excited thrum of voices ahead and dim lights that grew increasingly brighter drew me onward. Eventually, I found the crowd gathering and little knots of people clustered around bookies taking bets and promoters shouting about their fighters. I wound up standing on the periphery nearby two women, waiting for the fights to start. They were dressed entirely in black leather and chrome studs and were having an animated discussion about yo-gurt. Since everyone else in earshot was talking about this fighter or that and how they would or would not smash faces or eat dirt that evening, I was far more interested in the discussion of dairy products, because it seemed so out of its place and time.

"Greek yogurt is the best because it has that perfect mix of pro-tein and flavor," the first one said. She was taller and a bit stouter than Nadia, and of course much younger than me. "And ye can get it low fat."

"Who gives a toss about fat? Sugar is the issue," Nadia replied. "The Icelandic shite is pure dairy gold. They call it skyr. It's higher in protein and lower in sugar. It's got a wicked smooth mouthfeel."

"The fuck are ye on about mouthfeel for? It's not a gourmet-coffee tasting profile."

"Mouthfeel is a part of everything ye eat, ya cow. There's taste and smell, aye, but there's also a tactile component tae eating that most people ignore, and they shouldnae."

"So if I'm no thinking about ma yogurt's mouthfeel, I'm daein' it wrong? Is that what ye're sayin' tae me right now?"

"Not just yer yogurt. Everything ye cram in yer gob. Yer shite sandwiches and yer thin curries and yer weak tea."

The taller woman gasped. "Nadia! You fucking take that back. Ma tea is *not* weak."

That made me chuckle a tiny bit and they heard it, becoming aware of my presence. They turned as one and their eyes traveled up and down, judging and finding me wanting. Nadia spoke first.

"What are ye, a polis, dressed like that, all proper with yer cash-mere topcoat and yer mustache?"

"Not a polis. An investor."

"Investor? Like stocks and that?"

"In people. I require someone with unique talents and thought I might find one here."

"Well, Nadia here is unique as fuck," the taller woman said.

"Shut it, you."

"I'm sorry, okay? But ye are!" She turned back to me. "Look, ye want tae invest in sumhin? Put yer money on Nadia tonight. She's gonnay win it all."

"Shh!"

"Ye're fighting this evening, miss?" I asked.

She sighed in exasperation and glared at her friend before answering me. "Yeah. Bookies think I'm gonnay die in the first fight, but it's no gonnay go that way."

"Ah. Then they obviously missed something when they assessed yer chances. What did they miss? Are ye proficient in some martial arts, perhaps?"

"Competent, sure. But I cannae explain why I'm gonnay win. I just will."

"Against opponents who are far larger and stronger and perhaps more skilled at martial arts than you?"

"She's gonnay kill 'em all," the tall woman asserted. "And we'll make a killing on the odds too." She waggled a finger at me. "I was speakin' metaphorically there, but we'll literally be living for months off this."

"And ye are confident, I see. Besides risking yer own money and yer health, ye exhibit no nervousness at all about the coming match but rather stand in the back discussing yogurt."

Nadia shrugged. "I'm vegetarian, and I take ma protein seriously."

"As ye should. May I ask what odds are being given on ye right now?"

"Depends on the bookie. But I'm the long shot."

"What name are ye fighting under?"

The two women exchanged a glance. "The Weegie Goth," Nadia said.

"Excellent. Will ye excuse me? I have a wager to place. I do hope ye win."

"If I do and yer wallet gets swole, can I have a piece of yer winnings?"

"Ye can. If I can treat ye both tae tea afterward. Or yogurt, if ye prefer."

Nadia narrowed her eyes. "What are ye after? Are ye a pervert? Because we're no intae that. We're no intae men, in fact."

"Naw, nothing like that. As I said, I'm an investor. If ye win tonight, I'd like tae invest further. A business meeting only."

"Awright, sure."

I tipped my hat and moved off to find a bookie. I found an unsavory individual named Georgy Orgy willing to cover a thousand-pound bet at fifteen to one on the Weegie Goth to win the tournament and another thousand at five to one she'd win her first fight against someone named Hammerfist.

Georgy was a rail-thin sack of bones supporting a large nose and a sharp Adam's apple shaped like a wedge of cheese. His eyes had bruised purple bags underneath them, and he hadn't shaved for a few days. A mountainous brown-bearded man, obviously his muscle, stood behind him. Georgy moved and talked fast, like he'd sprinkled his morning muffin with a dollop of fruit compote and a kilo of cocaine.

"Why only five tae one in the first fight?" I asked him.

The bookie shrugged. "Just a hunch, ye know? I still think she's gonnay lose, but I watched her try out, ye know. She's got some moves and dodges like nothing I've seen, but she doesnae hit very hard, and that's where maybe I think she's holdin' sumhin back. I dunno if what she's got is enough tae win, but I'm no wantin' tae get soaked by a newcomer. Or by anyone, really. Fuck gettin' soaked."

"Are there any other women in the tournament?" I asked.

"Aye, there's one more. The Paisley Terror. Ye want tae bet on her too?"

"Naw, I was just curious. Who's the favorite?"

"Gallowgate Tate. He's won a couple of tourneys before. Four tae three on him."

I had brought the betting money separately and hadn't thought to go beyond the allotted money I was prepared to lose, but I emptied my wallet and put seventy-five quid on Gallowgate Tate to win the tourney.

"What, no another thousand?" Georgy teased me.

"This one's more of a lesson to me if my long shot doesn't pay off."

"Awright, awright, I gotcha. Here's yer ticket; come see me after tae settle up if ye win anything."

There were eight fighters in all, so there would be a total of seven fights, single elimination. Nadia would have to win three fights to take the whole thing. I hadn't seen any of the other fighters yet, but I had seen enough of them in my time to know that Nadia was undoubtedly the smallest and weakest of the lot.

The crowd had thickened during that time and I had difficulty finding Nadia and her friend again, but a gloved hand stuck up from the throng and waved at me. I made my way over.

"Saw ye place some bets with Georgy," she said.

"I did indeed. Win your first fight and ye can have my stake."

"Oh, aye? And what's that, then?"

"Two thousand."

Her eyebrows popped up. "Not bad. Anything for winning the whole thing?"

"I already promised ye tea." I'd be eighteen thousand ahead should she win it all, but winning the first fight would pay for an expedition to Australia. I required some quokka milk for an ink recipe, among other things, and it was ludicrously difficult and time-consuming to get.

"Ha. Fair enough. I'm Nadia," she said, though I had heard her name already.

"Aloysius," I said, tipping my hat. "Ye can call me Al."

"I'm Dhanya," the taller woman said.

"Excellent to meet ye both. Would I be correct in thinking this is your first pit fight, Nadia?"

"It is. Not ma last either, but it's the last time I'll get underdog odds like this."

"Do ye need the money for something in particular?"

"University. A flat that's not a closet. A bloody bed—"

"Because futons are *shite*!" Dhanya said.

Nadia grinned at her and then shrugged. "The usual."

"What are ye studying at university?"

"Gonnay be a certified management accountant. Live two lives, ye know, like Thomas Anderson. Pay ma taxes and help ma landlady carry out her rubbish. But once I'm off the clock I'm metal as fuck. Graduating in a few months."

It was at that point Nadia became more to me than a potential winning ticket. If she could both fight and handle the financials of MacBharrais Printing & Binding, she'd be an outstanding employee.

"Are you studying as well, Dhanya?"

"Naw, I code video games and set futons on fire. One pays the rent and the other's a moral obligation."

A man with a microphone and a portable battery-powered amp called for attention as the first fight was about to begin, so all bookies needed to close the betting. He introduced the first two fighters, who emerged from the crowded platform as their names were called and dropped down into the pit with the master of ceremonies.

There was no referee. There was, however, Georgy Orgy's bearded muscle, who patted down each fighter to check for weapons. It was bare-knuckle fighting until one fighter yielded or was knocked unconscious. The shouts of encouragement for the fighters were almost as loud as the shouts deriding the fighters and trying to get into their heads. The master of ceremonies had them square off on either side of him and asked if they were ready, then he picked up his amp and backed away.

"Fight!" he shouted once he figured he was safe, and the lithe, slim fighter known as Gunbarrel launched a flurry of punches and kicks at his opponent, Pisstaker. The latter was a squat man with bulging hairy arms and a broken nose, and he patiently absorbed the quick assaults of Gunbarrel, a weaker opponent who folded once Pisstaker landed a stunning blow and then finished him off by taking him down to the ground and choking him out with a hammerlock.

The second match featured the favorite, Gallowgate Tate, a tall beast of a man who was ripped and cut thanks to a high-protein diet and probably anabolic steroids; I imagined he received the attentions of Russian athletic scientists after they finished sculpting Ivan Drago in *Rocky IV*. Tate coolly watched his opponent, Dirty Clyde, circle him and dart in, but always reacted rather than initiated an attack. He blocked punches and kicks and waited for an opening in Clyde's guard. When he saw one, he struck savagely three times to the body and dropped Clyde to the ground. He didn't close but gave Clyde the opportunity to catch his breath, get up, and take some more punishment. Maybe Dirty Clyde felt he really needed a concussion to top off his proper whipping, and I'm pretty sure he got it, taking a roundhouse to the temple before collapsing in a heap. He had to be dragged away.

Both of the winners were probably double the size and weight of Nadia, but she was introduced next, and she dropped down off the platform into the pit to widespread jeers and a grinning opponent, a square-jawed blond poseur with slicked-back hair, called Hammerfist.

Georgy's bodyguard made Nadia take off her studded gloves and jacket. She had a black tank top on underneath. Hammerfist had to outweigh her by fifty pounds or more. I looked at the two of them square up, saw the bloodlust in the young man's eyes, and I was afraid for her. But Dhanya was grinning and chuckling by my side.

"Wanker has *no idea* what's coming."

Nobody did, except for Dhanya, apparently. When the master of ceremonies said, "Fight!" Hammerfist lunged with a lightning right cross at her head. I thought it would catch her, but Nadia dropped underneath it, spun, and lashed up with her foot, catching Hammerfist in the throat on his follow-through. He staggered back and fell on his arse, eyes wide and panicked because he couldn't breathe. Nadia stood back and waited as he gasped and wheezed, unable to get enough oxygen through a crushed trachea.

He waved her off, surrendering inside of five seconds, and the crowd fell to a shocked silence for a moment before erupting in a chorus of holy-shites and what-the-fucks. Had that been luck? If it was skill, why the hell was she a long shot? She dropped a bastard with one kick and was completely untouched. Hammerfist had some buddies help him out of there, and I hoped they'd be wise enough to take him to the hospital straightaway.

None of the bookies—and certainly no one who had placed a bet on Hammerfist—was pleased by this development.

I was sure the odds for her next fight would be interesting. Would she still be an underdog, or was she the favorite after a fight history that consisted of a single kick? Whatever the bookies decided for the second round, they'd all be hoping that she wouldn't win the whole thing, considering the extreme long-shot odds they'd given at the start. I had no idea how many bets had been placed— probably not many, but it wouldn't take many to clean them out. Georgy already owed me five thousand for the first fight and would owe me another fifteen if she won through.

Nadia's ability to stand unnoticed in a crowd and discuss the merits of assorted yogurts had evaporated forever. Everyone there would recognize her as the Weegie Goth now, the woman who ended a pit fight in less than two seconds with a single kick. Even if she wound up losing, no one would forget that first fight. That was something they'd never seen before. Word would spread, and people who hadn't attended that evening would be looking for her next time. When Nadia came up to the platform, Dhanya extended a hand down and hauled her up, and the two of them were mobbed by men who at first appeared to be well-wishers but turned out to be curious if that was a fluke or not and if she had a boyfriend.

They were not prepared for this, but Dhanya recovered quickly. She spread her arms in front of Nadia and said, "Oi! Back off and fuck off. It wasn't a fluke and she's got a girlfriend. That's all. Give her some space, ya bawbags!"

They gave her some space, but the jawing continued as the two women spied me and pushed their way in my direction.

"Help me form a bubble, Al," Dhanya said. "We need dressing rooms or sumhin. Nae privacy around here."

The next fight, thankfully, gave people a distraction.

The other woman in the tournament, the Paisley Terror, was an accomplished martial artist who had to fend off an extended and determined assault from the Broomielaw Kid, a ginger man who proved to be a smart fighter. He kept his distance and didn't let the Terror take him down—she was probably his equal in height and weight. He was betting that eventually she'd wear out and he'd be able to get a clean shot at her head. But she caught him out of position and delivered a swift kick to the nads. He had sense enough to wear protection, but it still froze him long enough for her to spin around and whip her elbow into his jaw. Blood and teeth sprayed out of his mouth, and he staggered back. He probably could have continued, but he was already looking at significant dental surgery and saw no need to incur additional trauma when his strategy had ultimately failed. He yielded, and that set up the semifinals: Pisstaker vs. Gallowgate Tate, and the Weegie Goth vs. the Paisley Terror.

It was a half hour or more before the fights resumed, though, because odds had to be calculated and new bets had to be laid. Nadia was giving everyone fits; more than one gambler came up and asked if she could take the Paisley Terror or if she'd just been lucky. Likewise, the Paisley Terror was getting questions about fighting the new kid. In the end I heard it was scored even money; no one wanted to leave their bollocks hanging out on this one.

Gallowgate Tate was favored against Pisstaker, though, and that went as expected, though it was a grind for both men. Pisstaker could both take it and dish it out. But Tate was just too big and too fast for him, and he chipped away at the smaller man's defenses until Pisstaker couldn't keep his hands up and block the haymaker that knocked him out.

Tate didn't leave the pit unscathed, however. He had a swollen eye and was favoring his left side, where Pisstaker had landed some punishing body blows.

When the master of ceremonies called out the Weegie Goth and the Paisley Terror, the roar of anticipation was genuine. Everyone—including me—was curious if it would be another fast fight.

The Paisley Terror was not stupid. She did not charge in but rather began to circle in a defensive position. Nadia just watched her, turning as needed to face her opponent, and kept her arms at her sides. Her lack of defense didn't tempt the Terror, however. She was sure there was a trap, and she didn't want to walk into it.

This continued for about thirty seconds and the cheers turned to boos, the crowd demanding that they get on with it. The Terror waved at the Goth to come on. Nadia smirked and shook her head, still not defending herself.

The Terror lunged forward, but Nadia made no move, and the Terror backed off, the whole maneuver being a feint to draw Nadia out. The Goth only smiled, and that enraged the crowd. They wanted action, not a staring contest.

The Terror finally stepped in to attack, a guarded strike that was little more than a jab to make sure that Nadia couldn't take her out with a kick. Nadia finally moved, setting her feet slightly apart as the Terror approached. I thought she was going to take the hit when she dodged at the last possible moment to her right, letting the fist pass over her left shoulder, and then she grabbed the wrist and held on as she attempted to get an uppercut through the Terror's guard. That didn't connect, but it got her right elbow up at face level and she whipped it into the Terror's teeth, followed immediately by a backhand fist that rocked her backward. Nadia let her wrist go so she could disengage. The Terror aimed a blind straight kick at Nadia's midriff as she fell back, but the Goth slapped it away to pass harmlessly to the left. Then she took advantage of the Terror's imbalance by lunging forward. The right jab was blocked, but the left cross behind it wasn't. It crunched into the Terror's nose and she went down. Nadia's boot was on her neck before she could roll away, and the Paisley Terror yielded.

That fight took longer but was no less decisive. Nadia was not only undefeated, she still hadn't taken a hit.

That set up a final showdown between Nadia and Gallowgate Tate. A known favorite and previous champion against a rather scary newcomer.

The thing I couldn't figure out was what kind of martial art she was practicing. I supposed it was close to krav maga, but I hadn't seen any signature moves. In terms of discipline she was outclassed by everyone, yet she indisputably won without discipline.

The next half hour was a remarkable test of evidence versus prejudice. According to the evidence we had—two wins and no damage—the Weegie Goth should have been the overwhelming favorite against Gallowgate Tate, who had two wins but was in significantly rougher shape. But Tate was huge. And he was a man. And he'd won before. Those were all facts, to be sure, but they weren't exactly relevant. The same facts applied to Hammerfist before Nadia applied her boot to his throat.

There were five bookies total and three of them made Tate the favorite, though not by much. Their books were lively on both sides. But Georgy Orgy and one other had Nadia as the favorite, and they saw plenty of action as men rushed to place underdog bets on Gallowgate Tate.

"Lookit them all betting on Tate," Dhanya said, shaking her head.

"That's good. It means the bookies will be able to pay us when we win," Nadia said.

A man pushed forward to ask the question that had been bothering me. "What style of fighting are you using?" he said.

"I fight according to the precepts of His Dark Highness Lhurnog the Unhallowed and sacrifice to him whisky and rare cheeses so that I may prove victorious."

"What?"

"She meant to say fuck off," Dhanya explained.

He scowled but did what she said, and I chuckled. "I haven't heard of Lhurnog before."

"Course ye haven't," Nadia said. "'Cause he's unhallowed, in't he? But ye can see him on the side of my van when we get tea after."

"Yer van?"

"She's got a wizard van," Dhanya said. "Wee shrine to Lhurnog inside. Icebox full of cold ones, glove box full of dank weed. It's pure tits. Half the people think we're gonnay go tae hell, the other half wish in their wee coward hearts that they could have a wizard van half so fine."

I just grinned at her, which was apparently the correct response.

"I'm just kidding about the weed. We have a box of salt in there distilled from the tears of men who try to harass us."

That made me chuckle. "I hope I get tae see this van."

"Oh, aye, ye will."

"It has a scene painted on the side?"

"Both sides. On the driver's side, Lhurnog sits on his throne of cheese with a glass of whisky in one hand, and in the other are some roasted men impaled on a lance like a kebab, about to be eaten."

"Excellent. What kind of whisky?"

"Whatever he wants, because he's a god. But that's not all. Lhurnog's in the background. In the foreground is Nadia riding a huge lizard, raising her studded fist to the sky. Eldritch energy swirls around it, because she's the wizard, see."

"This already sounds like the best van I've ever heard of, and if it isn't real I'm going tae be very disappointed."

"Oh, it's real. She's put so much money intae that thing. It's honestly why she needs this score tonight. She's broke because of the wizard van."

"Shh. Don't tell him that!" Nadia said.

"It's true, in't it?"

"What's on the other side of the van?" I asked, before they could begin arguing in earnest.

"Oh, naw, ye're gonnay have tae see for yerself," Nadia said.

I nodded agreeably and let some other people approach and ask questions or wish Nadia well, while I tried to think of where I'd heard of a god named Lhurnog before. I've either read or written contracts for most of the world's pantheons and didn't recall

Lhurnog being mentioned anywhere. They might just be having a bit of fun at my expense, which would be fine. But if not, who was this Lhurnog? It occurred to me that it could be a demon from any number of hells posing as a god, and that could spell trouble. It could explain why Nadia was so infernally good at fighting. Maybe following an extremely dangerous pit fighter back to her window-less van wasn't such a good idea.

When there was a small break in the jawboning, I asked Dhanya, "These sacrifices ye make to Lhurnog. It's just whisky and cheese, right? Nothing else?" I saw her lock eyes with Nadia for a second, then turn back to me, all seriousness.

"Aye. I mean . . . ye look a mite concerned there, Al. What are ye worried about?"

"Ye mentioned that in the painting, Lhurnog was about tae eat some impaled men like a kebab. So you're not involved in any of that, are ye?"

"Intae what? Impaling men? Or kebabs?"

"Well, delivering sacrifices to His Dark Highness."

"Oh! Naw, that's the sort of thing that Lhurnog takes care of himself. We do like a good kebab, though. Vegetarian, of course."

I wasn't entirely reassured by the answer, and my face must have shown it. Dhanya's and Nadia's lips twisted as they tried to stifle grins and didn't quite succeed. They were having a laugh, and that was good. If they had been serious, I would have had work to do.

The master of ceremonies made a big fuss for the main event, calling out the fighter's names and adding epithets on the end as they dropped into the pit and came forward. After a string of fluff for Gallowgate Tate, he called out the Weegie Goth and laid it on.

"Undefeated! Unbruised! And unknown until tonight! What fate awaits on her pugilistic date with Gallowgate Tate? Christ, that's all the rhyming I'm allowed to do for the rest of the year in one go."

Everyone expected a slow start, but the Weegie Goth charged immediately, which surprised Tate much more than it did the spectators, and we were damn surprised.

He aimed a straight kick at her midriff with his right leg to make her keep her distance, but she flowed around it and trapped his ankle under her left arm, then looked him straight in the eyes as she brought her right elbow down on his kneecap, blowing out all his ligaments and eliciting a howl of pain and anguish from a man who was normally a stoic fighter. She dropped his right leg, crouched and spun, sweeping his left leg and dropping him on his arse. He wouldn't be able to get up again without help, and she wasn't about to supply any. Nadia rose, stood over him, and said something that no one but he could hear because everyone was screaming over how fast she'd dropped him.

Gallowgate Tate yielded seconds later, and anyone that had held on to their shite up to that point promptly lost it.

Georgy Orgy was not the only bookie who didn't want to cough up the long-shot money when Nadia won. He and the others claimed Nadia must have cheated somehow. She had to beat up a couple of their bodyguards and slap away a pistol to convince them that, no, she was just a really good fighter and they'd better pay up before she stopped being polite.

Once we did get paid, we left the underground together, wary of anyone who might try to take us, but the spectators had learned not to mess with her. And that is how I met Nadia.

"Hold on, now, hold on. Ye cannae stop there just because I finished with the food."

[We can take a break, though,] I replied.

"I need to know things, MacBharrais."

[So do I. What is this thing we're eating?]

"Chicken adobo, Filipino style. Soy sauce, vinegar, water, minced garlic, and whole peppercorns. And chicken, of course. Served over rice and with a pint of stolen beer to wash it down, which is always the best kind of beer."

[Looks and smells good. What do you need to know?]

"How'd she become a battle seer? Are we going tae play any

video games that Dhanya worked on? And did she really have her-self painted on the side of a van?"

[We are not playing any video games, period. I suppose I can tell you the rest after we eat.]

"Wot, ye cannae shovel food in yer gob and type at the same time?"

[Feed me, damn it, please and thank you.]

For the record: Hobgoblin-made adobo is delightful, and stolen beer does taste better somehow than the kind ye pay for.

CHAPTER 21

The Wizard on a Lizard

Nadia's wizard van was parked on the street under a light, and it did not disappoint. Underneath the artwork it was one of those black work vans, the kind one sees everywhere and usually emblazoned with the logo of some plumber or construction contractor or flower-delivery service, except this one had the magnificent painted scene Dhanya had described earlier. The wizard figure riding a giant iguana—obviously Nadia, since the leather jacket and mohawk hairdo were unmistakable—was in the foreground, near the driver's window. Her clenched fist in the air summoned eldritch energies from the sky. She looked over her mount's head into the distance, where an enormous figure the size of a four-story tenement sat on a throne of aged cheddar or maybe red Leicester. In his right hand, dangling off the arm of the throne, he held a huge tumbler that must contain roughly the same amount of whisky as the liquid in an aboveground pool.

His left hand held a skewer, and the flailing bodies of men were indeed impaled and roasted crispy and ready to be eaten by Lhurnog, a large pseudo-amphibian humanoid with pale-green skin, yellow eyes, and the sort of knife-blade teeth one sees on anglerfish. He wore white robes with mystical symbols on them, but I checked to see if I recognized them and I did not. They were the sort of nonsense one sees in fantasy games and illustrations of this sort, and Lhurnog likewise seemed to be a marvel of the imagination more than anything else. Between Lhurnog and the goth wizard-on-a-lizard lay a field of fallen soldiers, the remains of some great battle, which provided some scale to the figures.

The scene was at once a relief and a mystery: Lhurnog was just some fantastical creation rather than anything real, but if Nadia wasn't getting her extraordinary gifts from a demonic pact, where was she getting them from?

"Tell me about Lhurnog. Who is he?" I asked.

Nadia shrugged. "He's made up, in't he? Ye can lookit him and say, oh, nice, a toothy frog monster, or ye can lookit that the way fantasy monsters are supposed tae be looked at, and examine what's he's on about, and then ye see a figure who symbolizes white patriarchy, the wealthy elite, and excess. But he's also the guy who will eat ye before ye can eat him. I like that part. He's a killer because he has to be. He's swimming with sharks."

"That. Is. Excellent. Who's the artist?"

"A friend from Australia whose parents were bastards and actually named her Sheila. She hates the jokes so she goes by Ozzy Peach, which I don't think is much of an improvement, but whatever lubes her tube, eh? She's doing book covers n' that now. Paintings for this game called Magic: The Gathering."

"Oh, aye, I've heard of that."

"Ye have?"

"I cannae play it well, but I like fantasy art. Especially anything to do with the Fae. May I see the other side?"

"Of course."

I walked around, and the passenger side of the van was a portrait of Nadia from the waist up, her right arm extended to the side and holding a straight razor, flat of the blade facing the viewer. Her arm pointed to the cab of the van, and above it was the word LIVING in block letters, and beneath it was ON THE EDGE. Her mohawk was tilted slightly to the rear of the vehicle, as if windblown by the movement of the van in operation. And her left hand, of course, was flicking the V, telling everyone to piss off, and her lip was curled in a sneer of disdain.

"That's pure brilliance," I gushed. "Do ye own a straight razor?"

"Hell yeah. Only part of me that's straight."

Dhanya sniggered at this.

"So, hey, Al," Nadia said, "I know that an invitation tae get intae a van is to be avoided at all costs, so I'm no gonnay do that. What I'm gonnay do is open the door and walk down the block so ye can look inside and see I wasnae lying. There really is a shrine in there to Lhurnog, and we leave him whisky and cheese. Melt the cheese intae fondue."

"Awright. So it's like worshipping a god ye made up?"

"Right. Because let's be real, Al: All the gods are made up. The rituals we practice are more important to us than the actual deities, in't they? Gods never do shite as far as I can tell. But rituals and ceremony are powerful things to us. They get things done."

She was half right, but it wasn't the time to provide the information she was missing. She unlocked the van and opened the back doors, then hooked a thumb over her shoulder. "We're gonnay have a smoke over there. Take yer time, but be careful yer brain disnae explode."

They walked away and I hauled myself up into the van. The interior was pure genius. The walls were draped in red velvet, and the ceiling was a tapestry replica I didn't recognize, featuring unicorns disemboweling men. A narrow black love seat on the right faced a custom shrine to Lhurnog on the left, which contained an altar with a triptych on top done in the style of Hieronymus Bosch's *Garden of Earthly Delights,* except that all the small human figures were Nadia in various goth outfits. It was at once the epitome of narcissistic excess and the ultimate satire and tribute. All these little versions of Nadia in states of pain, rapture, fear, and ecstasy, all for the glory of Lhurnog, who sat high in the center on his cheese throne with a whisky bottle in one hand and a tumbler in the other. He took his dram neat, I noticed. The altar was a sort of cabinet done in the shabby-chic style, whitewashed with some paint artfully sanded away in places to reveal a pale-blue layer underneath.

To either side of the altar, custom metal shelves had been bolted to the van walls through the velvet, thin steel towers with four slots each. On the bottom shelf were speakers. The next two featured raised rubber bases and brackets to secure bottles of whisky. They were designed so that the whisky could be displayed and appreciated but not tip over or break while the van was in motion, and she had bottles from Islay, Speyside, Highlands, and Lowlands available.

The top shelves contained a collection of high-end action figures from movies and comics—also fastened somehow, no doubt. I recognized Neo and Morpheus from *The Matrix,* Storm from *X-Men*—the one with the mohawk—and the others I wasn't sure about. But it was clear that Nadia knew what she liked, and she had the imagination and the personal courage to surround herself unapologetically with that which amused her.

There was a small sign—like a nameplate on an office desk but longer and crafted with custom sepia-toned calligraphy—resting on top of the altar: WHISKY AND CHEESE FOR THE GOB OF LHURNOG. And in front of that there was a crystal rocks glass, set in a secure base, and a small fondue set next to it with a porcelain bowl hovering over a votive candle. Both containers were empty, however. I knew where the whisky was, though I noted all the display bottles were still sealed and unopened. Where did she keep the cheese?

It was in the cupboard underneath the altar. There was an ice chest inside that contained small cubes of cheddar in a zipped plastic bag. There was also an assortment of sex toys next to the ice chest, which I was fairly certain I wasn't supposed to see. I decided right then that I wouldn't be sitting on the love seat.

Mounted on the wall above and around the love seat were shallow boxes covered with glass, as if they were museum pieces, because they contained actual museum pieces one might see in ancient weapons galleries. She had a khukuri knife, a katana and wakiza-shi, a medieval bastard sword, a kindjal, and a gladius. She may not have exhibited any disciplined martial-arts skills in the pit, but she certainly appreciated them and their history.

A glance forward confirmed that the cabin was upholstered in black leather and the finest of everything. She really had sunk a lot of money into this vehicle. It was undeniably the sweetest of rides.

I stepped out, shaking my head in wonder, and closed the doors, walking to the corner to join Nadia and Dhanya, puffing away on clove cigarettes. Ah, youth.

"So whatcha think?" Nadia said as I approached, chucking her chin at me.

"That van is absolutely mad in the best possible way. I love it."

"Ha. Excellent. Fancy a puff?"

"Oh, no, thank you. In my youth I would have joined you, but in my age I am vain about my white mustache, and tobacco would stain it yellow."

Nadia nodded and flashed a wry grin at me. "I get it. I am certainly not one to question anyone else's vanities."

"You still open tae having a cup of tea?" I asked.

"Sure. Tchai Ovna in thirty minutes?"

"Aye. See ye there."

A late-night pot would not go amiss. And the atmosphere at Tchai Ovna encouraged open minds. Not that I thought Nadia's was closed. Still, revealing the truth of the world is not to be undertaken in a sports bar. For I intended to reveal it to her. And I needed to convince her sooner rather than later, before my curse triggered.

Once we met and we had pots of chai in front of us, sitting in front of the fireplace opposite one another, Dhanya asked me the question I knew was coming: "So what d'ye do, Al, when ye're no crashing pit fights in yer cashmere?"

"I'm a printer. I own and operate MacBharrais Printing and Binding on High Street."

Nadia frowned. "That's it?"

"Of course that's not it. It's the day job. It's the cover. It's the mask I wear for the world, just like ye wear yer accounting-student mask to hide the pit fighting."

Her face relaxed as she poured herself a cup. "I've got tae say, Al, that's a fucking relief. I thought ye were gonnay bore me for a second there."

"Information control is the name of the game. It *is* the game. Some people think it's money, but it's no money at all. Information is what *gets* ye money."

"Attaboy, Al," Nadia said. "Ye keep talkin' like that and I'll be interested."

"Awright, how's this? I don't think ye won tonight because ye're a better fighter. I think ye won because ye knew something your opponents didnae."

Nadia and Dhanya both froze, their eyes locked on me. When Nadia spoke, her voice was low. "What do ye think I knew about my opponents, Al?"

"Oh, I have no idea. That is your secret to share or not as ye please, and I will no be offended if ye wish to keep it to yerself. But information control is how people with power keep it. And gaining access to information is how people with no power get power. Would ye agree?"

Nadia relaxed and sat back with her cup of tea, peering at me over the rim. "I would. Do go on."

"I have access to information known by only five people in the world. I'm no gonnay share that information with ye, but I will share the *existence* of it with ye. If ye're willing to perform a little experiment here."

"Maybe. What is it?"

"Ye will need to humor me a bit. Get up and try to lift the couch from Dhanya's end. With Dhanya on it. Do the best ye can, and then the knowledge comes after."

When Dhanya saw Nadia put her cup down on the table in front of us, she said, "Ye better no make me spill ma tea."

It was the equivalent of deadlifting a couple of hundred pounds from a very awkward position, and Nadia couldn't manage to get it airborne more than a smidge, effectively shoving it a tiny bit but no more. She gasped, defeated, and scowled at the couch and its occupant. Dhanya stared severely at Nadia.

"Nadia, I love fat people and I love ye too, but so help me, if ye say I'm fat right now because ye couldnae lift this couch with yer wee noodle arms, I will go outside and find a huge fucking spider and throw it at yer face."

Nadia's scowl evaporated as she laughed at Dhanya, and I grinned too. I withdrew a sealed Sigil of Muscular Brawn from my coat and gave it to Nadia. "This is information you didnae have until now. When ye're ready, break the seal and look at the symbol underneath the flap and wait a couple of seconds. Then try lifting the couch again. Dhanya, I recommend putting yer tea down beforehand."

They stared at me slackjawed for a few moments, then their eyes traveled around to see if anyone else had heard this. We were alone except for the employees and some people murmuring in the other room. It was late.

Dhanya shrugged, put her tea down on the table, and leaned back. "Let's do this."

"Right." Nadia popped the seal and flicked open the card, revealing the sigil to her eyes. It hacked her nervous and limbic system, infused her temporarily with the strength of a Druid, as Brighid intended, and she shuddered as the power coursed through her. It can have that effect the first few times.

She grasped the bottom of the couch again, thinking it would give her the same resistance as before but discovering as she lifted that, no, it was light as a waffle, and she sent Dhanya tumbling with a whoop as she lifted the end of the couch to her chest before realizing that she needed to stop.

"Oh! Shite. I'm sorry! For fuck's sake!" She set the couch down and Dhanya clambered back to a sitting position, cursing the whole while.

"Invigorating, eh?" I said. "Information is powerful stuff."

"What the hell did ye do tae me?" Nadia stared at her hands as if they held the answer.

"I gave ye information."

"Ye mean magic?"

I shrugged. "Call it magic or call it science. It's all information."

She curled her hands into fists and looked back at the stone hearth. "If I punch that chimney right now, will I make a dent?"

"Yes. Ye will also shatter most of the bones in your hand. I advise against it."

"How long does this last?"

"Not long. Another few minutes and ye'll be back to normal."

"Side effects?"

"None, apart from losing the strength ye currently have."

"Holy shite, Al, this is so much better than printing."

"And beating up people bigger than you is much better than accounting. Information, ye see. I can do things that border on the miraculous. But I must control that information, just like ye control the information you have."

Nadia dropped her hands to her sides. "So is that what ye want? I'll show ye mine if ye show me yours?"

"Aye."

"But my shite is no believable."

"And mine is? Ye wouldnae believe what just happened if I told ye, aye? There's a lot more where that came from. But I have seen what ye can do. So cough it up. I'm not yer average old man."

Nadia exchanged glances with Dhanya. They'd been together for a year at that point and they still are, wedded in all but name, since Nadia's family is the socially conservative kind.

Dhanya shrugged one shoulder. "It's up to you, love."

Nadia sighed and passed behind the couch and took her seat, retrieving her teacup and taking a long sip. I sat back and enjoyed my own, content to wait while she thought it through.

"Okay, fuck it. Let's see how this goes. Truth is, Al, I'm a demigoddess. Maybe."

My eyebrows rose, because that seemed to contradict her earlier statement that the gods were entirely made up, but it was also—to me, anyway—a plausible explanation that fit the facts of her abilities.

"Twenty-two years ago, ma parents were vacationing in India, visiting long-lost family and that, and . . . well, look: Ye know that Hindu tradition is littered with demigods, right?"

"Aye."

"Well, the demigods in Hindu tradition were humans that became gods, not the children of gods and humans like ye have in western tradition."

"Right."

"As such, while they were human, they procreated. Had children. But once they became gods, they blessed their children with this and that, good health or good fortune or whatever, and some of those traits got passed down. While she was on holiday in India, ma mum, bless her dark and conservative but secretly horny heart, hooked up with a man who was no her husband and who was descended from a demigod."

"She told ye this?"

"Fuck no. The man who impregnated her did. He found me about four years ago and explained why I didn't look anything like ma dad."

"A total stranger claimed to be yer biological father and ye believed him?"

"Only because I have his nose, ears, and chin, and he said I had a certain power. A power tae see what an opponent in battle would do before they did it. An ability tae see weak spots and exploit them. No super strength or speed. No long life or miraculous healing abilities. Just . . . a certain foreknowledge. Information, as ye said. And I knew it was true because I'd already experienced it. When I was in secondary, I got intae a fight in the girl's loo with Tiffany Tory MacFuckface and just destroyed her. She had it coming, believe me. She was a racist pile of mince. So when this stranger who could not possibly know about that episode identified exactly what had happened, I knew he was telling the truth. Or I thought he was."

"He wasnae?"

"I dunno. He had the dates for the holiday right, which was easy enough to confirm. But I cannae sit down with ma mum and say, *Hey, why did ye no tell me about the time ye cheated on Dad in India?* I can kick anyone's arse, ye see, but I cannae speak frankly tae ma mum. All I know is that I have this power and a stranger who has ma features told me it's because I'm descended from a demigod. It makes more sense than looking at ma dad and thinking I have his DNA. Ma brother looks like him and has no powers. So there ye have it. Believe it or no as ye please—I have days where I think it's all nonsense—but it's the only explanation I have. The power is real, but its origin is mysterious. I cannae even tell ye which demigod I'm supposedly descended from."

"And ye decided tae monetize that tonight?"

"Aye, but it took a while tae find out how tae do that. Underground pit fights don't exactly promote themselves at the local café bulletin board. I'm no gonnay get another score like that again, though. Word is gonnay spread about me. Even if I use a different name, they will be on the lookout for a teeny Indian woman with a mohawk. So what's yer story, Al?"

It was my turn to sip tea contemplatively before saying anything. There was no way to predict how people would take news that required them to shift their paradigms. Most of the time such news just bounced off them, the way horrific shite about a candidate bounces off a party's faithful because they can't face the fact that they voted for a monster and they may in fact be monsters themselves. Easier to just deny it all, call it fake news. No introspection required.

But Nadia might be different. She might have a mind capable of accepting new facts and discarding the old.

"What ye said earlier about gods was partially true," I began, cradling my saucer and holding the cup slightly above it. "The gods are all made up, but the making is no joke: They're also real, given the ability to manifest when they reach a critical mass of faith. They take up space but usually not on this plane. They dwell in whatever otherworldly dimensions humans have imagined for them. Call it magic or quantum theory or too much ketamine on yer cornflakes. Like yer foresight, it doesn't matter in practical terms *how* they exist, just that they do. The problem is, if ye have all the different gods of humanity prancing around on earth, it's gonnay become a nightmare super fast."

Dhanya snorted. "I'd say so. And by the way, I thought ye were gonnay tell us how ye got intae the printing business, so this is much better already. Five stars for defying expectations and coming out swinging with the batshite."

Nadia nodded and grinned her agreement. "Five stars. This has been an extraordinary tea."

"Thank ye. So with all these deities and their potential to royally screw us even more than we screw ourselves, ye need someone to keep the gods in their corners and leave us alone to live or die as we please. That's what I do: Keep the gods off our patch. And I do it with sigils like the one I just gave ye. There are many different sigils that do different things, and the knowledge is never written down but passed on through oral tradition. Information control."

They took a moment to digest this, then Nadia pointed at the card that was now just a symbol, its magic drained. "Ye can beat up gods with that sigil ye gave me?"

"Naw, but sometimes I have a go at the lackeys they send here. Monsters and demons and the like. I bind the gods with contracts that have severe penalties if they break them. Once they sign, they're bound, and they have to sign or the other gods gang up on them. But they always try to get around the contracts. They make unauthorized visits or perform subtle miracles and hope we won't notice. That's what all the sigils are for."

"Where do these sigils come from?"

"Two places. Sigils of power were originally invented in China by the Taoists, and they were primarily sigils of protection that we now simply call wards. But in the early nineteenth century, Brighid of the Tuatha Dé Danann—are ye familiar with her?"

"Aye," the women said in unison.

"Brighid added tae the Taoist sigils with a new set that had more active applications and were based off Druidic bindings. So, if ye'll forgive an analogy tae video games, it was like an expansion set. She introduced new mechanics, but the Chinese system still worked; they can use the new sigils and we can still use the old ones. Taken together, it's a system of knowledge that provides its very few practitioners extraordinary power. Those practitioners are called sigil agents."

"And you're a sigil agent?" Nadia said.

"Correct."

"Brilliant. Ya jammy bastard," Dhanya said, smiling.

I needed to check. "Are ye okay with this so far?"

Nadia gave a tiny shrug. "Well, I have questions, and I'm not sure I quite believe all the gods are real, but that sigil was real enough, so I'm willing to suspend disbelief for a little while, at least."

"Fair enough. Fire one of yer questions at me."

"Why did Brighid make all the new sigils in the nineteenth century? Why not earlier, or later?"

"Ah, excellent. A couple of reasons. First, there was a problem with the Druids at the time. There was only one of the old ones left, ye see, and he was in hiding until very recently."

"Hold up. This Druid who was in hiding in the early nineteenth century is still alive? He's two hundred years old?"

"More like two thousand, and he was hiding from a god for nearly all of that time. Brighid and the Tuatha Dé Danann needed some work done on this plane and couldn't get the Druid to do it, so she saw the sigils as a work-around. A few humans could get the basic work she needed done and the training time would not be as long or as intense as a Druid's would—the Druids take twelve years. These humans would necessarily have fewer powers and the potency of the sigils would last for only a limited time, but it solved a lot of issues."

"What issues? And are the Druids gone now?"

"I'm told there are a total of three Druids now and six more in training, but I only met the really old one once, by accident."

"He must have an epic case of arthritis," Dhanya said.

"Not at all. He looks younger than you, in fact. As for the issues, much of it had tae do with the advent of the Industrial Age. For the Fae, specifically, there was a lot more iron and steel around, and the earth simply wasnae safe anymore. But that brings us to the second reason Brighid initiated the system: photography. Gods didn't want there to be any evidence of other gods or pantheons being real, because that might weaken the faith of their followers. It was best for everyone if the gods stayed off earth—or, failing that, stayed off camera—so that people could continue to have their faiths and thereby fuel the gods' lives. So Brighid needed the Fae tae stay in the Fae planes, and all the other gods needed earth to remain evidence-free if not god-free, and sigil agents helped make that happen."

"How do ye make that happen, exactly?"

"The contracts I mentioned earlier require the gods to stay away except under very specific conditions, and they contain sigils of consequence that punish the gods who break them. I'm not sure what they feel, but I'm assured it's very unpleasant. They are also supposed to keep their attendants away, but that punishment is less severe or nonexistent, so that's where sigil agents are often expected to enforce the contract by other means."

"Awright, I'm gonnay need an example."

"Let's say a demon escapes from hell and wants to create a little hell on earth. Lucifer or whichever of his many names you prefer is bound by contract not to manifest here, but the innumerable demons of hell are not."

"Why not?"

"Because contracts are negotiated. Lucifer refused to take any responsibility for the actions of demons. And that is a common contractual dealbreaker among the gods; they all want some ability to visit the plane by proxy, so they give up their personal presence for the most part but steadfastly refuse to take any responsibility for their underlings. Their demons or angels or hobgoblins or faeries therefore make appearances on their behalf, but there's deniability built in. We can't really hold the gods responsible for the actions of an underling, because they always deny responsibility. But it works the other way too: We are free to capture or destroy those underlings when they appear, take any of their possessions, and so on, without fear of reprisal. Because if the deities get mad at us for defending our turf, then they're accepting responsibility for that underling's actions and are therefore in breach of contract. So, to return to the example, if a demon is found here on this plane, there is a Sigil of Cold Fire that will destroy them. It's a Druidic binding and it's much safer for a Druid to engage them, but we have that in our arsenal."

"You've slain demons?"

"A couple. It's rare. Mostly I deal with Fae of various kinds. The Irish, Scottish, and English varieties are all in my territory and present their own unique challenges, and the Germans have a set of interesting ones, and the Polish have a few nightmares, believe it or not."

"What is your territory?"

"The European continent, the Middle East, and the various countries that comprise Northern Africa."

"Holy shite. How do you take care of all this out of a print-shop?"

"Not well, I'm afraid. I'm barely hanging on. I could use a manager who knows her way around the tax laws and can handle herself in a fight if need be."

"Whaaat?"

"I ask nothing right now except for the chance tae tell ye more and make ye a lucrative offer."

"You're able tae make me a lucrative offer? I just made a fuck-ton of cash."

"As did I. But didnae I hear ye say ye wouldnae be getting a score like that again? A salary commensurate tae yer skills would be nice. Printing is a booming business when ye can run all sorts of other income through the books."

"What, ye're—ye're laundering sumhin?"

"Inefficiently and inexpertly, but yes. I have otherworldly revenue streams."

"So ye want me to cook yer books for ye?"

"And fight the occasional monster, yes, for a salary well above the industry average for a CMA. I think ye will find working for me exciting, challenging, and rewarding. A job like no other."

Nadia exchanged a significant glance with Dhanya, who shrugged, leaving it up to her.

"Awright, I'll hear more and take a look at yer offer. No promises."

"That's perfectly agreeable. Are you two partners, by any chance?"

"Yeah."

"Excellent. Well, then." I withdrew an entirely normal business card and handed it to Nadia. "Please call as soon as ye can tae arrange an office visit. In the meantime, I'll give ye both a parting gift." I pulled out the proper pens, two cards, and my seal. I drew them two Sigils of Sexual Vigor and prepared them for later use, then pushed them across the table. "The next time ye're in the mood tae enjoy each other's intimate company, unseal these sigils and look at them beforehand. You'll have an amazing experience."

Dhanya snorted. "What is this bollocks? Some kind o' sex magic?"

"Yes. Do not unseal those in public. Trust me."

I knew that they'd not be able to resist that temptation for long. Nadia called me after noon the very next day, and though it took a few visits to cement the deal, that was how we met and I recruited her to be my manager.

"That is a fine story, MacBharrais, but I have tae know: Does she still have the wizard van?"

[She does, and she still drives it. She completely replaced the engine and electrical system about three years ago and made some other improvements, but the paintings inside and out remain as magnificent as they were the night we met.]

"Will I get tae see it?"

[If we ever make it safe for you to leave the flat, absolutely.]

"Right. When are we gonnay do that, by the way?"

My phone buzzed with a text from Eli Robicheaux in Philadelphia.

The text read, *Can confirm S. Hatcher is Bastille. You'd better get over here and deal with it as soon as you can.*

[We'll start tomorrow. Fancy a plane flight to America?]

"I heard flying is a terrible way to both live and die."

[It is. But it's much faster than taking a ship.]

"Do I no need some kind of identification to fly?"

[Let me worry about that. You worry about being in a metal tube and wearing a seatbelt with a buckle made of steel.]

"Fuck no! Forget it, MacBharrais."

[I need ye with me, Buck.]

"I cannae stay here and watch the telly?"

[I need ye,] I repeated.

"Will there be snacks, at least?"

[Yes. Terrible ones.]

CHAPTER 22

The Secret of Salsa

I bought Buck a ticket to Philadelphia using Gordie's passport. Getting him through security, however, would require at least two sigils and maybe more, because there was no way anyone would look at the passport and then look at Buck and conclude that he was a wee sunburnt Gordie. Fortunately, Brighid had come up with something because all the sigil agents had to occasionally take flights with beings who had no government-issued ID and in fact were thought not to exist at all.

I wore a hat emblazoned with the Sigil of Seeming Absence and gave one to Buck as well, with the strict instruction not to remove it. It's a different effect than the Sigil of Swallowed Light. We'd appear on cameras, and we'd appear briefly in the vision of anyone in front of us, but then we'd disappear once the sigil took effect in their minds. People would see us at first and avoid the space we occupied but not be able to process that we were still actually there after a moment. The visual evidence that we were there would still be in effect, but they'd be unable to remember or process it. They'd blink and we'd be gone, and they'd see only whatever had been behind us before, because the brain is fantastic at supplying information like that and filling gaps. We had no luggage to check and I printed our boarding passes ahead of time. On a separate card—all black and about the size of a cell phone—I had drawn a Sigil of Swallowed Light and kept that in my pocket. I couldn't walk in and just take out the cameras: If security saw that their surveillance wasn't working, then they'd shut the checkpoints down. I needed them open just long enough to get on the other side of them.

So we walked up to security and scoped it out. I pointed out the X-ray machines and the metal detectors and the security personnel we'd have to slip past.

[There are cameras everywhere too,] I told Buck, [and somebody is supposedly watching them. If they're on top of things, they'll see us walk by security without them checking us and make a fuss. But do not respond. Once they're not looking at the cameras, they won't be able to see us either. Just keep walking.]

The true beauty of Seeming Absence was that not only did we sail past security without presenting passports or boarding passes, we didn't anger anyone who saw us queue-jumping, because once they blinked, we weren't ahead of them anymore.

Someone was watching monitors, to the airport's credit: a white man that I guessed was in his forties, with brown muttonchops connecting to his mustache but a clean-shaven chin.

"Oi, why did ye let them pass?" he shouted at the security guard as he emerged from behind a console to the rear of the security area and moved to block our path.

The bewildered security guard, who had blinked and ignored us breezing by, swung around. "Who?"

Muttonchops blinked and pointed at where he had seen us a moment ago. "These . . ."

"Where?"

Buck and I were already past him, and Muttonchops raced back to his console. I pulled out the card with the Sigil of Swallowed Light on it, and now they wouldn't be able to find us on camera again. I didn't want to cause a panic, however, so we moved quickly to our gate area and then ducked into a bathroom, putting the Swallowed Light away. Their cameras would turn back on now, and they could grouse about it but ultimately wouldn't ground any flights over it. We kept our Seeming Absence hats on once we took a seat in the waiting area, successfully escaping the notice of a couple of security guards making a sweep of all the gates. When it was time to board, we took our hats off and I used my official ID to get a command obeyed. I had to do this because if we just snuck past and pressed our boarding passes to the scanner, there was a good chance they'd think it was a glitch if each beep of the machine didn't match to a person.

"We don't need to show our passports," I told the flight attendant. "Just take our boarding passes."

She blinked and tried to shake it off and nearly did, but I kept the sigils in her face and repeated myself. "Of course, sir. Enjoy your flight."

Once at our assigned seats, we tore open a package containing a blanket and fastened the buckle on top of it to keep the steel safely insulated away from Buck's person. Once we got in the air, I unbuckled it for him and he relaxed.

We waltzed through customs in Philadelphia and met Eli Robicheaux outside of baggage claim, since it was a good rendezvous point. We took off our hats as we exited so that he'd be able to see us. He was dressed sharply now in a grey pinstripe suit and entirely unnecessary sunglasses, and a toothpick lolled in one corner of his mouth. His eyebrows rose above the glasses in disbelief as he took in Buck.

"Really? You contracted a hobgoblin?"

[Hi, Eli. Yes, I did.]

"Aren't they . . . ?"

"Wot? Small and pink?" Buck supplied.

"More trouble than they're worth?" Eli finished.

"Oi, I'm worth a bloody lot."

"I hope so. I imagine you're hungry for some real food?"

We were. Eli led us to the parking garage and loaded our carry-ons into his car, a nondescript sedan, and drove us to a Mexican restaurant called El Vez. Such establishments were scarce in Scotland and Eli knew it, so he was making an effort to give us a rare experience.

"Can't walk away hungry from a place like this. The chips and salsa will take care of you before you even get to the main course."

The interior of El Vez immediately delighted Buck.

"Wow, what is that thing on top of that thing?" he asked, pointing toward the bar. "Whatever it is, can I have one?"

The bar was circular, and rising from the ranks of tequila bottles and other liquors in the center of it, a pedestal at head height displayed a magnificent bicycle designed like a low-rider chopper, the frame a hot pink with a golden banana boat seat and gold handlebars and wheels. There was even a tube of white neon in the center of the frame to really make it pop.

[Maybe,] I said. A hobgoblin on a bicycle might be amusing.

We were led to a booth against the wall opposite the door, and said wall supported hundreds of small dioramas filled with Día de los Muertos scenes. Tiny figures of skeletons dressed in clothing, all of them singing or dancing, holding instruments or flowers or any number of things. All were exquisitely painted in great detail.

"I don't understand what I'm looking at here," Buck said. He was standing in the booth as we sat, because if he sat down, he'd probably disappear underneath the top of the table. "How did these tiny humans die?"

"They're not real," Eli explained. "That's art. It has to do with honoring one's ancestors in Mexican culture."

[You did a contract with them, didn't you?] I asked Eli.

"You mean Santa Muerte and the government of Mexico? Yeah, I renewed that recently." Eli's territory was all of North America except for the southern states; Diego took care of the South plus the Caribbean nations, Central and South America.

El Vez offered many different guacamoles, so we ordered three to start plus some chips and salsa and a round of margaritas.

"What am I lookin' at now?" Buck said, eyeing everything uncertainly since the cuisine was entirely foreign to him. "Is that green stuff smashed peas?"

"Smashed avocados. It's called guacamole. Take a chip and scoop up some and eat it." Eli demonstrated. Buck watched us carefully, wary of a trick, then he tried it and his eyes lit up.

"Hey, it's no bad."

"Right?" Eli said.

"Wot's the red shite there with bits in it? Chunky pasta sauce?"

"No, that's salsa. Tomato-based, but with peppers, onions, and cilantro, usually, instead of basil, garlic, and oregano."

"Sounds boring."

"It's not. Try some on a chip."

[Just a bit, now,] I typed, because he probably wasn't used to jalapeños, but I was too late. He had loaded up a chip with salsa and crammed it into his mouth as I hit PLAYBACK.

After the first couple of crunches, when the flavor hit his tongue, Buck looked pleased. But then horror suffused his features as the capsaicin in the peppers took effect and began to burn the tissues of his mouth and throat. I'd tried to warn him, because he'd probably never had anything with a little bit of spice to it, and moderation would have been wise.

He coughed and grasped for his water glass, his wee hands shaking, and some of it spilled and leaked down his chin and neck as he tried to put out the fire in his mouth.

"Gods below!" he gasped, slamming down the water, then fell back into the booth, his eyes rolling up. "Aww, yess. Aye. That's. That's the. Stuff."

"Holy shit, what is happening right now?" Eli said. Buck's skin had turned red instead of pink and he was sweating and trembling a bit, but now he had a faint smile on his face as he kept mumbling affirmations.

"This is beautiful. You're beautiful. I'm beautiful. I mean, pure beauty, right? Full of it."

[I think he might be high on salsa,] I said.

"Oh, aye," Buck said. "I like Mexican food. One bite is perfect."

Eli pointed to him and said, "That shit right there is not fair."

"Hey, MacBharrais, can we get salsa in Scotland?"

I nodded, and he started giggling.

"That's pure magic, mate. And all these dancing lights in the air. Where'd they come from? How'd ye do that?"

There were no dancing lights in the air. Eli shook his head. "Enjoy the ride, man. Al and I have business to discuss."

[We do. What have ye found?]

"Well, I walked into the CIA with a mask and a stack of authority sigils, making folks use their swipe cards and such, until I found someone who could tell me who Simon Hatcher was. And lemme tell you, it is some nerve-racking but giddy shit to walk into Langley and get what you want. I should have found out who killed Kennedy while I was there. Anyway: Simon Hatcher runs counterintelligence ops in the European theater, mostly against Russia. He's in charge of several code-named ops and has access to a budget. Meets your criteria, so he's probably your guy."

[Do you know what the ops are for?]

"No, I didn't have enough sigils to get details on everything. But I wrote down the names of the ops. They're about as balanced as a seesaw with an anvil on one end."

[What were they?]

"Shit like Summer Shoelace and Delinquent Maraschino. They have these random generators make those up, you know? Wildest one was Obstreperous Roquefort."

[Roquefort? Like the cheese?]

"Man, never mind the cheese. Somebody in the government typed *obstreperous* into a name generator. I had to look that shit up. Do *you* know what it means without looking it up?"

[Roquefort is a French word. A French cheese.]

"So?"

[Bastille is a French name. A place, actually.]

"Yeah, I knew that. Storming the Bastille started the French Revolution. Doesn't matter, man. I told you, those op names are randomly generated."

[But Simon Hatcher did not choose the name Bastille randomly. My point is that Obstinate Roquefort is probably a meaningful op to him.]

"It's *Obstreperous*. You don't know what it means either. Good."

[I know what it means. I tried to type it, but autocorrect is a bastard.]

Someone screamed in the booth behind my head, and I whipped around to see what the matter was. A woman was simultaneously trying to escape the booth and flail at something on her table, possibly trying to kill it. I was thinking it was an insect or a spider until she withdrew, and I looked at the table and saw three tiny Día de los Muertos figures sprawled among the plates and overturned glasses.

"They were moving!" she told me, apparently deciding that I needed an explanation. "They jumped off the wall onto the table! I swear!"

A low roll of giggles and snickers behind me told me exactly what had happened: a brief enchantment of animation from a mischievous hobgoblin. I nodded once to the lady, affirming her story but saying nothing, and turned back to my table. Buck Foi was lying prone in the back of the booth, holding his belly as laughter shook him and tears streamed from his eyes.

[That wasn't very nice,] I told him.

"Wot? Aw, come on. No harm done."

[She's going to have nightmares and probably require therapy.]

"She already has nightmares, and if there's anyone on the planet who doesn't require therapy at this point, I'd like tae know their secret. Yer bringin' me down, ol' man. I need another hit of salsa."

Buck clambered unsteadily to his feet and reached for the salsa bowl, but I knocked his hand away, shaking my head. The hobgoblin wasn't going to accept that, so he leapt onto the table, past my reach, and snatched up the bowl, tossing some of it down his throat.

"Auggh! Gods! Gah! Kack! Ugh! Oh. Aw. Yeahhh." He toppled backward off the table and crashed onto the floor, nearly senseless. We asked for our bill and I had to half-drag Buck out of there, since he couldn't keep his feet. Eli just kept apologizing to the bewildered staff of El Vez and left a huge tip. It was a shame we had to leave early; the food and drink were really good.

"Remember what I said about hobgoblins being more trouble than they're worth?" Eli said.

I nodded at him outside, ruefully. Buck had embarrassed me again.

"You've got a home address for Hatcher in Reston, right?" At my nod he continued, "We can catch a train down to D.C.—ride's about two hours—then get a rental car and be at his place an hour later."

[A late-night visit, then? Or more likely in the wee hours of the morning?]

"Yeah. He should be home, right? Easier to talk to him there than trying to talk to him at work."

[Let's go. I mean, after my hob sobers up.]

"We need to prepare some sigils anyway, I'm thinking."

CHAPTER 23

You Can't Handle the Truth

Eli took us to his place in the East Falls neighborhood. He had a flat—sorry, they call them apartments in the States—in Dobson Mills.

It was a lovely place, furnished in a hybrid style, like so many American things, that blended modern elements with Tuscan finishes on the moldings and edges.

I'd hoped to meet Eli's apprentice, Leonard Fort, but he was attending classes at college and wouldn't be around until the next day at the earliest.

I met Eli's family instead. His wife, Patrice, was a personal trainer and greeted me in gym clothes with her curly hair tied up with a scrunchy. Their two children, Camille and Pierre, waved shyly, then stared at Buck, wondering what they were looking at. They were sitting down to dinner as we entered and asked if we wanted to join.

"Welcome, Al. Did you eat already?"

[Yes, thanks. Please don't trouble yourself.]

"We're going to go back to my study and work on a few things," Eli said. "We have a late night ahead."

"You do?" Patrice's brow furrowed in concern.

"Yes. I'll explain later. But this is Buck. He's a little out of it at the moment. Don't touch him or make a lot of noise, okay, kids?"

Buck chose that moment to fart squeakily, and Camille and Pierre nodded, their expressions suggesting that they had no intention of going anywhere near Buck.

We deposited my stoned hobgoblin on the sofa and he instantly passed out, drooling on the cushions. Eli's pet, a curious English bulldog named Dumptruck, hauled himself up to the couch, sniffed Buck, and began to hump his leg. Eli and I started to object but then exchanged a glance, got out our phones, and snapped a couple of photos for later use.

"You're just gonna stand there and let him do that?" Patrice said to Eli. "Dumptruck! Stop!"

"We've gotta teach that hobgoblin about karma, and he won't learn if we don't record this," Eli said. "You shoulda seen what he did at the restaurant. Near scared this poor woman to death. Made a mess for the employees." His voice got all low and furry, the way it does when people talk to dogs. "You's a good boy, Dumptruck! Yes, you's a good boy!"

Camille and Pierre giggled, and Patrice sighed.

"G'wan outta here. Go on, you two. That's a terrible example to set."

We chuckled and went down the hall to Eli's ink room. It was similar to mine in the sense that there were lots of jars and cubbyholes and shelves, but it had a different aesthetic, almost more of a showroom than a work space. Eli had painted the walls a pale yellow and used a dark wood for the shelving so that the ingredients and inkpots were displayed almost like curios.

[Do you have the ink all ready for a Sigil of Reckoning Truth?]

"No, but I have the ingredients to make it. Certain Authority works just fine for most things."

[This isn't most things, unfortunately.]

"You got that right."

Eli pointed out an extra stool for me while he pulled down the ingredients for the Ink of Veracity, which included dust from the wings of the Madagascan moon moth.

[When did you get the moth dust?]

"Traded Shu-hua for it. She wanted dust from the cecropia moth, and I took a trip out to the Rockies to get some. Went camping with Patrice and the kids. It was nice."

While he got to work on that, he told me where to buy train tickets online, and I got us three seats for the train departing at ten P.M. I hoped Buck would be capable of functioning by then. There was no extant research on how long it took a hobgoblin to shrug off a salsa high.

When Eli pronounced the ink was ready, he drew up five Sigils of Reckoning Truth—far more than we would need. Two were for his later use and two for mine, which was kind of him.

[Do you know if Hatcher has any family?] I asked him. [What are we walking into?]

"I was gonna ask you the same. I have no clue. I just looked into him at work."

I looked up the address Codpiece had given me on a map app and switched to satellite view. Hatcher's house looked from above like a fairly posh spread for a government employee.

[Looks like new construction. Big lot. He's got a pool with a waterfall and spa.]

"So either he has a spouse raking it in, or he's inherited a load of cash, or . . . yeah. Maybe he's recently come into a windfall."

[And we already know he's used to dealing with numbered accounts, because he's Bastille. He might be legitimately well-off from something. Or he might be using laundered money to live large.]

"We should go in there prepared for trouble. If somebody in Tír na nÓg is helping him, then he might have some Fae protections around his place."

[Druidic wards?]

Eli nodded. "I'm not saying it's super likely. But we should be ready for it."

[Do you have your monocle? I didn't bring mine.]

Brighid gave every sigil agent a monocle that let them see a good portion of the magical spectrum. Incredibly useful but easy to lose or break, so we didn't travel with them.

"Yeah. I hate pulling that thing out, because I look damn stupid wearing it, but it'll be dark. Probably looks great on you, though. I bet nobody would look twice. You'd be just another Monopoly guy. Maybe I'll let you use mine."

We dragged Buck off the couch at nine-thirty and splashed some water in his face to wake him up, after a bit of shouting and shaking failed to do the trick. He blinked a lot and cursed and looked bleary but otherwise seemed all right.

[Do you have a headache?]

"I've got you, have I no?" he said.

We bundled him up to protect him from iron and headed to the train station. Buck was largely silent, trying to recuperate from his lethargy, and after a few minutes I snapped open a Sigil of Hale Revival for him and he felt much better.

"Why did ye no do that earlier?" he complained.

[I don't want this to become a habit. There need to be consequences.]

"I suffered enough! I had the weirdest dream. There was a bulldog or sumhin havin' a go at ma leg."

Eli chuckled. "That wasn't a dream." He pulled up a photo on his phone and showed it to Buck. "I think I'm gonna make that my new wallpaper."

"Aw, ye're a gobshite, both of ye!" he said. Eli just laughed while I composed a response.

[What's shite is using your magic in a way that humans notice. Stealing whisky and sausage leaves no trace of magic, and that sort of thing is allowed all day. What you did in the restaurant, however, broke the rules.]

He lowered his head. "Aye. I hear ye. I don't think I should take any more salsa trips in public."

We agreed on that, and then we filled him in on what we were about to do. Once we arrived in D.C., the cab driver at the station looked at us uncertainly but consented to taking us to Reston and waiting for us once Eli flashed a Benjamin at him.

Hatcher's residence was indeed far above his CIA pay grade. In the wan illumination of the streetlights, we could see that there was an awful lot of stone and groomed landscaping that I was fairly certain Hatcher wasn't maintaining himself. This sort of purchase should have raised flags somewhere, unless he'd carefully disguised what was going on. Or maybe such flags didn't get raised anymore in the general corruption of the United States—I wasn't up to date on their political bollocks except that it was a miserable cock-up on all three shifts, much like the UK except in the details.

Eli gave me his monocle and I scanned the grounds in the magical spectrum. There were wards on the walk leading up to the front door, confirming that Hatcher was getting help from someone in Tír na nÓg. We'd alarm him if we attempted to enter that way. Doubtless he'd have wards on the back entrance as well, which we'd be able to handle like the ones in front, but at least there we wouldn't have to break and enter in full view of the cab driver and the neighbors. Some plausible deniability would be good.

There was a sigil to handle basic wards and dissolve them, which Eli employed in the backyard. The sigil did nothing, however, to dispel or dissuade the troll guarding the premises.

He was hiding in the shadows of the back porch. Buck jumped out of the way of a fist at the last second, hollering, "Shite!" as it crashed into the deck, splintering wood.

"Owe you one, wee man," the troll growled, dressed incongruously in an XXXL black tracksuit and wearing an eyepatch. "And more besides. Won't forget losing an eye."

Buck popped out of sight and reappeared on the troll's shoulder as Eli and I unsealed agility sigils for ourselves. My hobgoblin poked the troll in his remaining eye and shouted, "Lose another!" before winking out of existence again. While the troll roared and covered his eye, swiping at us blindly with his left hand to keep us away, we drew our weapons. Mine was simply the cane, but Eli pulled two short iron daggers from somewhere and darted in, slashing the troll twice on the arm.

He felt it and grunted, but there was no other reaction, which we both thought odd as we backed off the porch. There wasn't enough room there to evade the troll.

"Shouldn't that have hurt him a bit more?" Eli said in an under-tone to me.

I nodded in the dark, which I'm not sure he saw. Pausing to type my answers during a battle was not the best way to win, so I'd be silent until it was over. But Eli was correct: The troll should have recoiled at the touch of those custom iron blades, and his skin should blister and pop like Durf the ogre's had, but he acted as if he'd just taken a minor scratch.

"Kill ye," the troll muttered, then fell silent as he cocked his head to listen for us and took a deep breath, trying to locate us by scent. "Yeah, ye better back off," he said, lumbering forward and finding by touch the post that bordered the steps. He grabbed on to it and used it to steady himself as he descended the steps. We were on some artificial-stone decking material now, bordering the pool on our left, and the troll was approaching cautiously and try-ing to hold himself defensively but advancing nevertheless.

"Buck, c'mere," Eli said, which gave the troll a clue where he was—next to the pool. I was to their right. The troll snarled and lurched toward Eli even as Buck scooted over to get close, and Eli tapped his shoulder. "Climb up." Buck leapt up instead and Eli gave some ground, taking three steps back and whispering to Buck as the troll roared and swiped a couple of times at the air in the direction of Eli's voice. Eli had to rear back to avoid the second one and shot a glance at me. "Follow up, Al," he said, then he flipped his grip on his daggers so that the tips pointed down. To Buck, he nodded that he was ready.

Buck popped them both out of the way just as the troll was coming at them for another swing, and they reappeared a few feet in the air directly above the troll's head, rotated a hundred eighty degrees so that they were facing the same way he was. Eli plunged his iron daggers up to the hilt in either side of the troll's neck as he fell, and Buck punched him in his left ear. Eli necessarily landed on the troll's back but didn't try to hold on. He just toppled backward and rolled away, and Buck likewise didn't stick around but launched himself toward the lawn.

The troll's reaction was instinctive. He reached up to the daggers, raising his arms and leaving his rib cage unprotected. That was my shot and I took it, darting forward and placing a straight kick into his left side, which I'd never be able to manage normally but could pull off thanks to the influence of the agility sigil. It staggered the troll just enough to tumble him into the pool, bleeding and blind. Trolls don't do well in water—their dense musculature means they float about as well as a cement block. But this wasn't a particularly deep pool, and he'd fallen in the shallow end. He stood up in short order, water up to his thighs, and bellowed a sort of layered roar, like a tuba snoring underneath a shrieking buzz saw and an ululating wombat.

"What the fuck, Al?" Eli said. "He should be disintegrating with that much iron in him."

I had no answer, so I simply shook my head and withdrew a Sigil of Muscular Brawn, opening it and taking it in as the troll fought against the resistance of water to get to the edge and climb out. I felt the strength flow into my muscles, and I gripped my cane like a cricket bat, sidestepping across the deck of the pool to meet the troll as he reached the side. Since he was standing in at least a three-foot hole, his head was conveniently positioned in what would be a high-strike zone in American baseball. I teed off on his face with everything I had, the carbon steel striking him directly on the forehead and the bone cracking audibly. His vocals abruptly ceased and he fell back into the pool, sinking to rest on the bottom and not moving. He wouldn't be getting back up again.

Fighting a troll does not lend itself to the sort of stealth one requires to surprise a target. As a species, trolls generally defy all attempts to fight them sneakily, and this one had made plenty of noise. So even though we'd not tripped any wards, someone in the house—either Hatcher or another bodyguard—had woken up sometime during the fight and found a gun. He used that to shoot at us through the windows.

I didn't know if he could see us well or if he was simply trying to scare us off, but I certainly did feel it when a bullet grazed my shoulder. I dropped to the ground and broke my silence.

"Buck! Get his gun."

"On it, boss." The air displaced behind him as he popped away and shortly returned with the gun in hand, a semiautomatic job. We heard someone howling inside the house.

"What'd you do to him?" Eli asked.

"Broke his nose. Don't worry, he can still talk."

"Good."

I got to my feet and used a Sigil of Knit Flesh on myself to stop the bleeding. That didn't stop it from hurting, so I was rather glad Buck had dished out a little punishment in return.

When we burst through the door, we discovered that it was indeed Hatcher and not another bodyguard who'd shot at us. He was a slightly sunburnt man with sandy hair and a middle-aged spread concealed under his powder-blue pajamas. His eyebrows were sun-bleached blond and kind of glowed against his flushed face. His teeth were abnormally bright as well, obviously having undergone a whitening treatment. But his combat training had been years ago and he hadn't been in the field for years, if ever, so he was no match for Eli. We had him zip-tied and bleeding on his living room carpet inside of two minutes. We let him say things like we had made a fatal mistake and we had no idea who we were dealing with and so on. That was all fine, because we needed to establish a baseline of behavior before we employed a sigil on him. I got out my phone and asked Buck to look around.

[Search for anything Fae, but carefully. He might have some dangerous shite.]

"Can I steal anything?"

[Maybe. Clear it with me first.]

"I love this job." He disappeared and Hatcher objected loudly.

I wondered why he bothered, and Eli spoke aloud what I was thinking.

"Man, if we didn't stop at the troll on the back porch and the gun you shot at us, what makes you think we're gonna stop because you tell us to when you're tied up and on your knees? Where's your situational awareness?"

"Fuck you."

"Fuck me, huh? Hmm. Is this a performative thing? The room is bugged and you know it, so you gotta act like you're not seconds away from shitting yourself?"

"Just know that anything you do to me is going to be paid back with interest."

"You'd have to remember it to get revenge, and you're not gonna remember any of this. Look, we know you're Bastille. We know you've been trafficking the Fae and doing something to them, and you've sold this whole business somehow to your superiors. What we want to know is exactly what you're doing to them and why."

Hatcher blinked a few times, clearly taken aback, though I wasn't sure which part had slowed him. That we knew he was Bastille? Or that we knew of his Fae experiments?

"I'm not telling you shit."

"Come on, man. We know about your secret op, we tracked your doughy ass down, and we handled your troll. We're not your typical home invaders. We can do things to your head to get the answers we need, but it'll leave some damage behind. We'd rather not do that. You come clean with us voluntarily and you'll wake up confused but otherwise of sound mind. That's a very good deal and you should take it."

"Who are you, then?"

"We work for Brighid, First among the Fae. She knows what you've been up to."

"Bullshit. You're Russian."

Eli blinked and looked down at himself to make sure he still appeared as he had that morning.

"Russia can do some impressive shit, I'll grant you," Eli said.

"Steal-our-elections-and-install-a-puppet-and-get-away-with-it kind of shit. But I don't think they have many brothers on their list of sleeper agents." He looked over at me. "I gave it a try. I think it's time."

I nodded my assent but typed a question. [You're clear on what we need to get in the short window we have?]

"Yeah, man. I'm clear."

Hatcher's eyes narrowed at me. "Why are you using a UK voice on your speech app? Are you from there?" His eyes popped wide open. "You're the asshole who called about Gordie, aren't you? That bullshit memorial in Edinburgh."

I didn't bother answering. Eli pulled out the prepared Sigil of Reckoning Truth and opened it in front of Hatcher's eyes. He flinched once, but then his eyes went glassy and unblinking.

"You're going to answer all my questions, aren't you, Simon?"

He gulped and then said, "Yes."

This sigil, my master taught me, was a variation on an enchantment applied to a sword the Iron Druid possessed, a legendary Irish weapon named Fragarach, the Answerer. That could compel truthful answers indefinitely and leave the subject unharmed, but our sigil was more of a spoon than a scalpel and was only effective for a limited time, so Eli dove right into it.

"Did you arrange the trafficking of Fae?"

"No, but I was involved."

"Who else was involved?"

"Gordie and Clíodhna of the Tuatha Dé Danann. And her intermediaries."

"Can you prove Clíodhna was involved?"

"No. She always worked through banshees."

"What are you doing to the Fae?"

"We're taking away their fatal flaw. Removing their vulnerability to iron. It disfigures them and drives them a bit crazy, but it works." We'd just confirmed that independently with the troll, so I knew we were getting good intel.

"And this is Clíodhna's idea?" Eli continued.

"Yes."

"Did she give you an ink recipe to deliver to Gordie?"

"Yes, a few of them." That was interesting. I'd only found the one. If there were other written recipes still around, I'd need to destroy them.

"Why does she want Fae immune to iron?"

Hatcher shrugged. "I guess she has enemies who use iron against the Fae. I don't care as long as I get to use them."

"Use them how?"

"Counterintelligence. Hit the Russians with monsters so they don't know how to hit back. It's all proof of concept at this stage, but so far, so . . . good."

That pause at the end was ominous, and Eli asked the next vital question quickly. "Where are you turning the Fae into these monsters?"

Hatcher blinked once, then a few more times in rapid succession, and my shoulders slumped. That was all we were going to get.

"Hey, what?" he said. "Hey. What'd you do to me?"

"Where are you turning the Fae into monsters?" Eli repeated.

"Fuck you, man. My head hurts. Jesus, what did you do?"

"Shit. Come on, get up," Eli said, lifting Hatcher by the crook of his arm so he could get to his feet. "Let's get you to bed."

Hatcher tried kicking Eli as soon as he was up, but Eli had been expecting that. He blocked it and sank his fist into Hatcher's gut. The agent doubled over with a wheeze and fell down.

"Dumbass," Eli said. "I'm tryna leave you here peacefully and you have to start your shit again. Let's try this one more time. You keep cool and I'll do the same."

Hatcher kept a steady stream of curses and dire promises of revenge going as Eli led him to the master bedroom, which turned out to be a spacious yet execrably appointed space. Had the man never watched a single interior-design show? He had a hunter-green futon sitting next to a turquoise armoire. He should spend an hour with the Property Brothers, for crying out loud; there was no reason for such barbarism. I hoped he had real furniture on order somewhere.

Eli got him lying down on his side on the futon—which Dhanya definitely would have set on fire—and then opened two sigils in front of his eyes in quick succession: a Sigil of Lethe River, which would erase the past hour from his memory, followed by a Sigil of Restful Sleep. Eli cut his zip ties once he'd nodded off.

"Well, at least it wasn't a complete waste of time," Eli said. "We don't have proof, but we know more than we did before."

I nodded, but there was still plenty we didn't know. Like where my hobgoblin was. I exited the room to go look for him. I heard some noises behind a door in the hallway and opened it to investigate. My hobgoblin was in there, perched on top of a glass display case and reaching into it.

[Buck, what are you doing? Let's go.]

The case was full of painted miniatures of the kind one uses in fantasy games like Dungeons & Dragons and Warmachine, and the desk in the room was clearly a hobbyist's work space. There was a spotlight lamp and a magnifying glass mounted on an extendable arm for detail work, a cup full of brushes, and little plastic bottles of acrylic paints. Buck was stuffing a canvas bag he'd found somewhere full of Hatcher's painted miniatures. "He was stealing Fae and doing science tae them. I want tae steal these and do magic tae them. It's only fair, right?"

[I'm too worried about Clíodhna to debate the morality of it with you. Congratulations on making a vaguely parallel argument. Did you find anything Fae in the house?]

"Naw. Just this wild shite here. He has a goblin army, can ye believe it? Painted their skin green and gave them these rubbish nonsense tattoos, the cheeky bastard! I'm gonnay have me a laugh with this and he'll be havin' a scream."

[Hurry up. We need to get in the taxi.]

"That's just wrong, that is. We should be getting in the van. The wizard van. Much as it pains me tae say it, I miss Nadia right now and wish she was here. Can we get a wizard van?"

I shook my head. [They draw too much attention, and I don't want any. That's why I try to look as boring as possible.]

"Except for yer mustache, eh, MacBharrais? That's well trimmed and memorable, like yer maw."

I left the doorway, and his cackling followed me. Eli was in the kitchen, wiping down Hatcher's gun to erase any fingerprints.

"I already got the doorknobs. You touch anything else?" he asked me.

I shook my head, and then he rifled through kitchen drawers until he found where Hatcher kept his sandwich bags. He put the gun inside one and then tossed it to me. "Hide that shit in your bigass coat and dump it at the station. With any luck, that's his service weapon and he'll get in trouble for losing it."

Hatcher was not going to enjoy waking up. We'd sent him to sleep with a broken nose, and he wouldn't remember who had socked him. Nor would he be able to explain the broken window he'd shot out, his missing gun, or the dead troll at the bottom of his swimming pool. Best of all—for us, anyway—Hatcher wouldn't remember that he'd been discovered and that he'd told us what he was doing and who was in on it.

Before we left, I peeked outside and turned on the pool lights to confirm that the troll's body was still in one piece. Normally the troll would have dissolved into a pile of ashes upon death, but apparently removing a Fae creature's vulnerability to iron also removed their convenient disposal. I worried briefly that we'd have to get rid of it, but then reasoned that Hatcher would have enough shady contacts to make sure it got taken care of.

"Gods below, MacBharrais," Buck said, appearing at my side and staring down into the pool. "He's uglier than a splash of bird-shite on yer sandwich, in't he?"

[Aye, but I'm sorry he had to come to such an end,] I told him. [I don't know what makes trolls happy in Tír na nÓg, but I have to think he would have been happier had he never met Hatcher and his crew.]

"That's true. The answer is screaming, by the way."

[What?]

"What makes trolls happy. Screaming in terror, anger, anything. They're happiest when others are upset."

[Sounds about right.]

We didn't talk on the taxi ride back to the station, except to answer Buck's questions about what he saw out the window. We tipped the driver well and then popped a Sigil of Lethe River in front of his eyes so he'd forget the last hour. He'd probably remember us getting in his cab originally, since that had been more than an hour ago, but he wouldn't remember where he took us, our field trip to Hatcher's backyard, or us emerging from the house via the front door later on with what looked suspiciously like a bag of loot in the hand of the small pink fellow.

Eli and I thought we'd have some time to talk at the station while waiting for the train back to Philadelphia, but it turned into a nightmare of trying to corral Buck: The hob had taken it into his head that the best way to spend a few idle minutes was to steal powdered donuts from the convenience store and then throw them at security guards, the pillowy soft thumps against their torsos leaving white impact strikes of confectioners' sugar.

"What the actual fuck, Al?" Eli growled at me. "Can't you control him?"

[Remember he blinded the troll and took Hatcher's gun away,] I said after I dumped the gun into a bin. Everyone was distracted by security officers rushing about, searching for whoever'd nailed them and then howled with mocking laughter, so no one was watching us. [You have to take the bad with the good.]

"No, I don't. You do. That little dude's gonna ruin your blood pressure, man."

Eli had a point. As sigil agents, we were supposed to first minimize what was revealed of the magical world, minimize what was recorded if the first couldn't be prevented, and then minimize what was remembered. My hobgoblin would have me struggling with all three.

CHAPTER 24

The Secret Lab

We got Buck onto the train and settled into a quad seat arrangement, with his bag of stolen miniatures on the fourth seat. He was tired after his shenanigans in the station and the fight with the troll, so he was quiet during the ride, examining Hatcher's paint jobs on the stolen miniatures, a great relief to Eli and me. We got out our phones and Signaled a conversation so no one could listen in.

Any thoughts on how to stop Clíodhna without getting our asses killed? Eli began.

We can't stop her, I replied. *Brighid won't intervene on a human's and hobgoblin's say-so.*

We'll never get solid proof, Al.

No, we won't. Checking her is going to be a next-level problem. All we can do for now is shut down things on this side.

Well, we kinda have, Eli said. *I mean, your apprentice shut it down by choking. He was the link.*

Aye. But why was he the link? Why did they come through Glasgow instead of here?

Because your boy Gordie was willing to use the sigils. There's no way a human's going to contain a pixie or a leprechaun or any of the Fae otherwise. And I'll add something else. He sent the first Signal and typed out another, his thumbs flying. *Coming through Glasgow was clever because the other sigil agents would assume you were on top of it. Even if we got alarms about Fae crossing over there, we wouldn't pursue it, because it was your territory.*

I nodded, mulling over the problem of the lab's location, then sent a Signal to Buck. He checked his phone when it buzzed and then looked over at me.

"I'm right bloody here, MacBharrais," he said.

I just chucked my chin at the message. It said, *That pixie you were trapped with: Did you ever get a chance to talk to her?*

Buck read it and responded, thankfully keeping his voice low. "Naw, Gordie had her knocked out the whole time. I just kept ma eyes closed once I figured out his sigil game and gave him pelters till he left me alone in that room."

Did he tell you anything about where you might be going? Any sense that you were staying in country or coming over to this one?

"I got the feeling I'd be staying nearby, but I don't know if I was right about that."

Eli said aloud to me, "All right, let's think this through," and then he began to type. I waited until the Signal pinged on my phone.

On the one hand, shipping the Fae across to the United States for science would make sense because Hatcher would want to be nearby to check on progress. But on the other, it's impractical when they have to come to this plane through Glasgow. Since we know Gordie was keeping them imprisoned with sigils, he'd probably need to accompany them if they were doing any lengthy travel. Did he ever leave the country while under your apprenticeship?

I just shook my head in reply, thinking he'd made a good point, and then I piggybacked on it. *They could shift using the network of bound trees, of course, but Hatcher wouldn't allow that until he could be sure he had control of them. Otherwise, they'd just take off to Tír na nÓg and not come back.*

Eli nodded. *Right. So they have to be doing their science in Scotland, or maybe England.*

Which means Buck and I will be catching the first flight back to find this lab. We'll just head to the airport from the train station. Thanks for your help, Eli.

Welcome. I'll monitor the plane-shifting around D.C. and see if I can catch them doing something. The troll might be taken care of, but we still have to find those other Fae.

The clurichaun might be providing clues if you look for them. Check for liquor heists in the D.C./Reston area. Especially near the river. They need a place for the undine to hang out.

"Oi, did I just see ye type *liquor heist,* MacBharrais?" Buck whispered. "Because I'm in. I wannay make Buck Foi's Best Boosted Spirits, like ye suggested. Let's get one of those motorcycles with a sidecar. We'll make it a wizard sidecar."

Too much attention, Buck. And those sidecars are rare enough that it makes them very easy to track down.

The hobgoblin blinked at me, uncomprehending. "Track how?"

When you buy a vehicle, it gets registered in your name, and the police use that to track them as necessary.

"Buy?" he scoffed. "We're not gonnay *buy* the sidecar, ya gormless bastard. We're gonnay steal that too."

I sighed in exasperation and Eli chuckled. "See? Told you your blood pressure was going to be a problem."

A Very Good Dug

I met the Druid who'd made sigil agents necessary just once, quite
by accident, some while ago. I was in Rome to consult the new
leader of the vampire underworld on how he might best avoid
confrontation with the world's pantheons, but it was twilight and
he hadn't risen for the evening yet, which left me some time to
myself. I chose to spend it enjoying a carafe of wine along with a
board of cheese, fruit, and miniature sandwiches at the Piazza
della Repubblica. The Caffè Piccarozzi had put out a few bistro
tables and canvas umbrellas that afforded an ideal view of the
Fountain of the Naiads, and so long as one was wary of pigeons
and assorted pickpockets who were preying on tourists, it was an
ideal place to relax and enjoy the charms of the city.

The charms were many, of course: It was Rome. Most of the
locals were loaded to the gills on espresso and in a hurry to get
somewhere, but in order to do so they had to negotiate a veritable
slalom course of slow-moving tourists who were craning their
necks around and gawking at the architecture, taking selfies and
completely oblivious that they might be hampering anyone.

I was chuckling at a near collision of tourists aiming cameras in different directions, when a man with a simply humongous hound—an Irish wolfhound, I believe—took the small table next to mine, and his dug sat right next to him without having to be told. We made brief eye contact as he sank into a seat, and I saw that he was a young man in his early twenties with wavy red hair. He seemed to be neither a tourist nor a local. I nodded politely at him and he returned it.

"Gorgeous dug," I said to him, on the off chance that he spoke English.

The hound's long tail immediately began to wag, and his tongue lolled out in a happy dug smile.

"Grazie," he replied, and reached for a menu wedged between the salt and pepper shakers. By then I would have turned my eyes away politely to afford him some privacy, except that the tattoos on his right arm were precisely like those of the Tuatha Dé Danann. He had the healing triskele on the back of his right hand and the band that continued up the forearm before wrapping around his biceps and disappearing underneath his shirtsleeve. Either I was sitting next to a god—which happened sometimes, since they sought me out—or I was sitting next to the legendary Iron Druid. A glance at the cold iron amulet hanging around his neck confirmed it.

"I beg your pardon," I said to him in English, "but your surname wouldnae be O'Sullivan, would it?"

Both he and the huge dug took more than a polite interest in me at that point, sizing me up, and I did the same to them. He had a sword strapped to his back, one of the shorter kinds, like an old Roman gladius. I guessed it was Fragarach, the Answerer, the sword of truth that could cut through any armor. Stealing that was supposedly what had landed him in trouble so many centuries ago.

He certainly didn't look two thousand years old, and a small ember of fury at that flared up inside me, for getting old is a terrible business, and I resented that he had somehow avoided those particular terrors.

"Who might be asking?" he replied, an American accent to his English.

"Al MacBharrais from Glasgow. I work for Brighid, First among the Fae."

He blinked and exchanged a glance with his dug, then leaned back in his chair. I wasn't sure if that meant he was relaxing or preparing to bolt out of his seat.

"Is that so? And what might you do for her?"

"A lot of what used to be your job. A lot of cleaning up after your bollocks, if ye don't mind me saying. I'm a sigil agent."

He regarded me evenly for a moment, then repeated, "A sigil agent. I've heard of them."

"Have ye, now?"

"I have. Don't be waving one around in my direction or I'll take it unkindly."

"Ach. Ye need have no worries on that score. Look, it's an honor to meet ye, sir. That's all I wanted tae say. I can leave ye alone."

"No, it's fine, Al. It's fine. I am simply wary of strangers. A bit paranoid, perhaps. I'm Atticus O'Sullivan, and this is my friend Oberon."

I chuckled. "Wariness is easy tae forgive. If you're even half as old as I've heard, I imagine those eyes have seen some shite."

"Indeed they have. I bet you've seen your fair share if you work for Brighid."

"I have," I admitted. "Not as much as Gladys, my receptionist, but a fair bit."

"Your receptionist?"

"She's Canadian," I explained.

The Druid's eyes shifted sideways to his hound, and he grunted in amusement.

"Oberon likes your mustache. He thinks I should grow one just like it."

I'd heard that Druids could speak with animals, but to have it confirmed like that was wondrous. The hound's behavior up to that point made much more sense; he could understand everything we said.

"Thank ye kindly, Oberon," I said. "Ye have some fine fur un-

derneath yer nose as well. Have ye ever asked Atticus tae wax it for
ye?"

"He says no," Atticus relayed after a pause. "He appreciates the
small but vital role of a mustache as a flavor saver, and would miss
licking his chops and reliving the savory deliciousness of sausages."

"An excellent point! I had not thought of that."

A server came over and asked the Druid what he might like to
drink, and the old man—I had to remind myself that he was im-
possibly old—peered at me. "If you don't have anything pressing,
Al, would you like to join us for dinner?"

"I'd be delighted." I was supposed to meet someone soon, but
he can wait."

Atticus ordered us a bottle of very fine wine and, after the server
had poured for each of us, raised a glass to me.

"It's refreshing to be with someone who knows what I am but
doesn't want to kill me or want any favors. It's rare, in fact. I'm
glad this chance encounter occurred." He stopped, considering. "It
is chance, isn't it?"

"Oh, aye. A happy coincidence that may not be so coincidental,
since there's this new vampire in charge. Ye may have heard."

Atticus nodded and Oberon snorted. "Leif Helgarson. Is that
who you're supposed to meet?"

"Aye."

"Be careful. He'll follow the letter, not the spirit, of the law, so
you must craft your contract precisely."

"Is he no tae be trusted?"

"He will try to take advantage of you and interpret the law as it
suits him. But he will also hold to his word, once given."

"Like the Fae, then."

"Aye, like the Fae."

We passed the most amiable evening together, talking about remarkable meals we'd had elsewhere even as we enjoyed another
one. Atticus paid frequent attention to his hound and bought him
a full dinner, so it was clear that they were genuine friends, not a
pet and a pet owner.

As the evening progressed, I slowly realized that dug was his lifeline. My gods, think of it: two thousand years! What could possibly anchor him to this world when everyone he'd ever known and loved had died, when he must be the loneliest man on the planet? I ask myself sometimes, at the relatively young age of sixty-three, why I yet remain, since my son hates me and my wife has gone on before, as have an alarming number of the fellows with whom I grew up. How much worse must it be for him? And how can he possibly bear it?

The answer sat before me, wagging his tail: He survived because of a very good dug named Oberon. Dugs are beings of pure love and devotion and broadcast hope to those of us who have only memories of such things, for they demonstrate by their existence that love and devotion still walk abroad in the world, and therefore it's worthwhile to live in it.

I gave him my card at the end of the evening, but I never heard from the Iron Druid afterward. That night of relaxation was the eye of a storm for him, a wee soft place and time in the chaos of his life. I'm fairly certain he was right back in a giant vat of shite just a few hours later.

Coriander tells me that life is very different for him these days, but better in all the ways that matter. He passed through the crucible of Ragnarok and did not escape unscathed, but he's finally free, no longer a fugitive from the gods, and he now has two very good dugs with him, wherever he is.

Would a dug come to hate me, I wondered, if I got one and the curse on my heid decided I had told him too many times what a good boy he was? Can a dug come to hate a man who loves him?

I didn't want to find out.

CHAPTER 25

Threats and Biscuits

Buck willingly accepted a sleeping sigil for the flight back across the Atlantic. Not only was he exhausted, but he didn't want to be conscious of being surrounded by so much steel. I took advantage of the peace to read the book I'd borrowed from the library but got upset about how people were manipulated into lives of forced labor. Upon landing, my cell phone pinged with voicemail messages. Nothing from Eli, however: They were from Nadia and D.I. Munro.

The D.I. did not apologize for planting a bug on me earlier, which I only realized I wanted to hear when I felt disappointed. But she had some relatively welcome news after her greeting.

"My colleagues in the National Human Trafficking Unit tell me that the names you provided are indeed likely involved in trafficking, based on their financial information, and they're grateful for the tip. However, they haven't found their victims yet but are relatively certain the suspects are communicating to them via phone. It will take some time to arrange surveillance, and they wondered if you might have any information on the victims' whereabouts. I wonder how you knew about these men when NHTU did not. Let me know."

I'd give her a call after I got out of the airport and pass along the addresses I had kept in reserve. Nadia's voicemail was a bit more urgent, however.

"Al, call me back as soon as ye get this. Someone named Clíodhna of the Tuatha Dé Danann wishes tae meet."

"Shhhhhite," I whispered, but it was audible.

"Wot?" Buck said, who was nearly dancing on his seat in his eagerness to deplane.

I typed my response. [Clíodhna wants a meeting.]

The hobgoblin's eyes nearly started from their spheres. "Is she waiting outside for me? She wants tae kill me, ye know."

[I do know. But, naw, you will not be meeting her.]

"But I'm tae be the topic of discussion, in't I? What are ye gonnay tell her when she demands ye give me up?"

[I will tell her you're under contract.]

"She's gonnay use some leverage, then. She'll offer ye gold first. Then she'll threaten yer friends and family tae get her way. It's what they do."

It certainly was. I thought of Durf the ogre, who'd flung himself at Nadia because someone had held his family hostage.

[I am not without leverage myself. But let's discuss this later.] I added that last bit because people on the plane were starting to turn around and stare at us. Buck continued his nervous dancing on the seat but kept his mouth shut. He knew he couldn't just pop out of there without causing serious alarm and we didn't want that, so he had to wait like all the humans.

There is something about getting off a plane that brings out the worst in everyone. Violations of personal space and nudging, utter rudeness and lack of courtesy that sometimes leads to snappish behavior. But since I learned to think of it as arising from a dire need to go to the bathroom, it's all made sense, and I can empathize and feel compassion for people rather than be annoyed with them when they get too close and huff and whine and so on. I recalled more than a few times in my life when I did not consider the needs of others when I had a dire need not to soil myself, and remembering those times in airports or in traffic has enabled me to entirely eliminate road rage from my life. Whenever someone shoulders past me or cuts me off, I feel like rooting for them instead of getting angry, and I hope they're able to make it to the toilet before disaster strikes. I cheer for the steadfastness of their sphincters and wish them long life and clean underwear. People think I am patient, but not really; I just get it. We are ruled by our bladders and bowels.

There was no one waiting for us when we got off the plane, and Buck relaxed a tiny bit at that, but then he was anxious to return home to the protection of my wards.

I texted the addresses of the trafficking victims to D.I. Munro and linked each to their respective pimps, reminding her that the victims required help and counseling, not an arrest record, and if all went well in that regard, with the traffickers rather than the trafficked getting a dose of justice, I might be able to help further in the future.

I didn't reply to Nadia until I had Buck safe at home, where nothing Fae could get to him.

Back in Scotland. Heading to Gin71, I Signaled her. *Initiating contact there. That's where to begin your search if I disappear.*

If ye disappear? Is that a thing that could happen, Al?

The Queen of the Bean Sídhe has been up to some naughty shite, and she knows that I know. If I disappear and you want a true challenge of your abilities, try to avenge me.

Ye'd better not die, by Lhurnog.

Sacrifice a bit of whisky to him for me?

Done.

I switched to text-to-speech for Buck. [While I'm gone to meet Clíodhna, it wouldn't surprise me if she sent another attack at you.]

"Aye, MacBharrais. I'll stay here."

[But it might not be Fae coming after you this time. She has the ability to contract with other parties.]

"What other parties?"

[You name it, she can probably find a way to hire them to kill you. It could be a human with a gun. It could be a demon with a five-foot-long spiked tongue.]

"Oh, aye, that's about as cheerful as a pair of bollocks on a biscuit. Thanks, MacBharrais."

[Don't answer the door.]

"I won't."

[I mean don't ask *Who's there?* or have the telly on. No sound to let them know ye're here.]

"What? I cannae watch telly? What am I supposed tae do, then?"

[Read.]

"For fun? Oh, I've heard of that." He waggled a finger at me and grinned knowingly. "That's kinky, that is. What ye got?"

I gave him my copy of the *The Wee Free Men* by Terry Pratchett and hoped he would enjoy it. Then I exited, waited to hear him lock the door behind me, and headed to Gin71.

Harrowbean smiled at me when I entered and made a small jerk of her head to her right. I followed her direction and saw a human male sitting at the bar, his mouth open and just staring at her, besotted.

"He'd rob a bank for me if I told him I needed a few pounds," she said.

"Too right I would," the man said.

"Good tae see ye, Al," she said. "Go ahead and have a seat and I'll come get yer order."

I nodded and picked a table far away from the bar. Since the man entranced with her would be paying attention to her every move, she wanted to make sure she could speak to me out of earshot, and I appreciated the quick thinking.

She came over and I explained what I needed via text-to-speech, which I didn't play out loud but simply held in front of her so she could read it:

Clíodhna has requested a meeting through my office. Please tell

*her she is awaited here now and escort her if she wishes. Separately—
perhaps first—inform Coriander and ask him to bear witness so
that Clíodhna doesn't consider violence.*

Harrowbean nodded but then looked back at the man sitting at
the bar, whose gaze was firmly affixed to her buttocks. If she exited
the building and took the Old Way in Virginia Court to Tír na
nÓg, he'd watch every step until she disappeared, and we couldn't
have that.

[Go,] I texted. [I'll take care of him.]

She exited, and I walked up to the man and held my official ID
in front of his eyes, which were still following Harrowbean until I
interrupted. If he wanted to obsess over faeries, I'd help him out
with that. "Go home and memorize the full text of *A Midsummer
Night's Dream*. You've always wanted to. Never come back here.
Maybe do a three-day juice cleanse."

"Great idea," he said, and he promptly fell off his stool in his
haste to leave. But he left out the side door without looking at Harrowbean, so that's all I needed. I'd settle up his bill later.

It took ten minutes for Harrowbean to return, and when she
did, she looked relieved that the man was gone.

[Bill me for his,] I said via text, and a couple of minutes later she
came back with my customary Pilgrim's and Coriander's favorite
as well. The herald himself joined me in my booth less than a minute later.

"Sláinte," he said, and we drank. "What news? I imagine we
have little time."

[The Fae that Clíodhna has trafficked here are being altered to
remove their vulnerability to iron. They're being controlled by a
man in the United States named Simon Hatcher. He confirmed that
Clíodhna is behind it, through he's only dealt with bean sídhe go-
betweens. But that's two witnesses naming her in this scheme.]

"Brighid will not be pleased to hear of Fae immune to iron.
How are they doing this?"

[We don't know that, or where they're doing it, though we suspect it's somewhere here or in England, since Gordie would have

needed to control them until it was done. The American lacks imagination, so he is using them to attack Russian targets. We killed the troll in Virginia, but there's still a leprechaun, clurichaun, fir darrig, undine, and pixie altered in the same way.]

Coriander opened his mouth to reply but I shook my head, forestalling him, for Clíodhna had stepped into Virginia Court via the Old Way and was approaching the entrance to Gin71.

I had never met her before, but I knew when she appeared in the court that she couldn't be anyone else. Goddesses do have a tendency to look divine. Plus, in the same way that Harrowbean and Coriander wore clothes more befitting the Victorian era than the modern one, she wore a waistcoat over a long-sleeved shirt with a grey string tie underneath her high collar. The waistcoat was white with a paisley pattern sewn in silver thread that caught the light and winked and shimmered as she moved, and I saw hints that the back was entirely silver. She wore trousers white enough to strike me snow blind, and her high-heeled boots were similarly white and spotless. She looked like she belonged on a runway in Milan, from the black hair artfully arranged to the smoky edges around her glittering dark eyes, including the haughty expression and arched eyebrows. She had three silver rings piercing her right one.

Upon her entrance, she caught the eyes of Harrowbean and nodded once in greeting. The bartender nodded back and pointed to our booth, and that's when Clíodhna turned her head and saw us. Her expression was carefully neutral as we rose to greet her, but it lingered on Coriander. Clearly she had not expected him to be there.

She took several elegant steps in our direction and spoke English with a pleasant Irish lilt. "Mr. MacBharrais, I presume? And Coriander, Herald Extraordinary. What a surprise."

We both bowed and welcomed her and invited her to join us.

"I was under the impression I would be speaking with Mr. MacBharrais in private," she said. "I have some words for his ears alone."

Coriander reached back to the table for his drink and drained it, gorgeously. If it had been filmed and broadcast, it would have sold any clear liquid at premium prices. Water, vodka, turpentine—it didn't matter. Watching him made one both thirsty and feel sated. When he finished, he set down his glass before speaking.

"Very well. But be aware that I will check on Mr. MacBharrais afterward. Brighid wishes him to remain in good health and under no threats, however veiled. And the same goes for his hobgoblin. I gently, respectfully suggest you allow him to speak candidly to you and that you speak candidly in return and think carefully before you act. I doubt you would wish to have a similarly candid conversation with Brighid in front of the Fae Court."

"A conversation regarding what, exactly?"

"Regarding contact with the American Simon Hatcher. The corruption of Gordon Graham. The unauthorized distribution of ink recipes and sigils. And attempts to grant the Fae immunity to iron." She began to respond, but Coriander held up a hand. "Best not reply. I will ask you to tell me three times, and a refusal to speak truth at this juncture could prove disastrous."

Clíodhna confined herself to a tight-lipped grin. "You are considerate for speaking so frankly, Herald. I wish you a good day."

He bowed again and took his leave. The Queen of the Bean Sídhe watched him disappear into Tír na nÓg before sitting down with me.

"It would appear we have much to discuss," she said as she slid into the booth. "Starting with that ambush. I did not expect to arrive here and be accused of such things."

"I did not expect you to be behind this either. In case this goes on for a while, I will need to use an application on my phone to speak, because of a curse laid on my heid years ago." In truth I didn't need to worry about it triggering on a first meeting, but I did welcome the excuse to slow down and speak precisely.

"Ah, yes. I heard you were cursed. Having just experienced the way you greet people, it's little wonder."

I switched to my phone. [Did you have anything to do with the curse laid on my head, or do you have any idea or knowledge of who may have done it?] One had to phrase questions carefully to the Tuatha Dé Danann, since they would seize upon any loophole to avoid answering. But in this case, the reply was unequivocal.

"No. I bear no responsibility for your curse and know nothing of who may have put it there, not even a rumor. I tell you three times. Should you wish to discuss earning additional curses in the future, we can do that."

Harrowbean arrived to ask Clíodhna if she'd like anything to drink, and while the faery consulted with the goddess over which flavor profiles she might enjoy, I took the time to compose my next words. When the bartender departed with an order, I pressed PLAY.

[Why did you cook up this scheme to render the Fae immune to iron?]

Clíodhna snorted. "I hardly cooked up anything." That was the sort of response I expected: A typical dodge was to seize upon a couple of words and dispute them rather than the spirit of the question. It was a marked contrast to the flat denial and oath of truth in response to my question about curses. She leaned forward the tiniest bit. "Let's backtrack, because I've missed quite a few miles of road if this is where we're at. Why do you think I'm responsible for the host of crimes of which Coriander accused me?"

She leaned back in her seat after that and took in the room, which was largely empty apart from a couple of tables. The evening rush was still hours away. Harrowbean returned with her drink and Clíodhna smiled graciously at her, but the smile disappeared as she turned her gaze back to me and raised her glass sardonically before taking a sip.

[It began with a hobgoblin named Gag Badhump, who said you offered him a fraudulent contract for service to be signed and sealed by me.]

"Pssh. Nobody trusts hobgoblins, for good reason."

[The reason is they're incorrigible thieves. They are not very skilled at lying or knowing when they're being lied to. But that's not all I have. Simon Hatcher named you under a Sigil of Reckoning Truth, witnessed by both myself and another sigil agent. Why would an American ever pull the name of Clíodhna out of his arse unless it was a fact? He was raised in an education system that doesn't cover the Fae at all except for Shakespeare's Oberon and Titania.]

The goddess shrugged. "Ye can't trust Americans either. Look at this planet we're on. Look at it! Cocked up beyond all recognition. Americans did that. I hear it's because they're all on drugs, ye know, and about a third of them are afraid of melanin."

I sighed in exasperation. Another non-answer. [Hatcher received a written ink recipe from a banshee, which he gave to my apprentice, and that—indeed, this entire scheme of trafficking Fae—would not have happened without your instruction.]

"I don't know this entire scheme you speak of. And I'm not responsible for everything the bean sídhe do."

Ah, yes, the standard god dodge: I'm not responsible for my minions. [We can find out from the bean sídhe exactly what you were responsible for.]

That elicited a wry grin. "I'm certain you'll not find a single bean sídhe who will corroborate your wild theories, Mr. MacBharrais. And neither will Brighid. Since you have absolutely no proof that I have done anything wrong and won't be able to find any, I strongly yet respectfully suggest you cease making accusations."

I'd been waiting for her to say something along those lines. There was, in the end, absolutely nothing meaningful I could do against a goddess. If she felt threatened enough, she could easily kill me and make sure my body was never found. It would be inconvenient for her but not a serious challenge. My path to victory lay in pointing out a convenient alternative.

[I could do that, sure. Except that hobgoblin is now in my service and someone keeps trying to kill him. First with barghests and then with an ogre named Durf. If there is no proof of wrongdoing to be found, as you say, then my hobgoblin should be able to live without fear, don't you think?]

"Ha!" Cupping her goblet of gin in one hand, she idly twirled the ice around in it as she cocked her head at me, thinking something through. I waited patiently until she made a decision, drained the glass, and then set it down, clapping her hands together once and rubbing them together. "So!" she said. "Let me see if I understand. I'm speaking entirely in hypotheticals, now."

I nodded and encouraged her to continue.

"If the person who did all these things you've been talking about—trafficking Fae, sharing secret ink recipes, and so on—were to simply stop doing them and cease trying to kill a thieving hobgoblin, then you would, what? Stop looking into the matter? Withdraw your accusations?"

[In broad terms, yes. This hypothetical person has Brighid's attention, you see. The First among the Fae is aware of the investigation and is quite curious to know whether she will need to get involved. She would most likely react poorly to the Fae becoming immune to iron.]

"Ye really think so?" Clíodhna said with her brows knitted together, but then she exploded with laughter. "Of course she would. It threatens a primary lever of control." She wound down then and traced her finger around the rim of her now-empty glass. "Hypothetically, then, a strategic withdrawal would be best."

[Agreed. No one loses face. The hypothetical mastermind becomes aware they have placed a toe over the line and prudently steps back behind it before anything truly unpleasant occurs. And my hobgoblin, instructed by me to remain silent on the matter, will be able to serve me on earth and in all the Fae planes without looking over his shoulder.]

The Queen of the Bean Sídhe nodded. "Ye know what, Mr. MacBharrais? I feel very strongly that everything will happen just as ye said. This hypothetical person will step back from this Fae-trafficking business and your hobgoblin will be safe."

[Hypothetically safe?]

"Really, truly safe. So long as this hypothetical person is also not threatened. As I said, I feel it will happen and that is a truth. I tell ye three times. That is the best I can do."

[Then I feel it shall happen also.] That right there was victory.

At least a partial one, and I felt proud because I'd managed to talk a goddess out of doing harm to my hobgoblin. But I couldn't seem smug about it or she'd slay me for being insolent.

"Good. Then I will take my leave and remember your kindness for the drink. I will remember everything else too, of course. That is not a threat, ye understand: It is simply a fact. I have captured Brighid's attention for many years to come because of your efforts. And so you have captured mine."

She rose from the table and I hurriedly typed out another question.

[What about Hatcher and the Fae he's corrupted?]

"I thought we established that I had nothing to do with that?" She chuckled at what must have been evident dismay on my face. "Come, Mr. MacBharrais, there are only so many problems ye can solve over a single drink. I mean, well done, lad, ye pulled on a thread and unraveled a good lot, and ye're wise enough to have a chat with me before doing something unforgivable. That alone sets ye apart from most humans. Ye have my respect, and I imagine ye play a mean game of chess. But the rest of this ye will have to confront outside the confines of a gin bar. And someday, Tír na nÓg will have to confront the fact that the Fae don't have to live in fear of iron if they don't want to." She raised a hand and waggled it goodbye at me. "Slán agat."

Something clicked into place for me—not a puzzle piece so much as a raw dose of empathy, a recognition that, in at least one sense, Clíodhna and I might be exactly the same.

"Is all this because—" I said aloud, then realized that I'd forgotten to use my app. And perhaps forgotten my good sense. It wasn't necessary to pursue this.

Except I wanted to know.

"Because what?" Clíodhna said.

I looked around at the bar and rose from the booth. There was Harrowbean, of course, and some cooks in the kitchen, and a couple of other patrons. But what I had to say was for Clíodhna's ears alone. She would never answer me where others could hear.

I gestured to the empty cobblestones of Virginia Court. "May I ask ye one more question, in private?"

She cocked her head, considering, then nodded once and preceded me out the door. She moved to the side as I came out beside her and waited for the door to close.

"What is it?" She crossed her arms and stared straight ahead at the wall of a building across the court. I adopted the same pose. It was not going to be a conversation for eye contact. It would be safer that way, and somehow we both knew it.

"My wife passed some years ago in a motor accident," I said. "And not a single day since that time has been so fine as the worst day when she was alive and with me. I have thought on more than one occasion that if there was some way I could bring her back, no matter how insane the trial tae make it happen, no matter how long it would take to get it done, I would do it. I would walk into Hades like Orpheus did to bring back Eurydice. I have that will inside ma breast. Because I swear tae ye the light of her smile warmed me more than the sun ever did. Even the memory of it is proof against the cold. And so I wonder, Clíodhna."

"Yes?"

"Hypothetically: Do ye think someone wants the Fae tae be proof against iron because they yearn for the old days? I mean the days of the Bronze Age, when iron held no sway and the Tuatha Dé Danann roamed the earth with the Fae as freely as humans do? And they're thinking, *If I can make the Fae immune to iron, then it will be like turning back the clock. It will be like reversing the worst thing that's ever happened in the world.* Because I would understand that. I want tae reverse the worst thing in the world too."

Clíodhna did not answer right away. In fact, she sighed to communicate that she'd be thinking over her answer a bit. I was patient. A couple walked through the court, and another, passing through on their way to somewhere else.

"I suppose ye might have a keen insight into the heart of the matter, if not the mind," she finally said. "Hypothetically."

"How so?"

"The old days are often mourned. We were freer then. The air was fresher, the grass greener, all of that. Ye have the right of it in that there's not a faery around who wouldn't wish to return things to that time. But we all know that we can't go back. Fand proved that when she had her rebellion against Brighid. The only direction we can move is forward."

"So they thought that trafficking was moving forward?"

"Immunity to iron is moving forward."

"But those Fae have hurt people. Killed people. They're in unforgivable territory as regards the treaty."

"Ah, here's where your empathy fails ye, sir. I was alive when there were just a few million people on the whole planet. How many are there now, five billion?"

"Approaching eight."

"Are ye, now! Well. If I truly wanted to return to the old days, I'd be slaying billions of humans, wouldn't I? Ye don't see anybody doing that. But I also don't give a slick selkie shite if a few humans exit early. The whole lot of you are poisonous—with the notable exception, perhaps, of your departed wife."

"That's kind of ye tae say," I said, though I wasn't actually sure it was.

"Well. I don't know about kindness. But I know I haven't spoken so much to a mortal in many a year. Can't say it was pleasant, but it was, at least, interesting. Farewell."

I nodded at her in farewell, and she retraced her steps to Tír na nÓg via the Old Way.

"Bollocks," I muttered. The secret lab was still secret. Where was it hiding, and who in all the hells had figured out how to grant the Fae immunity to iron?

"May I get ye anything else, Al?" Harrowbean said as I returned to my table inside.

[One more, thanks, plus a bar napkin and the bill. Remember to include that arsehole's tab on mine.]

"Coming right up, sir. And I appreciate ye getting rid of him."

I drew out my pen for doodling and fidgeted until Harrowbean returned. I settled the tab with her, took a swallow of my drink, and then wrote a list to help me think.

Corrupted Fae
  1. ~~Troll~~
  2. *Clurichaun*
  3. *Leprechaun*
  4. *Fir Darrig*
  5. *Undine*
  6. *Pixie*

The troll, thank the gods, was no longer an issue. But since Eli hadn't chimed in with any intelligence, he obviously hadn't found any leads yet. I'd have to generate my own. This problem of the corrupted Fae was mine to solve.

The undine was the strangest one on the list, to my way of thinking: What had they offered her that was more enticing than the waters she typically inhabited? Or had they threatened her instead?

I stared at the list until my eyes glazed over. I tried to shake my thoughts loose from the meaningless circle in which they were trapped by bringing the gin to my nose and inhaling the botanicals. Some people loathe gin and proclaim that they only smell medicine and rubbing alcohol, and while I never say anything because one's preferences are of course their own, I privately think they shouldn't have tried drinking shite gin. The Scots have discovered that gins, like whiskies, have some glorious tales to tell to the nose and tongue, if one is only open to exploring them. For me, I find their various scents invigorating, and it resets my mind somehow: I become open to possibility. I could also achieve the same state through meditation, but a nose full of a master distiller's craft had proven to be a shortcut for me.

I took a couple of deep breaths with my eyes closed, no tasting at all, and I realized that I'd forgotten a crucial fact. My eyes flew open, I set down the glass, and I circled number six on the list.

I checked the time: almost four in the afternoon. I Signaled Nadia.

Are ye free to kick some arse tonight? I need the battle seer.

How late? I was gonnay watch a movie with Dhanya.

Can ye reschedule? I need the van. Whisky and cheese for Lhurnog. The whole shebang.

You're gonnay pray to Lhurnog with me?

Aye. I'm thinking this will be a pretty good rammy.

Hell yes! I'll cancel the movie now, then.

I'll be at the office in about an hour.

She acknowledged that and I switched to Signaling Buck.

All clear, wee man. Safe to go outside. Get your arse back to Maryhill, where we first met. I need you to steal something for me.

That is the most beautiful message I have ever received, he replied. With that in motion, I downed the rest of my drink and motioned to Harrowbean once I stood.

[I need a good dug to wait in my office for a new contract,] I said. [I should be there in an hour or less.]

"I'll arrange it, Al."

I tipped my hat to her and hoped I'd get to see her again. If I actually found this lab it would be one thing. Taking it down would be another.

———————— • ————————

CHAPTER 26

Get in the Van, Pour the Whisky, Melt the Cheese

It was simple for Buck to pop into Gordie's apartment and remove the pixie cage I'd left behind. I was careful not to enter the building or get near it, really, since I didn't have my derby hat on and had no wish to be caught on camera entering the premises. We took the train from there back to my office, where a Fae packmaster waited with a barghest for hire. He was sitting across the whisky table from Nadia, who was playing hostess in my absence.

Buck hung back a little bit, not precisely comfortable around a barghest after the attack we'd suffered. I felt that too, but using one here was our best chance at finding the lab. I was betting that the lab also served as living quarters for these Fae now, since we'd heard no reports of them renting a flat in Edinburgh or anywhere else.

[We'll need your GPS tracker,] I told Nadia. The barghest would track the pixie for us, and provided it stayed in-country, we'd track the barghest from the van. If it the pixie was in Scotland or the north of England, we wouldn't even need a second tank of petrol.

While Nadia left to fetch the device, I wrote up the contract and paid the packmaster with a writ for an hour of agency services to be provided later. Bartering services in this manner was much easier than trying to figure out a form of legal tender between the planes and far safer than trading nebulous favors.

[Please explain to the barghest that this is a seek mission only. He'll have to carry a GPS tracker and remain corporeal as much as possible so we don't lose the signal. Halt within a hundred meters of the target and wait for us to arrive to fulfill the contract.]

The packmaster, a solemn faery with kind brown eyes, knelt next to the barghest and murmured to him in Old Irish. Nadia came back and he took the tracker and affixed it to a collar, which he then looped around the barghest's neck. Then he presented the pixie's cage for a target scent, and the ghost hound snuffled and whuffed at it, absorbing the smells. When he finished, he looked up at the faery and said something that sounded remarkably like, "Roof."

"He's ready," the packmaster said. "Would you like him to begin now?"

[Maybe not quite yet. Does he have an idea of which direction we're headed?]

The faery asked the hound something in Old Irish and the hound spun around a few times with his nose in the air, then sat down again. "Ohwhuff," he said.

"He says north."

[So we'll be staying in Scotland, then.]

"Aye. He can't track across oceans."

[Let's wait a half hour. I have preparations to make.]

The packmaster explained this to the hound, who lay down on the carpet, content to stay. I asked if it was okay to give him a roast, and the packmaster said that would be fine. He left as I tossed the meat into the barghest's jaws.

[I need to get some sigils ready for this,] I told Nadia. [And I should warn you that the Sigil of Iron Gall on your razor is not going to work on the Fae we'll be fighting. These are immune to iron and stronger than usual.]

"Fae immune to iron? I didnae know that was possible."

[Neither did I. You might wish to choose a weapon that's more immediately fatal.]

"The idea here is to be fatal?"

I nodded grimly. [These Fae have killed humans directly on this plane. That violates our treaty, and the punishment is capital.]

"I'll go home and get ma sword, then."

She left and Buck asked, "Awright if I go home quickly to grab a couple things too?"

[Like what?]

Buck flashed his perfect teeth at me. "I have a clever plan."

[Be back in thirty minutes or less. And bring my derby hat.]

He disappeared, and I went to my desk to press the stud that opened my ink library. I locked the office door and took off my topcoat, going through the many interior pockets and removing all the sigils I wouldn't be needing—sigils for contracts and the like. I had a couple of different sets, or loadouts, that I used when I knew I was walking into a certain kind of situation. This one called for some especially destructive sigils that I rarely used. One of them, the Sigil of Unchained Destruction, I had never used at all except when I achieved my own mastery. It was the last sigil an apprentice learned before mastery, and I unleashed it to prove I could do it, and then, of course, never managed to get one of my own apprentices to mastery. The one I had prepared had sat under seal for a good forty years. I wasn't even sure it would work anymore. Its potency might have faded after so long, like batteries left unused in a torch for years. I hoped I'd have no cause to find out.

Just as I finished my preparations, my phone buzzed. It was D.I. Munro.

"Mr. MacBharrais, I hope you're still at work? You haven't left for the day?"

"Aye."

"Good. Because I'm in your lobby. I'll be right up." She disconnected and I swore, fetching an ink bottle full of a navy-blue mixture that I'd need to replenish soon. I drew three quick sigils and sealed them, but it wasn't quick enough: D.I. Munro was mashing the office doorbell before I could finish. No matter; the door was locked, and she'd just have to wait until I was ready. Whatever she was here for was probably not good at all. Surprise visits by the police are never polite social occasions. She probably had backup if she had it in mind to arrest me for something, so that was why I prepared extra sigils.

There was no use calling to her that I'd be right there, because the office was soundproofed. She'd have to wait and get angry. And I'd have to figure out why she was here.

As I walked out of the library with my fresh sigils and shrugged on my coat, I spied the pixie's cage and the barghest sitting by the whisky table and realized I'd have difficulty explaining either or both to the detective inspector.

"Come on, pooch," I said, snatching up the cage and returning to the library. "Come on. Wait in here for a wee while, please? In here."

Barghests are smarter than any earthly hound. They might not understand my English the way they understood Old Irish, but they understood body language and intonation well enough. Since they were under contract and knew it—and I was also someone who occasionally produced a roast—I was temporarily someone to be obeyed. The huge hound shuffled into the library and sat where I asked, and I thanked him. I set the cage down on my worktable and hurried to my desk to close up the bookcase. Only when it was fully closed and I had typed up a text-to-speech welcome did I open the door and welcome D.I. Munro into my office, pressing PLAY on my app.

[Apologies. I was finishing up a very important email before the end of the business day.]

Two constables walked in behind her, as I'd feared. This was not the friendly fishing expedition in the coffee shop.

"How important can anything in this business really be, Mr. MacBharrais? Yer business is putting ink on paper. That's it."

[That is indeed it.]

Her eyes roamed the office, not looking at me at all. "Perhaps ye were up tae something other than an email. I'd be willing to bet ye were."

[How can I help, D.I. Munro? Are you here to tell me the trafficking victims have been rescued?]

"No. I mean yes, they have been rescued. The boys in Trafficking caught them as they were waking up for the night and most of them agreed tae give up their pimps, so la di da, thank ye very much, they won't be on the streets tonight and NHTU is very happy with ye now. But I am not."

She hadn't stopped looking around, even moving behind my desk and pulling out the chair to peer underneath it. But once that was done, she looked up at me with a scowl, and I tried my best to look concerned. I raised my eyebrows in consternation and typed, [Oh, dear,] just to make her explain. Though I suspected I already knew what she was looking for.

"Did ye know, Mr. MacBharrais, that inside that completely fucked room of Gordon Graham, your late employee, there was a smelly aluminium cage?"

[I didn't. I recall telling you and D.I. Macleod I was never there.]

"Right. Never there. Except I think ye were. I remember seeing ye there. And I remember thinking before I saw ye that room had a lot of jars full of shite the boys in the lab would get excited about. But I didn't see that cage for some reason. And in Gordon's bedroom, there were a lot of personal effects and a laptop I was going to investigate later. Then there's this strange gap in my memory, but I'm still sure I saw ye along with a wee pink man in that apartment. And after that time, well, ye know what I found in those rooms? That smelly cage that I hadn't seen before, but a whole lot else that went missing, including Gordon's laptop and all those jars and pots and that. Still, I couldn't place ye there for sure. Something was wrong with the cameras in the building, which was also strange. So damn strange I took precautions. I put a tracer inside that stinky cage, and what do ye know? It just reported that it's here. So where is it?"

Bloody hell, she was good. A good sight better at the business than Macleod. [It's not here. You just looked yourself.]

"Maybe ye have it in the shop, then. Where's it hiding? Because we know it's in the building."

[May I explain? It will require me to take a piece of paper out of my coat, but I will do it slowly. I promise I am not armed.]

She told one of her constables to get behind me, and he got out his baton just in case I was lying. I pulled out my official ID and showed it to her and she blinked, taken in by the three sigils there. I took the time to show it to the constables too, and once they were all open to suggestion, I gave them the prepared sigils I'd just made and said aloud, "I want you to break the seals on these cards and look at the sigil inside, then hand the cards back to me."

Under the sway of Certain Authority, they obeyed this command, exposed their minds to the Sigil of Lethe River, and promptly forgot the last hour, including the fact that I had just spoken aloud. I didn't like using Lethe River because it might cause someone to forget something vital to their own survival, but it was a stone cold fact that if I had used it in Gordie's flat on the day he died I could have avoided all this trouble with D.I. Munro. Easy to say in hindsight, but it didn't matter; I hadn't taken any Lethe River sigils with me that day.

In this situation, an hour's lost memory meant that the polis forgot why they had come to my office in the first place. And they were still under the influence of Porous Mind and vulnerable to further suggestion, so I took the cards back and put them in my pocket, along with my official ID. I smiled at them and returned to typing on my app.

[Thanks so much for coming by. I'll be writing a check to the Scottish Police Benevolent Fund straightaway.]

D.I. Munro squeezed her eyes shut and shook her head. "What? I beg your pardon, but . . . I believe I've had an episode of some kind. How did I get here?"

[In the company of these two constables. I imagine you have a car waiting outside.]

"Yes, but . . . why am I here?"

[You came to inform me that the sex-trafficking victims decided to cooperate against their pimps and that they will receive such aid as necessary to rebuild their lives.]

"I did? That doesn't make sense. I could have just called. And I wouldn't have needed constables to come along for that."

[No doubt you were on your way elsewhere and just stopped by. But it was a pleasure to see you, D.I. Munro. I hope I can assist the police again in the future.]

"Right. Well." She stood there, blinking and trying to recall anything, but those connections were gone. Not knowing how else to proceed, she said, "Good day," and exited with the constables. I locked the office door behind them and Signaled Buck.

Are you quite finished? I need you back here.

On my way, old man, he replied after a few seconds. He knocked on the door only seconds after that, and I let him in. He had that bag from Hatcher's house with him, along with my hat, and he was sweating and breathing hard.

"Bit worn out from popping so far and so fast," he said. "Do ye have anything nourishing, like chocolate-covered marshmallows?"

[No, those aren't healthy.]

"Naw, but they're important."

[Okay, I'll get you some or something similar. But I need you to take that cage back to Gordie's apartment and leave it there.]

"Now?"

[Right now. It's got a tracer in it somewhere, and the polis were just here looking for it. When they look again, I want it to be back in Maryhill.]

"I thought we were going after the pixie."

[We are. As soon as you're back and munch a couple of marshmallows.]

"Boff Bogdump's bollocks, I'm going to be worn out before we get started."

I wanted to ask who Boff Bogdump was—probably some infamous figure from hobgoblin lore—but Buck might be counting on that very thing to stall me, so I said, [Can't be helped. I'll get something to replenish you. Off you go.]

"Fine. But where's the cage, old man?"

I opened my ink library and fetched it, telling the barghest he could come back out and rejoin us in the office. Buck popped away with the cage, and I told the barghest to wait while I went out for a few minutes. There was a convenience store around the block, which didn't have chocolate-covered marshmallows but had the two items separately, and I decided that was close enough.

A quarter hour later we were all reconvened in my office, the swing shift was coming in to do the night's press run, and we were ready to go. I sent Nadia and Buck down to the parking lot off George Street ahead of me so I could speak aloud to the barghest without worrying about my curse.

"Begin your search now. Remember to stay a hundred meters away from the target, and once ye find her, wait for us to catch up. We're going to follow on roads using that tracker."

"Whuff," the barghest said, though I don't know how much of that he understood.

"Good boy. Find the pixie. Let's go."

He faced north and his substance melted away, becoming a ghost dog as he pursued the target scent we'd given him. I made sure to take my cane along and walked downstairs to join Nadia and Buck in the parking lot. Nadia was telling Buck about the rules, which all boiled down to him not messing up her ride or stealing anything from it. I joined them as Buck was giving her assurances.

"I swear on my maw's sacred lamb stew," he said, "I'll be a model passenger. I'll break nothing, steal nothing. I'll just be honored to ride in yer gallus wizard van."

"No pranks of any kind?" Nadia said, pointing a finger at him. "None."

"Awright. Ye wanna pray to Lhurnog with me?"

"Of course!"

"Good." She hauled open the back door of the van. "Hop in."

"Fuck yeah!" Buck launched himself inside and immediately sat on the love seat facing the altar, placing his sack next to it. Nadia turned to me.

"Want tae join us? Won't take a minute."

[Might be crowded. I'll get in the passenger seat. The dug's on his way.]

"Okay, we'll be quick."

Before I moved to the front, I saw her pull down a bottle of The Macallan and hand it to Buck. "You pour the whisky, I'll melt the cheese."

I didn't participate in the ritual for the very good reason that, with enough worshippers, Lhurnog might collect enough psychic energy to manifest, and then I'd have to quickly write a contract that forced him to stay off earth. The last thing we needed was a god running around eating men and inspiring wizards to ride lizards. Or maybe we *did* need that; we might be better off, I don't know. But for the sake of convenience I vastly preferred Lhurnog to be a vague idea in the ether, with only one place of worship—the van—and one holy relic honoring him thus far. I was doing my best to keep Nadia so busy that she never thought to produce a work of scripture that hallowed the Unhallowed.

I got into the passenger seat and did my best not to pay attention to the bloody prayers happening in the back. Flipping on the GPS receiver mounted on the dash, I waited for the signal to ping and give me a location. It took a few seconds, but a glowing red dot showed up heading north in the general direction of Stirling. That would be easy enough to get to, once we escaped the city traffic.

When the prayers finished, Nadia got into the driver's seat and got us on the road. The sun was crawling orange into the west when Buck spoke up from the back.

"Okay, the cheese is melted!"

"Good," Nadia called back. "Now you carefully eat it with that bag of crackers I gave you. Don't spill any!"

"This is the best," Buck said over the crackle and rustle of a plastic bag. "Only thing that could make it better would be a shot of salsa."

[Don't ever give him salsa,] I told Nadia. [He gets high off it.]

"He does? That's no fair."

[Eli said the same thing.]

The red dot on the GPS display stopped a few miles west of Stirling, near a wee village called Gargunnock.

I looked it up on my phone just to make sure there wasn't a convenient article describing a secretive research lab located there, but no such luck. It had an inn, a general store, and an old church. It was surrounded by sheep pastures, hayfields, and rural charm. There was also a table of rock that rose above it on the southern side, which someone had thought made a nice defensible position in the old days. There was supposed to be an old Bronze Age wall spread out along the base of it.

It was twilight when we hit the town. We had to go through it to reach the red dot; there was a road somewhere past the church that led uphill to the table, though it petered out before it reached the top. The tracker was near there.

The rock retaining walls lining the streets were capped with green carpets of moss and lichen, the soft furry kind one can pet. A few of the locals stared in shock and disapproval at Nadia's wizard van, and she smiled and waved at them.

"I love how ye can tell after ye pass someone in this van that they're gonnay turn tae their friend and shake their head and say, *Kids these days!* or sumhin like that."

[Or get the polis. You're suspicious and up to something.]

"Aye, that's happened, unfortunately."

Nadia had an official ID like mine in her glove compartment, which she kept for such occasions, telling the constables in question to simply let her go. It wouldn't do to have them search the van and find open whisky bottles in the back.

We turned off the paved road and onto a dirt one that wound

upward into the hills. A couple of sheep in a rolling pasture quivered and shot us anxious looks, transfixed by the sight of Lhurnog and the wizard lizard.

Houses were quickly left behind, and it became clear that the road was intended only for access to upper pastures. When it curved around to the right, away from the red dot on the GPS, I told Nadia we'd better park and walk the rest of the way.

"Gah. I hope we don't get stuck," she said, as the turf to the side was rather soft and muddy. I didn't know how much traffic the road got, but parking in the middle of it would be rude. We got out, squelched in the mud a bit, and Nadia fetched her sword from the back and inspected the rear of the van for any obvious signs of hobgoblin misbehavior. Buck grinned at her and shouldered his pack.

"Absolutely zero damage! I bet ye wish all yer passengers were so gentle on yer ride. Shall we be about it?"

Nadia had him fetch a torch out from under the altar before he got down into the mud. We'd probably need it if we were to spend any time at this, since the sun had set and we were walking under a lavender sky edging toward violet.

We found the barghest a hundred meters nearly straight uphill from the van. He was facing a copse of trees deliberately left standing to serve as a windbreak between pastures, as well as a habitat for various birds and other creatures.

I asked Nadia and Buck to hang back a bit so I could walk up and talk to the barghest without worrying about my curse.

"The pixie's in the trees, eh?" I asked him.

"Whuff," he said.

"Lead me to her, please, but slowly."

He walked on, and I waved at Nadia and Buck to catch up. The wall of trees grew before us, and I wondered how we'd actually find her in the darkness beneath the canopy. Pixies would have plenty of places to hide in a wooded grove like this. But the barghest stopped before the first tree directly in front of us and whuffed softly, his chin pointed up at one of the branches. I couldn't see anything, so I got out my phone.

[Buck. Call to her please, see if she's willing to talk.]

"Oi! Pixie!" he shouted. "I was the hobgoblin in the cage next tae yers in that shite flat of Gordie's. Can we talk? Are ye awright? We want tae help if we can."

A tiny voice responded from about halfway up the tree, though I still couldn't see anything. She had an Irish rather than Scottish accent, and I awarded myself some fleeting congratulations for tracking her down when neither Hatcher nor Clíodhna had been cooperative.

"Wee pink man. I remember seeing ye unconscious. Did ye escape somehow?"

"Aye, even so. I'm bound in legal service now tae the sigil agent Al MacBharrais. And Gordie's dead, so that's a joy and a justice tae the world."

"I don't think there'll be any joy or justice for me, hob. What's your name, by the by? We never got to talk."

"I'm Buck Foi. This here's Nadia, and the old man there is Al MacBharrais himself."

"Pleased to meet ye all. Or kind of afraid, really. I'm Cowslip. Are ye gonna kill me now?"

CHAPTER 27

The Rock of Gargunnock

B uck and Nadia both turned to me, and so did the pixie. The torch revealed her position, perched on a branch perhaps three feet above our heads. While Buck could probably reach her before she flew away, there was no way that Nadia or I ever could. Not that I was anxious to dole out death.

She wasn't quite a full foot tall. More like nine inches. She had some gossamer wings that shed pixie dust like a minor snow flurry, which sounded like pure magic until ye remembered that dust was simply flakes of dead skin, so if it *was* magical, then it was magical wing dandruff. She had on some nondescript grey clothing that camouflaged her against the bark of the trees, along with some very wee grey boots, but it only served to highlight her extraordinary pallor. A patch of dark hair—in a pixie cut, of course—was tousled around her scalp. Her eyes looked puffy and red from crying.

I typed a response to her question and held up my phone in hopes that she would be able to hear it.

[The treaty's been violated, but it's not necessarily your fault. I have broad discretion in terms of enforcement. So let's just talk for now. I'm not itching for a fight.]

"You're going to get one, though. Not from me, sir—from the rest of them."

[Are the rest of them nearby?]

"Sure they are. The lab's just over there against the rocks, behind the wall." She pointed past me, and peripherally I saw that Nadia and Buck turned to look, but I kept my eyes on her in case it was a trick. This whole thing might be a trap. She could be bait. We might be presenting ourselves as a fine, still target for a sniper.

[And why aren't you with them right now? Out here to distract us? Set an ambush, perhaps?]

"No," she said, sounding offended. "I'm out here because I don't like them. I'm not like them. They slobber and drool and drink wine and eat people."

[They eat people?]

Cowslip nodded. "Men they killed in other countries. They bring back an arm or a leg and roast it and take their time nibbling at it. They even ate one man's arse, and I said are ye barmy, why would ye ever want to eat an arse, and they said it was spicy. Can ye believe it? Spicy!"

[Ugh!]

"That's exactly what I says, sir, I says to them, 'Ugh!' and I contented myself with a nice flower salad, which is a salad with . . . flowers in it."

[Tell me three times, Cowslip: Are you here to ambush us or to let us be ambushed?]

"No, sir. I tell ye three times. I am here by my lonesome because I want to be alone."

[Fine. What have they done to you, and who are they?]

"They're not Irish or Scots. One of them said they are Americans, I think. Some group called See Hi Hey or something."

[CIA. Okay. And what did they do when they got you here?]

"They poked me with needles, but not steel ones. Made of something else. Special needles, they said. They injected stuff into me and it hurt. I had sweats and fevers and I shat my wee bed more than once. They said not to worry, that was normal, and I said no, ye bastards, ye can speak for yerselves if ye want, but it's not normal for *me* to shite the bed, so feck all yer poxy holes with a raw donkey cock. And after they were done, I looked rougher and older but iron wouldn't kill me. Plus I'm angry all the time."

Fresh tears coursed down her cheeks, and her tiny hands clenched into fists.

[I'm sorry, Cowslip. What hold do they have on you? Why don't you go home?]

"Oh, aye, why don't I just go home? Feckin' easy for ye to say, but ye don't know, do ye?"

[No, I don't. That's why I asked.]

"It's an addiction, sir. A bloody addiction. I have to keep getting their injections and do what they want or I'll die."

[How do you know you'll die?]

"I refused the shots for a while and I got so sick. It hurt so much. More than anything. And when they gave me a new shot, the pain went away. So I am well and truly bollixed. I have to do what they say."

[And what do they ask you to do?]

"Go places with the others. Find men and kill them. Take whatever papers we can find and then burn it down, leave no evidence. Don't let anyone see us or take a picture with their phones like ye have there."

"Tch. What a waste," Buck muttered while I typed my next question. "Think of the heists ye could pull off with a crew like that! And they're playing spy games."

[Have you personally, Cowslip, killed anyone?]

"No."

[Are you sure?]

"I tell ye three times, sir. They mostly send me in from above to disable their cameras."

[But the others have killed humans?]

"Oh, aye. They've developed a taste for ye, and the clurichaun brings a hatchet, a carving knife, some crackers, and a little jar of aioli with him on jobs now. It's just mayonnaise with some shite mixed in but he thinks it's super fancy, never shuts up about how good his bloody aioli is. But I like one bite of those vegetarian burgers—ye know, the new ones that don't taste like sawdust? Fills me right up."

[Fascinating. So where is this lab?]

She pointed behind me again, but I kept my focus on her. "Head that way and you'll see a wall of rock before ye get to the top of the table. A natural wall of rock in the hill, not the old man-made wall. It's like a wee cliffside. And there's a door in it now, hidden away. The lab facility is in there, built into the earth. That's where they hide."

[Who are they?]

"The rest of them. The fir darrig, who's a dirty bastard. The clurichaun and the leprechaun room together, drunk on Irish whiskey and wine. The undine has her own subterranean lake, and she's scary. And there are humans."

[How many?]

"I don't know for sure. I can't tell them apart. They all look stupid to me, like you. Except you have a fun hat and mustache."

Buck sniggered and Nadia grunted in disapproval.

[How do we get in?]

"I don't think ye do."

I looked around to make sure there wasn't an ambush coming at that moment. Nadia spoke what I was thinking.

"Look, Cowslip, if ye want Al tae overlook your violation of the treaty between the Fae and humanity, ye're gonnay have tae get us in there."

"I can't. I can get myself in but not you. There's all these security measures and defenses built in. You're on camera, by the way. This is the bound tree we use to shift to Tír na nÓg, so they have it under surveillance. They know you're here."

They didn't know anything for sure except that they were blind out here at the moment. The Sigil of Swallowed Light on my hat took care of that. If the CIA wanted intel on me or to train a weapon on my person, they'd need to do it with their actual eyeballs. I wasn't going to let a drone or a satellite take me out.

[Will you let me use a Sigil of Reckoning Truth on you?]

"No, sir, I've heard that leaves some damage behind, but I've not told a lie yet. I tell ye three times. And I'll answer any question ye have. I can't make them pay for what they did to me, so I need ye to do it for me."

She had been forthcoming so far and showed no signs that she planned to shift away, so I knelt down next to the barghest, removed the GPS tracker, thanked him for his service, and dismissed him before I continued. He didn't bark so much as borked a soft farewell before melting into the air.

[Do the humans have guns?] I asked Cowslip.

"Aye, sir."

[Are there more than ten of them?]

"Between five and ten is my best guess."

[So we're facing four Fae immune to iron and between five and ten humans with guns in a fortified bunker.]

"Right."

[Is there another entrance?]

"Maybe? I only know of that one in the rock wall."

[And this is where they have kept you since you left Gordie's apartment?]

"Aye."

[Were you lured to this plane by a promise of service from Clíodhna or one of the bean sídhe?]

She sniffled before answering and wiped at her nose. "Clíodhna herself."

I shook my head, suddenly sad. The poor wee thing was so unhappy. Clíodhna had preyed upon her hopes, and then Hatcher's people had preyed on her some more. Tricked, trafficked, and then trapped into forced labor, using the same methods that humans used on their own kind to press people into various services with little or no hope of escape.

"I'm sorry that happened to ye, Cowslip," Buck said. "I got fooled the same way. I'd be in there with the rest of them now, hating my life, if Gordie hadn't choked on a raisin scone."

I was looking down at my phone to type out another question when Nadia abruptly tackled me to the ground and shouted, "Sniper!"

Gunfire erupted. It was aimed at us, sure, but primarily aimed at the branches of the tree that Cowslip was sitting in. Bullets shredded and splintered the wood, and Buck cursed creatively the entire while. When they had emptied their clips and had to reload—yes, I purposely say *clips* instead of *magazines,* to make pedantic American gun nuts froth at the mouth—Nadia checked on the pixie.

"Cowslip?"

"I'm okay!" she squeaked, though I couldn't see her anymore. She had taken shelter behind a trunk or bough. Pixies were extraordinarily small targets.

[How many shooters?] I asked, not caring who answered as long as someone did. I couldn't see anything in the gathering darkness and needed a sigil to fix that.

"Lemme check," Buck said. He popped away, leaving his bag behind, and returned shortly thereafter. "Two. Up near the wall of rock that Cowslip told us about. Can ye see it without stickin' yer head up tae get shot off?"

"Stay down!" Nadia yelled, just before the shooters began spraying down the hillside again with their fresh clips.

I had questions. The CIA had obviously sent out someone to check on their loss of camera surveillance, but why had they initially gone after Cowslip instead of us? After going to all the trouble and expense to develop an asset like that, why did they decide to terminate?

The only possible answer was that they had the area wired for sound as well and heard her giving us everything. Since she was more likely to be taken out in the surprise first volley, they had targeted her first. But we couldn't be allowed to live either. We knew too much.

Bullets were hitting the hillside now. We had minimized our target silhouette, but they were going to keep us pinned down at the very least if not perforate us multiple times.

It clarified my thinking and resolve. When it comes to beings that are on earth without permission, my license to kill is absolute. I have no such license to kill other humans.

I do, however, occasionally run across the need. As in this situation, a self-defense scenario where it appeared that there would be no opportunity to negotiate. A minimized silhouette and the legendary inaccuracy of automatic weapons would not save us forever. We must either kill or be killed.

And rarely—yet always to my eternal shame—I actually wanted to kill. I'd never acted on such desires before, because other solutions were available to me that would let me face the mirror in the morning, and I supposed so long as one possessed a sense of shame, that was a weak moral code of sorts: *In the morning, and every morning after that, can I live with this shite I'm about to do, without self-loathing?*

But this was an extraordinary situation in which my wants and needs overlapped. I needed to survive this and get into that lab, and, pinned down as I was, I couldn't do that without a spoonful of lethal violence. That was enough to proceed. However, I also wanted these people who enslaved other beings yet sang of the "land of the free" to pay for their unforgivable cruelty and hypocrisy. They had literally created man-eating monsters but were no less monstrous themselves.

When they stopped to reload again, I leapt to my feet—*leapt* being a relative term for a man in his sixties—and pulled out the ancient Sigil of Unchained Destruction. I didn't see the gunmen, but I could dimly make out the miniature rock cliff in the hillside that hid the secret entrance to the lab. It was a darker slab in the deepening darkness.

One hand aiming the sigil and the other poised above it to break the seal, I held the sigil carefully still and hoped that it would work after all this time. If it didn't, I'd probably hear Nadia tell me to duck an instant before a bullet tore through me. I broke the seal, raising the flap and pinching it aloft so that nothing blocked the sigil, and counted:

One Ecclefechan.
Two Ecclefechan.
Three—

CHAPTER 28

The Corrupted Fae

The Sigil of Unchained Destruction is not quite like taking off and nuking a site from orbit just to be sure, but it's close. It's less wanton, more targeted, yet utterly irresistible. The aftermath looks like what you'd see if a helicopter news crew surveyed the path of a tornado through a trailer park. It's a cone of raw kinetic force that obliterates everything for approximately two hundred meters before deciding that's quite enough and it's time to fuck off and go to the pub.

It's a true cone of force, however. Aim the center at a point slightly aboveground, like I did, and you'll get a whole lot of that force scooping up the ground underneath the center. Or at least pushing it forward until it has nowhere else to go but up because that's the path of least resistance.

The resultant impact created a percussive boom and shockwave and threw up a whole lot of earth into the sky. It knocked me back on my arse. That would bring someone to investigate eventually, so we couldn't wait long before getting in there ourselves.

I looked over at Nadia and raised an eyebrow in question. *Okay to proceed?* She looked up at the expanding cloud of debris, clambered to her feet, and slapped at her clothes to get the mud off.

"Don't want tae get *too* wild here, but I think ye might've got 'em, Al."

"I'll say! Bloody hells!" Buck said.

"Did you kill them all?" Cowslip's tiny voice asked.

[The two shooters, yes. Don't know how much damage it did inside the facility.]

"Can ye imagine if William Wallace had been packing one of those?" the hobgoblin asked.

A keening noise made me think I'd sustained hearing damage from the detonation, until I realized the sound was coming from behind me rather than internally, and it was growing into a chorus. Cowslip squeaked in alarm as I turned around and she flew down to us.

"The bean sídhe are here!"

They were indeed. They had shifted in through the bound tree and were now spinning in slow gyres about the trunk, their glowing but vacant eyes staring at nothing, their open mouths wailing and ululating nonsense in a rising wall of teeth-grinding sound. There were no recognizable names being called. But I cast a worried glance at Buck. He had his hands over his ears and a wince on his face.

I walked over and gave him two sigils. "Agility and strength. You be careful."

"Are they gonnay have at us, then?"

I shook my head. Clíodhna wouldn't have sent them to do battle after we'd made such an amicable agreement. They were simply here to fulfill their function and herald the deaths of the Fae. [No. They're just telling us someone is going to die.]

"Incoming from the crater," Nadia announced.

I hurried over to give her the same two sigils and then popped the seal on the last pair for me, plus a Sigil of Feline Vision to help me see in the dark. I spread out to the right side, leaving Nadia in the center of our trio. Three shadowy figures silhouetted in the cloud of debris took shape, and I recognized two of them. The leprechaun's small stature was unmistakable, and the unsteady weaving of the clurichaun was a calling card. The other was of a height in between the two, perhaps four feet tall, and was most likely the fir darrig. They were rat-faced and rat-tailed bipeds who preferred to wear red coats redolent of hot rubbish juice. Temperamentally they were like football fans who didn't wait for an excuse to get into a brawl. They had an impressive vertical leap, and they liked to lay about them with a club-like shillelagh.

As the ol' cat eyes kicked in and the figures sharpened and brightened, the leprechaun leapt at me, the fir darrig bounced toward Buck, and the clurichaun stagger-charged Nadia in the center. I noticed that he was armed with something besides a gun this time—a hatchet in his right hand and a dagger in the left. (Did he bring the aioli?) Both the fir darrig and the leprechaun had shillelaghs cocked in their hands, which they brought down for an opening strike, and while I'm sure Buck and Nadia successfully dodged their opponents, I didn't. The burl on the end of the shillelagh smashed into my left cheek—the same one the barghest had shredded—probably because I was worrying about my companions and not paying full attention to the leprechaun.

But that got my attention.

Pain exploded underneath my eye, and I nearly fell over but managed to keep my feet by staggering back. The leprechaun landed on the soft turf and spun around, twirling his shillelagh as a manic grin split his face.

"Evenin', squire! Hee hee hee! Will ye be havin' some more?" And he came at me again, on the same side since he could no doubt see that I had my left eye closed and it would probably swell shut soon anyway. I rotated my left side back so I faced him with my right foot forward and my cane held defensively, and when he swung at me I pivoted to the left on that right foot to make him miss but whipped my fist down in that direction at the same time, my cane trailing along the line of my forearm until the end of it caught him high on the left cheek also. An eye for an eye. His appetite for cheery banter evaporated, and he growled at me instead.

"Oh ho," he said. "Bad move, me boy. I'll be eating your liver in a few minutes and feeding the rest of ye to the village dogs."

Judging by what Cowslip had told us about the corrupted Fae's new dietary preferences, that had probably been his plan regardless of whether I fought back or not, so if I was going to fall to this Irish blighter, I might as well go down the hard way.

I wondered where Cowslip had gotten to but didn't dare take my eyes off the leprechaun, even to check on the others. I heard some grunts and yelps of pain but had no idea who was making them.

The leprechaun was watching me move, trying to spot weaknesses, but it was still my left side where he'd initially tagged me. I was showing him nothing but my right side and a cautious defense. I'd opened a gash on his cheek and he had some blood sheeting down there, but his vision hadn't been damaged.

My long topcoat did me a service in the sense that it hid my hips and legs; he couldn't look at them and predict where I'd move next. But he was fast. Even sped up and stronger than usual, I had trouble fighting off his next attack, which involved him leaping at my face and then dropping his shillelagh mid-jump to latch on to my arm and lock up my cane with it.

I supposed I did not, in fact, fight it off, because he held on tightly to my arm and then swung a chubby and dirty foot at my chin and tagged me. My teeth closed on my tongue and I tasted blood, and the wee bastard cackled. Rather than try to shake the leprechaun off my arm, I simply went horizontal and dropped on top of him. The air whooshed out of his lungs as my full weight plowed him into the turf and the cane pressed into his diaphragm, making sure he was empty. I didn't want him to refill, so I shifted my weight, dragged the cane across his throat, and pressed down.

The leprechaun kicked me savagely enough in the ribs that I nearly rolled away, and he socked me good a couple of times in the ear so that I probably did sustain hearing loss after all, but this was going to be my best shot, so I endured it and kept up the pressure until the mad light in his eyes snuffed out.

The wailing of the banshees changed with his death. It didn't cease, but the mindless gabble altered to a slightly different mindless gabble. And it changed again as Buck Foi threw up his hands in victory over a still form and said, "That's right, ya bastard!"

But Nadia was still locked in combat with the clurichaun and having serious trouble with him. There was blood on her shirt from a stab wound—the first time, to my knowledge, that anyone had ever wounded her. How had he managed that? I hadn't thought it possible.

"Do ye need any help?" Buck asked, saying what I was about to say myself.

"Naw, piss off, both of ye!" Nadia snarled. "I'm gonnay leather this wee dick."

I scanned the hillside and the forest and then the sky to make sure reinforcements weren't incoming. The bean sídhe were circling around the bound tree still, screeching and ululating, and Cowslip was hovering high in the air behind the clurichaun, carefully keeping some distance between herself and the bean sídhe but also wary of what else might emerge from the mountain.

The clurichaun was cackling and barely upright but still keeping Nadia off-balance and defensive with wild swings of his hatchet and dagger. She kept giving ground, dodging his swings and neglecting to take advantage of several opportunities when his drunken follow-throughs left him vulnerable to a counterattack. Had she lost her gift, I wondered? If so, she could be in serious jeopardy, because she wasn't an accomplished or disciplined fighter otherwise.

Taking a few steps closer, I searched my inner pockets and fished out a Sigil of Knit Flesh that she could use on that stab wound. My face throbbed and my left eye was functionally useless due to swelling, but I didn't think it was time to look to my own relief.

"I'll catch y—urp!—eventually," the clurichaun said, feinting with the dagger and then swinging the hatchet instead, which Nadia ducked. "Ye look delicious, ye know."

He swiped again at her, this time a backhand, which left his torso open, and he raised his dagger to parry an anticipated strike from Nadia's sword. She did begin a swing that would have been blocked by his dagger, except that she rotated her wrist and dropped her arm, pointing the sharp end up, and then lifted it straight up his middle, opening a gash from his belly to his collarbone and even nicking his jawline. He instinctively curled in upon himself at that, and now he was open to attack from the sides.

Nadia turned her wrist again with the sword high in the air and caught him on the side of the neck with a downward chop. It lodged in his flesh and she let it go.

"Hurrk," the clurichaun said, sinking to his knees. He dropped his dagger to grab the sword and keep its weight from making the cut any worse.

"Looks like I caught ye instead," Nadia said. He threw his hatchet at her, feebly, which she easily sidestepped, and she hawked up a nice phlegm globber and spat it expertly at his face once he toppled onto his side in the grass. "May Lhurnog eat yer pissed and poxy corpse in the afterlife."

I handed her the sigil and she thanked me for it, popping the seal and waiting for the stab wound to close.

[How'd he get you? I didn't see it happen.]

"He was so drunk I couldn't predict his movements. He didn't know what he was going to do, so I didn't either. The agility boost saved me. Thanks for that."

The clurichaun gasped and died in the turf, and the howling of the banshees changed once again. This time, however, they were synchronized and singing the same nonsense syllables, a chorus of madness.

"Can ye do anything tae make them stop?" Buck asked. "That really gets on my nerves."

I shook my head. [One more member of the Fae to die here yet, if I'm interpreting their behavior correctly. That's either you, or Cowslip, or the undine hiding somewhere in the hillside there.]

Buck's mouth drew into a tight line, and his eyebrows knit together as he thought about it.

"We're all changed, is what ye're saying tae me now. Because the bean sídhe can't call out our old names anymore."

[Aye. It worries me.]

"Well, it's fated, in't it? The bean sídhe have the sight, like Nadia here, but different. If I'm gonnay croak and shite my drawers in the next few minutes, it doesnae matter if I stay here or go inside. Sumhin will get me either way. And if I am gonnay get got, I don't want it tae be out here tryin' tae keep ma shorts clean with cowardice. So let's go, old man. Once more untae the breach, as that English bastard Henry said."

I blinked at the reference. [You know *Henry V*?]

"Brighid's a goddess of poetry. We've been over this. And ye know I like Shakespeare, except when he killed Rosencrantz."

[Okay, if you're ready, we'll go. Nadia?]

"It stings and itches and I'm a bit light-headed, but it's sewn up, I think. What's the plan?"

[If Cowslip is right, there are at least three and maybe up to eight armed agents inside, plus the undine.]

A low roll of laughter bubbled out of Buck, and we regarded him warily.

"We can use some evenin' of the odds, am I right? I've got just the thing."

He fairly pranced away to where he'd left his bag on the ground and slung it over his shoulder, then waved at us as he jogged toward the cliffside.

"Come on, it's time for mayhem and that!"

CHAPTER 29

The Dripping Deep

Nadia and I shrugged at each other and followed. I'm not an excellent cross-country jogger, but the sigils hadn't worn off yet, so we were able to make it uphill as the dust cloud settled down. I got my first good look at the entrance to the CIA facility.

The Sigil of Unchained Destruction had punched a yawning black hole through the outer defenses, through which one could walk over pulverized rock. None of it was cement, which Nadia commented on.

"Shouldn't there be cement and steel rods and that?" she asked.

[Clíodhna probably built it all with the help of the local elemental. The rock was reshaped internally. No construction needed except for the electronics and security.]

There were steel doors, however, bowed and misshapen now and through which we'd have no trouble walking—no retinal scans or swipe cards needed. But there were most likely gun barrels in that darkness, waiting for us to step into their line of fire.

"That's a death trap right there," Buck said, jabbing his finger at what looked more like a mine shaft full of rabid bats than a secure intelligence bunker. "Nae chance in all the hells I'm gonnay walk intae that without knowing what's in there. So it was nice of Hatcher tae provide us with a bag full o' disposable minions, in't it?"

He upended his bag on the ground, and a mess of painted miniatures tumbled out. There were green-skinned goblins, as he'd remarked upon earlier, but many others as well. Trolls and dwarfs and elves with various swords and hammers and axes. They made a tinkling noise as they crashed into one another.

"Are those metal?" Nadia asked.

"Aye. Pewter, I think. Hard enough to put a hurtin' on and not be hurt by a brush-off."

"What do ye mean?"

"I mean this is how we win the numbers game." He drew in a deep breath and moved his hands in circles, spreading his fingers out over the figures as he spoke some words in Old Irish. When he finished, a tiny shimmer rippled in the air above the miniatures and they moved.

They stepped silently off their bases and grouped themselves by species, and Nadia whooped. "Fucking hell, Buck, that's as creepy as it is cool!"

The four squads hefted their weapons and stretched, and Buck nodded approvingly. "Time tae throw some magic at their science." I held up a hand as he drew breath to give them orders. "Wot?"

[Maybe throw both magic and science at them. Nadia, does your phone have a video-chat app?]

"Aye."

In less than a minute, Buck had a squad of painted armored trolls carrying Nadia's phone into the yawning mouth of the facility. It had Nadia's face on it, since we had started a chat outside and Nadia was using my phone. I wasn't sure how well the signal would carry in the facility, but this would give us our best chance to talk to someone and maybe negotiate a surrender. I'd coached Nadia a bit on what to say and promised her a new phone if they destroyed hers.

Buck waited a minute, then sent the remaining squads of miniatures in behind the trolls in case they needed "a military solution."

"Are ye controlling them individually?" Nadia asked.

"Naw. It's an enchantment of autonomous animation with only
basic goals given."

Nadia began shouting into my phone. Hers was on speaker.
"Hey! Any of ya tits still alive in there? We want tae help. Or at
least talk if ye don't want any help. Can we talk? Hello? Hello-
oooo?"

We were seeing nothing on the screen, and Nadia shot me a
questioning glance. I twirled my finger in a circle to indicate she
should keep going.

"Oi! Ya bastards! Someone pick up. I've got recipes. Books full
of elf erotica, people just nibbling on pointy ears for pages and
pages, and I promise you'll never think of ear foreplay the same
way afterward. I've got some fondue in the van. I know where
Jimmy Hoffa is buried. Elvis too. Mulder and Scully. Cagney and
Lacey. Thelma and Louise."

I had no idea what tangent she'd gone off on, but Buck chimed
in with "Starsky and Hutch."

"That's right, Starsky and Hutch. Turner and fucking Hooch.
And, oh, yeah. Hatcher! Simon Hatcher. We got Simon Hatcher. I
mean our people got him in Virginia. Don't ye want tae hear about
Simon Hatcher?"

That got a response, as I thought it might. Someone picked up
the phone and said, "Who is this?" The face on the screen was
poorly lit, a torch off camera providing the only illumination. It
was a white man in his late thirties or early forties, I guessed, with
some stubble on his chin and a tie loosened underneath his col-
lared shirt. His accent was American.

"I'm the one who put down yer clurichaun," Nadia said. "Time
to settle up all his outstanding bar tabs."

"Who are you?" he demanded again.

"Someone who knows exactly what she's doing," Nadia replied.
"Just wanted tae make that clear before ye say something like, *You*

have no idea who you're dealing with." She mocked his accent at the end of that, and I had difficulty stifling a laugh. "I have a really fucking good idea, awright? Ye're a twat from the CIA doing some illegal shite, and we're here tae stop ye. But that doesnae mean ye have tae go home in a box. We just need that undine ye're keeping in there and ye can go home and grind yer naughty bits against the corresponding bits of a consenting partner."

"What have you done with our operatives?"

"We killed them deid. They didnae give us a choice. But we're giving you one."

"What is it?"

"Just walk away and live to do some more spy shite in the future. Ye're free tae go but not tae stay. This operation's over. Cut yer losses and move on."

"Well—"

"Give me that," a new voice said, angry and male. The picture on the phone changed to an older white man, perhaps my own age, but clean-shaven and with a face twisted with rage and boils and burn scars. He looked like the picture of Dorian Gray, the corrupted one that showed all the sins written on the flesh. He might have been a handsome blond lad in his youth, but he had clearly been up to some wicked shite since then. Maybe some lab experiments gone wrong.

"That's him," Cowslip hissed, hovering over Nadia's shoulder. "That's the bloody doctor who did this to me!"

"Listen to me, whoever you are," he spat. "You've got maybe three minutes until a drone strike takes you out. You're outgunned."

Nadia checked with me and I shook my heid, pointing to my hat and reminding her that the sigils would make targeting impossible.

"I rather think it's you who needs tae be worrying, mate. Ye might have noticed we've taken out your gunmen and blown open the door with little trouble, and the Fae you've corrupted are in violation of a treaty with humanity."

"What treaty?" he spluttered.

"It's a need-tae-know thing, and now ye need tae know. The Fae are no allowed tae frolic about here and eat humans, and we're the folks who enforce that. Hatcher is mince, and yer operation's tits up. So come on out, eh? First round's on me after we take care of the undine."

"Hatcher is dead?"

"He's no deid, he's just neutralized. And there will be no more Fae for ye tae corrupt. We shut off that pipeline. So give it up."

"I can't give up, even if that's all true, and I don't think it is." The unnamed doctor sneered at the camera, and for me it was disheartening evidence that Saxon had been right: The scientists who willingly work for governments and their agendas might actually be the evil sort. At least this one was. It broke my heart to think of all the suffering and death that could be laid at his door.

"We will defend ourselves and our assets," he continued. "If you come in here, you'll get nothing from us but bullets."

"Awright, fine, but can ye let the others make their own decision? We'd rather no kill anyone, but if ye force us tae come in after ye, there will be no mercy."

"They're under oath every bit as much as I am, and they're also under my orders. If you come in here, you'll be shot."

Nadia sighed. "I do no like killing people who are trapped in a hierarchy, but you are different. Ye're a fucking bastard. Remember that I gave ye a chance and ye said no, and I'm very sorry about the others."

She switched off and handed the phone to me. I immediately launched my text-to-speech app and typed, [Activate your minions, Buck. Do whatever you had planned.]

The hobgoblin nodded once and then stretched out his right hand toward the facility, chanting some words in Old Irish.

"There. That should do it."

"Do what?" Nadia asked.

"Since it worked so well with the troll, I commanded them tae seek out the humans inside and gouge out their eyes. How they do that is up tae them. I assume they're going tae have tae climb up, and that's why it's good they're made of metal. The humans will slap them away, but they can fall down and just keep coming."

Nadia's jaw dropped. "That's bloody terrifying."

[Uh. Buck? Does that mean if Nadia and I go in there, your little minions will go for our eyes too?]

The hobgoblin blinked. "Shite. I didn't think that one through."

Nadia caught my gaze and shook her head, hooking her thumb at Buck. "I'm no gonnay be blinded by this wee man's wee men. Can we no just use another sigil tae blow the place up?"

Panicked screaming and gunfire alerted us that the miniatures had found some targets inside.

"Christ! Get 'em off me! Get 'em off!" a man screamed faintly. "Augggh!"

The hollering continued and intensified, and when one said, "My eye!" we knew that they had been at least partially successful.

"Awright, new plan," Buck said. "I'll go in there now that they're busy and get the guns. I'll have the wee folk stand down, then ye can follow."

The bean sídhe continued to screech out someone's garbled name, and I told him to be careful.

"Ye told me bein' in yer service would be dangerous, MacBharrais, but ye didnae say I'd be walkin' intae a hole full of guns. I want proper chocolate-covered marshmallows after this."

He crouched down and crept into the facility, conserving his strength, heading toward the gunfire and shouts. It wasn't a minute later that he popped into view next to us with a gun in his hand and dropped it at my feet.

"That's one," he said, and popped away again. He repeated the process twice more but brought phones back with him too, including Nadia's. He said, "That's all of them, I think, on the top floor. One of the humans is deid—fell down some stairs and broke his neck, but I couldnae tell if it was the doctor or not because I didnae go down tae check. I suppose there could be more people hiding downstairs. The other two I found are half blind—lost one eye but not the other—and they're trying tae call in backup and discovering that nothing works because that sigil of yours knocked out the power. I took their mobile phones tae be sure they couldn't make any calls that way. The wee men are comin' out, and they're gonnay get back on their stands and go tae sleep. Ye can come in now, but it's darker than a king snake's arsehole."

I picked up the guns and stashed them in my coat; I didn't want to leave them behind, in case someone else came along to investigate.

[Want to come with us?] I asked Cowslip.

"If ye don't mind," she said. "I don't wanna stay out here with the bean sídhe."

That was a good point. There was no telling what they might try once I was out of sight; best not give them an opportunity.

The fighting sigils faded away and my muscles and joints complained, but I doubted I'd need the boosts now. I offered Nadia a Sigil of Feline Vision and she took it.

[Need to renew the other ones?] I asked.

"I think I'll be fine without them. No drunk people inside, right?"

We followed Buck and Cowslip into the facility, Nadia using the torch she'd had Buck take out of her van earlier. It would reveal our position to anyone lurking in the dark, but we also didn't want to fall down a flight of stairs or feel our way by touch. The halls of the facility were the sort a fantasy author might say was *hewn from the living rock,* since they actually had been. The wailing of the bean sídhe continued outside, but they didn't follow us in.

Instead, we heard some cursing ahead.

"There's a room full of computers and that ahead on the left," Buck said, pointing. "That's where they are."

"Right. I'll get them sorted," Nadia said in a low tone, and she crept ahead, pulling a couple of zip ties out of her back pocket. There was no need to do anything but restrain them, and she had them bound and cursing us in a couple of minutes.

[Was the doctor in there?] I asked.

"Naw. My bet is that he's downstairs."

There was nothing to learn from the computers, since they were all powerless, so it left us with a single goal.

Buck exhaled slowly. "So. The undine."

[Where is she, Cowslip?]

"Down those stairs that Buck mentioned. It goes down for a while. There's a lake. Or a pond, maybe. She's in there, and she's scary. I don't wanna go."

[Okay. Stay here with Buck and guard the humans. Buck, please search them for ID and take it.]

"Got it."

Nadia and I went down the hall in search of the staircase. When we found it, the human that Buck had mentioned was sprawled motionless on the first landing, neck twisted unnaturally out of shape, and it was the doctor, doubtless on his way down to warn the undine of our approach or else to set up some kind of ambush. One of his eyes was missing, but the torch he'd been carrying still rested on the landing. Perhaps his depth perception had been thrown off and he slipped. Or perhaps he'd had one of Buck's little elves or goblins on him when he tried to take the steps and tumbled down in his panic.

I knelt down next to him with my creaky knees and fished in his lab coat until I pulled out an ID. His name had been Dr. Alex Larned, and I was grateful that the stairs had ended him. If he'd been alive, the treaty would have required me to hand him over to the Fae for punishment. They would have drawn out his death for a very long time. I pocketed the ID and left the torch where it lay.

The stairs kept descending for several flights down a chimney of rock. The two of us went down slowly, Nadia taking the lead, listening for anyone approaching.

The air grew colder and damper as we went, and soon the torch was the only light penetrating an absolute darkness, and I began to regret leaving Dr. Larned's torch behind.

"What do undines look like, Al?" Nadia whispered at the third landing. We still had several flights to go from what we could tell by the cone of the torchlight.

The light of my phone joined the torch as I typed a reply. [They're like naiads.]

"What's that?"

[They're like dryads, but moist.]

"Less of yer cheek, Al. What am I facing? Because this is not a negotiation for surrender, right? She's a pure monster, a people-eater?"

[If Cowslip is to be believed, aye. I had no trouble believing that the others had eaten people. The leprechaun told me he was going to snack on my liver.]

"Aye, and the clurichaun said I looked delicious. So what can an undine do?"

[I'm not sure, really. I haven't had this problem before. But I wouldn't go in the water.]

"Thanks for yer expert advice."

[Sorry.]

"Gimme one of those agility sigils at least. I cannae see fuck-all even with this enhanced vision, and I might need to move fast."

I gave her one and she absorbed it with her eyes before rocketing down the stairs, leaving me behind with only my phone for light. I followed at a much slower pace but soon heard her call up, "I cannae tell how big this pond is. And there's no anything much here at the bottom of the steps. A tiny beach and then it's a spooky Gollum grotto, in't it? If undines turn out tae be lamp-eyed motherfuckers eating raw fish and talking about their Precious, I want another raise."

I didn't answer, concentrating instead on not falling down the steps. But I did wonder what we could do if the undine didn't show herself. We didn't have any harpoons or tridents or even so much as a fishing pole. There was just Nadia's sword and my cane, and while I did have some confiscated guns with an unknown number of rounds in them, firing blindly into a rocky space was probably unwise.

My manager was right: There was hardly anything at the bottom of the steps. Just three or four feet of rocky sand and then black still waters stretching into more darkness. It was silent except for our breathing and the creak of Nadia's leather. I remained on the bottom step because otherwise I'd be crowding her.

"What do I do?" she asked.

[Stand there and smell tasty. You're bait.]

"What, she's gonnay come out o' there like an alligator or sumhin?"

[Yes. Maybe. I don't know.]

"How do I speed things along? Give her a whiff?" She had the torch in her left hand and held her sword in the right, and she waved her hands forward as if to waft her personal aroma over the waters.

[Aye, if there was an undine fishing show on the telly, I'm sure that's how'd they do it.]

"Well, I suppose this beats crouching over my desk doing the quarterly profit-and-loss statement."

I let the comment go unanswered for a while, and silence settled in. It occurred to me that if we were dragged into that water, no one would ever find our bodies. [Spooky as fuck, though,] I finally observed.

"Aye, I was just about tae say. Ye can meditate down here or go mad, and there's no much in between. But it's good. When I get home and Dhanya asks me how was work today, I can say it was all the weird shite ye promised me back in Tchai Ovna and then some, because I got stabbed by a faery whose veins probably contained more cabernet than blood, then watched a bunch of painted miniatures come tae life and hunt down secret agents in the dark, and now I'm undine fishing with my boss and might die. This is so much better than invoicing. So much." She chuckled. "I think this is ma favorite day of work ever. Thanks, Al."

I heard a swirl of water somewhere ahead and perhaps some light bubbles popping; in an area of water and rock walls, sound carried fantastically well.

"Whoa, hold on now . . ." Nadia said. She played the light over the waters in front of her, and I saw some swirls on the surface where it had been perfectly calm and glassy before.

"Duck low!" Nadia shouted, and I crouched down as deeply as I could even as she did, because her warnings were not to be taken lightly. There was a whoosh of sound like a tide hitting shore, and something took off the top of my hat and sheared straight through the steel handrails of the staircase.

"What the fuck?" I said aloud, for it was a spontaneous thing I wasn't going to type into my phone, and I stayed down in case whatever that was struck again. I had no idea what kind of weapon had done that, but I was wet now with water from the pond.

"My hair!" Nadia cried, and something inhuman screamed in response and launched itself out of the pond, half-seen in the light of her torch. Mostly I saw a gush of water and teeth, with some pale, gaunt arms ending in clawed hands stretching out for Nadia's throat. She fell away from it onto her back and bunched her legs up to her chest, successfully denying the attack by extending her legs and tossing the shrieking undine over her heid.

Said undine landed right on top of my heid, and I slammed painfully into the edges of the stairs, dropping my phone but not my cane. I instinctively slipped the cane in front of my throat to protect it and grabbed the other side with my left hand as the undine twisted and writhed until she faced me. Nadia swerved her torch around in search of her quarry and illuminated the creature from the side, a visage marred by pain and madness and teeth like scissor blades flashing at me. I pushed the cane away from me like a bench press, thinking it would prevent her from opening up my carotid and that I'd surely be able to fend off such a slight creature, which weighed no more than ninety pounds.

The undine objected.

Instead of trying to get past my outstretched arms and cane, she simply switched targets, grabbed my left arm, and bit into it. Those knifelike teeth tore through the cashmere of my topcoat and sank into my flesh, and fire lanced through my nerves as my grip loosened on the cane. My defense fell away and my neck was exposed, which is what she wanted. She tore herself from my arm, her teeth coated in my blood, and snarled prior to lunging in for the kill.

But a shucking sound and a jerk to her torso made her gasp and gurgle, and I was abruptly forgotten. Nadia had plunged her sword up under the undine's ribs and pierced at least half a dozen vital organs. The undine may have been immune to iron poisoning, but she wasn't immune to sharp pointy weapons. Nadia twisted the blade, which caused another tremor and moan, and then the undine's head slumped down and her expression went slack.

Nadia pulled the creature off and shone her torch on me. "Awright, Al? Sorry about that."

I confined myself to a tight nod, since I didn't have my phone, and searched in my pockets for a Sigil of Knit Flesh to use on my wound. The blood was flowing pretty well, and I imagined I'd have a hell of a dry-cleaning bill.

"Ach, she got ye a good one, I see. Well, she got me too." She swung the torch around to point at her heid. "Took off the top of ma mohawk. Wild stuff. That was a blade made of water, just shaped out of magic and whipped through the air before she came at us like an alligator after all."

It had taken the top off my hat as well. My sigil was probably ruined, but that was no matter. Had Nadia not warned me, or had I not ducked low enough, I wouldn't have made it.

"Now I know why the pixie thought the undine was scary," she said.

Once I'd given my arm some time to heal and Nadia found my phone, I explained that we needed to haul the body up to the surface. That was an awkward drag, especially over the body of Dr. Larned on the first landing, where I paused to pick up that extra torch, but we managed it and reunited with Buck and Cowslip in the control room. Their prisoners looked a little tousled and the worse for wear, what with an eye missing and blood streaming down their faces, but Buck proudly handed over their IDs. One was the middle-aged man with the loosened tie we'd spoken to briefly over the chat, and the other was a younger white woman with short dark hair and a square jaw.

[Excellent. Peek outside, won't you? See if the bean sídhe are still there.]

"Right." The hobgoblin and pixie exited together, chatting amiably like old friends.

I gave Nadia a Sigil of Muscular Brawn.

"What's this for?"

[I need these two agents dragged outside and dropped by the door. Then I need the undine and the three other Fae bodies piled up some distance away but nowhere near the trees.] Like the troll at the bottom of Hatcher's pool, they hadn't disintegrated to ash like most Fae did upon their death. The experimental treatments had fundamentally altered them, so we'd have to turn them to ash the old-fashioned way.

"Cleanup time, eh?"

I nodded.

"Do ye think that drone the doctor was talking about will get here?"

[If it was coming, it would have struck by now. I think he was talking out his arse.] I took her torch, because I needed to search the other rooms of this place before we left it.

There was a galley and several bunk rooms along with some lavatories and what looked like a medical lab, judging by the equipment inside, but there were no other occupants. The entire facility—especially its data and medical marvels—had to be destroyed. There was nothing I could do about data stored on a remote server somewhere, and Clíodhna knew precisely how to get the whole thing going again in the future, but wiping out this node, together with Hatcher's neutralization, should solve my problems for now. Happily, Brighid was a goddess of fire and had created the perfect sigil when one absolutely, positively had to burn it all down: the Sigil of Cleansing Fire. I had brought plenty of them for just that purpose, even though it exhausted my supply of ink for it and I'd have to get fire-salamander hearts to make more. There was a delay built into the activation so one could open the sigil in a room and have about ten seconds to get to a safe distance. I opened the first one on top of Dr. Larned's body in the stairwell, then climbed up and left a sigil in every room. I noted that the clurichaun's bunk room had a refrigerator stocked with bags of human fingers and labeled jars of aioli. That definitely needed to burn. The sigils ignited and filled the spaces with flames, and my back was uncomfortably toasty by the time I walked out of there. I wished I could say I exited in slow motion with sunglasses on as the entire facility exploded behind me, but it was just a building on fire with oxygen provided by the blasted door and whatever ventilation they had built into the mountain; no doubt there were camouflaged vents on top of the plateau.

The two half-blind agents started yapping at me when I emerged. Nadia had deposited them somewhat near the no-longer-secret entrance and informed them that I was the one in charge, and they had things to say to me. I ignored them and walked out to the neatly stacked pile of corrupted Fae, noting with pleasure that the bean sídhe were all gone and they hadn't been wailing a dirge for Buck Foi after all. They'd been singing the unknown name of the undine. I opened a Sigil of Cleansing Fire on top of the Fae and walked back to the agents.

I really wished I had those sunglasses, but the effect was no less cool in the dark. Or perhaps it was chilling. Seeing the bodies suddenly consumed by a pillar of fire as I strode toward them, the agents quickly ran out of threats and promises of vengeance.

Fire is our friend.

[Straight razor, please?] I asked Nadia.

"Sure." She dug it out of her pocket and handed it to me.

[Thanks. I need everyone out of sight in the van. I'll be there in a moment.]

Buck shouldered up his bag of miniature terrors and told Cowslip she was in for a treat. I waited until they and Nadia were in the van before I put away my phone.

"Now we can talk," I said. "I'm sorry about yer eyes. That's not what I was expecting to happen, and I really was hoping ye would all just walk away. But that mad scientist of yours wouldnae let it go. I just needed ye out of there because I had a monster to kill. But ye're the ones that made the monsters, are ye no?"

The woman spoke up.

"That wasn't us. That was Dr. Larned. We're just ops."

"I see. So ye're the ones who sent the monsters he made out to kill other people and eat them. Maybe I should do ye like those over there, eh?" I nodded my head at the burning bodies.

"No, no," the man said. "There's no need for that. Who are you, anyway?"

"A certain rare brand of law and order. An entirely different agency from yours. When it comes to the Fae on this planet, I have broad authority to right wrongs, and you have been very, very wrong. Hatcher in America is done for, just so ye know, and so is his pet troll."

The agents exchanged a quick glance before remembering that they'd probably given something away by doing so.

"Now, I can set the two of ye on fire right now and sleep well at night, knowing what ye did. I'm no interested in any rationale ye might have. But I am interested in what ye have in Area 51. I'll be merciful and let ye live if ye tell me what's down there."

"We don't know," the woman said.

"Aliens," the man said immediately afterward. "It was always aliens." The woman glared at him with her one remaining eye, and I chuckled. I hadn't really cared to know; I just wanted to see how they'd answer.

"I thought so. Thank ye. Awright." I pulled out my official ID and said, "I'm gonnay show ye who I work for." That got their attention, and so they were easily exposed to the sigils on my ID, which allowed me to command them to look at the next two very carefully. I proceeded to show them Lethe River and Restful Sleep, and they slumped back on the grass, unconscious. When they woke up, they'd see that their op was burnt down and they might even be in custody, but they'd have absolutely no recollection of how it all went wrong, how they'd lost an eye, or, most important, who'd done it. I used Nadia's razor to cut their bonds and made sure their IDs were spread out next to them. The CIA would have some explaining to do to Scotland, and Hatcher would take the blame.

I looked around at my handiwork and was satisfied. It wasn't the tidiest of resolutions, but it was a bandage on the wound, and it would heal so long as Clíodhna allowed it.

When I got back into the van, Buck and Cowslip were marveling at all the miniature goth Nadias depicted in the altar triptych. The bags of chocolate and marshmallows were sitting empty on the love seat and Buck was still chewing, recovering his strength. I returned the straight razor to Nadia and she drove us back down the hill to the village. It was marvelously quiet, and I was surprised. I thought surely some sort of law enforcement or fire department would have roused itself by now to investigate the thunderous explosion and subsequent fires up on the hill—especially since said fires were clearly visible when we turned off the road and looked back. But the village was dead silent.

I asked Nadia to pull over next to the Gargunnock Inn and soon realized why no one had paid attention to our raid: Everyone was inside watching football on the telly, with the sound turned up. Anyone still at home probably had the game on too. How much of the world could burn down, I wondered, while football was on the telly? How much magic and wonder was missed while people were distracted by something flickering on their screens?

[Buck, pop in there and steal somebody's phone really quick. The challenge is that ye must steal it and return it without them noticing.]

"On it!"

He popped away, and Cowslip laughed nervously in the back. "So, Mr. Sigil Agent sir, what's going to happen to me now?"

[I'm not exactly sure. What would you like to happen?]

"I'd like to go back to Tír na nÓg, but I can't."

[No, you can't.]

"Will you let me stay here?"

[Not with me, but maybe I can find you some legitimate service elsewhere.]

"I can't get my injections anymore, can I?"

[Sorry, no.]

"So I'm going to start hurting soon and I might die."

[You might,] I admitted. [But I have a plan.]

Buck returned triumphant, holding up an old flip phone. "Got one!"

[Nadia, please let emergency services know about the fire on the hill so the agents can be found.]

"A concerned citizen?"

[Can you do frightened and angry? Bonus points for both.]

Nadia called up emergency and gave them an earful. "There's a fucking fire on the hill and you lot are watching football! Just go outside and look, ye can't miss it! Pull yer thumbs out yer holes and do yer job!"

She hung up and tossed the phone back to Buck, who popped out to return it. "That should do the trick, eh?"

[Aye. Bottle of whisky on me. You choose.]

"And a raise?"

I grinned fondly at her. [A generous onetime bonus, I think.]

CHAPTER 30

Curses and Blessings

A call to my colleagues solved the Cowslip problem—or at least I hoped it would. Mei-ling agreed to take Cowslip in and attempt to treat her withdrawal symptoms and pain with sigils when they began; if Cowslip survived, Mei-ling would offer the pixie a legally binding service contract with her apprentice. That way, Cowslip wouldn't have to travel to Tír na nÓg much, if at all, and she could avoid being seen by the bean sídhe and thereby reminding Clíodhna that she was still around. It wouldn't be the life Cowslip imagined for herself, but it would be a safe one, and that was what trafficking victims needed and deserved.

It was a relief to tell the other sigil agents that I'd cleaned up my own mess. Clíodhna could try something again at any time, and we should remain vigilant, but more likely she would try something when we'd all passed on and hope the younger generation wouldn't think of her. I told myself that my colleagues were pleased that the matter had ended and that I had clearly suffered in the process of resolving it, since the black eye the leprechaun had given me hadn't cleared up yet.

Eli reported a couple of days later that, as far as he could tell, Hatcher had been demoted rather than fired for the immense cock-up at Gargunnock. The aftermath had caused something of an international incident, since Scotland wasn't fond of having one of its picturesque hills blown up, only to find out that it had been home to a secret CIA facility. Hatcher still had his shadowy offshore accounts to live on—we couldn't touch those—but at least he didn't have a squad of Fae—or anything else, really—to command. He wouldn't be running operations again soon, and Clíodhna wouldn't work with him anymore. We didn't know how he'd got rid of the troll corpse at the bottom of his swimming pool, but since nothing of the sort hit the news feeds, we assumed he'd taken care of it somehow.

I approved those short-term stays for the various deities who wished to go skiing in the Alps but let the other sigil agents know that something significant might happen there. I toyed with the idea of attending, just to make sure everyone behaved, but dismissed it since no one had invited me and I disliked the snow anyway.

With the assorted crises settled, there was finally time to sort through Gordie's inks and ingredients and either store them or dispose of them properly. A detective constable from Human Trafficking reached out to thank me for my information on those two pimps and said if I came across any more information like that, he'd be delighted to make use of it. And how *did* I come across that information, he wondered? Ignoring his question, I replied that I would pass on anything new that I learned.

Though I had no guarantee of any new information coming soon. Saxon Codpiece hadn't yet returned, and there was no way of knowing when or even if he'd be back. I imagined he'd wait until everyone thought he was dead and then return with dyed hair, a new wardrobe, and a new ridiculous alias, like Angus Crotchpot or Wallace Hungwell.

But I made a note to follow up with the detective constable in a few days to make sure the victims were being cared for. If it turned out agreeably, perhaps I could figure out a way to generate some new leads without Saxon's help.

D.I. Munro hadn't come around again and I hoped she wouldn't, though I simultaneously hoped I'd find a way to do her a good turn someday, since I'd been nothing but a source of memory loss to her so far. If she ever saw me in the company of Buck, the wee pink man she was certain had once punched her in the nose, I doubted I'd be able to shake her loose again.

On Thursday, I made my customary trip to the Mitchell Library and returned my borrowed book. I visited Mrs. MacRae on the fourth floor—her scarf was a riot of autumn colors this time—and asked her for help finding books in the occult or mythology section that dealt with humans being cursed specifically by deities, as opposed to witches or warlocks.

Her eyes widened a bit as her fingers began flying across the keyboard. "Are we feeling a bit cursed by God today, Mr. MacBharrais?"

[Asking for a friend.]

"Of course, of course. But even if your friend is cursed, they're still blessed in a way, if ye think about it."

[How so?]

"Well, gods so rarely do anything tae us. Or for us—I certainly got no help keeping my husband alive, for all my prayers. So it's kind of an achievement, in a way, tae be someone a god wants tae curse. Who were the good ones, eh? Tantalus. He deserved what he got, though now that I think of it, maybe that was a punishment after death rather than a living curse. Cassandra had a powerful curse on her, for sure. But ye know I've never been positive about that Ancient Mariner fellow. Did he really deserve to walk around forever undead and all his crew be killed because he shot an albatross? Not sure the scales of justice were functioning well on that day. But I defy ye to pick a day when the scales worked well for everyone."

I simply grinned at her.

"Oh, I'm babblin' on, in't I? Forgive me."

[Nothing to forgive. I find the case of the Ancient Mariner to be problematic as well.]

"I just feel so sorry for the crew, ye know? It wasnae their fault they happened tae be workin' with a pure bastard, yet they had tae pay for it with their lives."

[It certainly illustrates the dangers of living in the opium-addled imagination of a poet. And the principle of collateral damage.]

"Aye, collateral damage. It's a shame. So let me write a few things down for ye here . . ."

While she wrote down titles and catalog numbers, I thought about that angle a bit more. What if I'd never been the primary target of the curse but collateral damage? A deity may have been actually angry at someone else—another deity, most likely—and since they couldn't take it out on the god that vexed them, they took it out on . . . me?

That only made sense if someone was angry with Brighid. Attacking, compromising, weakening a sigil agent to get at Brighid— I could see that as a possibility. Some of the pantheons chafed at the necessity for contracts. It was an avenue of investigation worth exploring, at least, to discover who might have been motivated enough to do this.

I had to get to the bottom of my curses if I didn't want Buck to become collateral damage too and go the way of my apprentices. The clock was ticking, and I dreaded telling him about it, though I knew it was the right thing to do. He had the right to decide his own future, and I couldn't make that decision for him.

Leaving my service was the immediately obvious option, but we didn't know if that would work or not. It *might* work—it was even probable—but we couldn't know for sure. The curse may have fallen upon him irrevocably. Another possible salvation for him would be for me to shuffle off my own mortal coil; presumably the curse would be broken if I wasn't around. That didn't sit well with me, however. To begin with, there were inks to craft and hazelnut lattes to drink and people to be helped. There was also this librarian who quietly made my heart sing like no one had since my dear departed wife, and I wanted to listen to its song some more.

Better to follow Brighid's advice and eliminate the curse by eliminating whoever cast it.

Mrs. MacRae finished up and pushed a piece of note paper my way. Her fingernails were painted a bright orange, matching her scarf.

"There ye are, sir. Four titles to get ye started."

[Thank you so kindly, Mrs. MacRae.]

"Always a pleasure, Mr. MacBharrais. See ye next week, then?"

[Absolutely.]

I nodded farewell to her and took my list of titles to the stacks in search of a clue. I subscribe to the theory that answers cannot hide from us forever if we seek them long enough.

EPILOGUE

———— • ————

The Heist

Keeping a hobgoblin happy takes a little work, but it's always worth it. A happy hobgoblin tends to mess with yer life less, and might even save it. Buck had probably saved Eli and me from taking a bullet to something vital in Virginia. He'd most likely saved me again in Gargunnock. But besides all that, if ye ever have the power to make someone's dream come true and ye don't, then what kind of a selfish shite would ye be?

So Nadia and I cooked up a plan, and on a Friday evening, after the day shift went home—or, more likely, to the pub—I Signaled Buck to come down to the shop.

"What's all this, then?" he asked when he arrived. Nadia and I were at the whisky table, enjoying a dram. On the table next to the decanter rested a narrow cardboard box, taped shut.

"Got a gift for ye, Buck," Nadia said. She whipped out her straight razor and cut the tape sealing the box. "G'wan, then."

"What is it?"

"See for yerself."

He pulled back the flaps and removed some wadding until the contents were revealed, and then his eyes bulged in wonder and his mouth dropped open. "Whoa. Are ye serious? Are these ma labels? Stones and bones, these are ma labels!"

He pulled one out to admire it. The logo was a diamond shape inside a circle with text layered over it:

Buck Foi's Best Boosted Spirits

THE SWEETEST STOLEN HIGHLANDS WHISKY

HONORING THE LEGACY OF HOLGA THUNDERPOOT

SINGLE BARREL

AGED 10 YEARS

90 proof

We grinned at him and Nadia said, "We have pallets of bottles in the basement and a mixer, so ye can dilute it down from cask strength to ninety proof. One barrel should get ye about two hundred bottles if ye do it right."

"So all we need is the barrel?"

"That's right. Ready tae get in the wizard van and pull off a whisky heist in the Highlands?"

"Hells yes! Let's pour out a fine dram for Lhurnog!"

He popped out of the office before we could say anything else, and Nadia and I laughed. He was probably already at the van in the parking lot, dancing about and waiting for us.

We took off to the Highlands and picked a distillery that we knew would have a ten-year barrel lying around. It was dark when we arrived, but I got out with my derby hat on—a new one, since the undine had ruined my old one—and walked next to the van so that we wouldn't be caught on any security cameras approaching the building. I unlocked the warehouse door with a sigil. Buck chose the barrel and rolled it out to the van with a huge grin on his face. We got it loaded up and drove it back to the office, with Buck singing happy songs about the joys of stealing whisky.

On Monday morning, unbeknownst to Buck and shortly after the distillery discovered the theft, no doubt, a very well-dressed faery would visit the distillery with a suitcase of cash Nadia had put together. Using Gordie's passwords that Saxon had supplied, she'd drained all his illicit trafficking accounts and was now laundering it through our agency, replacing the twenty thousand I'd had to pay Saxon and much more. Hatcher's dirty money would be cleansed, and apart from giving Nadia a well-deserved bonus for saving my arse, we'd use it for agency business, a little scheme I'd thought of to help trafficking victims and to make one victim, anyway, a very happy hobgoblin without burdening us with the weight of guilt. The cash in the case would compensate the distillery for two hundred bottles of whisky and then some.

When we got the whisky back to the office, it was near midnight, but Buck couldn't sleep until we'd watered the barrel down in a mixing tub and filled at least one bottle, sealed it, and put a label on it. He beamed at it, laughed, and then wept as he hugged it to his breast.

"It's just so *beautiful*," he cried. "Thank ye, MacBharrais. And thank ye, Nadia. Why did ye do this?"

[You've earned it,] I replied. [You've been a good hob, and I appreciate your service.]

"And I appreciate the respect ye've shown for ma property since that first misunderstanding," Nadia said. "Plus, stolen whisky is the best whisky."

"It really is, in't it? Awright, shall we go upstairs and have a toast before calling it a night? I know ye must be tired. I'll bottle the rest and share it with the Fae Court later."

Back in my office, Buck cracked the seal on the bottle he'd just finished and poured us each a dram. He lifted his glass.

"A toast! Tae inks and sigils and straight razors, tae good bosses and wizards on lizards, tae outsmarting evil when ye can and kicking its arse when ye cannae do that, and tae distillers of fine spirits everywhere. Sláinte!"

I treasure such fleeting moments as that, little beacons of pure joy and contentment that last for a few seconds before passing into memory. They're always worth living and working for.

I'd let Buck distribute his whisky in the Fae Court and enjoy that high, and then we'd sit down and I'd tell him he might have only a year to live. It would ruin his day and he'd be justifiably angry with me, but I swore that together we'd figure out how to make sure he had plenty more days of heists ahead of him.

ACKNOWLEDGMENTS

Glasgow, you are brilliant. Thank you so much for being you. And that goes for the rest of Scotland; Kimberly and I loved our visit and cannot wait to return. You are, in short, magical, and the perfect setting for a modern fantasy. Should any reader ever wish to visit Glasgow, the locations mentioned (such as Gin71 and The Citizen and the mural of St. Mungo on High Street, to name a few) exist in reality and deserve a gander. The Mitchell Library has a fine section on the occult on the fourth floor, and I wish I could visit it every Thursday as Al does.

Incredible thanks to Amal El-Mohtar and Stu West for their Glaswegian expertise, and to Stu in particular for his advice on how the language should appear here. There are so many variations in the language and choices had to be made, but those choices are all on me. Anything that might seem off about the language is my fault and not his.

Gratitude to Charles Stross for some general conversation about phone hacking (again, if anything's wrong it's my fault) and to Victoria Schwab for introducing me to eighteen-year-old Bunnahabhain.

Thanks to Fran Wilde for her extraordinary kindness in showing me around Philadelphia.

My general gratitude and appreciation for fountain-pen manufacturers is boundless. Thank you for continuing to make such beautiful writing instruments.

Very specific gratitude goes to the Del Rey team for being absolutely spiffing publishers: Metal Editor Tricia Narwani, Alex Larned (yes, the namesake of the evil doctor), Julie Leung, Melissa Sanford, Ashleigh Heaton, David Moench, Keith Clayton, and Scott Shannon have all worked on this book, even though it's just my name on the cover, and they deserve infinite tacos and beer.

I consulted many works on the creation of inks in preparation for this work and used only a small fraction of the information gleaned; there's a remarkable history of chemistry and invention behind the medium of all our writing systems, and it's a very deep rabbit hole, if you like exploring such things. There are literally thousands of recipes out there. For an accessible overview, I suggest *Ink* by Ted Bishop. It will in turn provide an extensive suggested reading list, if you want more.

Regarding human trafficking, the volume I mentioned in the novel, *In Our Backyard: Human Trafficking in America and What We Can Do to Stop It* by Nita Belles, is an excellent starting point to understand how the sordid business is conducted, since it is so often glossed over in media stories and we are left to make frequently erroneous assumptions. It too will provide a bibliography for further research.

Thanks to Simone Alexander for her expert insight into the working conditions and safety of sex workers. Lastly, thanks so much to you for reading. Whether you're new to my work or a longtime reader coming from the Iron Druid Chronicles or my other series, I appreciate you giving *Ink & Sigil* a go and I hope you'll spread the word if you had fun. I wish you good health, an outstanding season for your football team, a ride in a gallus wizard van, and all the whisky and cheese your gob can handle.

About the Author

KEVIN HEARNE hugs trees, pets doggies, and rocks out to heavy metal. He also thinks tacos are a pretty nifty idea. He is the author of the Seven Kennings series and the *New York Times* bestselling series The Iron Druid Chronicles and is co-author of The Tales of Pell with Delilah S. Dawson.

kevinhearne.com
Twitter: @KevinHearne
Instagram: @kevinhearne

About the Type

This book was set in Sabon, a typeface designed by the well-known German typographer Jan Tschichold (1902–74). Sabon's design is based upon the original letter forms of sixteenth-century French type designer Claude Garamond and was created specifically to be used for three sources: foundry type for hand composition, Linotype, and Monotype. Tschichold named his typeface for the famous Frankfurt typefounder Jacques Sabon (c. 1520–80).